M000318128

LH"U
From the books of
Rabbi Eli and Tanya Kogan

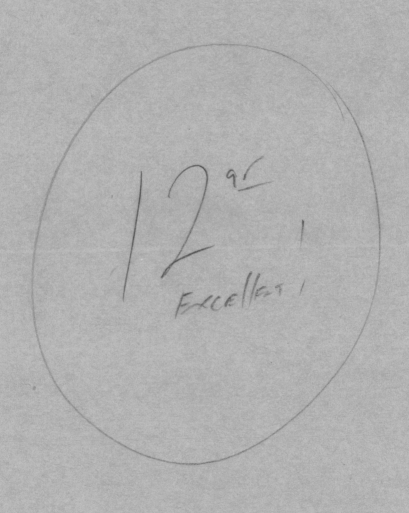

THE
SHAAR
PRESS

THE JUDAICA IMPRINT
FOR THOUGHTFUL PEOPLE

THE MIS

A novel by the
best-selling author of
In the Spider's Web

THE
SHAAR
PRESS

SION

CHAIM ELIAV

translated by
Miriam Zakon

© *Copyright 2000 by* Shaar Press

First edition – First impression / February 2000

ALL RIGHTS RESERVED

No part of this book may be reproduced **in any form,** *photocopy, electronic media, or otherwise without* **written** *permission from the copyright holder, except by a reviewer who wishes to quote brief passages in connection with a review written for inclusion in magazines or newspapers.* **THE RIGHTS OF THE COPYRIGHT HOLDER WILL BE STRICTLY ENFORCED.**

This is a work of fiction. Names, characters, places, and incidents are either the product of the author's imagination or are used fictitiously. Any resemblance to actual persons, living or dead, or locales is entirely coincidental.

Published by **SHAAR PRESS**
Distributed by MESORAH PUBLICATIONS, LTD.
4401 Second Avenue / Brooklyn, N.Y 11232 / (718) 921-9000

Distributed in Israel by SIFRIATI / A. GITLER
10 Hashomer Street / Bnei Brak 51361

Distributed in Europe by J. LEHMANN HEBREW BOOKSELLERS
20 Cambridge Terrace / Gateshead, Tyne and Wear / England NE8 1RP

Distributed in Australia and New Zealand by GOLD'S BOOK & GIFT SHOP
36 William Street / Balaclava 3183, Vic., Australia

Distributed in South Africa by KOLLEL BOOKSHOP
Shop 8A Norwood Hypermarket / Norwood 2196, Johannesburg, South Africa

ISBN: 1-57819-523-3 Hard Cover
ISBN: 1-57819-524-1 Paperback

Printed in the United States of America by Noble Book Press
Custom bound by Sefercraft, Inc. / 4401 Second Avenue / Brooklyn N.Y. 11232

THE MISSION

1

At 10 o'clock in the morning, Jeff Handler was greeted with an unwelcome surprise.

At 8:30, when he began his daily routine, he had no idea of what was awaiting him. At that hour he cheerily left his home on East 15th Street in Flatbush. He walked toward the parking spot in front of his two-story home and got into his 1982 Chevrolet, the new car he had bought the previous week. The motor roared to life and in a few moments he was cruising slowly down Avenue J and onto Coney Island Avenue, on his way to Manhattan. He had been taking this same route every day now for several years: a careful right turn onto Coney Island, merging into its traffic and putting on speed, and a left at Ditmas toward the broad boulevard of Ocean Parkway. Despite the heavy traffic and massive number of cars racing along with typical New York abandon, Jeff was calm and serene. Now was the perfect time for him to contemplate a *chiddush* that had occured to him during the *Daf Yomi shiur* this morning, and to contemplate the diamond sales that were awaiting him in the office. Everything was calm and quiet and absolutely routine. There was no hint of the great change awaiting him so very soon.

It took Jeff 45 minutes to reach his office on Manhattan's 47th

Street. He drove along Ocean Parkway to the Prospect Expressway and then merged onto the BQE. As he approached the Brooklyn Bridge he slowed down. A sharp right and he was on the bridge that stretched over the East River, linking Brooklyn to Manhattan. Beneath him the waters of the river flowed slowly; before him rose the glorious vista of Manhattan's skyline, its skyscrapers crowding one another and reaching towards the heavens. Always, as he passed over the bridge, he marveled anew at the city's magnificence.

As he approached Manhattan his thoughts turned to his boss, David Northfeld. Jeff was curious as to how their meeting would go this morning, after the bitter quarrel that had erupted between them the day before. When he returned home last night Jeff had been seething with fury. He had been tempted to call Northfeld and tell him unequivocally that he was quitting. But Jeff had a wise wife, practical and full of insight. Miriam had taken his foolish thought and banished it into the world of might-have-beens: "Where will you find such a good job, with a large company and a good salary, offering challenges and frequent bonuses? Remember Venezuela, Jeff!"

Yes. It was true: DEI was a very successful concern. But if she had known what awaited him at the meeting that was looming closer and closer, perhaps she would have agreed with his decision to quit.

Jeff merged onto the FDR Drive, a highway that curved alongside the East River. When he finally exited onto 42nd Street he was suddenly overcome by an inexplicable feeling of foreboding. Another 10 minutes and he would be in the office. He was already on the famed Fifth Avenue. One more turn and he would be on 47th Street, the center of the diamond industry. So what was this sinking feeling in the pit of his stomach, this sudden onslaught of tension constricting his chest and culminating, viselike, in a choking feeling in his throat?

Jeff slid into the parking garage in the depths of the building that housed, on its 10th floor, the company he worked for: Diamond Enterprises, Inc. DEI. He dismissed the strange feeling that had beset him so suddenly, waving it off like an annoying insect buzzing around his head. "Nonsense," he whispered, in a voice that came out clearly within the silence of the car. Surely it was nothing more than the meeting with his boss that was disturbing him. His boss, stubborn, inflexible, who wouldn't give in or admit to the truth.

That was all. Or was it? Why were the words of the Gemara suddenly running through his head: "Even if a man doesn't see [what will happen to him] his *mazel* (destiny) sees [what will happen to him]." Why?

He would try to avoid meeting with his boss today, he decided. It was possible that by tomorrow tempers would settle and emotions cool down.

The elevator brought him up to the glass-fronted office door. Jeff opened it and stood at the entrance.

"Hi," he said, with a quick smile at the secretary sitting behind the reception desk. Without awaiting a response he hurried into his office. He approached the small safe built into the wall. He pressed the secret code and the safe's door swung open easily. He pulled out a number of small envelopes that contained his valuable merchandise. Jeff then lit a fluorescent lamp whose white rays glanced off the wall and onto his worktable. He scattered the merchandise onto the desktop and began to count them.

The phone rang. It was the secretary on the line.

"Jeff?"

"Yes?"

"Mr. Northfeld wants to speak with you."

Jeff's heart thudded; he felt himself tense up.

"No. Don't tell me that."

"But I just did."

"You told him that I'm here?"

"You didn't tell me not to."

Jeff breathed deeply. "I don't want to speak with him today."

"So tell him that yourself."

"Do something to make him leave me alone today. Tell him whatever you want. Do you understand? After what happened between us yesterday, I need a break from him. It's the best thing for him, too."

"I understand what you're saying," she said quickly, "but he's waiting on the line. Get it?"

Jeff felt himself go cold.

"Okay. But I'm not responsible for the consequences."

The secretary sounded firm. "You most certainly are responsible. A person's behavior towards others affects their behavior towards him. And remember what they say: The boss isn't always right, but he's always the boss. Now, here he is."

Jeff tensely awaited David's voice.

"Hi."

The "hi," Jeff noticed, was fairly friendly.

He answered in frigid tones. "Hello."

"I'm glad you've come."

Now this was surprising. Such affability was not one of the more noticeable traits of his boss, not even when everything was going smoothly. And certainly not after the harsh words they had flung at each other yesterday afternoon. So what did he want? I'd better be very careful, a watchful voice hidden deep within him whispered.

And yet Jeff unbent just a little, and answered guardedly, "You make it sound like I don't get here every day. Why are you glad?"

Northfeld laughed lightly. "You're right," he answered, "and yet I am glad you've arrived. I've got something important to speak with you about. Later."

Jeff's curiosity, like his suspicions, were aroused. "Why not now?"

"Because things aren't quite clear enough yet. I'm awaiting an important call from abroad, from a certain country. The conversation between us depends on the outcome of that call."

Again, curiosity flared. "What is this 'certain country'?"

"You're very curious, my young friend."

The words carried just a hint of censure. They grated on Jeff.

"That's right. But, if you'll excuse me, you arouse my curiosity and then ask me why I'm curious?"

There was a moment's silence. Then his boss's firm voice rang out. "Just be patient, Jeff. I don't want to discuss this on the phone."

Jeff chuckled. His free hand gently rubbed his forehead, beneath the black *yarmulke*. This time his answer came quickly. His self-confidence when it came to his boss had returned.

"Who are you afraid of? You think someone is listening to us? Are we living in Russia?"

Jeff could hear David's rolling laughter.

"I see I was correct in deciding to speak to you, among all of our employees."

"I don't understand."

"You will, Jeff. See you."

Without warning the boss cut him off. Jeff held the receiver for a short minute, listening in some confusion to the dial tone: a sound that somehow reminded him of the long blast of the shofar on Rosh Hashanah.

Finally, Jeff replaced the receiver. He sat motionless and silent for a minute, then he lifted his head toward the ceiling, his eyes closed. He tried deciphering the mysterious words he had heard from David in the conversation that had just ended. How did the unusual dialogue tie in with what had passed between them yesterday? Was David planning on firing him? Or sending him to open a neglected office in some distant backwater, his only motivation being to keep Jeff far away? There had been some recent talk about opening new offices, subsidiaries of the main business in the United States. And what, exactly, was that "certain country" that he had mentioned? Jeff felt slightly resentful. He hated when things were left open and uncertain.

Suddenly he jumped from his chair. He hurried to the door of his office and opened it with a swift motion. He flew though the corridor with long strides until he was standing before the door that led to David's office. A brief hesitation, that he overcame with a firm nod of the head, and he knocked. Not awaiting a reply, he opened the door and stood on the threshold.

Northfeld was surprised at the sight of his unexpected and uninvited visitor. His gray eyes narrowed, expressing anger at Jeff's slight towards his authority as boss and president of the firm. But those eyes returned almost immediately to normal. David Northfeld recalled the mission that he planned on delegating to his employee. Now was not the time to stand on ceremony and assert his authority. His eyes even glinted with hidden laughter.

"Oh, I see that you are really curious. Curiosity can be a very helpful trait, when it comes to expanding one's knowledge. But in business, Jeff, and particularly in business negotiations, it's sometimes better to show a lack of interest. You understand that, I hope?"

Jeff didn't reply. His boss's eyes gazed at him like one trying to gauge a reaction. Jeff still stood in the doorway. Northfeld's voice shot through the silence of the room.

"It would really be a major error on your part, if you get too curious on the mission that's been chosen for you."

Jeff did not wait for an invitation. He entered the room, and with measured steps approached his boss's massive, luxuriously appointed desk. He dropped down onto one of the armchairs near the desk, crossed his legs, stared at the face of the man seated across from him in the black leather recliner. It was a face that radiated both authority and pride. Jeff waited, openly defiant.

Northfeld smiled. It was obvious that he was trying to create a pleasant, relaxed atmosphere.

"You want to know what mission I want to give you? Or the name of the country that I alluded to in our conversation?"

Jeff drummed his fingers on the desktop. Finally he said, "Is it a choice between the two? Can't I hear about this mission, and about this 'certain country'?"

"Perhaps. Why not? I just wanted to see how curious you really were."

Jeff began to lose patience. This unnecessary chatter really didn't fit in with his boss's character, and it was annoying him.

"Mr. Northfeld, can we get down to business?"

Northfeld accepted the rebuke without moving a muscle.

"Look, I'm wasting time, because I'm awaiting a telex from Moscow. It should be here any minute."

Jeff was shocked. He leaned slightly towards the desk.

"Moscow?"

Northfeld savored the moment. "You see, one word and you can hear about both the mission and the 'certain country' you were so curious about."

Jeff felt more and more uncomfortable. "I don't understand. You want me to go to Moscow?"

Northfeld lifted his head slightly. The jutting of his chin showed a fierce determination.

"That's right."

"To Russia? On business?"

"Yes."

"To the land of the KGB?"

Northfeld's face took on a softer cast. "Don't exaggerate, Jeff. It's not what it used to be. This isn't the Stalin era. It's true that the KGB still terrifies the local residents, but it's not like it was in the past. Besides, you're an American citizen. You've got nothing to be afraid of."

After a deep silence, he added, "Of course, that's as long as you don't get involved in matters that don't concern you and don't stick your nose into things that have nothing to do with the diamond business."

Jeff was wrapped in silence. Something about this did not appeal to him. His eyes skimmed aimlessly over the office walls. The wall hangings, brown running into red, brought home to him just where they were sending him: the country of the Reds. His fingers played restlessly with a gold Parker pen that lay on the desk. Northfeld quietly pulled the pen away from him. He did not like strangers touching his things. Jeff hardly noticed.

Northfeld pushed a bit. "*Nu,* so what do you say?"

"Nothing. This obviously has something to do with what happened yesterday. A punishment."

"I forget these 'yesterdays' quickly; I only remember tomorrow. But if you really want to know why I chose you, it's connected to your success in Venezuela a few months ago. With a sensitive topic such as doing business with the Russians, I can rely on you more than on the others in the office. You understand, you studied in yeshivah — Lakewood, I believe — and you have a good head for understanding the hard-headed Russian mentality that's inflexible and uncompromising."

"A topic that's sensitive — and dangerous, you meant to say."

Northfeld took a deep breath. "I'm telling you again, you're exaggerating. Russia is going through a profound change. The KGB also, even though it's still a very cruel secret police force. But there are many Americans now traveling back and forth who are never even aware it exists. Nothing happens to them."

Northfeld leaned over towards Jeff. He lowered his voice confidentially.

"Try to understand, Jeff. The Russians want to do business with the Americans. And as long as they want to do business they won't harm a neutral person who has come to Moscow for exactly that purpose. There's nothing to worry about. They have got good merchandise, small, exquisitely polished stones. A connection with them will help us get out of the grip of the Syndicate. Big profits, Jeff. You'll get a cut. The bonus will be greater than that of Venezuela. Got it?"

Jeff threw out his hands in a gesture that released some tension. "Of course the bonus will be bigger; the danger is greater. By the way, I assume the bonus goes to my wife if I don't return?"

He longed to ask Northfeld why he himself wasn't traveling, if the profits were so great. Let him keep the bonus for himself. But he didn't want to increase the tension between them.

"You're tough this morning," Northfeld said quickly. "But I forgive you."

Jeff stood up. "Is that it? Can I give you an answer tomorrow?"

Northfeld nodded his head in assent.

"By tomorrow I'll have the telex authorizing your trip."

Jeff did not answer. He was angry at his boss for working behind his back. He had already arranged a permit for him to enter Russia, without even asking him! But — he would keep quiet.

When he was standing by the doorway ready to leave, he felt himself pulled back by his boss's words.

"Remember, Jeff, if you refuse I won't send anyone else. The business will be lost."

Jeff turned to face David Northfeld. He didn't say a thing. He could hear an inner voice telling him: He's just trying to make you feel guilty.

"Bye," he muttered, and turned away.

"You're not going. And that's it. Period."

Miriam, Jeff's wife, stood in their living room, trembling with rage and nervous excitement.

Jeff laughed. "You told me yesterday that I shouldn't quit a terrific job that has so many new challenges. So here I am: I didn't quit, and I'm being offered an exciting new challenge."

Miriam burst into tears. Jeff was at his wit's end. He realized that refusing to go would ultimately lead to his losing his job at Diamond Enterprises, Inc. That wasn't what he wanted. On the other hand, this trip to Moscow frightened him. Maybe his fear was rooted in past history; still, fear wasn't something you could simply set aside. It existed. That was all. At the same time, he didn't know how to calm his wife and deal with her unequivocal refusal, that totally ignored financial considerations.

An idea flitted through his brain. "You know what? I'll do whatever my father tells me to do."

She didn't answer. He began to dial Israel, Ramat Gan, where his father and grandfather lived.

"Hello, Abba, how are you? How's Imma? Grandfather?"

"Is that you, Yisrael Yaakov? *Baruch Hashem*, we're fine. Why are you calling?"

"I'll get straight to the point. I'm a little confused and don't know what to do. My boss wants me to travel to Russia to finish up some business that he's begun. What should I do, Abba? Miriam objects very strongly. But if I don't go there's a danger that I'll be fired. That's what I think, at least."

The international line grew silent for a long minute. Finally, Jeff heard his father's voice.

"I don't know what to tell you. Today Russia is much less dangerous than it used to be. And yet — Besides, you remember that we're from Russia."

"I remember."

"And Grandfather left there in a way that got him into trouble with the authorities. Do you know about that?"

"Sort of."

"How do I know that they won't make trouble for the grandson because of him?"

Another silence.

"Look, Jeff. I think you should try to put the matter off. Use your brains, of course. It's a shame to lose your job."

"I hear. Do you want to speak with Grandfather about it?"

"Okay. If I come up with anything new, I'll be in touch. Bye."

"*Shalom.*"

Jeff turned to his wife, who had gone to the kitchen and was busy there, trying to release her tension.

"Okay, calm down. Abba says I shouldn't go."

A few minutes later, the telephone rang. It was his father from Israel.

"Look, I'm sitting with Grandfather, and he thinks you should go. He's very firm on the subject."

Jeff was shocked. He was simply dumbfounded.

"Jeff? Can you hear me?"

"Yes, I hear," he answered weakly.

"What happened to you? Why does your voice sound different?"

"You don't know why?"

"I understand. Here's Grandfather, he wants to speak with you."

"Yisrael Yaakov, how are you?" The voice was feeble with age.

Jeff answered quickly, "I'm fine, thank G-d. That is, okay."

"Look, Yisrael Yaakov, I want you to go. I have an important mission for you to do for me in Moscow."

"Okay," Jeff answered automatically.

"So you'll go?"

"If you want me to, I'll go." In his brain he was already weaving excuses, ways to get out of it.

"Look, Yisrael Yaakov, when are you supposed to be leaving?"

"In about two weeks."

"*Nu,* so you'll have enough time to come to Israel and hear what I have to ask you."

Jeff didn't understand.

"Why not on the phone, Grandfather?"

"No. Impossible. Only face to face."

"Are you afraid that someone is listening in?"

"Yes."

"Who?"

"What kind of question is that? The KGB!"

2

With a slow gesture, Jeff put down the receiver. His eyes, tense and half-shut, caught his wife's worried look. The phone's shrill ring had brought her running from the kitchen into the living room. Nervously she dried her fingertips on the edge of her apron. She saw her husband unconsciously rubbing his lower lip, and she understood: He had heard something very disturbing on this call. His forced smile did not fool her at all.

"Who was that?" she asked quietly, tensely.

He took a deep, liberating breath.

"My grandfather."

Miriam took a few steps towards him. "Why was he calling, all of a sudden?"

"My father told him about my proposed trip to Russia."

"Oh. What did he want?"

Jeff answered, trying to be nonchalant. "Couldn't you figure it out from my answers?"

Miriam dropped down onto the edge of one of the chairs and leaned heavily upon the table before her.

"I think I do understand. He wants you to go, right?"

Jeff did not answer. Miriam realized that she was on target.

"Why? Why does he want you to go to Russia? What's happened to him suddenly?"

Jeff walked over to the table but did not sit down. "You want to know the truth? I don't understand it."

"*Nu?*"

Jeff began to lose his patience. "What, '*nu*'? He refused to talk about it on the phone. He told me I should come to Israel immediately."

Miriam's head shot up, her eyes shocked.

"What?"

"That's right. It seems that the matter is very, very important. He was very upset and he told me to come immediately."

Silence.

Miriam's breath came quicker and shallower. "What can it be?"

"I don't know. I'm just as curious as you are."

"And what do you plan on doing?"

"What do you mean, what do I plan on doing? Even just for curiosity's sake I'll fly to Israel to speak with him."

After a moment's thought, he added: "Or, more accurately, to hear him out, to hear what he wants."

She was not placated. "And if he insists that you go, will you — will you listen to him?"

Jeff heard the hesitation in her voice, and the worry. She understood what he knew, deep down in his heart: One didn't say no to his grandfather, to Asher Yosef. And that was that.

The baby's cry could be heard from the second floor. Miriam made no move to go up and calm him down. Neither did Jeff. And yet, at that very moment he suddenly sensed a strong sense of attachment to this young son of his, this Ahreleh, named for his late *Rosh Yeshivah*, Rabbi Aharon Kotler, *zt"l*. For a split second Jeff felt as if he was distanced from reality. He saw himself far from home, somewhere in frigid Moscow, a city hostile and strange, with dangers lurking in every corner.

Neither said a word. Jeff dropped into a chair by the table. He rubbed his hands together nervously.

"Do I have a choice? Tell me, do I have a choice? You know very well that I have to listen to him. He's very obstinate."

Yes. She knew that her husband would have to listen. They always listened. When his grandfather, R' Asher Yosef Handler, had lived in New York, all of them, the whole family, listened to him. He was a reserved type, not given to speaking too much. "In Russia," he used to say, "we learned that one says only what one has to say and no more." Yet at the same time, he was a firm and domineering person. His requests to family members were commands that could not be questioned. Why? That was the way it was. And she, Miriam, though she felt affection for him — he was, after all, a good-hearted and pleasant man — had felt a burden lift when he decided, some years earlier, to move to Israel. It seemed to her that her husband had also breathed more freely, though neither, out of respect for his grandfather, had ever expressed any such thoughts openly. And now the command had reached them via telephone — a command, in her opinion, that was very ominous. *Even in Ramat Gan he will rule over us?* The thought flitted swiftly through her feverish mind.

She whispered, as though to herself, "Why did you have to call your father? Why?"

Despite the quiet tones, the complaint in her voice was obvious. A spark of anger rose within him.

"And why did I listen to you yesterday and not quit? Why?"

Silence descended once again, like a heavy fist bearing down upon them. Outside the hum of traffic could be heard, only a few cars were traveling at this late hour. Miriam stood up and wordlessly returned to the kitchen. At the doorway she stopped for a moment, turned her head, and asked dryly, "So what did your grandfather say? Why can't he reveal the big secret over the phone?"

Jeff blurted out, "He thinks the KGB is tapping his phone."

The answer once again reawakened Miriam's fears. She walked quickly to the dining room table. "What did you say? What's happened to your grandfather? Do you believe it's true? Is something really happening?"

Jeff laughed unconvincingly.

"Oh, come on. They have nothing better to do, the KGB, than listen in on the conversations of some elderly Jew who's almost 90 years old and lives quietly in Ramat Gan? It's all just an old man's hallucinations."

After a moment he added, "But I felt that he was under a lot of pressure."

Miriam returned to the chair she had just vacated. "I suppose you're right. It certainly seems like utter nonsense. But still, with all that, your grandfather is no fool. And if so, perhaps there really is something behind it."

She crossed her arms in a gesture of determination. "Just between us, tell me, Jeff, other than the fact that he ran away from Russia, do you know anything about him?"

"Actually, no. He never told us anything about his life in Russia. Yes, all we know is that he got into trouble with the Communists. But what exactly happened — he never said. At least, he never told me."

"*Nu*, and if so," she broke in, her voice mildly triumphant, "maybe he really is hiding something? Some terrible secret? Russia is full of terrible secrets! Maybe there is something behind his fear."

Jeff didn't rush to respond. Finally, thinking aloud, he said, "And yet, it seems ridiculous that the secret police of mighty Russia should be listening in on him. It seems that something is disturbing him greatly, making him feel persecuted. How can it be that we never noticed it before, through the years?"

He lifted his head and looked at his wife. "I wonder what's behind his fears. You know something? You've made me wonder. Maybe you're right. Maybe Grandfather really is hiding some secret."

Miriam responded immediately. "So you agree that it's frightening?"

Jeff nodded. "I don't know about frightening. Mysterious, certainly."

"That means," Miriam whispered, "that it's possible that for you personally, as the grandson of your Russian grandfather, it may be even more dangerous for you to travel than for an ordinary American citizen."

Jeff shrugged his shoulders. "Maybe. What do I know?"

Miriam continued. "That means that if you find out that such a danger exists, you'll stand firm against your grandfather's demands and refuse to go! Am I right?"

Her eyes stared at Jeff with a look that was both a question and a demand.

Jeff returned a look of such melancholy, there was no need to say more...

Two days later, at 5 p.m., Jeff landed at Ben Gurion Airport in Lod. His father, Moshe Aryeh Handler, came to meet him. The ride to Ramat Gan passed with pleasant father-son conversation. The reason for Jeff's visit didn't come up at all; both studiously avoided the topic. And yet, despite the easy, innocuous conversation, with all the "how are you's" — home, children, business, politics — an air of tension seemed to fill the white Subaru. Jeff longed to hear details of what was happening in his grandfather's house, and what was the reason for the summons to Israel. But he dared not ask.

Finally he asked one unavoidable question. "And how is Grandfather?"

His father gave an understanding smile. "Fine, thank G-d. Though he does have his illnesses, his heart problems, you know."

Jeff stared at the swiftly passing road. At the entrance to Ramat Gan, when they were driving down Jerusalem Boulevard near Haroeh Street, his father offered one more piece of information.

"Grandfather is very excited about meeting with you."

Jeff, too, was very excited. Nevertheless, he kept his emotions under strict control. He had decided to keep his cool; at all costs he would maintain a modicum of independence from the demands he would no doubt be hearing from his grandfather.

The car stopped near the two-story house on Gilgal Street. His grandfather lived on the second floor. Jeff's father let him go first. Jeff could almost hear his heart thumping, beating wildly within his chest, as he climbed up the narrow stairway. They rang the doorbell, and Jeff's father quickly opened the door.

Jeff found his grandfather lying on his bed in his darkened bedroom. Despite the fact that it was still daylight outside, the shutters were closed. Jeff approached his grandfather and kissed him on the forehead. His grandfather clasped Jeff's hand between his own and shook it, his happiness evident.

"*Shalom aleichem,* Yisrael Yaakov. How was your flight? Good? Thank G-d. Oh, I am so happy you've come. Maybe in your merit Hashem will allow me to fulfill my lifelong dream. Moshe Aryeh," the old man said, turning to his son, "give your son something to drink. Take him into the living room to sit down. And make me a cup of tea. I'll be there in a minute."

Very shortly Asher Yosef entered the living room neatly dressed. His weakness was evident, yet despite his advanced age and the fact that after his wife's death the previous year he now lived alone, he seemed to be coping quite well. Jeff's eyes carefully examined his grandfather's face, as he awaited his words. It seemed to Jeff that his father, too, was curious about what was going to be said.

His grandfather murmured the words of "*Shehakol*" and tranquilly sipped his tea. Finally he placed the cup on the table and turned to Jeff, a big smile on his face.

"See here, Yisrael Yaakov, I'm happy that you're traveling to Moscow. I want you to locate my old house. I want you to ask permission of the residents to go in. Understand?"

Jeff was not certain if he was hearing correctly. Or perhaps his grandfather's brain was deteriorating? He restrained himself and did not reply to such an odd request. Instead he asked, with every vestige of politeness that he could muster: "Where did you live?"

"Where did I live? I'll tell you in a minute."

His grandfather's forehead was deeply furrowed. Clearly, he was expending tremendous effort to recall the street name.

"*Oy,* it's 50 years since I left the house. Since the men of the GPO — today's KGB — jailed me at 3a.m."

The old man was silent for a moment. It was clear that his thoughts were in the distant past.

"What did they accuse me of? Simple! Counter-revolutionary activity and Trotskyism and who knows what else. I was a government official then, in the Foreign Ministry. And Comrade Stalin, may his memory be blotted out, decided to shake up the Foreign Ministry. That was his way: to fall upon a certain segment of the population so that everyone would be terrified and panicky, and to rule by fear. It was," again, the brow wrinkled deeply, "yes, it was in the year 1933 — in the winter — February. *Oy*, the road to Siberia was hard. Thirty-five degrees below zero. Do you hear, Yisrael Yaakov? Thirty-five degrees below zero!"

Jeff felt increasingly uncomfortable. His fingers tapped nervously upon the table. He threw his father an annoyed glance, as if to say: I had to come from America for ancient history? His father gave him a soothing wave of the hand, and he whispered, "Wait. A little patience. Grandfather wants something, I'm certain."

His grandfather's face lit up. "I remember! I remember the name of the street where we lived."

His fingers lightly smacked his forehead, jogging his memory. "How could I have forgotten? The street is called Krasno Bogatirski! That's right: Krasno Bogatirski. I want you, Yisrael Yaakov, to find the street and the house where we lived. It's the third house from the street's beginning. A two-story house. Do you promise?"

Jeff didn't reply. His face was expressionless, as if he hadn't heard his grandfather's request. But his grandfather didn't notice his reaction, or lack of it. Remembering the street name had awakened his memory of events from five decades earlier. He was back in the world of his youth, oblivious to the present.

"We lived there, Yisrael Yaakov, Father and Mother, two sisters, two brothers. *Oy*, many years have passed."

He straightened his bent form slightly; a spark of vital life shone from his eyes.

"And they were years of many adventures. Many, many adventures."

With difficulty Jeff hid his impatience.

"Yes, Grandfather, it's very interesting. Really it is. But you could have told me all of this by phone, don't you think?"

The old man grabbed Jeff's hand with his trembling, gnarled one. Considering the man's age, his grip was firm.

"I haven't told you anything yet, Yisrael Yaakov," Asher Yosef said in a tone of wonder. "You don't know what happened to me there, with the cursed Communists!"

His grandfather's eyes closed for moment. He let go of Jeff's hand and straightened his large black *yarmulke*.

"Today, for the first time, I will reveal one of my most closely guarded secrets."

He was quiet for a minute, and his breath came unevenly. And then he began to whisper, slowly, in a voice that sounded like a thin whistle. "I killed a man in Russia. Actually — I killed two men."

The old man's emotion was evident. The words seemed to stick in his throat. But finally he managed to blurt out another sentence.

"They weren't men, really. They were GPO agents."

3

Asher Yosef had trouble breathing as, with great difficulty, he revealed his life's closely guarded secret. The effort necessary for him to speak took an enormous emotional toll and left him weak. The old man leaned his head on his palm; his breath was labored. The memories that had suddenly awakened fell upon him with all their weight. His son, Moshe Aryeh, leaned towards his father and laid a gentle hand on his trembling shoulders.

"Father, you don't feel well?"

The words came out swiftly, fearfully. The heart disease from which his father suffered did not benefit from such outbursts of emotion.

Asher Yosef's breathed deeply and more calmly. He pulled his cup toward him and sipped the tea, which had cooled off completely. Moshe Aryeh calmed down somewhat, but occasionally he displayed his shock at the frightening secret that had burst upon them so suddenly.

"How is it, Father, that you never told me this story? It's incredible!"

Asher Yosef stared at his son with a dull glance. "All my life I believed that I wouldn't reveal this to anyone. That it would be buried with me in the grave. And today, too, I wouldn't have told it."

He pointed his finger weakly at Jeff.

"If not for our guest, your son Yisrael Yaakov, who is about to travel to Russia, the secret would never have been told."

Jeff fidgeted uncomfortably in his chair. He, too, had been taken aback by the revelation of this secret chapter in his grandfather's life. But, unlike his father, he felt this strange story was something of a threat. He believed that at some point the tale would have repercussions on his own life. At the same time he simply could not imagine his grandfather, that frail chassidic Jew, taking the lives of two members of the Soviet secret police.

"I still don't see the connection, Grandfather, between my trip to Russia, that, by the way, I'm not sure will take place, and your story."

He turned to his father and said, in a barely audible whisper, "This story seems just too implausible. I don't understand why and how he did it, if he really did. And to escape from Russia, the way it was then? Something here needs to be clarified."

The old man heard the whispered exchange. He was also quite aware of his dear grandson's cursory reminder that his very trip was in doubt. He lifted his eyes, gave Jeff an amused glance, a look that contained a spark of mystery as well.

"Ah, Yisrael Yaakov, I understand. You don't believe my story? I'm not angry. I wouldn't have believed it either, if someone had told me something like this —"

Suddenly he straightened his bent frame, like a soldier on parade, and declared: "But it is what happened! At my age, one doesn't lie to children and grandchildren. Do you understand that?"

Jeff accepted the rebuke without batting an eyelash. He waited to hear the rest of the conversation. Luckily, he had slept on the plane and wasn't tired out by his long flight.

His father, still concerned about the old man's health, asked anxiously, "Do you want to rest a little? Yisrael Yaakov will be here tomorrow too."

The grandfather shrugged him off, and a new vigor surged within him. "No, no! I have to tell this today. Yisrael Yaakov didn't come from America for nothing."

Father and son exchanged glances and decided to stay.

"I didn't kill them for no reason, those evil men. And I wasn't alone. But since then they are after me, I'm certain of it."

His eyes flitted from his son to his grandson, back and forth. "You don't believe me, hey? I'll tell you something. You know that I worked for a few years at the United Nations Center in New York. One day — it was in the year 1947 — someone approached me, a young Russian diplomat, and asked me in an offhand way, 'Do you happen to be Vladimir Paruskin?'"

His eyes gleamed with mischief. It was clear that he was enjoying the surprises he was springing on his children.

"Yes, that's another thing I never told you: my real name. I adopted the name Handler only when I came to the United States. The name Asher Yosef, my father, whispered into my ear, actually the day before he died of pneumonia. And it seemed that my new name saved my life."

"What did you tell that diplomat?"

"Naturally, I said that I didn't know what he was talking about. But I suspect he saw how I grew pale. Against my will, also, I blinked. And perhaps he noticed the trace of a Russian accent in my English. Do I know? But are you listening? He mentioned the name that was mine 15 years earlier, in a completely different country, as if there had been no World War, as if the entire world hadn't been plunged into chaos. And he mentioned it in New York, when I looked completely different and had another name. Isn't that terrifying? I am convinced that the NKVD had been on my trail, and that the diplomat was an NKVD agent. Don't you know that the NKVD were the heirs of the GPO, and the father of today's KGB?"

"But what could he have wanted?"

"Nothing, I suspect. Just to let me know that they know exactly who I am. And that the Soviets still want to lay their hands on me. Maybe they also thought that they'd put pressure on me to spy for them. That I shouldn't feel safe. Who knows?"

After a short silence he added, "They did manage to undermine my sense of security. Maybe they'd sentenced me to death in absentia. To tell the truth, I began to be afraid. I remembered well how Stalin had traced Trotsky to Mexico and had him assassinated there."

Jeff asked, with honest interest: "But Grandfather, how did they uncover your true identity?"

"I wish I knew. But you're asking about the Soviet secret police? They know everything!"

The old man stared with wide eyes at his impatient grandson. He understood the young man, living serenely in New York, the heavy baggage of his grandfather's memories far from his consciousness, light-years away from his way of life. It was very important to the grandfather that the grandson identify with him somewhat, at least now, when being asked to undertake a mission for him. Otherwise who knew, perhaps he wouldn't agree to take on the project in Moscow.

Asher Yosef closed his eyes and covered his forehead with the palm of his left hand for a prolonged moment of thought. Finally he began to speak incessantly; his son and grandson didn't dare to break the flow of words. He spoke in a slightly trembling voice, but clearly and firmly:

"For many years, my children, I haven't told you what I went through in those two years in Siberia. I can't explain, even to myself, why I hid it from you. Maybe it was my way of fleeing the nightmare. Or maybe the opposite: I wanted to keep the hard memory as a constant reminder of the pain. Or maybe I thought you wouldn't believe me."

No one answered him. Night had fallen upon Ramat Gan. Moshe Aryeh stood up and turned on the light in the shabbily furnished living room.

Grandfather continued. "As I told you, I was arrested before dawn. They, the men of the secret police, banged harshly on the door. And before I could open it, four of them broke into the room and ordered me to get dressed. My mother — my father was no longer alive — and my two sisters, Marisha and Irina, were left alone. I hurried to obey their command: they were the terror of the entire state. The terror of the nation. I didn't even have time to tremble. Their screams — 'Quickly! Quickly!' — paralyzed even my emotions.

"They took me in a black car with tinted windows to the GPO's central headquarters, without ever saying a word. I never saw my mother or sisters again."

Asher Yosef was silent for a minute. The memory of his mother and sisters brought a look of profound sorrow to his wrinkled face. It was clear to Jeff that his grandfather was now completely surrounded by the images of the past, of those days 50 years earlier.

"I was thrown into a small, dark, and frigid cell. From nearby cells I could hear screams, blood-curdling screams. It was clear that my fellow prisoners were being tortured. We knew that enemies of the government, or those whom the government decided were its enemies, were often tortured horribly by the GPO agents. In the past when we walked — hurriedly, of course — past the fearful headquarters of the secret police, we heard nothing. Now — I was alone, frightened, by myself in a tiny cell, knowing that soon, very soon, it would be my turn. What I had done wrong, I honestly had no idea. But as I have said, in Russia during those times one didn't have to commit a crime to be thrown into solitary confinement or even killed, after terrible tortures."

Another moment of heavy silence. He turned to Moshe Aryeh and asked, in weary tones, "Make me a cup of tea, please."

Grandfather sighed deeply. "To my great fortune, they didn't torture me. Until today I don't know why I deserved such kindness. After a short trial I was found guilty of sabotaging the Soviet economy and damaging the rights of workers, distributing false information on the Soviet government to foreigners, of Trotskyism and Zionism. Of course, all the charges were ridiculous; I had never done any of those things.

"The trial took two days. The judges sentenced me to five years of hard labor in a camp in Siberia. 'Reeducation camps,' they called them. They hoped to turn me into a productive Soviet citizen. They felt I needed five years of education.

"I was in Siberia for two out of those five years. The cold was frightful, sometimes as low as 45 degrees below zero. We worked like slaves from morning to night. Any slight infraction was punished harshly; some were even sentenced to death. Not many, but some. And many, in any case, died of natural causes, because they simply didn't have the strength to go on.

"Those villains once tied me to the back of a dog sled. The snow was almost waist high. The dogs raced off and I had to run after them, trying not to fall and be dragged through the snow. I didn't succeed, of course. I ran through the high drifts as long as I could, until I fell. Finally, they cut me away from the sled and left me, bruised and bleeding and completely drained, in the heavy snow. My friends in the camp saved my life. They found me and took me to their huts, where they revived me."

Asher Yosef told his son and grandson, as they sat mute, their eyes alert, of his failed attempt at flight, of his long confinement in solitary and how, finally, he and two fellow prisoners managed to run for their lives, to take advantage of the guards' drunken stupor to escape through the prison's gate unnoticed. It was during the summer months, after the snow had melted. When they reached the main highway they stopped a wagoner bringing hay to a local *kolchoz*, or farming collective. They forced him to give them a ride, hiding beneath the hayload. The frightened driver gave in to their demands, left his route, and sent his horses galloping eastward. Towards evening they reached the outskirts of a small village where he stopped.

"I jumped from my place," the grandfather recalled, "and put the knife that was in my hand to the throat of the wagoner, who trembled like a leaf.

"'Go! Go further!' I hissed threateningly.

"The terrified wagon driver begged me. 'Have mercy on me, my friends. In any case I am going to be punished harshly for not coming on time to the *kolchoz*. And if I don't get back there tonight, they'll kill me. Have mercy!'"

Grandfather told how his grip loosened somewhat. But his two comrades, non-Jews who'd fled with him, said, "Vladimir, haven't you heard? In any case, he's going to be killed. Let's kill him now, take his clothing and his horses and wagon. We need them."

Grandfather wouldn't agree. A Jew remains a Jew, no matter what the circumstances. The murder of an innocent man was not to be thought of. After some open confrontation he persuaded them to let the poor wagon driver free.

It seemed that his two gentile companions were right: freeing the driver had, indeed, threatened their own lives. In order to save his own skin the driver betrayed them to the GPO, revealing the precise location to which they had fled.

"At midnight two secret police officers were banging on the door of the barn where we were hidden. They weren't sure we were there, but they'd searched every corner of the small town, whose frightened citizens had cooperated fully. The darkness in the barn was thick and heavy. I decided to fight for my freedom, no matter what, so I unsheathed the knife in my hand. When one of the secret police approached, I jumped on him from the back and before he could recover I stabbed him in the heart. One stab and no more. A loud scream broke through the silence, a short, shrill scream, and then the body collapsed to the earth. The second GPO agent hurried to the spot from where the chilling scream had come. My two Russian comrades who had run away with me jumped from their hiding place, grabbed the man, and I took care of him too, with one terrible blow from my knife.

"The two Russian men didn't wait long. They took the uniforms of the two dead men and put them on. They left the barn, started the GPO agents' car that was parked outside, and swiftly left the village."

Asher Yosef sighed.

"I didn't manage to jump onto the car. They left me to my fate —"

Here, in the Ramat Gan apartment, he began to whisper. "Yes, yes, I saved their lives, and they left me. I was left alone in a hostile village, in a barn with two corpses."

Grandfather took a few sips of the tea his son had brought him. His hand, holding the teacup, trembled.

"At that moment, for the first time in my life, a deep despair seized me. At that moment, after many years, my soul cried out to the Creator."

Again, he grew quiet. This time, the silence was long and deep. Jeff crossed his legs. He could feel the curiosity within him growing. His resentment against his grandfather for having disturbed him with this sudden demand to come to Ramat Gan melted away. This unknown adventure of his grandfather had gripped him. And here was Grandfather's voice again.

"At that moment I remembered tefillin. My tefillin. And I made a vow."

4

Grandfather took another drink of tea from the cup that he now grasped in his hands. A few drops glistened on his scraggly white beard and then ran down, resting finally upon the faded tablecloth.

He smiled. "Don't think that I was an observant Jew then. Absolutely not. True, I wasn't a confirmed Communist like many of the people with whom I lived. Nevertheless, the rebellious spirit of the Bolsheviks had touched me also. Even my imprisonment seemed to me more like a mistake, or the result of the wickedness of the current government, or, perhaps, because some enemy had slandered me, rather than a failure of the Communist ideology itself. And yet it seems that a Jewish spark remained within my Socialist heart. There was one mitzvah that I tried to observe. I observed it because my father had asked it of me before his death, and not necessarily because I wanted to observe it. That was all."

His face took on a questioning look. "In any case, maybe it was because of this mitzvah that the urge to pray reawakened in me. Maybe."

Jeff moved uncomfortably in his chair. "What mitzvah?" he whispered.

His grandfather lifted his left arm up in a gesture of impatience, like one irritated by the interruption of his thoughts. "We'll get to that, Yisrael Yaakov, don't worry."

Again, he fell into a bemused silence, broken only by the sound of his sipping the tea.

"So where was I? Oh, yes. I was standing, in the dawning light of day, next to the barn in the village. Only G-d in heaven knows how alone I felt, so hopeless and unfortunate. The residents of the village — I didn't even know its name — hadn't yet woken up, but the roosters were already crowing in the approaching dawn, and dogs in various corners were barking, announcing that they were alive and awake. A few of them even turned up, growling at my unwanted presence in their village. I was afraid of the people; deathly afraid. I didn't know how they would react when they would see me, and I was particularly scared of their reaction when they would find the corpses of the two agents in the barn. I was in absolute despair. Is it a wonder, then, that my soul broke out in prayer?"

The old man breathed deeply and eased his grip on the teacup.

"Yes, in my heart I prayed. I prayed for a way to get out of this terrible trap alive. The strange thing was that in those moments I made a promise. A promise made to — I didn't know to whom. I promised that if I got out of this and reached a safe haven, far from the long arm of the GPO, I would search to find out what it meant to be a Jew. Strange, no? Because up to that day the matter didn't interest me at all."

The elderly man straightened up suddenly. His voice sounded stronger, clearer. Both his son and grandson noticed the change that had taken hold of him.

"And then, my children, then suddenly, like a light coming from an unexpected source, I heard myself make a vow:

"'G-d of the world, if You save me from this hell, if You show me the path to safety, I will return to Moscow, despite the dangers. I will return to my house on Krasno Bogatirski Street to get my poor, abandoned *tefillin*, that lie in that house.'

"That was my prayer. Strange! I suddenly believed that I wouldn't deserve to be saved, unless I saved my *tefillin* as well."

The old man turned wise eyes on his son and, particularly, his grandson. He looked eagerly for the spark of understanding and empathy. Uncomfortable under the scrutiny, Jeff asked quickly, "That was the mitzvah that you observed?"

The old man nodded his head in assent. "Yes. That was the mitzvah that I observed. My father, may his memory be blessed, had been a devout man; a strange bird in an atheistic state that trampled to death anyone who held on to his religious beliefs. And here, a day before his death, on the day he revealed to me my Jewish name, the one he'd given to me at my *bris*, he also revealed to me the secret of the *tefillin*. With tears in his eyes he begged me to put them on daily, and not just for a minute. And he also begged me to watch over them closely, for they were very holy, very valuable *tefillin*. They had been passed down as a family inheritance for generations, from my great-great-grandfather, who'd been a disciple of the holy Baal Shem Tov himself. My father told me that once the Besht had put these *tefillin* on, and had hinted to my forefather that they would guard him from all evil — he and all his descendants who would wear them. None of them, the Besht promised, would follow evil paths."

Suddenly the old man stopped short. He needed to rest a bit: the emotional upheaval had been too much for him. Jeff was subdued. Some dim feeling warned him that here, at this point, his troubles were about to begin. "Where are the *tefillin* now?" he asked.

"I hope that they are still there, in our apartment in Moscow. I hope so very much, do you understand? After I fled Russia I was never able to go back! No, not until today. And I haven't forgotten, even for one day, the *tefillin* that I left behind. I was never able to fulfill my vow. More than 50 years have passed. Do you understand now?"

Moshe Aryeh was very moved. "You see, Jeff, in your merit, we are hearing a piece of Grandfather's history that we'd never known."

Jeff didn't answer. *Who knows if this "merit" will really be meritorious for me*, he thought.

Moshe Aryeh turned to his father. "How were you finally saved?"

The old man's face shone. He was enjoying his descendants' growing interest in his hidden past.

"While I was still deep in prayer I heard the roar of a motor approaching from the dirt road that crossed the village. I jumped from my place and hid behind a bush that grew on a mound of dirt nearby. The black car, with a screech of brakes, halted next to the barn. Two GPO agents burst out of it like madmen. Their revolvers were pointed at my two comrades from prison, who were pulled out of the car, their hands tied behind them. Their faces were terrified. My heart beat wildly. I wanted desperately to know how the GPO had managed to get on their trail so quickly. I crouched in my hiding place, paralyzed with fear, almost unable to breathe. And from my shelter I stared, wide eyed, at what was happening.

"The officers of the GPO pushed the fugitives whom they'd captured behind the barn. After a few minutes I saw my fellows, their hands untied, dragging the two corpses into the car. I thought I would pass out at any minute. I was certain I was going to be spotted. Surely they would soon begin to search the area. And me — I had no place to go. No place to hide. I was also certain that my fellow prisoners had betrayed me, that they'd accuse me of the murders. I knew that my fate was like theirs — sealed. I knew what punishment awaited me when we'd be returned to the camp. Death."

Grandfather spoke slowly, tranquilly, but with a voice full of emotion. His story had taken hours; after long years of silence everything had come out, every tiny detail. He told his son and grandson how the GPO agents had searched for him, while the village farmers had looked on silently. How they had been so close to him, and how his prayers had clearly been answered and he had not been detected. After the agents had left, one of the local farmers had hidden him in a bunker dug beneath his house. He had spent two days in the dark bunker, surrounded with the smell of mold and the aura of fear.

"The GPO agents returned to the village to look for me. They came to my host's house too, and even discovered the underground bunker, but they didn't find me. My 'host' found out that I was Jewish. When the secret police had left, I heard a woman's voice call me.

"'Come up right now.'

"I did as I was commanded. I realized that this must be the farmer's wife. I rushed up. Not far from the entrance to the bunker a woman awaited me, her face angry and full of hatred.

"'You lied to my husband and said you were not a Jew, filthy *zhid*. They told us that the third fugitive, that's you, is Jewish. They took my husband, Ivan, for questioning because of the bunker that they found in the house.'

"I was quiet; I didn't know what to say. I was afraid that any word would enrage her more. Who knew what the consequences would be?

"'You're lucky, *zhid*, that I don't give you up to the GPO. But then we'll all be lost. Get out of this village as fast as you can. Understand?'

"'I understand,' I answered weakly. I was ready to go out the door and leave the hut, come what may, but her wild cry brought me to a halt. 'Where are you going, you stupid Jew? Do you want every informer in the village to know that we've hidden you here? Wait!'

"She rushed to the other room and brought me clothing belonging to her husband. I took my prisoner's uniform off and in a few minutes had become a typical Russian farmer.

"'Now,' she said, 'you wait here. In a half-hour my uncle's car will arrive. He knows about you. I had to tell him. He said he would get you forged documents. You'll travel with him to Vladivostok. And I don't want to hear anything more from you.'"

Grandfather sighed, remembering those bygone days. He described the gentile who brought him to Vladivostok and left him in the middle of the city late at night.

"And there, again, on the street of that strange city, thoughts of the *tefillin* came back to me. I tried to banish them from my heart, but did not succeed. Do you understand me?" he suddenly asked his son and grandson.

"Understand, no," his son replied. "But I'm very moved by your story."

"It's a long story, how I managed in Vladivostok. How I finally smuggled myself onto a Japanese freighter, how the Japanese sailors believed my story when they found me in the middle of the high seas, and how they agreed not to return me to Russia, but to take me to

Japan. There I was granted asylum. At the first opportunity I emigrated to the United States. But that's all another story. A tale in itself."

Grandfather tapped Jeff on the arm.

"Your father has asked why I never told him this chapter in my life. Today I will reveal the secret, the reason. For 50 years I have been dreaming that one day I would be able to fulfill my vow, to return to Moscow and find my *tefillin*. The memory of them helped me to survive during my long flight from Russia. And because I hadn't managed to make my dream come true and fulfill my vow I decided not to tell anyone what had happened during those days, for without those *tefillin* my salvation could not be complete."

The old man grew silent once again. His breathing became irregular. Jeff felt his grandfather's hand, still holding on to him, begin to tremble uncontrollably. But Jeff didn't move. He waited for what his grandfather would say next. He already knew.

"And now, Yisrael Yaakov, I have heard from your father that you are going to travel to Moscow. I am begging you, pleading with you: Find the *tefillin* that are undoubtedly still hidden away in the wall of the room where I lived with my mother, my brothers, and my sisters — who knows if they are still alive."

He looked at his grandson beseechingly.

"I beg you!"

5

eff lowered his eyes. Though he had suspected such a request was coming, still, hearing his grandfather say it left him stunned. He stared at his shoes: he could not deal with his grandfather's eyes, begging and commanding at the same time. A storm raged within him, a maelstrom of anger, impatience, and pity for his grandfather who could be so obsessed with a pair of *tefillin*, holy as they may be, that he did not see the dangers he might be bringing down upon his grandson's head.

Jeff gently pulled his hand from his grandfather's grasp, stood up, and, avoiding the question, said: "Grandfather, it's late. It's been too much for you. Go to sleep and we'll continue tomorrow."

The old man's features grew shocked and uncomprehending. "But Yisrael Yaakov, you haven't answered me! I want to know: Are you going or not?"

Jeff could feel the impatience grow in his breast. "We'll talk about it tomorrow, Grandfather. I haven't yet decided. I have to think about it."

The old man tried to get up. His palms gripped the table for support, and after considerable exertion he managed to stand. Now, upright, he said indignantly: "What's there to think about? Haven't I explained myself well?"

"Grandfather, you've explained everything perfectly. But it's not clear yet if I'm traveling or not. My boss hasn't made the final decision."

The spark in the old man's eyes dimmed somewhat. Jeff's father, Moshe Aryeh, who had also stood up, hastily interrupted. "Yes, Father, everything's okay. Don't worry, he'll go. He wants to think about it awhile. That's understandable."

The old man stared at his son and grandson, who were preparing to leave the apartment. He leaned heavily on the table; it provided some support. Why was his instinct telling him that his beloved grandson was avoiding his question? A sudden fear gripped the old man, piercing his heart like a bolt of lightning: his grandson would not go. This silence, this refusal to give a clear answer, worried him. He couldn't conceive of why his Yisrael Yaakov wasn't excited about this mitzvah that Hashem had prepared for him, had almost dropped into his lap — the mitzvah of saving a pair of holy *tefillin*; *tefillin*, moreover, that had been handed down in their family from generation to generation. Wasn't this an enormous *zechus* that had fallen into his hands? And had he, Asher Yosef, at this very moment lost his last hope to see those holy *tefillin*, to feel them with his hands and, perhaps, merit to put them on once more, one final time before he left this world? Had they no pity on their old father, who had suffered such tortures and pain?

Jeff and his father realized that Grandfather wanted to tell them something, but some inner force was restraining him. Asher Yosef's mouth opened a bit, his eyes followed them with a wild and haunted look, a look of despair and sorrow. He stared at his son and grandson, already standing near the door, prepared to bid him good night.

Suddenly he collapsed. He fell back into his chair and burst out in bitter, uncontrollable tears. His son, Moshe Aryeh, raced to his side to try and calm him. Jeff also approached the chair, and whispered to his father, "I can't stand this! Tell him, tell Grandfather, that I've decided to go. You'll see; that will calm him."

"Father," Moshe Aryeh whispered to his father, whose tears still streamed down his face, "Father, enough. Enough! Yisrael Yaakov has told me that he will go. Enough! He'll try to find them, your *tefillin*. Enough, Father, enough!"

The words were effective. Slowly the old man calmed down. Jeff hurried to the kitchen to make another cup of tea. While he waited for the kettle to come to a boil, he carried in a glass of cold water.

"Drink, Grandfather, drink. It will do you good. I don't understand why you thought I wouldn't go. I just wanted to think a little. What's the matter with you?"

Though Grandfather was much calmer, he didn't even try to explain his sudden fit of weeping. He was already past that. "I have to explain to you where the *tefillin* are hidden, there, in Moscow. Of course, this all depends on whether the city or someone else hasn't already destroyed the house. If the house, heaven forbid, is no longer there, at least I'll know that I did whatever I could to save them, and I didn't just break my vow. Perhaps, because of my sins, it was simply decreed otherwise."

The old man, recovered, stood up and walked swiftly towards his bedroom. All evidence of his hysterical weeping had vanished, as if it had never happened. The fleeting thought passed through Jeff's mind: perhaps the crying and collapse had been staged only to influence him to agree to the trip to Moscow, a means of pressuring him.

After a short interval, Grandfather Handler returned to the room. His son and grandson sat quietly around the table. Asher Yosef held an old, folded piece of paper in his hand. He, too, took a seat and placed the apparently timeworn piece of paper on the table. Slowly, he unfolded it. The men stared at it, at the faded lines scratched upon it, uncomprehending. The old man didn't hurry to explain its meaning; he stared longingly at the marks, that seemed so strange to Jeff and his father.

Finally he spoke. "This is a diagram of our small apartment on Krasno Bogatirski Street. Many years ago, a few years after I'd moved to New York, I drew the apartment and the exact place where the *tefillin* had been hidden. I drew it because I was afraid that over the years I would forget. Here, thank G-d, I can show you the exact location, so that if you get there, you'll find them."

He glanced at his grandson's face, which remained impassive and expressionless. Grandfather seemed oblivious; he was completely taken up with the rescue mission, hardly aware of his surroundings.

"You see," he turned directly to Jeff, "you see? This is the room in which we lived. From here you go out through a narrow hallway that leads to the kitchen. Here, can you see it? Here, on the left side, is the communal kitchen of all the families who lived in the apartment. We only had one room there. Do you understand? That was the way it was, then. So go back to our room. Can you see it? Here is a window that looks out on the street. We lived on the first floor. Here, in the square drawn on the paper, is the window. Now, on top of the window, that is, on top of the thick frame around the window, on the left side, is a shaky brick. From the outside you can't see a thing. Carefully touch the place, until you can feel it. Pull it out slowly, slowly, do you hear? Slowly! You don't want it to fall apart in your hands! And when you put your hand in deep, to the right side, you'll find the *tefillin*. Understand?"

Jeff looked at his grandfather, and didn't know whether to laugh or to cry. On the one hand, he was moved by his fervor. On the other, he was shocked by how far removed his grandfather was from reality. Seeing that his grandfather awaited a reply, he asked, speaking in as calm a voice as he could muster, "And how, Grandfather, do you think that a simple American citizen, who doesn't speak one word of Russian, who knows nothing of Moscow, will get to this house? And how can I get into it?"

Grandfather smile understandingly; at the same time, he waved away the objection.

"You'll find the place easily. I rely on you. I am convinced that G-d will put the right words into your mouth and you'll succeed."

He grabbed his grandson's hand again, as if to strengthen his request.

Jeff felt himself growing impatient. He realized that arguing with his grandfather was useless. The man was obsessed with his dream and no logic would sway him now. Jeff knew he had no choice: he must go. It was a question of life and death, the life or death of his grandfather. Upon his return he would explain to Grandfather that the mission had failed. He would tell him that the house had been destroyed, or some such excuse. After all, white lies were permissible in order to keep the peace.

Jeff looked at his watch. It was 10 p.m. Time to go. He stood up; his father followed. He hoped he could still catch *Ma'ariv* at Itzkowitz's in Bnei Brak.

"Good night, Grandfather. It was all very informative, and also fascinating. I'll admit, I was moved by your story. And don't worry, I'll go to Moscow."

The old man, too, stood up and escorted them to the door. A glimmer of hope shone in his eyes and a flash of color painted his wrinkled cheeks. His eyes gleamed. As they walked down the stairs, they heard his voice follow them: "But Yisrael Yaakov, remember that it is Russia. Not America! Be very careful there. The KGB is full of evil men, and very cruel. Murderers! They are everywhere, suspecting everyone, and you must be very, very careful. Promise me!"

"Yes, yes, I promise. Good night, Grandfather," Jeff said, glancing towards his father walking quietly beside him.

"Do you know what a mess your father has gotten me into?"

"Your grandfather, you mean," his father retorted.

"Okay, my grandfather. And just to keep me calm, he manages to add that I'm putting myself into deathly danger during this search for his *tefillin*. What's going to be? Is it a mitzvah that one must give one's life for? What should we do?"

His father could hear the fury and despair in Jeff's voice, but he said nothing. He simply didn't know what to say. Finally, he mumbled, "Go and ask a *rav*."

Jeff landed in New York early in the morning. His wife, Miriam, met him at JFK. She came to hear what news he brought from the Holy Land, from his grandfather's house. She drove him back home in absolute silence though, containing her curiosity as best she could. The tension in the car was palpable. Finally, as they drove on the Belt Parkway on their way to Flatbush, she could not wait any longer. She spoke, trying to sound nonchalant and unconcerned.

"You're going?"

Jeff didn't rush to reply. At last, he said, "Yes. I'm going."

She felt her body go limp. Hardly aware of it, she closed her eyes and almost let go of the steering wheel.

"What are you doing?" Jeff yelled.

She had almost crashed into the car in front of her; she'd practically forgotten that she was driving. At Jeff's shout she opened her eyes in fright and hit the brakes hard. The screech sounded like a wail.

"Is this the way you plan on keeping me out of Moscow?"

He was tired from the flight and angry that he had agreed to his grandfather's pleas. But he immediately regretted his sharp words to his wife. In the meantime, she retorted, "That's the way a person drives when she hears her husband is traveling to Moscow."

Again they sat in silence until they reached their home. She parked in front of the house, and helped her husband with his luggage. She gave him a steaming cup of coffee, sat across from him, and threw him a glance.

"Tell me," she said.

And he told her. Told her the entire story, from beginning to end. Finally he summarized the whole thing in one sentence. "And I decided to go, despite my own inclinations and fears."

His wan face showed how he awaited her reaction. But Miriam sat quietly, her eyes half shut, her head stiffly erect, like one paralyzed. After a few moments she roused herself, opened her eyes, and said, "I've changed my mind. I agree to your going."

He stared at her in obvious shock, his voice edged with surprise. "What happened to you?"

"Nothing. I simply understand your grandfather."

"Fine. I understand him too. But that's it? You're not afraid anymore?"

"I'm very afraid. But 'a messenger to do a mitzvah does not come to harm.' Until now, you were just going for business, and I was much more frightened. Now this is something entirely different. This is a mission."

"And you believe that there is a chance that I will find the *tefillin*, or even manage to search for them? What's the matter with you?"

"I don't know. In any case, the trip is now different."

Jeff sipped the last drops of coffee and whispered, "Abba told me to ask a *rav*."

"It's always a good idea. In any case, we never know why heaven drops these things on us. Maybe the entire idea of the business trip came only so that you could help your grandfather with his *tefillin*. Who knows?"

After a thoughtful pause she added, "Actually, there's no maybe about it. It's a certainty!"

She stood up, her eyes bright. "I'll say a few chapters of *Tehillim* every day. And may Hashem watch over you."

She hurried to the kitchen. She didn't want him to see the tears falling down her face.

"I am happy to see you," David Northfeld greeted Jeff, as he stood before him the next morning in his office. "What have you decided?"

"I'm going."

Mr. Northfeld's face lit up. He stuck his hand out over the polished mahogany desk and pressed Jeff's hand warmly. The two exchanged smiles.

"A wise decision, absolutely. I'll tell the secretary to call the travel office. They'll make all the arrangements, visas, tickets, everything."

"Fine."

The boss lowered his voice, like one sharing a secret. "And the bonuses, as we agreed on."

Jeff nodded in assent.

Northfeld's face grew more serious. He held his Parker pen in his hand, waving it in warning.

"Remember, Jeff, this is a unique trip. It's Russia, not America. You understand the difference, I hope. It's a police state. The secret police, the KGB, runs the country. The KGB head, Yuri Andropov, who is very clever and very brutal, has the power, not Prime Minister Brezhnev. They'll follow your every footstep and action. They'll follow you day and night. Your hotel room will be bugged; they'll record you even when you talk to yourself. Try not to call the office or your home. Any word you say that they don't like can mean trouble. I'm asking you: Don't get involved. Don't change dollars on the street, with cab drivers, or anyone. Most of them are KGB agents. They'll inform on you immediately. At the airport you'll be met by a man from Intourist, the official Soviet tourist agency. Do business only with him. Do you hear?"

"I hear, I hear!" Jeff was losing patience. Here he was hearing his own fears verbalized, and in almost the same words that his grandfather had used.

"Usually the Intourist men speak English. But remember! Even with them, be cautious. Don't get too friendly. They are undoubtedly agents of the secret police. Don't ask them too many questions. Mind your own business and don't seem too interested in anything else. Remember! Your visa is good only in the city of Moscow. Don't ask to go anywhere else, to Leningrad for example. That will seem suspicious to them. Try to finish your business as fast as possible so that you can fly home in a few days. Clear?"

"Very clear. And thanks for the scare."

"It's not a scare, Jeff. They're good rules of caution. That's all."

Jeff nodded his head, as if in agreement. He felt a surge of self-pity for the terrifying situation in which he had suddenly found himself trapped. But there was no choice: forces more powerful than he were dragging him towards an unknown destination. His rabbi had told him he was obligated to take the trip. He had, in fact, calmed Jeff down somewhat, but he had not been able to completely quell the fears that had grown within him.

The night before the trip, almost at midnight, the telephone rang, breaking the silence of the night. Jeff wasn't expecting any calls. First, he tried to ignore the shrill rings, but after a short hesitation he lifted the receiver. Before he could say anything he heard a voice with a heavy Russian accent speaking in broken English.

"The man travels tomorrow to Moscow?"

Jeff felt his ire flare up. "Who are you, sir, and why are you interested in my itinerary?"

The voice answered with still another question. "But the man travels to Russia, yes? Tomorrow at 8 in the morning I ring your house's bell."

The connection was broken; the man had hung up. Jeff held the receiver for a few seconds, staring at it without really seeing. *Was this unknown voice the first sign of things to come, there among the Communists?* he thought grimly to himself.

T he bell rang at exactly 8 o'clock the next morning. Jeff was furious with himself for not having sneaked out earlier. Somehow he had not believed that the mysterious midnight caller would actually show up, exactly to the minute as promised.

Jeff was sitting in his kitchen eating breakfast. His muted conversation with his wife centered around the preparations necessary before his night flight to Vienna, and from there to Moscow.

For that first minute Jeff hesitated. Should he stand up and answer the door, or ignore the ringing bell? Finally Jeff decided to stay where he was. Maybe the person ringing the bell would give up and leave if he saw that the inhabitants were ignoring him.

Another ring, shrill and long, broke the morning quiet.

Miriam jumped up. Jeff signaled to her to stay where she was. She turned startled eyes to him; his answering glance conveyed heavy tension.

"What's the matter?" she whispered, frightened.

He put his finger to his lips as one demanding absolute silence.

With a gesture he let her know he would explain later. In silence he tried to calm her down, but he felt her panic growing.

"Is it connected to your trip?" she whispered.

He nodded his head in assent and again gestured for her to be quiet. Ignoring his request, she said, "It's already begun, the fears, the dangers, and all the rest?"

Jeff's face reflected his own doubts and ambivalence. The tension in his eyes grew, or so it seemed, at least, to Miriam.

The jangle of the bell could be heard once again, sharper and longer than the previous one. It was followed by loud knocks on the door itself. The baby, in his room on the second floor, burst out into loud wailing. Miriam rushed into the hallway and climbed the stairs to his room, never noticing in her hurry to get to her child that the mysterious man at the door would realize that someone was home. Jeff was trapped.

"One minute," he called, as he stood up and walked towards the door. He felt rather foolish: surely the caller wouldn't believe that he hadn't heard the doorbell until now.

Jeff opened the door. Now here was a surprise: Before him stood a man in his 30's, dressed like a typical yeshivah student — black suit, black hat, a bristly beard on his chin. Not an American, Jeff could see that at a glance.

"Good morning. May I come in?"

Jeff hesitated, not rushing to respond to the greeting. He examined the stranger carefully, from head to toe, and simply was at a loss. The word KGB loomed large in his consciousness, inescapable.

"What do you want?" Jeff asked coldly, holding the door only slightly ajar.

The stranger seemed surprised by the frigid reception. In any case, he tried to smile as he asked, "Are you Mr. Jeff Handler, traveling tonight to Moscow?"

Jeff waited. Harsh thoughts flashed through his mind: *Where did this stranger get such detailed information? What does he want of me? Who is he? And what should I do now?*

Jeff had no desire to confirm details of his trip. "You're mistaken. I'm not going."

The man seemed shocked. "Impossible!"

Jeff laughed loudly. The laughter broke some of the tension roiling within him. "What do you mean, impossible? I know whether I'm traveling tonight or not!"

The young man stood stock still. "But they told me that the gentleman travels tonight, and that he will do business in diamonds."

Jeff kept his cool. "Who told you that?"

"I was told."

Jeff felt a growing impatience. "By whom?"

"We from Russia, we don't say more than we have to."

Jeff felt the blood rush to his face. His cheeks grew scarlet with anger, as he shouted, "Tell me right now who told you about my trip, do you hear?"

The man backed off slightly. Clearly, he was insulted by the cool reception accorded him.

"But the gentleman has said that he doesn't travel, so why should you care who said it, if the information is incorrect?"

Jeff gave him a withering look of scorn. He was certain that this was a well-disguised KGB agent standing before him, anxious to make a connection with him. His talks with his grandfather two days before had had a strong influence upon him. Though the wheels of his mind were turning frantically, Jeff could not find a sensible answer to return to the man. He felt defeated as he said, "You know what? You're right. I am traveling to Moscow tonight. What do you want from me? What's wrong with my going?"

The stranger calmed down. Jeff could see that clearly. He returned to the door, gave an apologetic laugh, and said, "Everything is okay with your trip, Mister. You're suspicious of me for nothing. I was a refusenik in Moscow, and I managed to get to New York. I learn in a yeshivah here. My name is Michoel Borochavitski. You can check me out in Yeshivas Mir here in Flatbush. And I —"

Jeff's patience came to an end. Because of his deep suspicions, which had grown day by day, he did not believe a word that the man standing before him had said.

"*Nu*, so what do you want?" he asked shortly.

"My younger brother is still there, Mr. Handler. Like me, he too is interested in Yiddishkeit. I want to send a pair of *tefillin* with you for him."

And before he even finished speaking he had whipped out a small package wrapped in plain brown paper and handed it to Jeff.

Jeff stared indifferently at the stranger who called himself Michoel. His hands didn't reach to take up the proffered package. He knew that he must be careful. The serious suspicion grew that this was an attempt to trap him. Of all things, *tefillin*! Maybe the Russians already knew about his grandfather's *tefillin*? Were they hinting that they knew everything? When he reached Moscow he might be asked some difficult questions about this pair of *tefillin*. He had paid strict attention to the warnings from his boss and from his grandfather on how he should act in foreign territory. Now maybe they were trying to trap him into illegal action, as a way of paying him back for his grandfather's flight and the murder of two agents of the secret police. After all, the Soviet secret police were famous for being almost omniscient. Moreover, these *tefillin* could, in their hands, serve as evidence that he planned on pursuing anti-Soviet activities through Jewish holy objects, which were banned in the Soviet Union.

Jeff was tempted to call his boss and cancel the trip. But he realized that this was a futile thought. Though he desired to do it with all his heart, he simply lacked the courage to take such a step.

Jeff turned his eyes to the strange man and said, "So it's like what I said at the beginning: I am not going to Russia. You've made a mistake, young man. I pretended I was going just out of curiosity. Goodbye."

He quickly slammed the door and returned to the kitchen. Jeff finished his breakfast in silence. He *bentched*, his heart awash in a storm of emotion.

Jeff reached JFK three hours before flight time. He simply could not stay at home. Although his wife usually didn't drive him to the airport, this time she chose to. They did not exchange a word all through the trip from Flatbush to the airport. Jeff stared sternly at the passing scenery, at the cars and buildings passing swiftly by, as if this were the first time he was seeing them. He took a deep breath, in an attempt to release the tension in his chest, tension curled as tightly as a fist.

They went directly to the Pan Am terminal. Immediately upon stepping into the large hall, Jeff stopped, rooted to the spot.

"What's the matter?" Miriam's voice gave off concern.

"The man is here," Jeff said in controlled anger.

"What man?"

Jeff lost what little patience he had. "*Nu*, the one who paid me that friendly visit this morning."

Jeff pointed to a young man who stood out in his garb of the average yeshivah student: black suit, white shirt, dark hat perched on his head. He stood a short distance away, like an island amidst the waves of humanity washing over him. Fortunately his back was facing them, and he didn't notice Jeff's arrival. Jeff could see Borochavitski eagerly scanning the faces of the passers-by. Clearly, the Russian was looking for someone.

"Oh," his wife exclaimed, "that's him? I didn't see him this morning."

Jeff didn't take his eyes off the student. "You didn't miss anything," he said shortly.

"Do you think he's looking for you?" she whispered.

His impatience grew. "How should I know? I hope not. But I am certain he is. It's driving me crazy, that he came to the house with a pair of *tefillin*. Do you think they want to hint to me that they know my grandfather's story?"

His wife was quiet for a long moment. In the meantime they both stood, unmoving.

"Jeff," she said.

He turned to her. "Yes?"

"Tell me, maybe your fears are exaggerated? Maybe he really is a yeshivah student wanting to get a pair of *tefillin* to his brother in Moscow?"

Jeff nodded. "Could be. But if so, why is everybody frightening me? Why did my boss warn me to behave properly in Moscow, keeping my eyes open? Why did my grandfather remind me that the KGB no doubt still remembers his flight and murder of their two agents? Even the travel office told me: 'Remember, Jeff, you're going to Russia. Don't take anything from anyone in the airport. Stay away from any funny business, from anything that smacks of the illegal. Don't let the taxi drivers or elevator boys in the hotel persuade you to change dollars for rubles on the black market. Don't talk politics at all. Don't change your itinerary, and listen to the instructions of the authorities.' Wow! So what do you want me to do now? Do you think these warnings, that I've been hearing for days now, haven't had their effect? Is it any wonder that I'm a bit nervous and suspicious of everything and everyone?"

He was quiet for a minute, and then added, "And I honestly believe that the criminal file against Grandfather is a serious one, and my fears are wellgrounded."

Miriam sought refuge, again, in silence. Finally, though, she spoke. "So maybe — maybe you should cancel the trip. Let's turn around and go home."

Jeff waved the suggestion away.

"Too late! It's impossible to go back."

Suddenly he grinned. "You explained to me that a messenger doing a mitzvah doesn't come to harm, right? So what's happened now? Besides, do you want a husband who gives up when things get tough? Who surrenders when he already knows what he must do — to take on the mission that his grandfather has placed upon him?"

Miriam did not answer. She knew that he was right. One could not just run away from the battlefield.

The yeshivah student suddenly noticed Jeff. His face lit up. He made his way through the crowds. Jeff immediately raced towards the check-in counter for European-bound flights. He tried as best he could not to meet the other's eyes. But Micheol Borochavitski, as he claimed to be called, followed right behind him. Now he was at his side, his eyes pleading.

"Maybe, Mr. Handler, you'll take the *tefillin* to my brother?"

The young man grabbed Jeff's arm. Jeff shook him off firmly.

"I told you I'm not going to Russia." (*"Don't take anything from anyone."* The warning rang through his head.) He turned towards the clerk, handing her his passport and ticket. The yeshivah student gave up and disappeared among the crowds.

The clerk did her job efficiently and with complete indifference. She signed what needed to be signed, checked the baggage's weight, gave Jeff a seat assignment, at his request, near a window. But at the end, as she returned the ticket and passport to Jeff, she smiled.

"Going to Moscow, sir?"

"Yes."

"Take care of yourself and have a good trip."

Again — a warning. As if he needed still another.

Jeff left his wife and turned toward passport control. He disappeared behind a glass door and after an hour and a half of waiting finally boarded the DC-9 on its way to Vienna. There, after a layover of a few hours, he boarded the Aeroflot plane.

The plane landed at Chermentyevo 2 Airport, near the Soviet capital. The time was 9 p.m. A three-hour flight from Vienna had brought him, suddenly, to a new reality: the reality of the oppressive Russian regime of Leonid Brezhnev, prime minister of the Soviet Union, and Yuri Andropov, KGB chief and strongman of the Politburo, the ruling arm of the Communist state. The change from the Pan Am plane, with its lighthearted atmosphere, to the Topolov jet of Aeroflot, was astounding; the contrast was marked. Jeff noticed the deep silence of the travelers, the majority of whom were Russians returning home from abroad. He did not see a single passenger chatting with his neighbor. The stewardesses, too, did not speak much. No, he did not see fright on people's faces, as the western media had sometimes described; the faces of his fellow passengers were impassive, rather than suspicious. Their faces revealed nothing.

Jeff waited patiently at Customs Control. This would be his first real encounter with the Communist world. From here on, he had to keep his eyes open, scrutinize every move made by the authorities. Every detail was important, when he would set off in another day or two on his search for his grandfather's home in this city. He knew that Customs inspections here were serious business. His eyes took in the care with which the agents searched through the passengers' luggage. They did their work silently and cheerlessly. Occasionally they whispered a question.

When his turn came he prepared himself for a cross-examination on every article in his luggage. And now, much to his surprise, after the official checked his passport and entry visa, and held a two-minute consultation with another official, they released him, without even searching his bags. This worried Jeff slightly: He could not decide if this was a good sign or a bad one. He certainly could not find any logical explanation. Except — No, he did not want even to think it; it was too terrifying.

A young man waited for him at the terminal's entrance, a sign in his hand bearing Latin letters which spelled out *Jeff Handler*.

Jeff approached the man and shook his hand. He knew that this was an Intourist representative, who would accompany him all through his trip to the city. He had been promised that his guide spoke a fluent English and would act as his translator. Jeff did not doubt for a moment that he was a KGB informer as well, who would follow his every move. He had been afraid of this even in New York.

"Good evening. My name is Gregory Butbinick," the Russian turned to him, speaking softly. "I hope you will enjoy your stay with us," added Gregory politely, before leading Jeff to the old state-owned automobile that would take them to Moscow.

After close to two hours' travel, the car reached the gates of the Russia Hotel, the huge hotel where the Soviets housed their official visitors.

Jeff greeted the doorman with a friendly wave. The man, dressed in a green uniform, nodded sternly. He stood outside the glassed-walled hotel. The function of this doorman, Jeff was to learn later, was not to offer assistance to those entering the hotel. Rather, his main job was to keep Soviet citizens out of the building. Black marketeers, who dared work right under the noses of the police, seeking tourists in order to sell them stolen merchandise and to trick them by exchanging dollars for forged rubles, offering ten times the rate that the tourist would receive through official channels. Tourists also claimed the attention of curious Soviets, interested in chatting with Westerners in order to learn about their way of life.

Jeff entered the hotel through a revolving door that led to the lobby. At first glance the area seemed totally empty. The atmosphere surrounding him was somber. The lobby, built of gray stone and aluminum, was narrow and long. Jeff's new friend, Gregory, led him towards a booth that looked like a ticket-seller's stall. Jeff showed the man inside his Intourist reservation, his passport, and his entry visa. The man studied the passport carefully and disappeared behind a door that was behind a small desk.

Jeff waited tensely. Gregory did not bother explaining the reason for the delay. After a short wait he heard a voice behind him calling in English, with a heavy Russian accent: "Mr. Jeff Handler."

He swung around. He could feel a momentary twinge of panic. He was standing before an aging woman who was staring coolly at him. She spoke without hesitation. "I am from Intourist. Your papers, please."

After a short scrutiny she returned the identification papers to him, but not the passport or visa. She also gave him a green-colored card.

"This, sir, is your travel permit. You must carry it with you at all times. Your passport and visa will be returned when you leave the hotel. You must show your permit whenever someone in authority asks you to."

"Okay." Jeff could feel the Soviet halter growing tighter around his throat.

Gregory left, telling Jeff that he would meet him in the lobby at 8 o'clock the next morning. Jeff took the elevator to the sixth floor. There, near the bank of elevators, a young woman sat at a desk. She was absorbed in a book, whose torn binding testified to its continual use. Jeff soon learned that a porter — called a *dzornie* — was stationed on every floor, responsible for keeping everything in order. These, too, were KGB agents. This young woman was obligated to report daily to her superiors on every movement she observed on her allotted floor: who came and when, who left and for how long. Jeff filed away this disturbing fact in his brain.

"'Allo," the young woman called out, as she heard the elevator door open, "your travel permit, please."

Jeff handed her the card, and she gave him the key to his room, number 636.

"When you leave the room give me the key and I'll return your permit to you," she told him in poorly spoken English.

Jeff went into his room, a medium-sized room, very simply furnished. The red carpet rolled out on the wooden floor was in urgent need of a good cleaning. The dust that clouded the window did not lighten the atmosphere. Jeff looked around him. He had heard much about the listening devices and wiretaps that were found in every hotel room in Russia, and he tried hard to locate them. His efforts, though, were fruitless. He gave a close look at the telephone, by far the most suspicious object there. Finally, he comforted himself with the thought that it did not really matter; he was alone in the room and did not plan on talking to himself and criticizing the Soviet regime. Wiretaps could not pick up thoughts. At least he hoped so.

Jeff approached the window. Across from him, he could see Red Square. He thought of photos he had seen in *The New York Times* of soldiers on parade in October, on the anniversary of the Soviet Revolution. And now here he was, staring in the night at the empty square. At his right stood the Kremlin, hiding its terrible secrets behind its red walls. From his room he could see into it just a little. In the distance stood the churches with their onion-shaped domes. In place of the crosses that had stood atop them for generations loomed five-pointed stars, symbol of Communist Russia. All the buildings in the area were dark; only the churches of the Kremlin were illuminated by lanterns that flickered all through the night. The deserted streets, cold and lifeless, added to the dejection that lay heavy upon Jeff's heart. Jeff could see also the Moscow River flowing nearby, the flickering lanterns of the Kremlin walls playing games of light and shadow upon its quiet waves.

Jeff could not pull his gaze away from the Kremlin and its secrets. On the plane here he had read with interest a report in *The Times* on the latest prisoners taken by the KGB, Jewish refuseniks who three days earlier had held a protest march in front of the Kremlin. And now here he was, Jeff — Yisrael Yaakov — standing near these silent walls, a free Jew from a free land, while beneath the Russian quiet a great Jewish drama went on. Looking at these dreadful walls, so close to him, he felt ashamed that he had read those newspaper reports without giving them much thought. Even now, he was not particularly disturbed. Thoughts of how he would carry out his mission to Moscow, how he would smuggle his grandfather's *tefillin* out of an apartment whose very existence was in doubt, disturbed him much more.

The real reason for his visit to this city — the diamond business — was completely forgotten.

7

Jeff woke up before dawn in a cold sweat. He sat bolt upright, trying to remember where he was. Blackness engulfed the room entirely. After a moment of haziness it came back to him: he was in Moscow, in the Russia Hotel.

He got out of bed and went to the window. Carefully, so as not to make unnecessary noise, he pushed away the heavy curtain. The flickering lights of the lanterns illuminating the Kremlin walls sneaked into his room. Red Square was silent, the silence of death.

He turned the light on in his room. His watch told him it was 3 a.m. Jeff got dressed. He did not have the patience to stay in bed. He had two days to stay in the city, and he had to find his grandfather's *tefillin*. He had to prepare his plans. The business of the diamonds he would take care of, *im yirtzeh Hashem*, without problems. He had no doubts on that score.

But what of Krasno Bogatirski Street? How would he get there? How would he find it? He did not have the faintest idea how to go about it, and what to do. Already last night he had realized that there was no phone directory in his room. Strange. Had there been one, perhaps he could have found a street map of the city.

After some interminable moments of hesitation he carefully opened the door of his room. He looked down the corridor, right and left. The corridor was empty, with only a flickering yellow light illuminating it. There was silence throughout the length of it, the serenity of the early morning. He did not see a sign of the Intourist porter near the elevators. Still, he did not rush. He waited for a long minute, one that seemed to last forever. Finally, he silently slipped out of his room, locking the door behind him. His fingers trembled slightly. You're just nervous, his brain reassured his beating heart. Finally, he walked towards the elevators, the shabby carpet obscuring the sound of his slow steps.

"Good morning. Is the gentleman suffering from insomnia?" The voice was hoarse and the English broken. He recognized that voice.

Jeff stood still; his heart missed a beat. Then he calmly turned around towards the voice, as if nothing was disturbing him. Before him stood the Intourist representative. She had appeared from out of nowhere, it seemed to Jeff.

"Good morning," Jeff replied. "No. I don't have insomnia." He gave her a forced smile. "It was just hard for me to fall asleep, out of excitement. After all, it's my first visit to Moscow."

She listened to him stone faced, not even blinking.

"And where are you going?"

Jeff was dumbfounded for a minute. Then he spoke. "Oh, just for a walk in the hotel. I want to go down to the lobby. This is a large hotel; I don't know of one in New York that's bigger. You have something to be proud of."

The attempt at pleasant conversation did not succeed.

"Look, sir, I won't stop you. This is a free and democratic country, where every citizen, and certainly every tourist, can do what he wants."

"How nice. Thank you." Jeff decided to continue on towards the elevators.

"One minute, sir!"

She put out her hand. Jeff did not understand what she wanted at first.

"You've forgotten the instructions, Mr. Handler. Your key, please."

Jeff again smiled in confusion. "Oh, you're right, I forgot. Sorry."

Nervously, he rummaged through his pockets. Finally he pulled out the key and put it on the small desk. In exchange, the hall porter handed him his travel permit.

Jeff mumbled his thanks and hurried toward the elevators. After an infuriating wait the elevator arrived and he disappeared into it. A few seconds later he was in the empty, darkened lobby. At first he considered leaving the hotel. But he quickly changed his mind. He still did not know the ways of this country; why should he endanger himself for nothing? And maybe he would find what he was looking for in the hotel itself.

He looked for a public phone. At first glance, he did not see a single one in the lobby. He paced back and forth upon the stone floor, the sound of his footsteps breaking the silence somewhat. Finally he entered a dark passage that led to the gift shop, and there he found a phone booth. Much to his disappointment, though, even here there was no phone directory.

With slightly quicker steps he turned towards the lobby. An older woman was waiting for him there.

"I'm from Intourist," she said without hesitation. "May I see your permit?"

Jeff remembered the instructions: Hand your permit over to any authority that demands it of you.

Jeff pulled out the green card and gave it to the hard-faced woman with feigned indifference. She gave it a long stare and then turned suspicious eyes upon him.

"Mr. Handler, can you explain your wandering about?"

At first he was tempted to joke with her, to tell her something about the magic of Moscow at night. But he immediately realized that humor was not a recognized currency in this place. When he did not answer the woman continued.

"And what were you looking for, if I may ask, in the telephone booth? Who did you want to call at this hour? Do you have some enemy in this city whom you've decided to wake up?"

Jeff made a gesture of dismissal. "Why do you think so?"

"What do you think I'm supposed to make of this early morning visit to a public phone? By the way, why didn't you call from your room?"

Jeff grabbed her last words like a life preserver.

"Exactly!"

She cut him off. "Oh, exactly? You also believe the lies the dirty capitalists spread in their failing countries, that we listen in on our tourists' telephone conversations? That's why you chose to use a public phone?"

She approached him and whispered coldly, "And what do you think, if we wanted to listen, couldn't we also tap a public phone? The boys of the Cometee know their business."

Jeff knew that "the boys of the Cometee" meant the KGB agents. But he didn't understand what this unsympathetic woman was driving at, aside from getting him out of the lobby and back to his room and his sleep.

"You didn't understand what I meant to say." This time he hurried to reply. "I said, 'exactly,' that I had no intention of calling. I could certainly have called from my room. I don't think the rates are particularly high. Certainly, it makes more sense than to wander through a cold lobby at this hour. Madame, I was looking for a phone book. For some reason, there is none in my room. Even more surprising, there is none here either. How do you make phone calls here in Moscow?"

The woman gave a wave of her hand. "There are no phone directories in Moscow, except in the hands of the authorities."

Jeff gave her a glance of incomprehension. He did not dare ask why. Later, much later, he learned that the regime did not approve of people knowing too many other people. A telephone directory could be a dangerous weapon to the security of a dictatorial state.

In the meantime, a change swept over the face of the woman in charge. Her eyes narrowed tensely. Jeff watched her closely. Her voice suddenly softened.

"But what do you need a telephone directory for? Perhaps I can help you? Do you have acquaintances in the city whom you want to speak with?"

Jeff was certain that she suspected something. He carefully chose his words, still uncertain that he was saying the right thing.

"I didn't want to phone anyone; I don't know a soul in Moscow. I'm looking for a map."

The woman's eyes opened in surprise. "A map?"

"Yes. A map of Moscow. A street map. That's what I do in every city that I visit for business purposes."

"Hmmm — interesting. A map, in the middle of the night."

Jeff laughed. "Not really. I woke up and decided to pass the time until morning looking at a map."

The woman unbent a little. It seemed she believed him. She allowed herself a swift, scornful thought on the strange customs of visitors from the West.

"That I really can't help you with. Go out tomorrow and you can find one at a subway station."

"*Spasibo*." He thanked her with one of the few Russian words he knew.

The woman did not move. She continued to stare at him. He realized she was waiting to see what he would do. Jeff decided to return to his room. The difficulties of free movement in this city were beginning to become clear to him.

Dimitri Grasimov, KGB officer, was nervous that morning. Yesterday had not been a day that would bring credit upon him among his colleagues. In the morning he had sent his men to follow a small group of Jewish refuseniks who had settled themselves near the city's central telegraph office. They had demonstrated in front of the passers-by, particularly before the foreign journalists coming to send their telegrams to their western newspapers. This had been the third time they were demonstrating in front of the building.

The KGB officers had gritted their teeth over the demonstration. They could not handle it as they would have liked. The hungry eyes of the reporters from *The New York Times* and *Le Figaro*, the influential French paper, and others would not allow the KGB the freedom of violent response to the demonstrators.

"Don't touch anyone." Thus Grasimov had warned his hard-faced men. "Stand by the side and just watch them. Right after the demonstration follow them; when you are near their houses, you know what to do."

Chagrined, Grasimov thought of the end of the affair. He paced the floor of his office, nervously and tensely. When his men left Dzerzhinski Square, where the KGB headquarters were located, he did not think anything out of the ordinary would occur. They proceeded to the demonstration in their Chekha automobile. The demonstrators were sitting on the building's steps. When they saw the KGB automobile approach they quickly cleared the entranceway, so that they could not be arrested for disturbing the peace. Nearby, as always, stood foreign journalists who quickly photographed the KGB car.

The agents stood silently, awaiting the end of the demonstration. Their instructions had been to openly follow the demonstrators. The purpose of the surveillance this time was, as explained to them, to limit the refuseniks' movements and increase their feeling of suffocation. Nothing more than that. Not to openly persecute them, or the Western countries would erupt in an outcry over the human rights situation in Soviet Russia. Brezhnev was interested now in minimizing the tension with the West and he needed public opinion that was not openly hostile to him.

Dimitri Grasimov's men returned to their headquarters after a short time. They were upset.

"Did something happen?" he asked, seeing their downcast faces.

"They're getting more and more out of hand!"

"We know."

"So why don't we teach them a lesson?"

"Instructions from higher up. General Andropov makes the decisions. But what happened today?"

"We waited for the demonstration to end, so that we could follow them. What happened next has never happened before. The square grew suddenly full: thousands of young people, and some older ones, walking back and forth without a destination. It got more and more crowded, and after 10 minutes the demonstrators, the ones we were supposed to follow, couldn't be found anywhere. They simply disappeared. We can't absolutely prove that the crowds were part of the demonstration, but the fact is that they used the crowd in order to escape."

A day after the event, Grasimov still felt the bitter feeling of failure. Recently he had not succeeded in bringing a single accomplishment to the attention of his superiors. His promotion was on hold, and the bitterness in his heart grew. The fact that he was Jewish, he suspected, was also contributing to the delays in his promotion after long years of service.

At first he wanted to flare up at his men for their failure, which was his failure as well. He wanted to put them in their place, he wanted to explain to them exactly what he thought of their negligence, how damaging it was to the interests of the state and the party. But he felt weakened, when adding this to the previous lack of success in dealing with the refuseniks.

Thoughts of failure led him to think of the problem at home. The problem with Igor, his 19-year-old son. The student.

regory appeared in the hotel lobby at precisely 8 o'clock in the morning. Jeff Handler came down from his room at 8:30. He'd already managed to *daven Shacharis* and to eat some of the food he had brought with him: melba toast and hard cheese. For the next two or three days, he knew, he wouldn't taste anything cooked. In Moscow there was no kosher restaurant, and certainly no *kashrus* supervision.

The two men shook hands. "Good morning, sir," Gregory welcomed him with a tight, forced smile. The Russians, it seemed, were not big on smiling. *Understandable*, thought Jeff.

"*Dovroye utro*," Jeff answered in Russian, adding a warmer smile. But Gregory did not compliment him on his knowledge of the Russian language.

"We're traveling to the Ministry of Commerce now," Gregory hurried to inform him. "They've told me that your meeting is scheduled to begin in an hour."

Jeff returned a polite, "Okay."

"Have you returned your key?" Gregory asked. "You have your travel permit? I don't want to get into trouble over it."

Jeff put his hand into his coat pocket and pulled out the green-colored card, waving it in front of Gregory's face. This pressure was beginning to get to him.

Gregory did not answer. He just nodded his head in assent and walked out the glass door. Jeff followed closely behind. Outside, a black car awaited them. Jeff did not recognize the make. Gregory opened the door for him and Jeff entered, sitting down in the back seat. Gregory sat beside him. The driver did not wish them good morning; absolute silence reigned. Jeff hoped his relations with Gregory would warm in the course of the day. He was, after all, at this stage at least, Jeff's main source of information.

The car glided slowly, trying to merge with the traffic that was beginning to flow heavily, to the rhythm of the city. Gregory did not tell the driver their destination. He already knew.

This meeting at the Ministry interested Jeff as much as yesterday's headlines. His eyes passed over the street signs that whizzed by, that were hung onto the corner houses. He decided not to show a marked interest in the subject so as not to draw Gregory's attention. The Intourist agent sat, motionless, beside him, occasionally turning for a split second in order to see what his American client was doing. Though he tried to watch him furtively, without Jeff's knowledge, Jeff's sharpened senses detected the careful scrutiny.

Jeff did not manage to read any street names. The Cyrillic letters, so different from the Latin ones, were strange to him. Finally, he decided to take a calculated risk.

"What's the name of this boulevard?" he asked, trying to sound casual. His tone of voice announced that if he got the answer or not, it did not really matter much to him. Still, Gregory threw him a searching glance.

"Kalinin Boulevard. Why do you ask?"

Jeff shrugged. "No reason, really," he answered quickly. "I'm just curious."

Gregory did not answer, and returned to his thoughts.

The car continued to speed, passing several streets. Jeff hoped that G-d would help him and he would manage to identify the street where his grandfather had lived. Finding the street was, at the very least, the first step in his rescue attempt.

He dared once again. "And this street?"

"Ordinka Street," Gregory answered offhandedly.

After a few minutes they reached a square where they made a sharp left turn. Jeff took a deep breath, trying to maintain his composure.

"Excuse me for my questions: What's the name of this square?"

Gregory lifted his eyes; there was just the hint of a smile in them.

"Now, mister, we have crossed Dobrinin Square. In another few minutes we will reach the famed Gorky Park, and from there we will get to Tchaikovsky Street. Would you like the tour to continue?"

Jeff could hear the irony in his words. Did this irony conceal something that Jeff did not know, or was it simply the Russian trying to teach the curious American something?

"No, no, thanks, Gregory. It's my weakness: wherever in the world I find myself I'm always interested in the street names, the parks, the famed buildings. My hobby."

Gregory turned a little towards Jeff. His face showed rising interest.

"Really? Famous buildings and parks, I understand. But street names?"

Warning bells began to toll within Jeff's breast. Still he managed to meet Gregory's stare, his face pleasant.

"Don't you understand? For the atmosphere! I love to really feel the city I'm visiting. The sound of the street names adds to the general atmosphere. Every person has his own preferences—"

Gregory shrugged. "Yes, every American with his own eccentricities."

Jeff reacted quickly. "That's our democratic way."

"Yes! Your tragedy! Everyone does whatever he wants to do. Your capitalistic society is disintegrating. Crime, murder. We know all, Mr. Jeff Handler."

"Thanks," Jeff answered shortly. He decided to cut the conversation right here. The warning he'd been given in New York suddenly echoed through his brain: "Absolutely don't get involved in political debates!" The Russians, he thought, apparently like to entrap strangers, getting them to condemn the Communist regime. Then the KGB steps into the picture— And he, Jeff, wanted only to return safely to his home in New York.

Jeff changed the subject. "Where are we now?"

"In a suburb called Krasno Farsonya."

Jeff's heart missed a beat. His eyes raced over the scene passing by from the car window. The words echoed in his head: "Krasno Bogatirski." Could that street be nearby?

Gregory noticed Jeff's sharp reaction, but made no indication. Carefully, trying to sound casual, Jeff asked, "What is Krasno Farsonya?"

"Farsonya is the ancient name of the place. Krasno means red; that is, the red Farsonya."

For the first time Gregory gave a wide smile.

"You're looking for atmosphere, my American friend? I'll tell you. Here in this area the workers fought in the revolutionary times, in 1905, against the czar's army that shelled them. When they put down the uprising, the czar's soldiers brutally massacred the populace."

Jeff did not answer. He was afraid to ask the next question but, in a moment of weakness, it somehow escaped him.

"Are there other streets or areas called Krasno?"

"A strange question. Why do you ask?"

Jeff truly did not know what to say. He was furious with himself: Almost without thinking, he'd practically given away his terrible secret.

Fortunately the car pulled over just then and Gregory informed Jeff that they had reached their destination. A feeling of relief enveloped Jeff. He hoped that Gregory's interest in his strange questions would now abate.

But — he was wrong.

Dimitri Grasimov stood up in his small office. A man in his 50's, he was rather short but solidly built. His face was determined, his lips thin and tight. When he arrived at his office a short while earlier he had not bothered taking off his heavy coat; he had not even doffed his rabbit fur hat. Here he stood, immersed in his melancholy thoughts, thoughts that left him completely demoralized. Particularly galling thoughts, since his superiors apparently shared the same feelings. Who knew what they thought of him, Dimitri, up there in his superiors' sealed offices. The KGB had no sympathy for the pain of an agent who failed. Here you had to bring results: suspects, dismantling of subversive organizations, creation of fear among potential cultural criminals, and the like. Bitter indeed was the lot of the one whose mission failed, who did not show results. Dimitri Grasimov pondered the fate that awaited him. And if that was not enough, now he had the problem of Igor. His Igor, his only son.

Grasimov stood in the center of his room, with no set goal or destination. His feet took him, almost unconsciously, to the window. From this window, on the third floor of the KGB building, Grasimov would enjoy watching the passers-by running through the streets that met at Dzerzhinski Square. There was pleasure in the knowledge that all those people down there trembled before him and his friends; as they passed by these streets they did everything in their power not to be noticed. They avoided eye contact; they had no idea what the consequences of such contact could be. This gave Grasimov a feeling of power, a feeling of having control over the destiny of others, in his ability to determine their fates. The pride of power filled his heart.

And now, at this moment, on this cold, wet autumn day, he suddenly felt the power of those who controlled him, who could determine his own fate. No, no. His recent lack of success and bad luck did not have to reach the desk of Yuri Andropov, the all powerful, in order for him, Dimitri, to come to harm. There were many small-minded men who hated him (perhaps for his Jewishness, too, though anti-Semitism was outlawed in the Soviet Union), who would see to it that news of his failures would reach the proper circles. He knew full well that they could determine his fate in a way that was causing him, Dimitri Grasimov, to be very frightened. Yes, he knew it well. Hadn't he himself done it in the past to his own friends in the secret police? The NKVD, as it had been called then.

For the first time in his life he felt that if something terrible befell him, it would be a punishment that he deserved. A strange feeling for someone who had grown up an absolute atheist, on the beliefs that the world was a totally physical place, without any spiritual dimension whatsoever. It would truly be a fitting retribution for all the colleagues who died or disappeared or had been tortured — because of him.

Grasimov poured himself a brimming glass of vodka and swallowed it in one gulp. His face took on a yellow tinge.

A knock. Grasimov lifted his eyes towards the locked door. It was a confident knock, firm and forceful. Grasimov sharpened his senses.

"Not now." He spoke harshly to the anonymous caller. Then he listened cautiously for a reaction. He could hear footsteps growing more distant. Grasimov took a deep breath. His arm reached for the Smirnoff vodka. The sound of the bottle hitting the empty cup was the only sign of life in the silent chamber. A moment later, the cup was empty once again.

Oh yes, Igor. The new worry. It seemed to Dimitri that the future success of his only child was assured. A top student, mathematics degree. Continued education in electric engineering. With the help of friends and some quiet KGB-style pressure, a good job.

But recently a terrible problem had appeared. One of his men, in charge of watching secret student activity, had photographed a subversive group of Technicom students meeting in the Marinovaya Rosha Forest near Moscow. He'd brought the photo to Grasimov, who had immediately identified Igor. The shock was terrible. Grasimov's terrified glance was not lost on the "*tauton*," as the KGB spies were known. But he had lowered his eyes, as if he had noticed nothing. Grasimov worried over the possibility of the picture making the rounds through the building, reaching the desks of his good friends who would see to it that the damning picture would receive the widest possible attention. They would know how to use it well.

"Good luck, my friend," Dimitri shot the compliment at the young agent who had brought him the photo. The agent's back straightened proudly, but Dimitri did not notice. He pretended to stare at the picture so that the young man would not notice the fear, worry, and lack of confidence in his eyes. But as he looked at the photo he could not see anyone else. Only Igor. The countenances of the others seemed fuzzy somehow; Igor's face grew larger and larger, like some kind of monster. He was sitting on a tree trunk next to a tree that grew high in the sky. In Grasimov's fevered imagination the tree seemed to become a gallows. A gallows prepared for him, a KGB officer, Dimitri Grasimov, of course.

He raised his eyes to the young man standing silently before him and looked at him with interest.

"Is this the only copy?" he asked cautiously.

The agent was perplexed. He did not know what to say.

"I asked you something." Dimitri's voice sounded firmer, more in authority, this time.

"I don't know," the other answered hesitantly. "I brought the film to the lab. After developing they told me to rush here and bring it to you."

Dimitri's eyes narrowed. The last sentence sent warning bells ringing in his head.

"They told you to rush here and bring me the picture. Why?"

The young spy's confusion increased. His lack of experience melded with his lack of self-confidence.

"I don't remember exactly. Maybe that's just the way I understood it."

He waited for a moment, a moment that seemed an eternity. Suddenly he banged his finger on the desk and said, with a firmness that frightened Dimitri, "Yes, I'm sure. He told me to rush."

Dimitri did not respond. Had the men in the lab realized that one of the students in the photo was his son, Igor? Was the blow about to fall upon him?

The arm stretched out a third time for the bottle of vodka. This time, he didn't bother using a cup.

9

The conference at the Ministry of Commerce, in the department responsible for the diamond industry, was held in a business-like, intense atmosphere. Seated across from Jeff were several skilled, tough officials whose job was to get the most out of the negotiations. The debate concerning the type of polished diamonds that Jeff was interested in purchasing was not simple. The question of price, too, took some time to resolve. Even after hours of discussion the chasm still had to be bridged.

Generally, during all the negotiations that Jeff had handled until this one, he was patient all through the protracted discussions. He was the type who kept his cool, listening well and weighing each word that his adversaries uttered. But this time he found it difficult to concentrate. He was impatient, too quick to answer the questions put to him, even as he became furious at himself for such behavior.

Gregory, sitting next to him, clearly noted Jeff's agitation. Gregory lit himself a cigarette. Some sensor within him told him that this Jeff Handler was not simply an innocent diamond merchant, like one of those from Belgium who appeared from time to time. It did not seem that he was merely interested in doing business. He had no proof but a deep instinct hinted that the diamonds were merely a front — in this case not a very successful one.

And yet his suspicious behavior was almost too obvious. Gregory had already heard this morning from Intourist of his client's nocturnal search for a telephone directory, certainly unusual and strange behavior that begged for attention. In their trip here, too, to this business meeting, there was something disturbing and suspicious about Jeff's questions about the city and its streets. But if Jeff had criminal intentions towards the Soviet Union, he would undoubtedly have been more careful. His behavior, the behavior of an amateur, surely precluded the possibility that he was a spy.

Gregory stood up from his seat and wandered towards the window. His cigarette burned down; the butt scorched his fingertips. Outside, traffic was very light.

The voices around the negotiating table rose several octaves. Gregory turned towards the participants. The argument over price had not been solved. Suddenly Jeff glanced at his watch; his eyes registered surprise. He had not realized that the conference had lasted over three hours, much longer than planned.

Jeff began to pull the papers he had placed upon the table towards him, hastily stashing them all in his attaché case. He stood up quickly and asked that they continue the meeting the next day. Gregory scrutinized his every move. He did not understand the reason for the hurry. His suspicions returned in full force. Jeff apologized to his hosts, telling them that he was still tired from his long and fatiguing flight. He wanted to go back to the hotel to rest up. The Russian officials acceded to his request without batting an eyelash. The American businessman's hurry was of no importance to them.

As they sat in the car on the way back to the hotel Gregory noticed that his American guest no longer seemed interested in the city's street names. Jeff sat, silent and withdrawn. Gregory, too, did not speak. When they were close to the hotel Jeff straightened up and asked, "Does Moscow have a synagogue?"

Gregory looked offended. "That's a slightly insulting question."

Jeff felt uncomfortable. "Why?"

"Of course there is a synagogue. We allow freedom of religion here.

Didn't you know that? Fascist propaganda loves to give us a bad name."

Jeff answered quickly. "Of course I knew that. But I didn't think Moscow had Jews who needed a synagogue."

Gregory calmed down somewhat. "You're somewhat correct, mister. There are very few Jews in this city, and in the Socialist Republic, who still need a synagogue. Most of the Jews grew up in the lap of the Revolution. Religion is, when all is said and done, reactionary and the Russian — even the Russian Jew — is a forward-looking, revolutionary person who is implementing the Socialist dream."

Gregory's chest swelled with pride; his eyes gleamed. Jeff was amused. He was certain that Gregory did not really believe the drivel he was intoning with such ceremony. The man was simply reciting the cliches they had taught him in his tour-guide course. The Russian playacting went on.

Right next to the hotel entrance, before Jeff had left the car, he asked Gregory, "Can you take me to the synagogue this evening?"

Gregory acted surprised. "That will be a little complicated."

"Why? After all, there is freedom of religion in Socialist Russia."

Gregory could hear the irony in Jeff's words. He also realized that he had been backed into a corner.

"Okay, I'll arrange the matter."

Jeff did not understand what matter needed arranging. He could not recall having to make any arrangements in New York when he wanted to daven *Minchah* with a *minyan* during his busy Manhattan workday. But he did not ask questions. He remembered. He was in Russia. In Moscow.

Dimitri Grasimov took the incriminating photograph and stashed it deep into his attaché case. That night, if his son Igor returned home (the last time he was missing for a week, and no pressure could get him to reveal where he had been), he would show him the evidence. This time his wife, Natasha Alexandrova, would not be able to save her son from his, Dimitri's, wrath. What had happened to this new generation, with its complete lack of discipline? Why was it secretly rebelling against the socialism of its parents, who were laboring so hard to create a socialist paradise for future generations? Grasimov did not understand. But what disturbed him most was the possibility that his son's mischief might again cost him his KGB promotion, for who knew how long this time. He needed the promotion to collect a generous pension when he left the service.

Suddenly he banged his clenched fist harshly onto the table, letting loose all of his concealed rage. In a flash, he came to a decision. He would not wait until evening. Now, right now, he would go looking for his pride and joy, his Igor. He would pull him forcibly out of the university and confront him with his awful, deviant behavior.

He entered the black Volga that was at his disposal. He drove it away.

Anatoly Dobrovitz was shocked.

He walked slowly, stunned, down the bustling sidewalk of Ulitza Machabaya, the street where Moscow University is located. He had just left the admissions committee of the mathematics department. The members of the committee had tested him for five straight hours. They had hurled particularly difficult and complicated questions at him. As a top mathematics student throughout high school he had approached the tests with full confidence, free of any doubts.

But immediately upon his entrance today, he had sensed the hostility built up against him. A sense of despair whispered to him that these honored professors wanted only to fail him. Unlike his friends in his class whose grades had always been lower than his own, he had had to undergo a difficult test on which, upon its completion, he had been given an "F." That is — failure.

The bottom line was that his request to join the Department of Mathematics had been denied. The admissions committee members had pretended sympathy, but on his question of why he had had to take such a difficult test, there had been no answer, other than some meaningless muttering. But before he had left the room, shaken and upset, one of the members of the committee had mentioned casually, and with a clear lack of sensitivity, that the fact that he was a Jew had tipped the scales against him. Naturally, this had been said in such a way that should Anatoly complain to the university authorities, the committee could deny everything. After all, anti-Semitism was outlawed in Russia.

Anatoly walked into the corridor and saw his Russian friends still wandering through the department. When they saw the ashen pallor of his face, without the trace of a smile, they understood that their friend Anatoly had not been accepted. They did not bother to hide the scorn that spread across their Slavic faces. He realized that they understood the reason for his rejection. His Judaism. A Judaism of which Anatoly himself knew nothing. He knew only one thing: They hated him for it. It had been in high school that he first experienced the bitter taste of active anti-Semitism.

Anatoly hardly saw the pedestrians. They seemed to his glazed eyes to pass as shadowy figures, as ghostly spirits. His blasted hopes blurred his vision completely, and pulled him into a chasm of despair. From these depths he suddenly felt a growing fury, which grew into a desire for vengeance. Vengeance against the anti-Semites of whose existence he had just learned. Vengeance against society, that for some reason would not give him what he deserved. He was Russian, a Muscovite, and he loved the city in which he had been born. If so, why was he rejected, without a reason, on the threshold of the scientific career he had always dreamed of?

Anatoly did not have the courage to return home. How would his mother, a supervisor in the Soviet education system, react? He didn't have to report to his father: an army officer, he had been killed during the war in Afghanistan. His father, like his mother, had been a dedicated Communist. Now how would his mother take his rejection, because he was a Jew?

Anatoly walked aimlessly through the streets. Without any destination he turned left to the Nikitaskaya Ulitza, the street that led to the zoological museum and the famed Mykovski Theater.

Suddenly he felt a push that almost brought him down to the ground. He turned to see who had shoved him. But again he was pushed, this time forward, by the press of a crowd that was racing like one being pursued by the enemy. Dozens, perhaps hundreds, passed him by in the mad race. Anatoly leaned against one of the shop windows in order to avoid being trampled. Finally he grabbed a young man firmly and stopped him in midrun.

"What's going on here, comrade?"

The young man was startled by the sudden stop. He pulled away with a powerful gesture and joined the others without answering Anatoly's question.

His second try was more successful. "*Yevrei?*" asked the young man whom Anatoly had stopped.

This was the first time that Anatoly had answered that particular question without hesitation.

"*Da.*"

The young man cast thoughtful eyes upon him and answered. "There was a demonstration of several refuseniks near the telegraph house on Olache Gorkva. When the KGB arrived to take them for interrogation we appeared in large numbers, as if we were taking a stroll. The demonstrators quickly joined us and now we're all leaving the area as fast as we can. Now please let me go."

The arm was freed and the boy, again beginning to run, yelled after him: "I advise you to get out of here too. Our good friends in the Cometee can surprise you and ask you some unpleasant questions."

Anatoly instinctively listened to him and joined the crowd.

At that moment his eyes lit up. Now he knew how he would get vengeance for his humiliation at the hands of the admissions committee.

10

At 5:30 in the afternoon Gregory arrived at the Russia Hotel. Jeff was waiting in the lobby. Gregory saw the impatience in Jeff's sour face. But he did not bother to apologize for the delay, and Jeff would not dare ask him why he was late. Gregory turned wordlessly towards the exit, Jeff following on his heels. The black automobile that they had ridden in that morning was already awaiting them.

Jeff opened the car door. Suddenly he stopped. Gregory lifted his eyebrows in surprise.

"Is the synagogue far from here?" Jeff asked.

Gregory did not know what he was getting at. Hesitating, he finally answered, "Not really. A few minutes' drive."

"And by foot? Walking?"

"Say a quarter of an hour. Why do you ask?"

"Am I allowed to walk to the synagogue?"

Gregory's face hardened. "Allowed? Of course you're allowed! I thought you were in a hurry to get there. And besides, it's cold. It's always better in a car."

"I understand. Still, I prefer to walk, if it's not hard for you, of course."

"No, no, it's not hard," Gregory said courteously. He shut the car door with obvious reluctance and let the driver leave. Jeff and Gregory began to walk toward the synagogue, silent most of the time. Gregory occasionally glanced at Jeff and noticed how his gaze continually fell on the dark lettering of the street signs attached to the corner homes. Where did this strange interest in street names come from?

Jeff suddenly wheeled around to face Gregory, whose expression still bore traces of suspicion. Gregory, trying to hide his confusion, quickly asked, "So what do you think of Moscow?"

Jeff smiled. "Beautiful. A beautiful city. I imagined it differently."

"How?"

Jeff did not answer. He realized that if he told the truth he could get into trouble. He had certainly noticed the frozen miens of the Muscovites. One hardly saw any people speaking to each other in the streets. What a difference from what he was used to in the Western world. Perhaps the reason for the silence was the fear of getting entangled by a word that was not appropriate or that the regime might not like.

Gregory did not ask him again.

Silently, one next to the other, the two walked on for close to 20 minutes, until they reached the synagogue gates on Archipova Street, a small street that eventually turned into major thoroughfares in both directions.

So here it is, the thought flashed through Jeff's mind, *this is the place that I read about in the Times. Here is where daring young Jews meet on Simchas Torah, demonstrating the fact that they are Jews.*

He felt goose bumps creep like a snake up his back.

Jeff lifted his eyes, deeply moved, and stared at the two wide white columns that reached up so high and supported the dome which covered the entrance steps. This was it, then, the last place of prayer that was left to the survivors of Communist Moscow. Amazing!

Jeff slowly walked up the wide steps that led inside. For a moment he forgot about his escort, who clung tightly to him, whose face he would have preferred not to see right now. He noticed two old, bent men sneaking glances at him the moment that they entered the building. Their faces, wrinkled like the tributaries of a river, and their eyes, sunken in their sockets, turned away from his glance. One was wearing a faded cap, the other a Russian fur hat. At first Jeff wanted to stop them to chat, Jew to Jew. He would pull out his own broken Yiddish in order to communicate. But he held back at the last instant. He remembered Gregory and turned around to see where he was. Strangely, Gregory had remained standing upon the steps. Jeff noticed that he was whispering to a tall young man wearing black. A flash of worry coursed through him.

Gregory gave him a cold smile and motioned to Jeff that he should go inside. He would wait outside. Jeff walked in carefully, as if suspicious of something unseen and lurking.

In the small *beis midrash* slightly more than a *minyan* of men were gathered. They glanced swiftly at the stranger who encroached upon their impoverished fortress, then quickly turned their attention back to their *siddurim*. Jeff felt uncomfortable. This encounter showed him a different side to the Judaism that he knew at home. The men murmured their prayers quietly; Jeff did not know if they were pronouncing the words correctly. He also noticed several men who stood near the entrance, who were not *davening* at all, just watching. Who were they?

Jeff waited for the prayers to end. At all costs he wanted to speak to one of the congregants. He felt that this was his chance, now that Gregory was not standing next to him, to discover the address he wanted to locate. At least that is what he thought. He never dreamed of what would happen next.

Dimitri Grasimov pulled over near the university building on Machabaya Street. He left the car with quick steps and entered the building itself. Around him stood students doing their best not to make eye contact with the stone-faced KGB agent striding through the corridor.

Dimitri met his son in one of the hallways. He grabbed him by the arm. "Come!" he commanded.

Igor was frightened. "Has something happened?"

"We'll talk somewhere else, not in front of everyone."

"Okay, Father, but has something happened? And please let go of my arm. Everyone is staring!"

Grasimov loosened his hold on his son. But he did not answer the young man's question.

"Has something happened to Mother?"

"No," he answered shortly.

"So to whom?"

"To you!" The reply sounded like a command.

Fear almost paralyzed Igor; he knew something dreadful was about to happen.

"Me?"

"Yes."

"What happened to me?"

With a quick gesture Dimitri pulled out the incriminating photograph.

"Can you explain to me what this is?"

Igor gave a hurried glance and paled.

"Do you recognize the place?"

"Father, let me explain." Igor tried to defend himself.

His father interrupted him. "Too late! It's already in our archives, in Lubianka! Too many people have seen it."

They reached the entrance gates. In a moment of kindness the sun spilled over the Moscow street, blinding them with its radiance. Grasimov grabbed his son's arm once again. "Look around you. I can already see Victor Malenkov's men around me. Do you know who he is? He's the officer who's trying to get rid of me. They're already following me, you fool! Thank you for the help you've given your father and his career."

"But Father —"

"Now keep quiet! Come back home with me. Then we'll see!"

The prayers ended. Jeff turned around and saw the three men standing motionless not far from the entrance to the synagogue hall. They were dressed like civilians and they stared at the congregants, their looks relaxed and indifferent, as if what they were looking at interested them not at all. Yet with all that, Jeff, the visitor, felt their presence was disturbing, even to the few men who had gathered to pray. Jeff noticed that none of the congregants gave either the three men nor himself even a hasty glance. Were they merely reserved — or were they frightened?

The congregants began to disperse. Jeff tried to make eye contact with at least one of the men who passed him by, but almost all of them avoided his gaze. They walked by him as if he did not exist. Jeff, perplexed, did not know how to react. In all of his travels, in the United States and abroad, he was used to being greeted by fellow Jews with a warm and welcoming hand. Again he asked himself, was this behavior merely a manifestation of a coldness, a reserve? Or something more sinister?

He began to walk around, trying to draw attention to himself. Finally he decided to walk to the exit so that he would actually bump into one of the men. His plan was successful: A Jew walking beside him whispered to him in Yiddish with a heavy Russian accent, "From America?"

"Yes. From America," Jeff answered, also in a whisper, looking ahead of him without turning towards the Jew speaking to him.

"New York? Washington?"

"New York."

"*Oy vey.*"

"Why *oy vey*?"

"The Jews have troubles there."

"Troubles? Why?"

The old man finally turned his face towards Jeff and stopped walking.

"Everything is okay there?"

"Yes. Why not?"

The Jew's face plainly showed his disbelief.

"Under the capitalists it can be good?"

Jeff, too, stopped in his place. Though the conversation was a strange one, he rejoiced in it. He hoped to draw the Jew out.

"Why can't it be good under the capitalists?"

The Jew scratched his forehead concealed beneath his faded cap and waited for a moment before replying.

"Don't you have poor people among you?"

"Sure."

"And homeless? Don't you have homeless?"

Jeff found himself growing impatient. His glance fell instinctively upon the three men still standing motionless near the entrance door. Their gazes were riveted upon Jeff and his companion. He felt a touch of fear as he noticed that Gregory, too, was suddenly standing close by, waiting for him, Jeff. When had he come into the synagogue? Hadn't he said he would wait outside? He remembered the old man standing next to him and whispered, "Yes, there are homeless."

He noticed a mischievous twinkle in the old man's eyes. "And hooligans who wander through the streets of New York?" he asked in a lilting voice.

"Yes. Why do you ask?"

The old man raised his voice slightly. Perhaps he wanted his words to reach the ears of the men standing by the synagogue door.

"*Nu,* so how can it be good there?"

His voice held a note of triumph. Jeff felt insulted. The American patriot within him was stirred. He forgot the rules of caution that he had learned before embarking on his trip. He asked the man, whose name he still did not know: "And how is it here in Russia? In Moscow?"

"Very good."

Jeff decided to give him back what he had gotten. "You have poor people."

"None."

Jeff was surprised. "None? How can that be?"

The old man brought his mouth to Jeff's ear and whispered to him, with a giggle, "Because we're all poor!"

Jeff saw that the KGB men hanging around the entrance were still watching them with interest, as was "his" Gregory. He marveled at the daring of the unknown Jew who was so directly thumbing his nose at the Soviet regime. An inner voice whispered: "Caution! This may be an instigator standing before you. He wants to trap you!" Outwardly, though, he maintained his composure.

"And you don't have hooligans here, like we have?"

The Jew gave a dismissive gesture. "What are you talking about? We have a strong regime. Comrade Brezhnev takes good care of matters." His voice carried the ring of finality. "*Nyet!* Here there are no hooligans wandering through the streets like by you. They are afraid, simply afraid, of the authorities."

Jeff made no reply. In his thoughts flashed the answer he would have loved to give: "*Because you are all afraid of Comrade Brezhnev.*" But better to stay quiet. And yet, in order to keep the conversation going, he continued. "And the Jews?"

"It's good for the Jews too. Why shouldn't it be good for them?"

The last sentence came out in Russian, which he immediately translated into Yiddish. Jeff noticed that he was squinting in the direction of the three uninvited guests. Clearly the man wanted his last sentence to be understood.

Jeff and the local resident were now standing near the exit door. Jeff was a little upset; he felt his golden opportunity dissolving before him. He decided to take the initiative.

"Where do the Jews live in Moscow?"

The Jew gave him a surprised look. "Everywhere! What kind of question is that? Do they live in a ghetto in New York?"

Jeff gave a forced laugh. "Heaven forbid! In New York, too, the Jews live everywhere. But still, there are neighborhoods that have many Jews living together. Jews like to live together."

The old man again paid his debt to society. "Of course, in countries such as America, where there is anti-Semitism, they want to live together. But here? In the Soviet Union? There is no need!"

Jeff could not tell if the man himself believed what he was saying or not. But he decided that he would not back down.

"Still, there must be places where many Jews live in the city. No?"

The old man shook his head back and forth in thought. Finally, he murmured, "Yes, let's say that outside the city there is a neighborhood where many Jews live. The place is called Mala Chobka. There's a large market there once a week, a Jewish market. You get off the train at the Mala Chobka station if you want to go there."

They were now right near the exit, a few meters from the KGB strongmen. As they opened the synagogue door the old man lifted his head and asked, "Actually, what are you doing in Moscow?"

"Me? I'm a diamond merchant."

"And why are you interested in where the Jews live?"

"No real reason. A Jew is interested in other Jews."

"Hmmm. I understand. Do you know anyone in Moscow?"

"No. This is my first visit to the city. I've heard of the Kremlin, of Red Square, and other places."

The Jewish Muscovite looked interested.

"What other places have you heard of here?"

Jeff felt a rising pressure in his chest. His moment had finally arrived.

"I've heard, for example, of a large museum called the Hermitage."

The man burst into laughter. "That museum is in Leningrad."

"Oh, sorry. But the library of Baron Ginsburg is here."

"That's right, that library is in Moscow."

Jeff furrowed his brow as if trying to remember other Moscow sights.

"Gorky Park. Kalinin Bridge."

"Yes, the park is a beautiful place. The bridge is a little far from here. It spans the Moscow River."

It was time: Jeff "remembered." "Oh, I remember another place. Krasno Bogatirski. I think it's a street name. Is that right?"

The old man gave him a piercing, suspicious glance. They were now standing on the steps outside the building.

"That's right. It's a street name. Where did you hear of it?"

Jeff hesitated. "I don't remember. Maybe someone on the plane told me that he lives there. I don't remember."

The man looked at him again. Finally, he closed his eyes and muttered, "Hmmm — interesting. No. I don't know that street name. Good night."

And without another word he went on his way.

A short Jew had been walking slowly behind them. Now he jumped quickly next to Jeff and whispered to him in Yiddish, "Be careful of the man you've just spoken to. He's an informer." The man said no more, disappearing into the rapidly darkening street.

Jeff turned around. A shudder of fear raced through him. Gregory was standing there, silently watching. He had heard the conversation. For the second time he had found out that Jeff was interested in a Moscow street. Krasno Bogatirski.

Dimitri Grasimov paced back and forth in his small apartment without uttering a word. His son, Igor, sat on the faded sofa and did not take his eyes off his father. Grasimov's steps were hurried and swift; his hands were clenched behind his back. For half an hour after he had returned home with his son he had walked in this manner. Igor was afraid. He knew his father. He knew that at moments such as these he could make tough, even cruel, decisions. As a member of the Cometee — that is, the KGB — his father had never shown mercy to others. He had served in the KGB for many years. Igor did not know if his father had killed suspects or criminals with his own hands, in the fulfillment of his job. It was certainly possible. Igor always tried to push those thoughts away, but now they flashed before him against his will. Igor did not particularly love his father. Especially since the time that he, Igor, had happened to find out that he was a Jew. He had been furious that his father had never revealed to him this strange and confusing fact.

His father approached him with hasty steps. Igor backed away. In instinctive self-defense, he picked up his arms to protect his head from a possible blow. His mother, her maternal senses alert to the growing storm, jumped out of the kitchen where she was frying potatoes and screamed in a shrill, thin voice: "Don't touch the boy! Do you hear?"

Dimitri stopped for a moment. His eyes, emitting sparks of a murderous rage, took in the furious and severe face of his wife, then turned to his son cringing on the sofa. Natasha Alexandrova approached, a rolling pin in her hand. She stood near the couch, her stance that of a woman prepared to defend her young.

Dimitri assessed the situation. No. He had no intention of coming to blows in the house. In the past he had felt the strong arm of his wife, and each time it was connected to the education of their son. Igor had always refused to toe the line. Now Dimitri retreated a little. He sat on the chair nearest to him, covered his face with his hands, and sighed. Igor exchanged a swift glance with his mother. They heard Dimitri whisper to himself, "I'm destroyed — you've destroyed me — destroyed me."

Igor relented a little. He whispered cautiously, "But Father, I don't want to do you any harm."

"I told you, it's too late. The damage is done. The picture of you with that gang of hooligans is surely in the hands of my enemies. They'll use it against me. What do you think, I won't pay the price of your hooligans? You've destroyed me!"

Grasimov was silent for a moment. "Particularly because I'm a Jew."

Suddenly he rose with one motion. His rigid face appeared from behind his hands. It seemed that he had recovered from the trauma. The change in his mood was astounding. He announced determinedly, "I have decided to send you to a re-education center. There you will get treatment that will restore your sanity. Yes, education and rehabilitation — that's what you need! Do you understand?"

Natasha Alexandrova, shocked, did not say a word. Igor, too, was silent, in a total state of shock. In these closed institutions they treated the patients like madmen, with medicines and injections. Many did, indeed, lose their minds after all the dedicated and caring treatment.

He longed to get up and flee anywhere, wherever the wind would blow him. But he sat, paralyzed.

Suddenly the sound of an approaching car engine broke the silence. Dimitri picked up his head and looked out the open window. To his horror he saw a Volga, the kind used by the KGB. A young officer jumped out. Grasimov knew him well. Yevgenyev Patrichovski was his name. He strode quickly towards the door of the Grasimov home. Silence reigned in the house; the knocks on the door could be heard clearly. Dimitri felt his legs weaken in fear. What did he want? Was it finally — them?

The door opened. The officer handed Grasimov an envelope. He opened it with a trembling hand and impatiently pulled out a short letter. He read its contents. His face paled. He muttered to his wife, "I'm going with him. I hope to come back soon."

11

T he two stood motionless near the steps of the synagogue, each staring at the other. Jeff gave a forced smile; Gregory responded with one of his own. The Russian's eyes did not reveal his inner thoughts. Had he heard the question Jeff had asked the Jew or not? Jeff waited another minute on the wide steps. He slowly buttoned his heavy coat and put on his gloves; the weather was growing colder and colder.

"Shall we go?" Jeff asked in a friendly tone.

"Yes, let's go," Gregory answered with ostentatious politeness. He even waved his right hand in front of him, as if inviting Jeff to show the way down the steps.

Their slow progress up Archipova Street towards Ploshad Nagina and from there to Lubianka was acceptable to Jeff. It gave him a chance to conceal the confusion that had possessed him. It was absolutely clear to him that Gregory was no mere Intourist representative. Gregory was a puppet, and the string that was pulling him was undoubtedly fixed in one of the KGB offices; that was certain. The question was: If Gregory's suspicions had been aroused, would he report them? To whom would he report? Jeff felt that he had not been careful enough. Now what should he do?

For a short while they walked in heavy silence. In order to demonstrate his composure Jeff looked at the passers-by, at the Russian automobiles racing past them, at the ancient buildings with their heavily ornamented entranceways and the austere new buildings rising up next to them. But his thoughts constantly wandered back toward Gregory and his reactions. According to Jeff's itinerary he was to spend the night in the city, meet tomorrow morning with the Ministry of Commerce officials to finish off the business, and then fly to New York. Jeff glanced at his watch. Seven p.m. That meant 20 more hours or so in Moscow. A lot could happen in 20 hours. The hours left until his flight seemed to him like an eternity. He felt a covert flash of fear in his heart. The surroundings suddenly seemed hostile, though he could not explain why. He felt a wave of longing for New York, for Flatbush, his home, his family.

He glanced quickly at Gregory, who was walking next to him; the Russian responded with a glance of his own.

They were now on a street which ended in a huge area that Jeff had already identified last night: the famed Red Square. He came to a sudden halt; instinctively, Gregory stopped too. He looked at Jeff but was silent, not burdening him with unnecessary questions. Jeff, in order to quiet his fears somewhat and also to radiate a sense of calm for Gregory's benefit, decided to become a bit of a tourist.

"Wonderful! Just magnificent!" he murmured.

His eyes roamed over the large plaza. At this evening hour only a few people milled about, well wrapped in their overcoats. The lanterns had already been lit, casting light upon the Kremlin walls, making them a bit too mysterious for Jeff's taste. He lifted his head toward the church tower that rose up beyond the walls of the Kremlin. The five-pointed Communist star soared high upon its spire. For a moment a thrill passed through him: Here he was, standing by the walls that concealed the evil empire! From his vantage point in New York the Kremlin seemed like an object that lay far beyond dark mountains. And now — here he was!

Among the flashes of fear that coursed through him he felt the refreshing pulse of wonder. In his imagination he could see Brezhnev, prime minister of the USSR. At the same time he remembered the fearful Yuri Andropov, the strongman, head of the KGB. And here he was, Jeff Handler, standing a stone's throw from these mysterious walls and the terrible secrets of oppression that they contained.

Suddenly he felt a light jolt, like a small electric shock. Against his will he looked at Gregory's face. Who knew, perhaps tomorrow these forbidding walls would know something of Jeff Handler as well? His right hand moved instinctively towards his chest, near his heart, shuffling through his jacket pocket. He wanted to feel his American passport, his insurance policy against all harm. But it was not there. His fear grew. Where could it be? A difficult moment passed until he remembered that it had been deposited in the hotel. The subsequent relief brought on a slight headache.

Gregory watched Jeff's reactions with interest. He noticed how Jeff seemed to wake up. The tension that he had been laboring beneath all day seemed to have disappeared. To where?

"Do you like it?" he asked.

Jeff smiled. "It's very beautiful. You feel free, liberated, standing here —"

Suddenly he stopped, cutting off his words in midsentence. He felt that he had spoken absolute nonsense, and did not know how his escort would react to it.

Gregory burst out laughing. He pointed towards a dark brown, rectangular area: "Over there, you can see the mausoleum. Inside lies the embalmed body of the father of the revolution who brought the freedom that you're feeling now."

"The body of Lenin." Jeff finished the sentence, to show off his knowledge.

"That's right," Gregory continued. "Vladimir Ilyich Lenin. If you want, we can arrange a visit there tomorrow."

"Gladly."

"And we," Gregory continued significantly, "guard with all our strength the freedom that Comrade Lenin bestowed upon us. We guard it inflexibly before all the enemies of our nation."

Jeff did not respond. He remembered the iron-clad rule: Don't speak about politics and don't voice independent opinions. The last sentence seemed very strange to him: to guard the freedom from oppression — by oppressing. And yet he kept his silence.

Gregory gave a cold, tight smile and added: "And our socialist revolution has many enemies, both inside the nation and outside."

"I understand," Jeff answered, nodding his head sagely. In his heart, he wondered: Had his escort meant to send a hint, an arrow to his heart, because of Krasno Bogatirski?

The two crossed Red Square. They walked down the street until they reached the hotel entrance. There they parted with a warm handshake.

"Good night," Gregory said demonstratively.

"*Dosvedania*," Jeff showed off the vocabulary that he had picked up from the Russian-English dictionary he had bought in New York.

Dimitri Grasimov returned to his office in KGB headquarters in Lubianka, overlooking Dzerzhinski Square. Impatiently he took the elevator to the third floor, moving toward his office with hasty steps. Most of the offices were already empty and abandoned at this late hour, and the narrow corridor was eerily quiet and dim, lit only with a single bulb. Despite the news that had dropped like a bombshell, he had not forgotten the humiliation of his weakness before his wife and son. As he stood in front of his office door fumbling nervously in his pocket for his keys, he bit his lip. The anger he felt at himself when he remembered how he had lost control grew even greater now that he recalled that embarrassing moment. Luckily, the note from Yevgenyev Patrichovski had gotten him out of the house. Otherwise, who knew how the degrading scene would have ended.

Grasimov sat down at his desk. He reached out toward the heavy black telephone, but at the last minute did not pick it up. The palm of his hand gently tapped his forehead, while his eyes grew narrow. Yevgenyev Patrichovski entered the room. Grasimov lifted his weary eyes towards him. Finally, after a silence that lasted some minutes, Grasimov asked in a whisper: "Do you see in this something suspicious, something that must be dealt with?"

Yevgenyev shrugged his shoulders, in a gesture that showed that he did not know, and kept quiet. Finally he said a few cautious, noncommittal sentences: "It's impossible to know. The American has only been in Moscow one day. And the mistake he made, it seems, was too big and too noticeable, until it seems almost that he did not make a mistake at all."

"Meaning?"

"Simple. If he had illegal plans and plots against the Soviet Union, he would not have shown such a lack of caution."

Grasimov did not reply. He waved the paper back and forth. His thoughts were far away.

"Are you listening to me, young Patrichovski?"

"I'm listening."

"It's possible, it's very possible, that we're talking here about a young, arrogant, self-confident American, who thinks he can act any way he likes in Moscow, just the way he acts in New York. It is possible.

"But," Grasimov straightened himself and stood up, his palms leaning on his desk, "but my guess is that something strange is certainly going on here, something very strange, worth checking into."

Yevgenyev Patrichovski approached the desk. With a nod of his head Grasimov allowed him to sit on the lone wooden chair that stood near the table that served as his desk. Grasimov himself remained standing.

"What's so strange?" Yevgenyev allowed himself the question. "What happened, after all?"

A slight grin played on Dimitri Grasimov's face.

"Here comes an American to Moscow. He has entered the Socialist Republic for the very first time. And after all the lies and slanders that he's heard about it in the newspapers and television of his country, what interests him, Yevgenyev? He's not interested in the Kremlin. Doesn't want to see the mausoleum where Lenin is kept. Doesn't want to buy tickets to the Bolshoi or the Mykovski Theater. Nothing. What interests him? Hmm?"

Yevgenyev finished the sentence for him.

"Krasno Bogatirski."

"That's right, Krasno Bogatirski," Dimitri repeated the street name heavily and with emphasis, "a small street in one of the city's suburbs. You want to tell me he heard that street name in New York? On Wall Street maybe? Or maybe from one of the Mafia godfathers? Where?"

Yevgenyev's hands lay on his knees. He gazed straight at his superior. "And suppose he did hear that name in New York. Maybe in Washington, in one of the secret offices of the CIA? Who knows?"

Dimitri Grasimov thoughtfully stared out the window. The dim lights of Moscow pierced through the glass. Yevgenyev felt that something about this incident was troubling his superior. In Yevgenyev's eyes it was no more than another opportunity for an investigation that might lead to an exciting discovery of treason or espionage, even though, at first glance, it hardly seemed likely. But he felt that the man sitting opposite him, on the other side of the desk, was more disturbed. Perhaps it was worth investigating what was bothering Dimitri? He enjoyed the thought.

Grasimov sat down again and leaned back in his chair.

"What's his name?" he asked laconically.

"Jeff Handler," came the reply.

"What's he doing in Moscow?"

"What we know he's doing?"

"Of course. The rest we'll find out."

"Diamonds. He came to buy precious stones. The prices in Moscow are apparently good for these bourgeois businessmen."

Grasimov digested the information rapidly. "And where was he when he showed interest in the city's most illustrious street?" The mockery in his voice was apparent.

"In the synagogue!"

Grasimov was surprised. "The synagogue? He's a Jew?"

"At least that's what it looks like."

Dimitri Grasimov did not move. Yevgenyev could see the emotions roiling within the man. Slowly his face grew grim and set; he pursed his lips, a well-known mannerism when he was coming to a decision. Patrichovski waited silently for him to continue. Still, he could not understand what was so disturbing about the news that some young American who arrived two days earlier in Moscow had casually asked, during a visit to a synagogue, where a certain street was located.

Without warning, Dimitri gave a somewhat frigid smile. He could not decide what lay behind the appearance of this Jeff Handler here in Moscow. That is, he did not know yet. But he would use the circumstance in order to raise his stature in the eyes of his superiors here in the building. He had to succeed! And even if there was nothing behind it he would have to create something, so that they would recognize him and appreciate him. Perhaps they would forget about his son Igor.

He suddenly turned to Patrichovski with marked friendliness:

"Listen, we'll take care of this young man, with the utmost caution, with brains and cunning and, most important, completely and decisively!"

He stood up and approached Yevgenyev, who got up as well. The two men stood side by side.

"We'll work slowly, Yevgeny. Slowly until he falls into the net that I've spread beneath his legs."

Yevgenyev perceived the wicked spark that gleamed within the eyes of more than one officer in that building. It was a spark ignited as they imagined their prey flailing helplessly in their hands.

Anatoly Dobrovitz reached his home in one of Moscow's suburbs in the afternoon. The tall drab buildings of the neighborhood where he lived seemed to him even drearier than usual. He entered one of the dark entranceways, climbed wearily up the stairs, and when he reached the second floor banged harshly on the metal door.

After a few seconds the door opened. Anatoly's mother, Katya Nashtarova, gave him a frankly curious look. Anatoly, in return, gave a smile that could not conceal his nervousness.

"Do you have good news for me, Anatoly?" Katya asked hesitantly.

His smile wavered. He knew what news his mother was awaiting. Katya noticed that he was avoiding her eyes. He did not rush to reply; instead, he tried to make his way to the other room through the small opening that his mother had left in the door.

The Dobrovitz family was fortunate: They had an entire apartment, two small rooms and a kitchen, at their disposal. As compensation for his father's death as an army officer in Afghanistan, they had merited getting this apartment. Anatoly, the only son, had a bedroom to himself, enabling him to occasionally invite friends to listen to music, chat, or do homework. Now he tried to rush to his room without the necessity of giving a full report to his mother. It just was not the time for it.

His mother, though, was an energetic woman. Despite her job as an educational consultant, she did not always follow the advice she gave to principals and teachers in the schools that were under her guidance. Now she blocked the passageway with her body, not letting her son pass.

"I asked you something! Anatoly!"

The words issued forth like a military command. Anatoly returned her gaze. His mother's unquestioned authority infuriated him now, as it had never done in the past. Their eyes met, the mother's piercing ones, the son's determined ones. She realized that something had happened.

"What's the answer, Anatoly?"

A terrible fear whispered inside of her that something had gone wrong in his admission to the university.

"You asked if I had good news for you today, right?"

His mother noticed his emphasis on the "you."

"It's both for me and for you, no?"

Anatoly hesitated. Finally he lifted his chin defiantly.

"No! Today it's not the same thing!"

Katya Nashtarova did not weaken. "Can you please explain yourself?"

"I'm not certain."

"In any case — "

Anatoly took a deep breath. From childhood on he had avoided open confrontation with his mother. She always had to be right. Because of the fact that she was a teacher by profession, Anatoly knew, she suffered from a slight form of megalomania, a belief that all of the wisdom of the universe was hidden somewhere in her skull, between her neck and her narrow forehead. It was insight and wisdom greater than anyone's except, of course, that of Josef Stalin. She had continued to adore the "light to the nations" even after his death and despite Khrushchev's terrible revelations, at a party convention where she had been a community representative, of Stalin's sins and excesses. She also did not believe the tales that had become known in the past years of his cruelty and the "gulags" he had created in Siberia, this Comrade Stalin. Her deep faith in Communism and in the unity of the Soviet republics had often infuriated Anatoly in the past, though he had been careful not to express his feelings. But now his fury had risen to a destructive point. He felt surprised that he was able, despite his wrath, to maintain his composure.

"Explain myself? It's hard."

His mother was silent, her face frozen. He had never refused her before. He had never been so firm when they had conversed, particularly when she had made demands of him. She saw a new aspect in his behavior, a change in the determination and defiance that was written on his face, something she had never noticed before. Anatoly felt his heart lift somewhat. This was the first time he had failed to bend to his mother's will during the first round of a debate. This feeling of liberation helped diminish his immediate feelings of anger at his mother's pointed questions.

Her voice remained interested. "But you can try, my sweet Anatoly."

Anatoly heard the word "sweet" clearly. He knew his mother had not used it because of a sudden burst of affection. He believed she loved him, but never, absolutely never, had she openly verbalized her feelings. No maternal hugs, no goodbye kisses when he traveled to the Komosol summer camp at the outskirts of Odessa. It had always seemed to him that her fanatical devotion to the building of Soviet society and the strengthening of Communism somehow clashed in her eyes with her love for her only child. He had carried the hurt deep in his heart over the years. And now her "sweet Anatoly" had indicated a greater distance between mother and son.

"You're right. I can try. For me, today, there was good news. For you, no! Do you understand?"

Her gaze turned angry. Her brows curled in an uncontrollable shudder. He recognized this involuntary movement; it occurred often during angry debates between her and anyone who did not believe in the righteousness of the Communist cause in the full sense of the word. His mother was a true fanatic.

Now she asked the question openly. "Have you been accepted to university?"

Anatoly did not answer. He took a step forward and demanded in a clear and determined voice: "Let me go to my room."

Much to his surprise, she acquiesced. She moved aside as he walked into his room. He heard her slam her door in fury, a slam that shook the walls of the apartment, perhaps the walls of the entire building. This was his first indication of his mother's powerlessness. No, she was not happy with him: This was his first victory against

Communism, the Communism that had thrown him out of university because he was a Jew.

Jeff walked unhappily up to his room. He was upset at the thought that he had behaved so stupidly in his first steps in Moscow. He did not have to be an experienced spy to know that he should have been a lot more careful. He knew well that this Gregory had not been glued to his side for nothing. The broad smile Gregory had given him at their parting worried Jeff more than anything. Clearly, it was a smile of victory; he had something to tell his handlers in the KGB building. In Jeff's imagination he could already see the interrogator appearing in his room. Or perhaps the operative would meet him in the lobby tomorrow, invite him over to his house for a chat — and who knew where it would end. He would ask him about his strange interest in Krasno Bogatirski Street. Jeff's imagination worked feverishly; he must fabricate a series of believable excuses in an attempt to allay the well-known suspicions of the Soviet secret police.

He threw himself on the bed completely dressed, not even bothering to remove his shoes. For a minute he was startled; the screech of the springs protesting beneath his weight had caused him to think that the bed was collapsing under him. *They want to conquer the world, but they can't make a normal bed in a hotel room,* he thought bitterly.

Suddenly he panicked. He sat up quickly on the bed. He had spoken the sentence out loud! Had they not warned him in New York that he should not even talk to himself in Moscow, certainly not in an official state hotel? State-of-the-art listening devices were scattered in every corner. He remembered how he had laughed when cautioned not to talk to himself. The warning had seemed so foolish; and now here he was, talking to himself! Speaking out loud — and look what he had said! It was clear to him that someone, somewhere, had recorded his incriminating words. What a fool he had been! Now he had supplied even more evidence to the KGB; now they had a lovely excuse to come tomorrow morning and asked him some questions.

Jeff cracked his knuckles in nervousness. Perhaps they would come this evening? Tonight? Maybe before dawn, as was their custom? Or maybe he was imagining the whole thing? Oh, how he longed to be back home in New York!

Jeff shook his head decisively, as if to banish his murderous thoughts from his feverish brain. He stood up and approached the window that looked out on the center of wickedness concealed behind the walls of the Kremlin. His eyes latched onto the five-pointed star, symbol of the Communist folly, that gleamed in the light of the lanterns. He opened the window, despite the cold of the night. A gust of cold air blew in and chilled his bones. He could not explain why he had opened the window at that moment; perhaps it was just some sort of instinct, a reaction to the choking feeling of imprisonment that had him and his overworked imagination in its grasp.

Jeff remembered that he had not yet *davened Ma'ariv.* He washed his hands and began praying fervently. It had been a long time since he had stood in such humility during the long moments of *Shemoneh Esrei.* The focused prayers eased something within him. As he prepared for sleep, the soothing verse ran through his mind: "Wait silently for Hashem and wait longingly for Him; do not compete with... the man who executes malicious plans."

Just then, the telephone rang.

Dimitri Grasimov calmed down somewhat. He began to weave the long-range plans that would let him trap the American who had appeared from out of nowhere. The KGB archives included a list of all the names of known CIA agents; there was no mention of Jeff Handler. Strange. Perhaps they were really talking about an eccentric young American? Dimitri would have to be careful not to make a fool of himself.

Grasimov took the last cigarette out of the case that lay on his desk. He took a deep drag on it. The light cough that followed was uncomfortable, but he ignored it. The possibility that there was nothing in the story of the American depressed him a little.

Suddenly he straightened in his chair. He stubbed out the cigarette in the ashtray and curled his right hand into a fist. He pounded it into his left hand with all his strength, until his fingers ached.

"It can't be," he said out loud.

Yevgenyev, startled out of his thoughts, looked at his boss in surprise.

"What can't be?"

Grasimov held his tongue. He had forgotten that someone else was in the room with him and thus had allowed himself the outburst. His gaze softened, trying to conceal his confusion from Yevgenyev. His eyes gleamed with spurious good humor.

"Nothing, Yevgenyev, just some personal problems bothering me. Who doesn't have some?"

Yevgenyev nodded his head in understanding, in assent. Naturally, he did not believe Grasimov's assurances. And if he had known what Grasimov was really thinking, he would have realized that he was correct.

For what was bothering Grasimov, bothering him very much, was: What was the American looking for in Krasno Bogatirski Street? Why particularly that street? Why? Why?

12

Jeff was frightened. The sharp ring of the telephone tore through the thread of his melancholy thoughts. He sat up, almost by reflex, in his bed. His bloodshot eyes stared at the heavy black instrument. The ringing would not stop. Jeff lowered his legs from the bed onto the floor, but did not stand up. He hesitated over whether or not to pick up the receiver or wait until the strident, frightening ringing would come to an end. In New York, at home, if he did not pick up a phone the shrill jangle eventually ceased; here, it seemed, the Russian telephone behaved differently, at least in his room in the Russia Hotel.

Jeff finally got out of bed and thrust his arm out towards the instrument. His hand shook slightly as he picked up the receiver.

"*Dobro Notcheh, vas vizivayet zagranitza* (Good evening, you have an overseas call)."

"*Ya nye ponimaye Poriski* (I don't understand Russian)," Jeff whispered the all-important sentence he had memorized in New York: I don't speak Russian.

The operator immediately switched to English.

"You have a call from New York."

Jeff recovered his composure immediately, and felt a vast relief. The tension that had overtaken his entire body melted away within seconds, followed by a splitting headache. He ignored his throbbing temples and answered, "Oh yes, thank you!"

"Jeff, how are you?" the voice came from afar.

It was his wife, Miriam.

"Fine. Very good. Excellent. I'm enjoying every minute."

"Good, I'm glad. How's business?"

"Hmmm — thank G-d, fine. I had my first meeting today at the Ministry of Commerce. Tough negotiations but, okay. Tomorrow I hope to close the deal, *im yirtzeh Hashem.*"

There was a short silence. Then he heard his wife whispering once more.

"And what about that other business?"

This was it! He felt that the dangerous question would blow up the entire conversation. His wife had whispered it, the question, as if she thought the KGB only listened to conversations that were spoken out loud. As if they did not care about whispers. Nonsense!

"Everything is fine," he replied quickly. "How are the kids?"

His diversionary tactics failed miserably. "The children are fine, thank G-d. But what about that matter. You know very well what I'm talking about!"

Jeff bit his lips until they hurt. Of course he knew what matter she was referring to. But how could he change the subject? Should he just hang up and end the conversation, without even wishing her a good night from frigid Moscow? He began to shake his left leg back and forth in an involuntary movement.

"I told you, everything is fine! Why do you keep asking? Miriam, let's end this call. I'm tired. Good night."

"Wait a minute, Jeff. Just a minute! Remember, I'm all alone at home, and you're far away. I want to talk a little more."

Jeff felt his body grow weak. He was terrified of continuing the conversation. He knew that someone was listening to every word, but he had no way of warning her not to speak of the topic of his grandfather's *tefillin.* Death and life in the hands of the tongue. Here it was, the old saying, in practical reality. What should he do?

Without much of a choice he continued. "It's cold here, very cold. Fifteen degrees below zero. And how's the weather by you?" He tried once again to take the conversation away from the matter that was of such interest to her.

"It's cold here too, but not below zero like it is in Russia. But Jeff, it seems that you're avoiding the issue. Why don't you tell me about the other things?"

"Okay, I'll tell you. I took a walk around the Kremlin walls. To read so much about the Kremlin and Red Square, and suddenly you're standing there — it's very exciting, no?"

"I understand, but —"

Jeff interrupted her harshly. "And I went to visit and *daven Minchah* in the only *shul* in Moscow, on Archipova Street. What an impressive synagogue!"

"Yes, but what about —"

Jeff continued remorselessly. "Listen, Miriam, the hotel I'm in, Russia Hotel, is gigantic, it's built on a huge plot. In general, Moscow seems to me a lot prettier than I imagined. And I think that when I come here again, and I do intend to return, you'll come with me."

"Me?" Her frightened voice came clearly over the line. "Never!"

Jeff was satisfied. The conversation had taken an entirely different course. Thank G-d. He allowed himself a satisfied grin.

After a moment her voice came through again. This time it was determined.

"You know what? I am prepared to come with you to Moscow. I can tell that you're avoiding my question, about that street, I can't remember its name. Believe me, I'll come — and find it!"

Jeff thought he would faint. His right hand leaned on the wall of the room, while his left pulled the receiver away from his ear. *What is she doing to me?* came the frightening thought racing madly through his mind. Why doesn't she understand that she was putting him in danger with her candid speech?

Jeff could hear the quiet voice issuing from the receiver that was still held far from his ear. Now she began to yell: "Jeff! Hello! Hello! Jeff, do you hear me? Hello! Jeff, Jeff! Hello?"

Finally, when he did not answer her cries, a click could be heard. The dial tone hummed in his ears, sounding like the siren of an ambulance racing to a hospital. In the heat of fury Jeff threw the receiver down. He had never regretted a conversation like he regretted this one. On legs still weak, he walked back to his bed. But before he could fling himself down on it he stopped and turned around. He lifted the receiver again, examined it minutely looking for listening devices. He found nothing: no wire edging out of the instrument to who-knew-where. After a few seconds he replaced the phone. What a fool he was! Did he think the Russians were so stupid that they would not conceal the fact that they were listening in?

After several hours of sleeplessness he finally dozed off. Again, it was the phone that broke through his slumber. He jumped up, instantly awake. The morning was peeking in through the window, from behind the heavy curtain.

Morning broke, and Anatoly Dobrovitz stayed in bed after a long night's sleep. For a full day he did not budge. He could hear his worried mother's desperate cries as she banged her fists on his locked door, begging for a sign of life. He did not bother answering. It was as if he gained power and enjoyment from the knowledge that his mother was worried about him, a simple maternal concern. To Anatoly, the student who had been kept out of university because he was a Jew, it was important to hear his mother's pleas. Ultimately she was betraying herself, her faith in Communism, the faith she had tried to pass down to him. For here she was, worrying about him as an individual, as her son, not as a mere piece of the Soviet nation whose only function was to help build the centralized socialist society. How wonderful that her attention and worry were focused upon him.

Finally he gave in. "Don't worry, Mother. I'm fine."

The cries outside his door diminished. The sign of life that he had given, it seemed, had calmed her down.

After a few more wasted hours, time seasoned with humiliation and fury, he got up lazily from his bed. It was almost midnight. He went to the area of the tiny room that was his own private sanctum, towards a chest of drawers. The top was strewn with piles of paper covered with mathematical scribblings and geometric figures. Anatoly grabbed them with a quick gesture and threw them down to the floor. He would not need them any longer. Then he forcibly pulled the chest of drawers away from the wall. He pulled out a recording of American jazz that a close friend, whose father was an officer in the Moscow militia, had given him to conceal. Listening to such music was forbidden; it was considered politically and socially subversive, and woe to him who was caught enjoying it. Anatoly's friend would occasionally come to his house, and there they would "sin" by enjoying the banned music.

Now Anatoly took the illegal record and plugged in the old record player that he had bought cheaply from a Georgian anxious to get rid of it. At the time Anatoly had not asked him where he had gotten it. He put the record on and turned the volume up as high as it would go. The loud music with its wild American rhythms burst through the open door and could be heard throughout the area. It was the perfect method to get the police over; perhaps even the KGB would be interested. Anatoly did not care.

His mother raced once again to the locked door.

"Anatoly, what are you doing? It's against the law! And at night yet!"

Anatoly, too, raised his voice. "And the heads of the university aren't going against the law? You're a Soviet citizen, right? I'm a Jew, I can't be a student? Aren't there equal rights in your country, between your citizens?"

"Anatoly, stop it at once," his mother's voice came out, a wail. "Have mercy on me. I'll try to do something tomorrow for you in the Ministry of Education. Have a little patience."

"I won't be patient, do you hear me?" He roared, so the words would be heard over the sound of the music. For several long minutes he was silent, as the record moved smoothly round and round. Miraculously, not a window in the adjoining houses opened with the angry demand that the music cease at this midnight hour; the sleep of the Soviet workers was undisturbed.

Suddenly his mood changed. He disconnected the record player, and the silence of night once again reigned in his room and his neighborhood. He opened the door of his room, a smile of triumph on his face. "Did you see, Mother? Not one neighbor complained. No one called the police. Do you know why? Because they all want to hear that music. They're sick of this. I tell you — they're sick of you and your socialism! That's it exactly! They're sick of it, like I'm sick of it!"

His mother did not respond. She glared at him furiously, but at the same time felt powerless. How she longed to get back at him for the heresy he was spouting. But she knew that now was the time for her to hold her peace. Who knew what else her angry son, offended as he was, could do?

"Good night," she said quietly.

Anatoly grinned but did not answer. When she turned towards her room he barked after her: "Don't bother with me at the Ministry of Education. There's no need. I've learned everything I can learn in university today. The most important lesson I could have had."

Without another word he returned to his room and slammed the door behind him.

The next morning, at 6 o'clock, he awoke. He put together a small package of clothing and some personal belongings that he loved. His mother, who had heard him moving about, quickly got dressed and came out of her room.

"Anatoly? Where are you going?"

"Me? I'm going to Archipova, to the synagogue there. I don't know when I'll be back."

"Not that! Just not that!" his mother screamed.

He did not even turn around as he walked towards the station and the train that would take him to the center of the city.

Dimitri Grasimov spent a little more time in his office. He sent Yevgenyev home, but he still sat, lost in thought. Before Yevgenyev had left, Grasimov had asked him to turn off the lights. Better that way: The darkness liberated the thoughts that coursed wildly through his brain. Slowly, he examined once again the opportunity that had come to him.

Clearly there was reason to suspect that this American was not merely an innocent diamond merchant. The unusual questions he had asked at the synagogue on Archipova Street surely had unusual answers. With all that, Dimitri discarded the idea of inviting him for a short, friendly investigation. In these days of tension between Grasimov's country and the United States, with the background of nuclear disarmament talks, the big bosses were being very careful, behind the Kremlin walls, not to do anything that would antagonize the Americans. He knew that despite the stern speeches of Brezhnev and Andropov in the last weeks regarding the threat of nuclear war if Washington refused all of the Kremlin proposals, his government wanted to sign a treaty with the Americans at almost any price. They would not allow him to increase the tension, that already was so strong, by arresting an American tourist, even for a short investigation. If he would do so, Dimitri knew full well, he would be thrown out of office, if not worse.

He hoped that by tomorrow morning he would have photographs of the man in his office. Yevgenyev's men, who were still loyal to him, would see to it that he would be photographed without knowing it in the lobby of the Russia Hotel. The photographs would go through regular channels to New York. He was already impatient to hear the report from their men in the field in New York on the tourist and his true identity. Dimitri was disturbed by the thought that they might not recognize him at all. He believed that there was no American agent of whom they did not have detailed information, more or less. But of Jeff Handler — not a trace. Perhaps he had not been sent by one of the spy agencies? And if so, then what? Again, he felt the hope rise that he, Dimitri Grasimov, would manage to get to the bottom of the mystery. Even his sworn enemies in the KGB would not be able to stop his promotion in the halls of the Cometee, and when he would retire in a few more years he would be able to spend the rest of his life in the *dacha* that the regime and the party would give him, in reward for his faithful service. There he would finally be able to busy himself with the small things he so yearned for: fishing, reading, and perhaps writing spy novels. Suddenly, his own personal fate seemed intertwined with the fate of some unknown American who had happened to land in Moscow. Strange, the ways of destiny.

Grasimov went down to Dzerzhinski Square. A huge statue of the man of iron — Dzerzhinski the Pole — stood there. A man with an oddly shaped, short beard and an unusually sharp mind, he had been the founder of the Cheka, precursor of the KGB, the man who had repulsed the West's first efforts to destroy the Soviet Union from within. Usually Grasimov did not spare a look at the statue that he passed daily. Now he remembered the joke that was connected to it. The statue was located at the back of the KGB building; Moscow wits would say that Felix Dzerzhinski had been found guilty and sentenced to stand in eternal solitary confinement. Grasimov sometimes identified with his solitude.

Only a few people were walking outside. The night was cold. White snowflakes drifted lazily down upon him in an elegant shower. For a moment he allowed himself the luxury of enjoying the crisp, cold air. Then he disappeared into the automobile that awaited him at the entrance gate. He hurried home.

"Where is Igor?" The words burst out of his mouth, a direct question. For some reason he had imagined that he would find his son still huddled on the couch in the same position as when he had left him when called to his office. And here it was, their less-than-spacious house, empty. His shouted question brought his wife out of the kitchen. Her expression was frozen and serious. She looked penetratingly at her husband, standing by the door shaking off the snow from his coat and fur hat. She did not answer; she merely returned to the kitchen.

He carefully locked the door behind him and asked once again, "Where is Igor?" This time his tone was threatening. His wife, Natasha, came out of the kitchen. Standing straight and tall, she approached him and hissed, "Igor? Igor has run away!"

His eyes narrowed in surprise. "What do you mean, run away?"

Natasha spread her arms out, as if to emphasize her words. Then she wiped her hands on her apron with a gesture that clearly showed her growing fury. She turned her back on him and marched into the kitchen, but Dimitri jumped ahead of her and blocked her way.

"I believe that you understand, Natasha, that I deserve a full and detailed report."

She gave a frigid laugh. "Your working hours in the Cometee are over now. Don't you ever take a vacation from investigations?" After a short silence she continued, her revulsion apparent: "Investigations, investigations. Every day, investigations."

His lips tightened and a spark of anger flared in his eyes. But now, not like in the past, his wife was not intimidated.

"I have time off from strangers. But not from your son."

"That's right, Dimitri Grasimov, the famous, and perhaps cruel, investigator. You won't like to hear this, but your son has decided to take some time off — from you."

Now it was too late, Natasha knew. In another minute her beloved husband would go wild, and another few household items would find their way to the garbage, after the treatment that they would get at the hands of the drunken boor she had married. She saw how he approached her, his fists balled up tight. She did not move a muscle. This time, she decided, he would hear everything.

"And you," he screamed, "you let him go?"

Her voice was quiet, without a trace of fear. She herself did not know how she found the composure. Perhaps because she had already accepted the consequences of this encounter.

"Me?" she mocked his scarlet face. "Me? Stop him? That's your problem, and the problem of all your friends there in Lubianka. Haven't you figured out yet that the world has changed? Here too, Dimitri, the children and the adults aren't afraid, the way they used to be afraid in the past. That's it! Listen here, Dimitri, you think that you rule over everyone through terror and fear. That's the past, Dimitri! Outside, it's not so noticeable. But if only one person is prepared to stand against you — that's the end of the reign of the KGB! It may take a year, two years, ten years! But you should start looking for a new job. Did you really think, in these days, you would be able to stop Igor from leaving?"

"Where is Igor?" he screamed, like one possessed.

"I told you," she shouted back, suddenly losing her control. "He's run away! He told me we'd never find him. And what did you think: that he would voluntarily agree to go to a psychiatric hospital — is that what you call that place? Re-education — of his own free will? It's a new Russia, even in the house of Dimitri Grasimov, big man in the KGB."

She stood before him defiantly, like one ready for battle, fists upraised, lips clenched, facial muscles tense, and eyes filled with contempt for the fear that she saw, or hoped to see, for the first time in his own.

His voice went down several decibels. His wife's fearlessness frightened him. He was not used to it, despite her occasional outbursts in the past. He asked in a more patient voice, like one accepting his fate: "Where did he go, the boy?"

"Ah," another frigid smile. "Ah, suddenly he's 'the boy.' A boy whom you worry about. In front of him you showed that only your career was important to you, and that he'd endangered it. You weren't ready to hear a word that he had to say. And now he's 'the boy,' the sweet one whose fate so concerns you. Very nice, Dimitri, very nice indeed."

Dimitri did not respond. He accepted with forced humility the insult that was hurled at him like a fist. Again he asked, "Where did he go?"

"I know where? Put your agents out in the field! Maybe he went to Tashkent, to Ukraine, to Georgia, to Siberia. I know where? And maybe he's smarter, and is holing up somewhere in Moscow. What's important is his announcement that we would never find him."

The furious fist finally found its way into the palm of his other hand. Without looking at her again he sat down at the table. She gave him one last scrutinizing look before disappearing back into the small kitchen, returning to the potatoes she was peeling. She had managed to get some a few hours ago from one of the peddlers, at a very good price. The man had been anxious to get rid of the produce that he had smuggled out of the communal farm where he worked. After a few minutes of deep silence she heard her husband's cry: "Of course I'll put agents on it. I've got to search for him, before Malenkov's men do. Do you understand?"

His voice was slurred. Clearly, his bottle of vodka had once again become his faithful friend in time of trouble. After a few long minutes she could hear him announce in hoarse tones, "And I, I, Dimitri Grasimov, swear that I will find him. I will find him. I will!"

Then she heard a loud thud. She rushed into the room. Grasimov was lying on the floor, his eyes shut. A bottle of vodka stood on the table, two thirds of it empty. She approached him, bent down and listened closely. Slowly, slowly she could hear his labored breathing. She returned to the kitchen, to the potatoes.

J eff lurched out of bed. Once again, it was the nerve-shattering ring of the phone frightening him into wakefulness. He hastily washed his hands and murmured a quick "*Modeh Ani*," as his heart thudded wildly, then rushed to the ringing instrument. This time he decided to pick up the receiver at once, in order to allay his fears. He grabbed the receiver and put it next to his ear, but all he could hear was the dial tone. He replaced the receiver, wondering who it was who had upset him so for nothing.

He dressed quickly. He planned on putting on his *tallis* and *tefillin* and *davening* in his room. Then he would have a little of the diminishing supply of food that he had brought with him from New York, and would await Gregory's arrival in the lobby. He would go with him to the second vital meeting at the Ministry of Commerce, and then sit and count the hours until the night flight that would take him out of Moscow. He hoped, with all his heart, to finish his business on a positive note, not to disappoint his boss.

It was 10 minutes to 7 in the morning. No need to rush: The meeting was called for 10 a.m. Jeff opened his suitcase and pulled out his *tallis* and *tefillin* bag. What upset him was that he would not have good news for his grandfather. He felt that he was a first-class failure. He could not forgive himself for his lack of caution. What would he tell the old man waiting so anxiously in Ramat Gan for his grandson to return with the holy pair of *tefillin?* What could he say? That he would do better on his next visit? He was not coming back to Russia, no matter what happened! Jeff just could not handle the oppressive atmosphere that surrounded him. The fears he had felt yesterday were quite sufficient for him. In the future he, Jeff, would fly to Florida, to the diamond exchange in Ramat Gan, to Los Angeles, to Caracas. Anywhere, but not to Moscow! But what would he tell his grandfather?

The thought weighed him down as he pulled out his *siddur.* He wrapped himself in the *tallis.* He had already straightened his left arm in order to put the *tefillin* on it, quietly murmuring the prayer that precedes it.

And then he heard the knock on his door.

He lifted his head from the *siddur.* His fears returned, stronger than ever. For a moment he stood motionless in the center of the room, in one hand the *siddur,* in the other the *tefillin.* Wide eyed, he stared at the locked door, his ears straining. His breathing came slower; if he could, he would have stopped breathing completely.

The knock repeated itself.

His brain got into high gear. Who could it be?

Another knock.

He noticed that the knocks were light. No authoritative knock, these, in the manner of police or secret agents. Or perhaps, the thought went through his mind, this was their way of not frightening their "customer"?

Jeff waited for another knock. If it would happen, he would go and answer the door. What could he do? He was in a strange country, in Russia, in Moscow. Yes, there it went: this time, three knocks, somewhat firmer than the others.

"*K'to tam?* Who's there?" he asked in Russian, having hastily looked it up in his Russian-English manual.

"*Ya,*" came the reply from behind the door.

Jeff did not recognize the voice. He asked, again, "*K'to* (Who)?"

"*Ya.* Gregory."

Jeff relaxed a little. But not completely. There seemed no reasonable explanation for Gregory's sudden appearance at his door, not when they had agreed to meet at 9:30 in the lobby. It was only 7 o'clock. Was Gregory alone behind that door?

Jeff opened the door. There stood Gregory, by himself, smiling broadly at Jeff's stony face.

"I see that you're trying to speak Russian, Mr. Handler. Now say after me in Russian, *dovroi utro* — good morning."

Jeff felt better and decided to answer in the same pleasant vein. He still did not dare ask why Gregory had come so early to the hotel and why he had come up to his room. Still, he decided to contribute to diminishing the tensions. He pulled out his manual, skimmed through it, and said, *"Rad vas videt. Kak dila?"* (I am happy to see you. How is everything?)

Gregory laughed loudly and turned back to his fluent English. "You didn't answer the phone, so I decided to come up to your room."

"We decided yesterday to meet in the lobby at 9:30. It's only 7 o'clock now. Has something happened?"

"No. Nothing."

Jeff sat down on his bed and took a deep breath. "And so —"

Gregory noticed Jeff's tension. He wanted badly to know what was bothering this American tourist so greatly. His behavior was a little strange. Did he have something to hide?

"Mr. Handler, nothing happened. I saw yesterday in the synagogue that you actually prayed, and didn't just visit like most of the Jewish tourists. I understood that you are a religious Jew. Are you really religious, or only in Russia?"

At first Jeff did not know what to say. Suddenly he remembered that he was still wrapped in his *tallis*.

"I don't understand your question, Comrade Gregory. Don't you see that I am really a religious Jew? Here—" he grabbed the *tzitzis* at the end of his *tallis* and waved them in front of Gregory's face. "Do you know what these are?"

And then he showed him the *tefillin*. "And these?"

Gregory indicated his assent and understanding, but stayed silent. Jeff continued. "Yes, I am really a religious Jew. Why do you ask?"

"I thought maybe you would want to go to the synagogue this morning too. I've escorted Jewish tourists there before."

Jeff was shocked by the goodwill of this Soviet citizen. To help a Jew *daven*? For some reason, he could not believe in the pure motives of this young Russian, this Communist who was surely against all religion. Nevertheless, he decided to accept the offer. *Shacharis* in Moscow, in a *shul* yet! And perhaps he would be able to make some progress in the matter of his grandfather's *tefillin*. Perhaps? Who could know the hidden paths of *hashgachah*?

They went out into the street, to be greeted by a shower of snowflakes drifting lightly down from the slate grey sky onto the immobile, expressionless faces of the few passers-by. They walked with difficulty on the white-coated sidewalks to the synagogue. The weather was cold but refreshing. They walked silently, one next to the other, each wrapped in his own thoughts. Jeff was still disturbed. What did Gregory want? Who had ordered him to get out of bed and bring his American charge to the synagogue?

Finally, after a walk of about half an hour, the two reached the corner of Archipova. As they stood not far from the synagogue, Jeff finally found the courage to ask his young escort: "Am I allowed, Gregory, to ask you a question?"

Gregory gave him an amused look. "Of course it's allowed! Haven't I told you that this is a free country?"

Jeff kept his composure in the face of this declaration.

"I wanted to ask: Why did you ask me before, in my room, if I was really a religious man or if I just wanted to go to the synagogue?"

Gregory shrugged. "I wanted to know."

"Why are you so interested?"

"I'm always interested in finding young men like yourself who believe in G-d."

Jeff, who had already begun to go up the wide steps that led to the synagogue entrance, stopped. Gregory, too, came to a halt. Jeff gave him a searching glance.

"What's your problem with that?"

"I have no problem, personally. It just seems strange to me."

Jeff felt a tightening in his chest. "Strange? Why?"

"Strange? Because here in Russia we have no such phenomenon. Do you understand, Mr. Handler? We're progressive! This backwardness belongs only to a small group of old people, like the ones you met yesterday, like the ones you will meet here once again today. But the last vestiges of the phenomenon will disappear within the next few years."

Jeff was quiet. In New York, or in any other place in the world, he would have known how to reply to such nonsense. But here in Moscow, it was advisable to keep quiet.

He heard Gregory ask, "Don't you think so?"

The desire to debate rose in Jeff's heart. "No. I don't think so. And if you want, I can explain why!"

A rash offer, Jeff himself would admit to it. He had been told to keep quiet. He hoped that Gregory would not take him up on it.

Gregory merely made a grimace of astonishment and barked out one word: "Interesting."

They climbed a few more steps and now stood at the entrance door. Gregory quickly opened it and motioned to the American tourist to him into the synagogue. But on the threshold, Jeff turned his head to Gregory. "Tell me, when the Communist revolution broke out 65 years ago, was the Jewish religion and belief only a matter for a few old people?"

Gregory looked confident. "Without a doubt. Why do you ask?"

"Look, these believing old men were young 60 years ago, correct?"

"Correct."

"So, they didn't just start believing in G-d and keeping the commandments today. They did so then, when they were young, right?"

"Right."

Jeff celebrated a small victory. "So the conclusion is: Religious belief isn't a matter of youth or age. It's contingent upon the person."

Gregory would not give in easily. "With all that, only the elderly now come to the synagogue. And old people have this custom: They die."

"And there are no believers among the young? Are you certain?"

Gregory waited for a moment before answering. His eyes traveled over Jeff's face. Jeff could not not decipher that look. Finally, Gregory said nonchalantly, "Truthfully, I don't know. Maybe there are."

They entered the *shul*. Jeff could see a few old men. Some were already wearing *tallis* and *tefillin*, others were just standing around.

When he entered some turned to look at him, but then they almost in-
stantaneously turned back to their *siddurim*. Near the door, like
yesterday, stood several men, their hands clasped behind their backs,
their bearing military, looking around without even blinking.

"I have another question."

Gregory turned a pleasant face to him, a countenance that seemed
to say, "Ask away."

"Why did you say that there are tourists who are only religious in
Russia?"

Gregory rubbed his hands together vigorously, to try and restore
some of the body heat that the winter's cold had robbed.

"Yes, Mr. Handler, there are Jewish tourists, a little impudent perhaps, who, in New York or London or wherever they live, would
never visit a synagogue. But only in Moscow do they suddenly long
to pray. You think we don't know why? You think we're blind, that we
don't realize that their goal is to arouse subversion and unrest among
the Jews? They think that it will be easier for them to meet Jews in the
synagogue and to get them to rebel against the government. That is a
terrible return for the hospitality we show them. I think so, don't
you?"

"Do you take these things personally, Gregory?"

"No, Mr. Handler, if you are truly religious, that's something else
entirely. It is your prerogative to pray. That's why I asked you that
question."

Jeff did not answer at first. He again tried to uncover what lay beneath the words, but could not figure it out.

"Is that why you came early to the hotel? And that's why you were
willing to walk such a long way in the Moscow cold? It's rather
strange, no?"

Gregory burst out laughing. "I told you that we're a country that's
hospitable to guests and we take care of our tourists."

Jeff heard and kept quiet. He did not feel tranquil. It was clear to
him that something else had caused Gregory to want him to return to
the synagogue. He would have to be very careful: Something here
was not clear.

The Mission | 117

Anatoly walked down the stairs to the Metro station near his house. His eyes were riveted to the railroad tracks. But he did not even see them; nor did he notice anyone among the hundreds of people milling around the platform. His lips were tight and his brain, like a snake pit, was full of venom and bitterness. Several people actually looked at him; the moment he felt their stares piercing his back he turned around and faced them, and they swiftly looked in any direction but his: right, left, towards the decorated ceiling of the station or the railroad tracks. Anatoly sensed them avoiding his gaze. The thought flashed through his head: Were these the *tauton*, the KGB agents who shadowed people on foot? Were they already on his trail? Had his dear mother managed, in the name of the socialist nation, to report her rebellious son to the proper authorities? He waved his hand in derision, as if to wave off an annoying insect: *Let her do what she wants. I don't care.*

The deep humiliation that he had suffered at the university was still stronger than any other emotion. Stronger than fear, stronger than the self-destructive route that he sensed he had embarked upon. With his having been orphaned, his father an army officer dying for the homeland in some stupid war in Afghanistan; with his mother an energetic educational supervisor; with her burning and naive belief in the Party's principles — with all that, he had been shut out of the university only because he was a Jew. If so, the entire regime could go to the devil for all he cared.

The train arrived and slowly came to a halt. Its doors opened wide; people came in and out. Anatoly entered like one being led to his destiny. The train began its journey slowly, then picked up speed, disappearing into the dark tunnel. Anatoly stood, though there were empty seats. He hardly noticed that he was standing; he had no idea how long he was traveling. When the microphone announced "Metro Ploshad Nagina" he got off. He did not bother checking whether his suspicions were correct, whether he was being followed. Let them! He got onto an escalator and reached Ulitza Salonka, the street that would bring him to Archipova Street, where the synagogue was located.

Anatoly breathed deeply, the frigid and clear early morning air entering his nostrils. The fresh oxygen flowed through him. He needed several such breaths in order to re-ignite the courage in his heart.

He had never been to this synagogue, or any other. The whole idea was far removed from him. He had, though, heard of the young Jews who openly scorned the KGB and who in full view of everyone entered the synagogue on Jewish holidays. He had heard, but the news had not made any special impact on him.

He reached narrow Archipova Street. Anatoly walked upon the sidewalk across from the house of prayer that rose above it. The closer he came to the imposing building, the slower he went. He found himself breathing heavily. What was this emotion? Fear? A final retreat before he took the courageous step that he had decided on? He knew clearly that just the act of climbing up those wide steps meant that he was burning many bridges behind him. Every decision had its price. To climb up those steps now was his violent protest, a protest that would reach the heavens, against the injustice the Soviet system had done to him.

He lifted his eyes toward the back of the building. His gaze wandered over the white marble pillars that reached high up to the ceiling of the building's entranceway. On the wall opposite him he could see indecipherable writing, in unfamiliar letters. *Probably Hebrew,* he thought to himself — he knew almost nothing about it. The building impressed him with its size, with the tranquility and nobility that it radiated. Moscow was filled with beautiful buildings in the style of the preceding century, from the days of the czar. *Yes, but this is a Jewish building.* It was the first time in his life that Anatoly felt an emotional attachment to something Jewish. He examined the strange new feeling and grinned. *What those professors could do to a person with just one expulsion!*

A few minutes afterwards he crossed the street. He stopped for a moment and then climbed the steps leading to the building. He opened the entrance door, blinked in the dimness of the lobby, opened the wooden doors that led to the sanctuary itself, and entered. Other than the pounding of his heart and growing confusion as to where this rebellious journey would lead him, nothing happened. The scene that was revealed before him was very strange. A few men, mostly elderly, were wrapped in some kind of white garments. They were fooling around with small black boxes that were on their heads. Others leaned over books, not saying a word, not blinking an eye. *Were these Jews?* Anatoly wondered confusedly. He noticed, also, the men standing quietly near the door. He knew very well who they were, but ignored them completely.

In a corner by the table he saw a young bearded man sitting and shaking back and forth, gracefully, in front of a large book. What was that?

Anatoly walked toward him. The man continued to study the open book before him without lifting his head towards the young stranger who stood not far from him.

Finally, Anatoly took another step. He approached the table, squinted in order to see what was written in the large book, without success. After a hesitation of a few seconds he sat on the edge of the bench, not taking his eyes off the young man so engrossed in his studies. He spoke in a whisper, in Russian. "*Ti mozesh naotchit menyah yevreiskoi histori'i* — Can you teach me Jewish history?"

The scholar, surprised, lifted his head from the Gemara. He contemplated the young man toying with illegal questions, right next to the agents of the KGB who stood nearby and heard every word.

He answered firmly, "*Idi i uchi! Shto ti chotzesh ot menyah. Ya nyeh utchitel* — Go and learn; what do you want from me? I'm not a teacher."

Anatoly was surprised. He stood up, disappointment in his eyes. He turned away from the young man who had rejected him and stared into the magnificent room. He noticed Jeff, standing nearby. Jeff's tailored suit broadcast the fact: This was no Muscovite. Jeff looked at him curiously. This young Russian was wearing Western-style jeans and a baseball cap, like his American counterparts, with the brim facing backward. He also wore a short leather jacket. Clearly, he did not belong among those who regularly attended this synagogue. Jeff wondered what a young Russian rebelling against the Communist mode of dress was doing here during morning prayers. Their eyes met in mutual interest. Jeff felt that this young man, despite some confusion, radiated strength, anger, determination and, with all those, a spark of warmth and humanity.

Jeff turned to Gregory, standing next to him. "What did that young man want from the man learning in the corner?"

"He told him that he wanted to learn Jewish history."

"And what did the man say?"

" 'Go learn,' he said. 'What do you want from me? I'm not a teacher.' "

Jeff did not understand such an answer. At that moment he did not know that he would, in the future, understand it well. But at this moment he decided to celebrate a small victory over Gregory. He smiled. "*Nu*, you see, Gregory? Here is a young man in Moscow looking for religion!"

Gregory did not answer. Instead, he gave Jeff another mysterious smile, a smile that said little.

No one paid any attention to Anatoly. That bothered Jeff. If he had any courage he would approach him and try to chat. But he felt that such a step might harm the young Russian. He stared at the young man when he left the hall. The frigid reception, it seemed, had disappointed him.

Jeff noticed one more thing. The moment the young Russian left the synagogue, one of the quiet men standing near the door came to life. The sphinxlike figure lifted his palm to his mouth and spoke. Jeff assumed that some kind of miniature radio was hidden in his hand. After a minute the man gestured to one of the others to follow the young Russian. The agent nodded and left.

Jeff watched and longed to be home.

14

"So nothing happened?"

The words were said in overt surprise.

"No, Comrade."

"He didn't say anything? Not one careless word?"

"No. No."

Silence, for a long moment. Grasimov gazed with narrowed piercing eyes at the man standing before him.

"In any case, what did he do?"

"He prayed. He prayed like a Jew prays."

Grasimov hesitated. "And on that street, you know —"

He made as if to try and remember the street name.

"What was the name of that street he asked about yesterday?"

The man standing before him quickly volunteered the information.

"Krasno Bogatirski."

Grasimov moved uncomfortably in his chair. His eyes narrowed. It was hard for him to admit to himself that he was confused. But that was the reality. Sitting here in his office, he asked himself a question:

If the American had inquired about another street in Moscow, would he still feel the same tension? He suspected not. But what was this Handler looking for in, of all places, Krasno Bogatirski?

Grasimov opened his eyes and saw, somewhat to his surprise, that the man was still standing in front of his desk. The man looked at the KGB officer nonchalantly, as if uninterested in the obvious nervousness that was displayed on this man of power.

Grasimov lifted his hand, in a gesture of dismissal. "*Spasibo*," he whispered casually. The man, without answering, spun around and disappeared out the door.

Grasimov stood up and began pacing the floor of his small room, from the window to the door and back again. On one wall the flinty eyes of Leonid Brezhnev, president of the USSR, stared at him, as well as those of Grasimov's superior, Yuri Andropov, the man who could do anything, the true ruler of Russia who placed his fear upon everyone through the KGB. Grasimov always thought of Andropov in terms of that obsolete capitalist word: Boss. For some reason, the concept flew through his brain now. And if he would succeed in uncovering the connection of the American to Krasno Bogatirski Street, would the boss be pleased with him? The thought made him breathe rapidly. Why did it worry him so?

A knock at the door. Grasimov lifted his head in surprise. It was early, before office hours. Who could it be? Grasimov liked to come early in order to speak with his undercover operatives. The mind was clear then. But who could be here at this hour?

"Yes," he said in authoritative tones to the unknown person on the other side of the door.

The door opened. Victor Malenkov, Colonel Malenkov, stood on the threshold, a thin smile on his lips. Suddenly Dimitri remembered his rebellious son, Igor. Where was he, that hoodlum? Malenkov had no doubt come about him.

"Hello."

"Good morning."

"How are you?"

"Thank you, excellent."

A lie: Grasimov never felt excellent when meeting with Malenkov. Malenkov had more than once tried to undermine his position at the

KGB and Grasimov was convinced that his promotion had been blocked time after time because of Malenkov's slanders. And no matter how illegal it was in Soviet law, there were times when Malenkov's big mouth spouted anti-Semitic slurs. It happened after no more than half a bottle of vodka — and it did not have to be fine Smirnoff, either.

So what did Malenkov want from him?

Malenkov did not wait for Grasimov to invite him to sit down. He dropped down into the only unoccupied chair in a corner of the room and looked quietly at Grasimov's thoughtful face.

"So early and you're already in the office?"

Malenkov did not answer, but just gave an all-knowing, mysterious smile, one that announced that he was concealing something. At least that was what it looked like to Dimitri, who would have given more than one month of his measly salary to get this one out of his office.

"And you?" Malenkov finally replied. "So early?"

Grasimov took a deep breath. "Investigation, you know."

A short silence.

"Who was it today?" came the inescapable question.

"Some American. Nothing out of the ordinary."

Victor pulled out a cigarette case from his jacket pocket. He held onto it with both hands, not bothering to take out a cigarette. Grasimov watched his every move.

"Maybe I can help?"

Grasimov felt himself unable to resist. It always happened: Malenkov would offer assistance, and in the end throw a wrench in the wheels. Yet through his own weakness he, Grasimov, would volunteer information to Malenkov, though he wanted to keep it to himself. He was furious with himself over this weakness, but he did not have the strength of character to rebel. This, despite the fact that Victor Malenkov was actually in a lower position than he was. Still, Malenkov exhibited a far stronger personality.

"A young American, claiming to be a diamond merchant, sniffing around Moscow in places where you won't find gems."

"For example?"

Grasimov, against his will, continued to speak.

"He's interested in the synagogue in Archipova —"

Malenkov put the cigarette case down on the desk, with a movement that was far too swift for Grasimov's liking. He interrupted. "He is a Jew?"

"Yes," Grasimov answered sullenly.

Malenkov eased himself back in the chair, until one could hear the wood cracking beneath him. He said nonchalantly, "A Jew? Like you?"

Grasimov's face reddened. "Yes, like me," he hissed. "So what?"

Malenkov felt he had gone too far. He straightened up and said softly, "Nothing, Dimitri, nothing. Just a fact. No offense intended."

He laughed loudly.

"No offense meant this early in the morning. I haven't even had one cup of vodka."

After a short silence he spoke, as if giving an order: "Go on."

Grasimov did not have any desire to continue. Yet continue he did.

"This American, this Jew, is interested in some Moscow street."

"What street is that?"

"Krasno Bogatirski. Do you know where it is?"

"No, I don't," Malenkov admitted. "And what is there, on that street, that so interests the American?"

Grasimov knew full well what, from his point of view, was interesting on the street. But he did not say a word about it.

"I don't know."

"And if so, what are you investigating so much?"

Grasimov decided to be careful with his answer. "I'm not investigating so much. I'm investigating! I want to know. Actually, I have to know. Isn't that so, Colonel Malenkov?"

"Yes, of course," Malenkov hurried to reply. Grasimov caught a trace of mockery in his voice. He bit his lip lightly. And again, the disturbing thought: *What does he want now?*

"What do you plan on doing?" Malenkov asked.

"I don't know right now. That's the reason I got here early."

Grasimov had an interest in displaying to Malenkov his loyalty to his job, to the party, and to the security of the socialism of Mother Russia.

Malenkov asked, "How much time will this man of yours be in Moscow?"

"I think until tonight. Why?"

"Maybe you can shake him up a bit. A short conversation would help even an American citizen."

After a moment he added, "Do you want to give him to me?"

Grasimov reeled, but his face did not show his internal conflict. That was all that he needed, for Malenkov to take charge of the affair. He had no idea of the sensitive nature of Krasno Bogatirski.

"It's not worth it, Victor, just not worth it. I'll make certain he returns to Russia and we'll solve the riddle."

"And maybe your suspicions are groundless?"

Grasimov shrugged. "Maybe? Will this be the first time that suspicions turn out to be wrong?"

Malenkov grinned. "And sometimes the suspicions are found to be groundless even after the suspect has confessed."

"That's true. And is it particularly pleasant?"

Malenkov waved him off. "I never think about things being pleasant or unpleasant. A man is dead? He's dead! Guilt and suspicion have nothing to do with it."

Grasimov felt an aversion to this man and his callousness. *In any case, I'm a Jew*, a strange internal voice declared. He shuddered at the thought, and decided to change the subject.

"You've come here to me. Why?"

Malenkov gave him a searching glance. "The meeting in the forest, you know, the pictures of the participants."

Grasimov did not answer. He knew. Malenkov had gotten hold of the evidence of his son, Igor.

The scent of danger was strong in the air.

From the synagogue Jeff returned to the hotel. The second, decisive meeting with the officials in charge of diamond sales was scheduled for 10 a.m. He still did not know what the results of the meeting would be. The officials were being too obstinate, in his opinion, on the price. He had not managed to convince them that he represented a serious and large concern, even though he understood from things they had said that they were familiar with his company. He was preparing himself for failure in the negotiations; much to his surprise, he realized that he did not care very much. He wanted to leave Moscow as soon as possible and was not prepared to stay there even one more day in order to advance his connections with the Russians. True, their merchandise was particularly clean and beautiful. Still the pressure that he felt in this city, the suspicions and fear of unpleasant encounters with the regime because of his careless conduct in the matter of Krasno Bogatirski, had taken away the desire to stay in this place.

Jeff came down to the lobby at 9:30 exactly. Gregory was already waiting for him, friendlier than he had been before. Jeff did not like it. You never knew if the Soviet citizen was showing the emotions he really felt, or if he was under orders from some sinister party apparatus.

"Ready?" Gregory asked cheerily.

"Yes," came the laconic reply. He would keep his distance from this confusing man. For some reason he felt a strong aversion, not to say hatred, for him.

The officials in the diamonds section of the Ministry greeted him warmly. The debate over the price continued, but in a more relaxed and calm manner. Jeff used all his persuasive powers to try and show them the great possibilities that could open up if they could come to terms. His company represented diamond interests all over the globe. The problem, Jeff realized in the course of his fervent speech, was that sitting across from him were gray officials, functionaries, bureaucrats, and not businessmen who would be making a profit from their deal — and so all his words did not really interest them. They heard him out politely, nodded their heads pleasantly, and when it came down to terms, they stood firm in their refusal.

Jeff looked at the large box in which the merchandise he hoped to buy was placed. Yesterday they had poured out the diamonds onto the table. He had liked what he had seen. His boss had agreed to a first purchase of up to a million dollars — "and after that we'll see," as he'd told him in New York. The amount they were demanding was much higher than that. Occasionally one of them would walk away, it seemed, for consultations. Too bad he could not meet with the unknown person with whom they were speaking. Jeff felt that he was wasting his time.

The telephone suddenly shrilled. The top official picked up the receiver. His face seemed struck by shock. He listened patiently and quietly to whatever was being said on the other end, said a goodbye, and replaced the receiver. After another minute, in which he seemed to be digesting whatever he had heard, he began to speak in rapid Russian to the others sitting at the table. Jeff did not understand a word that was said, except one, that was repeated several times. KGB.

His heart began to pound.

15

Jeff looked at the inscrutable faces of the Ministry of Commerce officials sitting across from him on the other side of the table. He cast a fleeting glance at Gregory, sitting close by, a glance both instinctive and almost against his own will, as one looking for help. Immediately, though, he brought his attention back to the men sitting across from him. Jeff could palpably feel the difference in the air, though he did not know what it was. The face of the head official softened a little and it seemed to Jeff that the shadow of a forced smile played on his lips. The faces of the other functionaries, too, seemed to lose some of their Siberian coldness. During the long moment of silence he turned again to Gregory, who looked surprised.

The head official said something to Gregory in Russian, who translated: "He said that they've decided to finish the business up, and to agree to your terms."

Jeff laughed lightly, though he did not feel calm. This sudden Soviet generosity was inexplicable; suspicious, even.

"Okay, great! Okay!" He reacted with a typical American show of feeling. Then he added, in quieter tones, "What happened, Gregory? Did they tell you why?"

Gregory shrugged. "No. They didn't say anything."

Jeff was quiet. He was well aware of the Russians staring at him, though he feigned indifference.

"Interesting," he said to Gregory's obvious evasion. "I heard the word KGB in that one's conversation," he added, nodding towards the head functionary.

Gregory did not rush to reply. He turned toward the head bureaucrat, Alexander Gamov by name. Gamov's sharp, sly eyes, which Jeff had noticed at their first meeting, absorbed Jeff's question.

"Tell him, your American, that he heard correctly. The KGB recommended to us to finish the deal and not get stuck on petty details like price."

Jeff heard the words without moving a muscle. It seemed that even a mundane business deal in diamonds was connected to the secret political arm of the state, the KGB. How did these people live? But he immediately realized that the KGB intervention this time might be connected to his suspicious interest in certain areas of Moscow life. His interest in Krasno Bogatirski Street, for example.

Jeff took a deep breath. In order to cover his confusion he pulled out a pack of Lucky Strikes. He offered the open pack to the others sitting back in their chairs. With the exception of two, all refused. Jeff put the pack back into his jacket pocket and waited for developments.

They were not long in coming.

"Yes, Mr. Handler," Gregory translated the words of the head official, who was smiling broadly, "we agree to finish up the deal. I understand that you are disturbed by our security awareness. True, we needed KGB authorization for such a deal. We had to first clarify the uprightness of the American firm that you represent."

Jeff did not respond.

Alexander Gamov's voice softened. His crafty eyes flew from side to side.

"Look, Mr. Handler, yesterday we were inflexible in our negotiations, not because we're rigid by nature. We simply wanted to buy time, until we could get the proper authorizations."

He took a deep breath, and spread out his arms. "And now, we've gotten them."

Suddenly he laughed. "The KGB, Mr. Handler, is not as terrifying as people say. Here, you see, it has given you and your company business and the prices you've asked."

Jeff smiled and thanked them. *"Bolshoye spasibo."*

Yet in his heart he did not believe a word of what the man had said. He remembered his boss in New York (*When was that? It seemed years ago. And yet the conversation had taken place just four days earlier!*) telling him that the Russians had carefully checked their firm and its reputation, and made certain its employees were not secret agents of the CIA. If so, what was the meaning of this heartfelt explanation that this official was giving him — and what would happen now?

The authorizations were swiftly written out. The initial investment was substantially lower than the Russians had demanded. Jeff signed on the documents despite his suspicion of this sudden surrender. He gave the diamonds one last check. The glittering gems, those of half a carat, simply took his breath away with their beauty and clean look. The Russians certainly did good work. After he had satisfied himself looking at his newly purchased merchandise, the officials collected the stones and placed them into the large box, inscribed with both Jeff's name and the name of his firm. To his surprise Jeff noticed that one of the officials stood up and took the box with him as he left the room.

Jeff did not understand. "Where is he going? Those are the diamonds that I've bought!"

"Don't worry, Mr. Handler. They're yours. We're just putting them back in the safe."

Jeff moved uncomfortably in his chair. "I'm not getting them now?"

For that was the tradition in the world of diamond trading: After a handshake at the end of the negotiations, and the declaration of the words '*mazel* and *berachah*," the purchaser immediately takes possession of the diamonds, transferring payment within a few days to the account of the seller. And now the Russians were trying to cheat him.

"Mr. Handler, we don't give the merchandise until we've gotten paid."

Jeff felt the blood rush to his head; his anger dispelled any fears.

"What are you talking about? Don't you believe me? You've checked out my company. Surely you've found out how honest we are in our dealings. All diamond deals are based on mutual trust. If there's no trust, there's no deal!"

Jeff was honestly angry. He had never gone through two such difficult days of negotiations in his entire career. He did not understand this approach; no one had warned him of it at home, in New York.

The Russian tried to pacify him. "Mr. Handler, it's not a question of trust. It's a question of custom. It's possible that failures in the past with unfair merchants have brought this about. Truthfully, we don't really know why."

He waved the document that was lying before him.

"The contract has been signed to everyone's satisfaction. Go back to New York, transfer the money through the usual channels, and we will send the merchandise to you."

Jeff was now dealing with a situation he had never faced before. He hesitated for a moment, wondering if he should accept the proposal despite the risk of being entrapped. In the passing of a moment he decided to gamble.

"Okay," he muttered.

Everyone stood up, shook hands courteously, and said their goodbyes. A cloud of suspicion, though, continued to weigh heavily on Jeff's heart.

That night Gregory escorted him to the airport. They did not speak very much en route, although the atmosphere was cordial. As soon as Jeff had passed through passport control, Gregory disappeared. And then, as he stood by customs, Jeff heard a steely voice call out his name in heavily accented English.

"Mr. Handler, we'd like to ask you a few questions."

Anatoly Dobrovitz slowly descended the wide steps of the synagogue. He had no particular destination. The determined and inexplicable refusal of the bearded man in the synagogue to study with him left him even more confused. Anatoly could not understand why he had behaved in such a manner to him. First Anatoly decided to go down the street, then he changed his mind and decided to go in the opposite direction, to crowded Slanka Street. He would make his way to the banks of the Moscow River. Perhaps the slowly flowing waters would calm him down a little.

Suddenly he turned around. He had the strangest feeling that he was being followed. Yes, about 50 yards behind him a man walked alone on the quiet, narrow street. Anatoly continued walking. The man did not seem particularly threatening, even if, for a moment, he had thought he had seen him somewhere before. The man was tall and thin; his face was sharp edged, and his small mustache emphasized the point of his nose. Anatoly decided to get away from him.

When he reached the corner he felt a soft arm fall on his shoulder. Anatoly pivoted around, frightened. The tall, thin man gave him an affectionate grin. Now Anatoly remembered: He had seen him in the synagogue, standing immobile next to the door of the sanctuary. What did he want from him?

The man whispered one word.

"Cometee."

That was it. Anatoly realized at that moment that he was in for it. It figured that his mother, loyal Communist that she was, would inform on him. Anatoly gritted his teeth. A terrible rage raced through him, like the flow of a mighty river.

"Hello."

Anatoly answered with all the calm that he could muster from within. "Good morning."

"How are you?"

"Thank you, fine."

The thin, tall man grimaced; Anatoly did not understand the gesture. He did not take his eyes off the man who had called himself a KGB agent.

"What is your name?" Anatoly heard the question being asked, and felt a surge of impatience. The passers-by walked near them, not sparing them a glance. In Moscow one only looked ahead.

"My name," he said, after a long wait, "is Anatoly."

"Family name?"

"Dobrovitz. Anatoly Dobrovitz."

"What are you doing here?"

Anatoly shrugged his shoulders. "Nothing."

The tall man's face grew serious. "Nothing?"

"That's right. Just walking."

"Hmmm. Interesting. A Soviet citizen simply walking in the middle of the week, at the beginning of the day. You don't look like a parasite."

"That's right. I'm not a parasite."

"Do you work? Where? Are you a student, maybe?"

"I want to study."

"And why aren't you studying?"

The tall man strolled over to the corner and leaned on the wall. Anatoly realized full well that he was trying his best to be pleasant.

"Because I wasn't accepted to the university."

The tall man bent over a little. His eyes showed surprise.

"Why? Are you lazy?"

In the first moment Anatoly longed to tell him the bitter truth, how he had failed because he was a Jew. But he did not know how he would react, this agent of the regime. KGB agents had never been great lovers of the Jewish people. Anatoly did not know if confiding in him would help him or bring him to harm. Finally, he answered, "It happened."

The tall man did not reply. His eyes stared at Anatoly as one trying to learn from the expression of his eyes what was happening in his heart. Anatoly looked from side to side, waiting for this encounter to end. He still did not understand what the man wanted from him.

And then came the direct question.

"What were you looking for in the synagogue?"

Anatoly's heart skipped a beat. "Just walking around. Another place to walk through."

The tall man gave a frosty smile and said, "Instead of the university?"

Anatoly played the innocent. "What do you mean, instead of the university? I am familiar with the buildings of the university; I've walked there a lot."

The tall man straightened; it seemed to Anatoly that he added a few inches to his height. He laughed, and his mustache seemed to do a Russian dance.

"Anatoly, you understand full well what I've asked you. Instead of learning in the university, you've decided to learn in the synagogue?"

"No. Why do you think so?"

The man again put his arm softly on Anatoly's shoulder.

"We heard you, young man. We heard you ask the bearded man sitting near the table in the synagogue. We heard you ask him to teach you from his ancient books."

Anatoly did not answer. He had, indeed, behaved carelessly. He had been so involved in his anger that he had not realized that the KGB agents knew what was going on inside.

The agent continued. "Don't you know that learning religion is against Soviet law?"

Anatoly kept quiet. Now he understood the behavior of the bearded man, who had so brutally rejected him. Anatoly knew that by law one could study religion, but not teach it. How had he been so stupid, with his open and direct request?

"Can I see your identity card?"

Anatoly unwillingly pulled it out of a pocket in his leather jacket.

The man stared at the card, making certain the face standing before him was the same as the one on the photo. He skimmed over the ID card, and finally returned it.

"My young friend," the KGB agent said, "let me give you some advice. Don't go near that building. You're a Soviet citizen, no? Try harder in your studies. Be a good citizen. What a shame for you to get into trouble. I think you've understood my message well. I am keeping you in mind. Do you understand what I'm saying? As a Moscow resident, I hope that you do."

Anatoly did, indeed, understand his message. He did not answer, simply nodded his head in assent.

Suddenly the agent threw out one more question.

"I didn't notice where you live."

"Me? I live on Krasno Bogatirski Street."

16

Jeff stopped short, alarmed. But he did not turn around towards the speaker. He was too upset. Just minutes before he was certain that Moscow, with its atmosphere of tension and insecurity sitting heavily upon it like a thundercloud, was behind him. In only a short while he would be on the plane taking him home, to freedom, and in his hands a successful deal. Instead — he was trapped. Was the swiftness with which they agreed to close the deal nothing more than a net they were spreading around him in order to take him in for investigation at the very last minute? And all because of his interest in a certain street in Moscow?

Jeff took control of his thoughts and whirled around. Before him stood a meticulously dressed, middle-aged Russian man. The suit he wore was much more elegant than those usually seen in Moscow. One would almost say that he had bought it in a store in the free world. (Perhaps he had?) His face was wide and beefy, with a strong Slavic cast. The pleasant expression on his face could not conceal coarse character, a crudeness and harshness that was particularly noticeable in his eyes.

The man put out his hand; Jeff shook it weakly, hesitantly.

"Excuse me, Mr. Handler, I am the Intourist representative here in the airport."

Jeff felt a little calmer, though his tension did not dissipate completely.

"Pleased to meet you."

The man laughed lightly. "I wanted to know, Mr. Handler, if you've enjoyed your two days in Moscow."

Jeff wished he could eat him alive. *That's what you stopped me for? To ask me such a stupid question, you had to scare me like this?* But he did not give a sign of his anger. He was well aware of the man's sharp glance, that pierced through him like a newly whetted knife. What did he mean with that question?

"I enjoyed it very much, Comrade?"

"Podgorov, Yuri Podgorov."

"I enjoyed it very much, Mr. Podgorov."

Podgorov bent his head in appreciation.

"I am happy to hear it. What impressed you particularly?"

Jeff put his briefcase down on the ground. For some reason he suspected this conversation would take longer than he had expected.

"Oh, what do you mean, impressed me? A new world has opened before me! A civilization that is completely different from the one in which I live. It's fascinating."

The Russian's eyes expressed surprise and astonishment, but Jeff could not tell if it was sincere or not.

"A better civilization than yours?" the man asked quickly.

Jeff took a deep breath. Was this the trap? "Two days is too short a time to make a decision like that," he replied. "It's different. That's all."

During the course of the conversation the Intourist (KGB?) representative was holding his hand. It seemed to Jeff that he was checking to see if it trembled or if he was sweating. Impatiently he waited for this nerve-wracking and meaningless conversation to come to an end so that he could go on his way to the exit gate and board the plane.

The Russian thought for a moment. Finally, he said, "Oh, I understand. I'm glad to hear it. Intourist wishes you a good flight, sir."

"*Spasibo,*" Jeff replied, in a show of goodwill to the Russian representative.

The two separated with a rather forced friendliness. When Jeff finally turned to go on his way, breathing a deep sigh of relief, he heard the Russian call: "Excuse me, Mr. Handler, one more question."

Jeff gritted his teeth and answered, "Yes?"

"Excuse me, Mr. Handler, do you plan on visiting Moscow again?"

Jeff was surprised. What did the question mean? But he was not interested in looking for answers anymore. He quickly responded, "What a question, sir. I told you that my quick visit to the city was fascinating. In two days one cannot get to really know it. Besides," Jeff winked, like one sharing a secret, "the business was good too. Certainly, sir, I will return to visit again."

The flood of words was received by the Russian with a stony face, without a smile. After a short silence the Russian said, "Thank you, sir, I'm already welcoming you for your next visit."

Somehow Jeff felt a hidden threat in the words. He could not decide if his exaggerated fears were somehow raising imaginary suspicions, or if this Soviet citizen was truly hinting at something Jeff could not quite understand. In any case he did not spend long worrying about it. He hurried to exit gate 12. From a distance he could see the line of passengers winding around the counter where the clerks were checking tickets. At the moment that he joined the silent group in its slow progress he vowed that his feet would never again tread the streets of Moscow. The past two days had been more than enough adventure for him. Somewhere in his unconscious mind, though, he saw the image of his grandfather crying somewhere in Ramat Gan. He would be terribly disappointed by Jeff's declaration. Jeff would do everything in his power to persuade him that there was no chance of finding the *tefillin*. Two days in Moscow were enough to convince him that the mission that had been placed upon him was absolutely impossible.

Once in the airplane he leaned back comfortably in his chair. He was fast asleep even before takeoff.

The bearded man sitting and learning at the table in the synagogue raised his head. He had followed Dobrovitz's exit from the synagogue with his eyes and had noticed the man who had walked out behind him. In front of the scholar lay a pad on which he would jot down notes connected to his learning. He bent over it now, swiftly turned page after page until he reached a blank sheet, and hurriedly scribbled a few words. Then he ripped it out slowly, casually, trying not to call attention to himself. Finally he put the note onto the page of Gemara that he had been learning in a way that the top of the sheet stuck out a little. He unhurriedly closed the Gemara, leaving it on the table. He stood up and walked toward the *aron kodesh* in order to kiss the *paroches* before leaving the building — an action he did very infrequently.

Not far from the scholar's customary place sat a man in his 50's. His face was lined with marks of suffering. He sat wrapped in a tattered coat and faded cap, one that almost covered his eyes. He sat here often, gazing at the few congregants in the synagogue. From his place he could see the people behind him and the exit doors of the synagogue. He, too, had clearly seen Anatoly's exit. Behind his indifferent gaze he had etched onto his memory the figure of the young man whose name he did not know. Perhaps one day in the future he would have to meet this young man.

He saw the bearded man stand up and walk towards the *aron*. He, too, got up, standing across from the scholar. The scholar bumped into him, as if he had not noticed him until now. He grabbed the older man by both arms and said loudly, so that those men standing by the door could hear, "Excuse me."

"It's okay."

The man in the shabby cap took the hint. He turned towards the table and began returning the books lying on it to their place on the shelf. He took the Gemara in which the bearded man — who by now had left — had learned, and he swiftly pulled out the note hidden within, returned the Gemara to the shelf, and walked out. In the bathroom he read the note and destroyed it. Then he pulled out a small pad from his pocket and scribbled a few hasty words. He pulled the page out of the pad, folded it several times, and jammed it into his pocket. With quick steps he walked out to the street, his eyes scanning the horizon for a sign of Anatoly.

He saw him farther up on Archipova Street, just as the KGB agent had finished talking with him. The man walked behind him, keeping him in his view. Anatoly walked down the steps to the closest train station, Ploshad Nagina. The older man followed him, keeping a cautious distance between them. Anatoly stood, lost in thought, on the platform, looking blankly at the railroad tracks that disappeared into the darkness of the tunnel. Slowly the stream of travelers grew, as more and more people awaited the train, due any minute now.

When it finally pulled in, it slowly came to a stop, and the doors swung open. A stream of humanity disgorged itself onto the platform; another stream of Muscovites just as swiftly flowed into the newly emptied railroad cars. Anatoly boarded. The other man entered through another door. But even before the train had begun to move toward the next station he had made his way towards Anatoly. After a short moment he stood not far from him. When the train had reached the Ploshad Comsomiliskaya he bumped into him and thrust the prepared note into his hand. Anatoly, shocked, felt fear grip him. He quickly turned the other way, but before he could catch a glimpse of the man who had bumped into him the man had disappeared through the open door into the flow of humanity streaming towards the Metro exit.

Anatoly took a seat. He could feel his tension rising. He held the note in his hand, a piece of coal burning his palm. He dared not move his clenched fist through the entire journey. He felt paralyzed by fear of unknown eyes staring at him, wondering if he would read whatever it was that the mysterious stranger had left in his hand.

He thought about getting off at the train's next stop, of trying to find a quiet place far from anyone's eyes in order to solve the terrible mystery now clutched in trembling hands. But finally he got off at the Krasno Varuto station. He walked upstairs, bought the first newspaper that he saw, and looked for an empty bench in one of the small gardens. After he had spread the newspaper open before him he cautiously unfolded the note.

"Tonight," it said, "at 7:00, at the Ploshad Revoluzai Metro station. Hold the book *The Three Musketeers* by Alexandre Dumas in your hand. Follow the man who will be holding Tolstoy's *Anna Karenina*, with the newspaper *Izvestia* under his arm."

Anatoly read the note a second time. He could almost hear himself whisper soundlessly: "Ploshad Revoluzai. Seven o'clock. *Three Musketeers*. Alexandre Dumas. *Anna Karenina*. Tolstoy. *Izvestia*."

He slowly ripped the note, pretending all the while that he was reading the newspaper spread over his knees. He did not dare raise his eyes to see if anyone was watching him. He tore the note into tiny pieces and stashed them in his pants pocket. When he stood up, he decided, he would spread the pieces among the various garbage cans in the vicinity — and not all together in one garbage can, either. His fear painted a picture of some unknown man collecting the little pieces and slowly pasting them together.

Anatoly stood up and began walking about aimlessly. What should he do now? Should he ignore the note or follow its instructions? Was this a trap or the opening to new hope? What should he do?

Anatoly stopped near a garbage can. He pulled out a few pieces of paper from his pocket and thrust them inside the half-empty bin. He continued his slow progress on the paths of the park. Old men absorbed in reading *Pravda*, Moscow's daily newspaper, ignored the young man walking tranquilly on this cold, wet day. He halted for a minute: Maybe these oldsters were not as indifferent as they seemed? The opposite, perhaps — were they spies?

All at once his steps quickened. A sudden, daring impulse called upon him to take the challenge. He would go to the rendezvous, whatever the consequences. He repeated the details in a hoarse whisper. "Ploshad Revoluzai. Seven o'clock. *The Three Musketeers*. Alexandre Dumas. *Anna Karenina*. Tolstoy. *Izvestia*."

17

The next day, towards morning, Jeff saw from his airplane window the New York skyline soaring proudly skyward. He felt joy like that of a released prisoner returning home. His wife, Miriam, awaited him in the airport, as excited as though she had not seen her husband for years.

On the way home she reviewed the events of the three days that had passed since his departure.

"You don't know what it was like! In Tzipporah Chavah's class they said *Tehillim* for your safety. There was so much worry, so much fear; everyone was concerned about you."

Miriam lapsed into silence, as if completely immersed in the driving. Her eyes were riveted onto the road disappearing beneath the car's racing wheels. Suddenly she added, not looking at her husband: "I said *Tehillim* too."

"Thanks."

Jeff could hear the slight tremble in her voice as she continued. "What do you mean, thanks? Believe me, I was furious with myself for having let you go. I don't know — I was horribly afraid."

Until then Jeff had not reacted. Now, though, he saw the need to calm her down.

"*Nu*, really, from far it seems worse than reality. It's true: I actually went to pray in the *shul* and met some others *davening*. I spoke with some people. It wasn't so bad."

Jeff knew he was not telling the truth. But to keep the peace, to keep her calm, he would beautify the Soviet reality a bit.

When they were already close to Brooklyn she asked, "Was the deal a success?"

Jeff was intentionally enthusiastic. "Thank G-d, more than we expected!"

He would not mention the KGB interference, he decided, and how they pressured the Commerce Ministry officials to finalize the deal. Even now, remembering the facts sent a tiny worm of fear snaking through his heart.

"And the other thing?" Jeff heard her hesitant question.

"You mean the *tefillin?*"

"That's right, your grandfather's *tefillin.*"

"Nothing."

"Which means —"

"Which means, quite simply, that the idea was always completely unrealistic; I wouldn't quite call it stupid —"

Jeff stopped for a moment, reflecting, then continued. "Yes, it was stupid. I understand Grandfather, and his deep connection with his *tefillin,* but it's not realistic."

"Did you at least try?"

Jeff passed a weary hand over his forehead. The fatigue that had beset him after two days of tension was beginning to show. He closed his eyes for a second in an involuntary movement. But even in the tiredness that was engulfing him he hurried to answer, his eyes still closed.

"Did I try? Of course I did! But it's impossible. I saw how they were all suspicious when I just asked an innocent question about Krasno Bogatirski Street. I admit that the affair gave me some pretty scary moments."

He did not continue. He did not want to frighten his wife, nor did he himself really want to remember those stressful moments when he had asked his questions in Moscow.

But his wife would not let up. "The KGB?"

The car pulled up in front of their Flatbush home. It was a wonderful feeling, and a good way of avoiding his wife's direct question. Jeff hurried to the trunk of his car, and with a swift gesture pulled his luggage out and made his way toward the house. It had been a long time since he kissed the *mezuzah* with such fervor.

As they were drinking their steaming cups of coffee in the kitchen, Miriam repeated the question that was bothering her.

"Did you have anything to do with the KGB?"

"No. Why do you think so?"

She raised an eyebrow at him. "Didn't you say you had some scary moments?"

Jeff waved her off. "You didn't understand. I meant that I was afraid because the atmosphere there is very oppressive. Maybe because of all we've heard over here about the Russians."

Miriam could tell that Jeff did not want to pursue the subject. She decided to hold her questions for a more convenient time.

"Do you want to sleep a little or have breakfast?"

"To *daven* and then sleep," he answered.

As he stood up, she thought of still another question. "And what will you tell Grandfather?"

Jeff turned toward his wife.

"The exact words I'll use, I still don't know. But naturally I'll explain that the entire business is crazy."

"Be careful not to hurt his feelings."

"Of course."

Jeff was already standing at the bottom of the steps that led towards the bedrooms on the second floor.

"Jeff?"

He held onto the banister; his extreme fatigue was beginning to affect his balance.

"What?" he asked wearily, with growing impatience.

"This is your last trip to Russia, I hope?"

Jeff grinned tiredly. "Yes, this was my last trip to Russia. The first and the last."

He began to climb the steps. As he stood next to his bedroom door he murmured to himself, "But what do I know? *Bli neder,* this was the last trip."

At 10 to 7 Anatoly Dobrovitz was already standing at the steps that led to the Ploshad Revoluzai station. In his hands he ostentatiously grasped a copy of Alexandre Dumas's *The Three Musketeers.* Hordes of men and women streamed around him, people cold and frigid, in the Moscow manner. It had been years, if ever, that Anatoly had stood and watched the passers-by. Always, until now, he had been part of the flow streaming in from the suburbs to the city center, from the city center to the suburbs.

Now he stood in the station, watching and thinking. In his own eyes he seemed like some tiny island standing in the center of a river, the water flowing endlessly around it. This river of humanity, indeed, did flow, while he stood upright. An interesting thought flitted through his brain: Was this a reflection of his new personal situation in the Soviet community, now that he had placed himself standing firmly against it? In truth, this meeting that might take place in a few minutes, was it not more evidence that he had become a desert isle, unchanged by the waves and eddies of the river of Soviet humanity that ebbed and flowed around him?

Remembering the upcoming meeting his eyes followed that man, this woman, looking for the one who would be holding *Anna Karenina* and the latest issue of *Izvestia.*

Anatoly tried his best not to draw attention to himself, not to arouse suspicion. He did all he could to maintain a calm facade. He hoped that none of the people passing by — you could not be sure of any of them — would notice the tension that had him in its grip.

Then he saw him. Not far away, walked a tall thin young man wrapped in a long coat. His hands were jammed into his pockets; under his arm he clutched a copy of *Izvestia.* On top of the newspaper one could clearly see the book *Anna Karenina.* Anatoly's heart beat wildly. He straightened *The Three Musketeers* in his hands so that the man would see it. At the same time, he tried not to stare at the approaching stranger, but without much success. The man was already near him. Anatoly stood, paralyzed; he had no idea what he should do. Actually, this was the first time in his life that he was taking part in underground activities. With all the paralyzing fear he still felt a tiny surge of joy, of revenge against his mother, the Russians, the university, the professors who threw him into the streets.

The man came closer. Anatoly fixed his eyes upon him, but the other man avoided his gaze until he was right next to him. Then his eyes beckoned Anatoly to follow him. The stranger even bumped lightly into him, as if by accident, and then went on his way, down into the depths of the station.

Anatoly longed to follow directly behind him, but a healthy sense of caution whispered to him to wait a bit. One could never know if someone was looking at him or not. Anatoly glanced at his watch, as if to check the time, waited another minute, lifted his head and looked around like one searching for someone. Then he made an obvious movement of surrender, as if there was no reason to wait any longer. If someone was watching him, Anatoly hoped, he would see these movements and understand that he was an honest citizen.

Anatoly then descended into the Metro station, his eyes searching for the tall young man holding on to *Izvestia.* He found him easily and walked toward him with measured steps.

"He's gone down into the station," the spy assigned by the KGB to Anatoly Dobrovitz whispered into his miniature transmitter. *"Go after him,"* the official whispered back.

The tall thin young man entered one of the trains, Anatoly following behind him. Moments before the doors closed, the man jumped back out onto the platform. With a speed that he had not known he possessed Anatoly managed to follow just one second before the doors shut and the train moved away. The thin man could immediately make out the infuriated and sour face of the agent who was following them, but the KGB operative could not manage to get out of the moving car.

The two, Anatoly and the thin man, did not exchange a single word. They stood quietly among the milling crowds waiting for the next train. It arrived, and they entered. Casually, they sat down next to each other. The thin young man opened his copy of *Izvestia* and began to read attentively. Anatoly opened *The Three Musketeers* and pretended to read, though his eyes did not take in a single word. They were not doing anything unusual: All around them the other passengers did the same, silently immersing themselves in their reading. Muscovites would never make casual conversation with someone whom they did not know well.

Anatoly suddenly heard his neighbor whisper. "Do you really want to learn Torah?"

The man did not lift his eyes from the newspaper. It looked as if he were sounding out the words of the article he was reading.

"*Da*," Anatoly answered. "Yes."

"Why?"

"I want to know more about my people."

"Is your mother Jewish?"

Anatoly did not understand the question, but he answered quickly, "Yes."

"And your father?"

"Also."

"What does he do?"

"He was killed. He was an officer in the Red Army. He was killed in Afghanistan."

"And your mother?"

"A supervisor in the Education Ministry. A sworn Communist."

The stranger lifted his eyes for a moment; he stared at the window across from him. At the same time he inspected the faces of all those who stood around them with a hasty, cautious look, to see if anyone was listening to their conversation. Then his eyes returned to the newspaper.

"You understand that your life will be in danger from now on?"

Anatoly did not rush with an answer. He had not thought of this particular point until now. Finally, he said, "Yes. I know."

The other continued. "Investigations. Perhaps jail."

"I know."

"Why do you want to learn?"

"Because I am a Jew."

"And until now you weren't?"

"It's only now that I feel like one."

"Why?"

"They wouldn't accept me in the university because I am a Jew."

The whispers ceased for a moment. The thin man again scrutinized his fellow passengers. The frozen faces all around them showed no interest whatsoever. Good. Anatoly strained to hear the next words.

"In 'Bubba's' apartment. Tonight at 8 o'clock. A lecture. Get off at the Viyokovskya Station. Go up to the street and they'll wait for you there. Hold *The Three Musketeers* in your hand. I'm getting off at the next stop; you continue traveling."

The thin tall young man left at the next station. Anatoly continued looking into Dumas's *The Three Musketeers*. But he did not read a single word.

18

rasimov shifted uncomfortably in his chair. He tried to fathom where Malenkov was headed. He knew with painful clarity that Malenkov would see to it that the story of Igor would be spread throughout the ranks of the KGB. It was to be expected that he, Dimitri Grasimov, would be called upon to supply clarifications to someone. Even if he got out of the investigation safely, it would certainly be most unpleasant, and it would obviously not endear him, not to his own superiors nor to those beneath him. Grasimov could see past the expression of the man sitting across from him. It was the serious, thoughtful expression of one whose goal was to understand what lay behind a man's every movement and gesture. And, at the same time, it was the expression of a cat's wicked enjoyment as it slowly plays with the mouse trapped between his front paws.

Malenkov rubbed his hands on his knees and stood upright. Grasimov watched him with veiled concern. From his perspective, Malenkov had gotten everything he wanted. Grasimov, in his confusion, had not denied the story of Igor, who had been wandering through the streets of Moscow with enemies of the regime. Malenkov came to a clear conclusion. He knew that if the tale was a lie, Grasimov would have been furious, would have cursed and raised a complete ruckus. But the fact was, he had remained silent. He must know of his son's swerving from the path of Communist ideology. And that meant that he himself was covering up for him! Grasimov, a KGB agent! The fact was, he had not reported his son to his superiors in the Cometee, had not warned his son or followed him, had not reported him to the investigators who would have interrogated him, as he should have, both as a KGB member and a loyal Soviet citizen. Now the great question was how loyal was he, Dimitri Grasimov himself, to the institution he served. Malenkov patted himself on the back: Here, he had managed to bring down the dirty Jew a little, the Jew who acted as if he was the faithful servant to the regime and the KGB.

Malenkov held out his hand to Grasimov. His handshake was strong, but the hand that met his, Grasimov's, was weak and shaky.

"My friend," Malenkov said in a soft voice, "I've got to go now. We'll talk again of this."

Standing by the door he turned around and asked, "Where is your son now? In the house?"

Grasimov's expression was blank as he answered, "I don't know. He's run away, after I told him I was going to send him to a re-education camp."

Malenkov looked surprised. "Good. I see you were heading in the right direction."

Grasimov's fury finally erupted. "What did you think?" he screamed in a sudden outburst. "You thought that I would let him go free with his counter-revolutionary ideas, those ideas that you and your friends haven't managed to suppress? Did you think I wouldn't do my job even if we were talking about my son, my only child?"

Malenkov gave him an amused glance, but did not answer. There was a thin, frigid smile pasted onto his lips. Wordlessly, he left the room.

Igor wandered through the streets of the city for several hours. Thoughts of escape surfaced in his mind, of flight to the Ukraine or even Vladivostok, at the other end of the huge country, or to any place where he could avoid the long arm of his rock-hard father. His father, he knew, was not the sort of man with whom he could come to a compromise, to a cease fire that would allow them to live together despite their differences. His father, like all his comrades in the KGB, was not prepared to accept a new reality, the new winds that were blowing throughout the nation. These new and revolutionary ideas could not be destroyed by the power of fear, of investigations and torture, that Igor's father and his KGB cohorts had used for so long. Still, perhaps if he would disappear for a short while he would be able to find — once the storm had quieted down — a path of co-existence. There was always the hope that his mother, who was on his side, would manage to change his father's mind.

But he did not flee. At least, not now.

Instead he went to Kazi Minki, one of the Moscow suburbs. There, he ascended to the fifth floor of a tall building. The long corridor was unlit. The one light bulb used for that purpose had long since been stolen by one of the residents for his own use. Igor walked carefully and slowly, staring at the many locked doors. There was no sound from behind any of them. He strained his memory until he had found what he was looking for. He walked to the third doorway and knocked lightly. No one answered. Several older people passed by in the hallway, giving him piercing and curious glances. Igor tried his best to look nonchalant and waited for them to vanish behind the doors of their own small apartments. Afterwards he knocked once again, this time a little harder.

The door opened. A bony-faced woman, whose thin brown hair was sternly pulled back, attacked him with a suspicious, frightened glance.

"What do you want?"

"Is Yuri home?"

The woman spat out a decisive, "No," and quickly tried to slam the door. Igor, faster than she, placed his foot between the door and the threshold.

"Get away from here!" The woman raised her voice and gave the command in a shrill tone.

"When will Yuri be back?" Igor asked quietly. "I want to know."

The woman looked back at him with terrified eyes. "And I don't want to tell you."

"You will tell me. He's my friend, and he's in great danger. I have to speak with him."

The woman was motionless for a moment, staring at him with eyes which still spoke of her initial fears.

"What kind of danger?"

"Danger. Great danger. I have to speak with him."

The woman was not sure she understood him.

"Danger?" She repeated the terrifying word. "Danger, to Yuri? Yuri will be back in an hour."

Suddenly she awoke, as if from a dream. She opened the door and forcibly pushed Igor out. Panting, she blurted out a few words. "Go! Go away! You, I know what you are. I know who you are, you, yes, you infiltrator. The KGB sent you. Go, get away from here!"

She slammed the door with such violence that the narrow hallway seemed to shake. A few doors opened, a few anxious heads peeked out, only to disappear again hastily.

Igor stood, embarrassed, in the dark and silent corridor. Only one small beam of light came in through a small window at the end of the hallway, a beam of light that would allow him to find his way out of the building. There, in the building's courtyard, he would wait for Yuri Primakov, until he arrived.

Anatoly Dobrovitz was excited. His underground meeting with the man in the train filled him with pride. The feeling that he somehow belonged to a rebellion strengthened from moment to moment. On his way home it seemed to him that everyone passing him could see the change in him. He tried walking to one side; unfortunately, it was this very fact that caused several passers-by to give him surreptitious glances. The looks startled him, igniting within him a concealed and dim flash of fear. In Moscow people usually walked without looking at one another, and certainly without making eye contact.

Anatoly rushed to his mother's apartment. He did not greet her, just hurried to his room. Only a few minutes had passed when his mother knocked on his door. At first he hesitated, wondering if he should open it or not. But when the knocks continued he stood up from the bed where he sat when he returned.

She stood before him, her eyes questioning. He understood those eyes, but decided not to answer until she actually asked him the question that was lying so heavily upon her. For a long moment they stood silently, opposite one another. Anatoly could not help but grin slightly at his mother's discomfiture.

Finally, she asked it. "Were you there?"

"Where?"

Her growing impatience was reflected in her voice, growing slowly louder. "You know!"

Anatoly continued on his way. "No. No, I don't know. I was in many places. You wouldn't like some of them."

He saw how his mother's eyes narrowed and how she bit her lower lip.

"I am interested," she finally muttered, "I am interested in knowing if you went to the synagogue in Archipova, to the quacks and charlatans who hang out there."

Anatoly took a deep breath. Now that he was making contact with those in the underground who were searching for their Jewish heritage, he did not want to arouse his mother's suspicions too much to his secret actions that were to come. Now it was his job to calm her down and lull her overwrought senses.

"No. I didn't go to the synagogue."

Though she tried to conceal her feelings Anatoly could feel his mother's relief. *That's good,* he thought. *Let her believe that despite my anger against the regime, I am still following the socialist, Communist path through my deep faith.*

Then he heard the surprising question. "Why not? Why didn't you go there? You said you would."

Anatoly gave her a searching glance. He tried to understand where she was leading this conversation.

"I didn't go there, because it really has nothing to do with me. I don't know if I am a Communist like you. But Archipova — that's not for me!"

His mother gave a satisfied smile. Her obvious feeling of victory suddenly enraged him. He would not give her this small satisfaction. What particularly infuriated him was that she was ignoring the problem of what had happened to him in the university, ignoring the humiliation that her son had undergone only so that she could go on believing in the equality of Soviet citizenry.

"That's right," Anatoly began to speak hurriedly. "That's right, I don't belong there. The komosol education did at least one thing for me. But why do you call them quacks and charlatans?"

"Because they are," came the firm answer.

"You don't know them at all, these Jews, and yet you are so certain?"

"That's the way it is." Her words had the ring of finality.

"How are they greater quacks and charlatans than the professors who wouldn't let me into the university with all sorts of formal excuses, when they told me afterwards that the only reason for my failure was the fact that I am a Jew?"

His mother gave him a cold look. "It's not the same."

"Why isn't it?"

"Our Soviet society will one day reach perfect equality. Those there in Archipova are living in the past. We, in contrast, are living in the future."

"Yes, yes, I've heard the speeches. Future! Future! Future! In the meantime we're sacrificing already for generations, living all our lives in suffering. Tell me, how have relations with the Jews changed since the Revolution? How? Tell me, how?"

He approached his mother with a threatening movement. Of course, he did not intend to hurt her, but still she backed away. At that moment she had no desire to enter into an argument with her son. Enough that he had felt an instinctive repugnance and had not entered the synagogue. Anatoly, for his part, explained her silence as a result of the fact that she knew that he was right. But as a loyal citizen she could not admit the truth. *And she talks about hypocrisy,* Anatoly thought.

Night fell upon Moscow. Dim lights twinkled from apartment windows, from cheerless and unattractive housing in the suburbs. Anatoly dressed quickly, wrapped himself in his father's military fur coat, a poignant reminder of the man who had fallen in battle. He put a fur hat on his head, warm gloves on his hands, and turned to the door.

"Where are you going?"

"To friends."

"Now? At this hour?"

Anatoly leaned nonchalantly on the threshold of the open door. He stood to one side, like a leaning tower of Pisa, and stared at his mother from the corners of his eyes.

"Is this the first time that I'm going out at night? What's the matter with you?"

His mother was silent. She herself felt she had gone too far. A deeply felt fear whispered to her that this was different, this was not like the other times he had gone out at night, those other times he had hung around with his friends and returned in the early hours of the morning. But it was clear to her that she could not articulate these fears openly.

Anatoly waited a long moment for some kind of reaction. When it was not forthcoming he jumped over the threshold, said a quick "Good night," and disappeared behind the door that he locked with overdone politeness. His mother listened silently to the sound of his footsteps going down the stairs to the street.

eff awoke the next day and traveled to his office in Manhattan.

"Hi," the receptionist greeted him warmly.

"Hi," he answered, a little embarrassed, but with a wide smile.

"How was it?"

"Okay," he answered evasively, as he hastened towards his boss's office.

His boss stood up to greet him with a smiling face.

"Hi. Are you all right, Jeff?" David Northfeld asked graciously.

"When I came back from Caracas you didn't ask about my welfare," Jeff answered, seeking to provoke him. "It seems that you thought something would happen to me in Russia. And yet you sent me anyway!"

Northfeld seemed embarrassed. Jeff broke out into laughter, trying to dissipate the uncomfortable atmosphere that his failed joke had evoked.

Northfeld laughed with him, though the laughter was a bit forced. Jeff, regretting his words, inwardly raged at himself for his habit of speaking without thought.

Northfeld returned to his armchair and waited for Jeff to speak. The two stared at each other for a long moment. Jeff was searching for the words to begin his description of his unpleasant adventure in a way that would make it clear to Northfeld that this was his last trip.

"Let me make it clear: it was not a pleasant trip."

"I understand."

"To be perfectly honest, it was frightening, suffocating, and it didn't leave me with a very good feeling."

Northfeld narrowed his eyes a little. Where was his emissary to Russia headed with this conversation?

"The main thing is what you've achieved, my young friend. Difficulties are part of the price we have to pay."

The boss's voice had taken on a slightly more authoritative tone, different from the friendliness of the first moments of their encounter.

"A very high price," Jeff said offhandedly, moving his eyes to and fro in order to avoid his boss's gaze.

Northfeld leaned over his desk towards Jeff, sitting on the other side.

"*Nu*, Jeff," he said heartily, "we've exchanged our blows. Now tell me what happened. Did they put you into jail? Is that what you're so hostile about?"

Jeff allowed himself a smile. He wanted more than anything to maintain his distance, to make certain that his boss would understand that this was his first, and his last, trip to Moscow. And yet he did not want to push him too far.

"No, no, they didn't throw me in prison. But there were times when I thought that would happen to me."

Northfeld stretched in his chair. "I don't understand. You went to Moscow with official sanction. You had a visa, you stayed in a hotel that they assigned you to, took part in business that they knew you would take part in. If so, what happened? Why did you think they would arrest you?"

Jeff crossed his legs and pulled a cigarette out of his jacket pocket. He offered one to his boss, who politely refused.

"Try to understand. Russia is Russia. You can never know."

Northfeld gave Jeff a piercing glance. "Something seems strange to me, Jeff. Others also travel there and return, travel and return, and they don't have these feelings. They just don't. Okay, they admit that it's not the greatest place in the world to live, but they didn't feel your fears. And your American passport is also a kind of protection, isn't it?"

"They didn't feel it. I did."

Northfeld, amused, joked with Jeff. "And maybe you were busy with something besides diamonds?"

Against his will, Jeff's face took on a serious cast. Northfeld saw the sudden change that came over him. Something stirred within him; alarm bells began to ring in his head. Suddenly he awaited Jeff's reply. His casual remark, thrown out without serious thought, had turned into something serious. Could it be? Could Jeff be hiding something?

Jeff burst into laughter. Northfeld did not believe in its sincerity.

"What could I have been doing there? Do you think I'm in the pay of the CIA?"

Northfeld chose to conceal his suspicion beneath a veil of good humor. "Maybe. What do I know?" he laughed, giving Jeff a mischievous look. "Actually, you do look a lot like a secret agent."

Jeff did not care for the joke. After all, he knew full well that he was, indeed, hiding something.

"Mr. Northfeld, why do you think such strange things? On one day's notice you told me I was flying to Moscow; the next day you think I'm an agent of the CIA? Do they train agents in one day? Really, now."

Northfeld was silent. Jeff's obvious need to lay his suspicions to rest actually increased them. If he were as pure as the driven snow, Northfeld reasoned, he would have gone along with the joke, rather than dismissing it with this flood of words. So? Could he actually be a CIA agent?

Nonsense! But with all that, he could not rid himself of the feeling that his messenger to Moscow — the man he hoped would become his permanent agent there — was hiding something, something not necessarily connected to the diamond business.

Jeff again felt furious with himself. Just as in Moscow, so in New York, his chatter was getting him into trouble. Why did he have to mention his fears in Moscow? Why hadn't he realized that Northfeld would cross-examine him to understand why he thought they would put him in prison?

Northfeld liberated him from his increasingly uncomfortable thoughts.

"*Nu*, Jeff, enough foolishness. Let's get down to business. How did it go?"

"It was fine. Two meetings and the deal was done."

"Two meetings? With the Russians? They're well known for being tough negotiators!"

After a short pause he added, with a smile of goodwill, "And that's the reason I sent you there."

"Thanks," Jeff murmured in answer to the compliment. *Thanks for nothing*, he added to himself.

"That's right, two meetings."

"How did you do it?"

"You want to know the truth? I don't understand it either. At the second meeting they rushed to complete the agreement at the price I offered."

"Strange. Very strange."

Northfeld suddenly lifted his head and stared at Jeff. *Maybe,* came the mad, silly thought to his head, *maybe they — the KGB — have recruited him? Could that be the reason they concluded the deal so quickly, at such an advantageous price?* He knew the idea was completely crazy. But with all that was going on, who knew? Stranger things had been written in the newspapers.

He roused himself from his reverie. "*Nu*, Jeff, to business. Where's the merchandise?"

Jeff put on a mysterious face. "They've kept it!"

Northfeld was shocked. He began to speak, held himself back, leaving his mouth hanging slightly open. Finally he murmured, "I don't understand. I asked you where the merchandise is."

"And I answered you: They've kept it!"

Northfeld crossed his arms on his chest. "What do you mean, they've kept it?"

"This is what it means: The Russians won't give the merchandise until they've gotten the money."

"Why? Do they think we're thieves?"

"Maybe," Jeff answered with feigned indifference.

"They don't believe in a handshake and a '*mazel u'berachah*'? It's not like the diamond exchange here?"

"No. These are government officials who really don't care if you make the sale or not."

"*Nu*, so"

Jeff understood what his boss was leading up to. He interrupted him in midsentence. "And that's why it's worth doing business with them. Their merchandise is clean and top quality. They don't mind cutting down the stone, so long as it is completely clean."

After a pause he added, "What we have to do is transfer the money to the bank whose name we will get from the Russian consulate in Washington. We'll receive the merchandise via return mail. That's it."

"Can we trust them?"

"Other salesmen whom I met say that we can, that except for one case, when the wrong merchandise came, merchandise not as good as what was ordered, they've never caused problems."

Northfeld stood up. Jeff followed his lead. They shook hands and parted. Northfeld did not take his eyes off Jeff's receding back, not until he had left the office and closed the door behind him. Afterwards he threw his arms out in a gesture of surprise, settled himself back into his armchair, and turned to the pile of papers on his desk. But some part of his brain still wondered about the change that had come over Jeff.

Jeff returned home still worn out from the adventures of the past days. Tired, also, from his unpleasant conversation with his boss. He walked up to the second floor hoping to grab a quick nap before *Minchah*. A few minutes after he lay down in bed, his eyes already closing, he sat up, rubbing away the sleep that had begun to dim his eyes. "How could I have forgotten? I have to call Grandfather!" he said aloud.

He reached for the telephone, then suddenly came to a halt. Could he be sure that no one was listening in? He burst into laughter at the silliness of the thought and yet put on his shoes and jacket and went outside to use a public phone.

When he opened the door he noticed a truck pulling out from in front of his house and roaring away at high speed. He walked to the corner. The public phone was out of service. Jeff grumbled but walked to the next phone booth. He threw in some coins and dialed Ramat Gan.

"Hi, Grandfather, how are you?"

"Hello," the voice sounded strained and a little hoarse.

"Yes, Grandfather, it's me, Jeff, your Yisrael Yaakov."

Jeff closed his eyes and put the receiver closer to his ear.

"Who is it?" he could hear the distant voice.

"It's me, Grandfather. Jeff, Jeff Handler, Yisrael Yaakov! Your grandson. I've just gotten back from Russia, from Moscow."

The voice in Israel seemed to come to life. "Oh, it's you! You're back?"

"Yes."

"*Nu?*"

"Look, Grandfather, it's not so simple."

"Simple or not, nothing in life is simple. I asked you: *Nu?*"

His grandfather's voice was suddenly firm and lively. Perhaps the hope that Jeff would have good news for him gave him new spirit. It hurt Jeff, it hurt him terribly, to disappoint him. But he had no choice. Jeff took a deep breath, put his mouth to the receiver and in a loud voice told his grandfather the sad truth:

"Grandfather, try to understand, in two days in Moscow I couldn't do a thing! Do you understand?"

"No, I don't. I don't understand. Why didn't you stay there another few days?"

"Grandfather, the Communists are still in power there. The KGB is everywhere. I tried to ask where the street was, and they began to follow me. No one would talk to me, and tell me where to go."

The line went silent, a deadly silence. After a minute he could hear his grandfather's despairing voice. "There's no goal that can't be reached, Yisrael Yaakov. You need the will and you need the fear of G-d."

Jeff accepted the insult that had been hurled at him from the Holy Land. But he would not surrender: His grandfather simply had to accept reality and give up his dreams.

"Try to understand, Grandfather, I see this as an impossible mission. Do you see? I went to Moscow only because you asked me to. I— I didn't want to go. But in these two days I saw that it's impossible. I won't go again. It's dangerous. I have a wife and children, Grandfather, your great-grandchildren, even if you don't remember them."

Not a word came from the other end. Long, and expensive, minutes passed. Jeff began to worry.

"Grandfather, Grandfather, do you hear me? Has something happened?"

The quiet voice from Ramat Gan spoke. "Yes, yes, I hear you. I hear you better than you hear yourself."

After a short silence, the grandfather added, "Okay, good. Good night."

The conversation ended.

Jeff walked home slowly, his steps heavy.

20

A few minutes quickly passed and Jeff entered his home once more. He walked slowly towards the stairs that led to the second floor, to his bedroom. His heart was heavy. The fact that he had disappointed his beloved grandfather deeply disturbed him. He knew that he had destroyed the hope that had begun to flicker when his grandfather learned that his grandson was traveling to Moscow — the hope that the *tefillin*, so holy in his eyes, would be found. But what could Jeff do? This brief, two-day visit was sufficient to show him that the thing was just impossible. Finding those *tefillin* was an incomparably complex project. Actually, given Jeff's standing as an American tourist in Moscow, under KGB surveillance, it was more than complex: It was impossible.

Jeff halted midway on the steps. His footsteps, heavy as they were, were muffled in the burgundy carpet; still, in the deep silence that lay upon the house he could make out the dim thump of his footfall. He stopped, gripped the banister more tightly, and took a deep breath. Was this some strange weakness overtaking him? Perhaps; Jeff did not really know. Suddenly he saw the figure of his grandfather before him. In his imagination he could see him pacing his bedroom, perhaps taking the pills he was to swallow every morning. Or perhaps not: Perhaps he did not care anymore to take care of his failing health, now that his goal in life could not be accomplished. Jeff could not imagine how his grandfather's *Shacharis* prayers would pass, now that he had received the bitter news. Maybe Jeff had even brought on his grandfather's — Jeff shook his head firmly, trying to banish the terrible thought. *Why am I to blame? What do they want from me? That I should do the impossible?*

Jeff took another deep breath and continued up the stairs. He knew very well that if he were to search for the *tefillin* in any other city in the world, the chances of finding them would be greater. In any other city, the effort might be successful. In Buenos Aires, in Caracas, in Rome or Amsterdam or London, even in African Nairobi, he might be able to find them. At least there was some chance of it. These were places where one could speak freely, without fear, to other people, where one could go anywhere without being asked too many questions. You could make your mission public without being afraid of being accused of espionage or subversive activities or damaging public security or who knew what else they might attribute to you! But in Moscow? *Haven't you seen for yourself,* Jeff tried to persuade and encourage himself, *those big, suspicious eyes that opened whenever you merely asked the question: Where is Krasno Bogatirski Street?* But how could he explain to his grandfather that he would have to live for months in Moscow before he could possibly make his move without arousing suspicions? And how could someone live in that crowded city, where one man never spoke to the next for fear of saying the wrong thing? A city where no one knew the sweetness of a passing smile, of a simple, pleasant greeting, because of the mutual fear, the fear that someone might suspect you and your motives. He felt sorry for his grandfather, to whom he could never explain these feelings. He simply wouldn't understand them, because of his age, because, also, of his obsession, his madness — yes, madness — about this pair of *tefillin* that he lost more than 50 years earlier.

Jeff reached his room and flung himself down on the bed. He was tired. No more than tired; he was exhausted. Yet despite his determination to sleep, he could not close his eyes. A storm of emotion raged within him, a terrible typhoon that swept him up against his will. What could he do?

The telephone lying beside him shrilled. Jeff streched out a weak hand to lift the receiver. Maybe this caller, whoever he was, would free him from the bonds of these wild, inescapable thoughts.

"Hello," Jeff whispered dully.

"Hello, Jeff," his father's voice, coming from Israel, came through. "Jeff! What's going on? What have you done to your grandfather?"

The voice had the edge of hysteria. But Jeff was indifferent to its sound: He was listening to a voice in his own heart screaming the words again and again: *And what have you done to me? Why did you put this impossible mission on me? And when I tell you it's impossible, I am responsible?*

But none of these words were uttered, of course. Instead, he whispered into the receiver, "Abba, I'll call you back. Hang up, please."

There was a moment's silence, the silence of surprise. Then came a voice, fierce with fury: "Tell me, Jeff, what does that mean? What kind of *chutzpah* is that? What's happened to you? That's how you answer me?"

Jeff sat down heavily on the bed. The heavy fatigue had vanished, replaced by nervous tension.

"Abba, I'm hanging up! I told you I'll call you back. Do me a favor, don't ask questions."

His father's anger grew even stronger.

"Tell me, two days in Moscow have corrupted you completely? You've forgotten your manners, your respect. First you tell your grandfather that you won't fulfill his request to you in Moscow —"

Jeff hung up, thrusting the receiver down onto the phone. He felt himself shaking. He was afraid, truly afraid, that someone was listening. These Soviets, perhaps they wanted to know what he was looking for in Moscow, in addition to diamonds. He knew, as every citizen of the free world knew, that their arm was long, like the tentacles of an octopus encircling the globe. He did not need them to learn more about his mission in Moscow from his home phone.

He jumped from his bed and rushed to leave the house once again. He decided to drive to Boro Park and call his father from there. It was a good idea, he decided, to use a different phone each time he called Israel. Perhaps he was overdoing it but — you never knew. Now he had to hurry. He had to call his father while he still had the chance to explain why he had cut him off, while he still could cool down the older man's increasing wrath. Another hour or two would be too late.

He took the steps two at a time, down toward the front door.

Suddenly all the phones in the house came to life. He stopped for a moment and lifted his head, then immediately continued to walk toward the exit. He tried to ignore the shrill rings that so annoyingly followed him. When he reached the door he noticed his wife, who had apparently just returned from shopping. Her hand was reaching out towards the phone.

"Don't pick it up!" he screamed impatiently. His wife, taken aback, reflexively pulled her hand away, like one who had gotten an electric shock.

"What's the matter?" she cried, obviously confused.

"I'll tell you later, when I get back."

Her confusion increased. "Where are you running to?"

"Later. Later. Understand?"

As he hastily locked the door he could hear her voice. "Jeff? Does this have something to do with your trip to Russia?"

Jeff opened the door once again. His head peeked through. With his finger on his lips and a strange, stern look in his eyes he motioned to his wife to keep quiet. He suddenly remembered his hotel room in the Russia Hotel where — as every visitor knew — microphones were hidden, and the KGB listened in on every breath that its occupants took.

Jeff hurried out and turned on his car. He raced to Boro Park and there, on the corner of Thirteenth Avenue and Forty-Fifth Street, parked his car and hurried to the closest public phone to call his father in Israel.

Anatoly Dobrovitz was completely lost in thought. He sat on the subway, curled up in his oversized army jacket. The railroad car was full, but complete silence reigned. Everyone was quiet. Only the clack-clack of the steel wheels rolling on the railroad ties could be heard, or the occasional roar of the motor as the train picked up speed after one of its many stops. Occasionally his glance would fall on the faces of the people sitting across from him, at the people standing nearby, and for a few seconds on his neighbors to the right and the left of him. Everyone's faces were frozen, a Siberian frost. Were any of them following him? Anatoly realized that he was now traveling a path from which he could not turn back.

Trying to distract attention from himself, he looked at his watch. 7:30. About 20 minutes to reach the station where he was to get off. "At exactly 8 o'clock," the stranger he had met on the Metro had told him, "they will be waiting for you." So he would be 10 minutes early. Good; it was better that he come early. Or maybe not? Maybe it wasn't good? Maybe they would be suspicious if they saw him hanging around for 10 minutes? He would have to act completely natural, to hide all signs of fear, all of his emotions, before this unknown encounter with the illegal study group in Judaism.

The train screeched to a stop in the Viyokovskya Station. Anatoly got off and slowly walked up the stairs to the street. He hoped that the hordes of Muscovites walking near him did not hear the thumping of his heart. He stopped when he reached the street. The flow of people continued around him, scattering in many different directions. The air was cold and dry, despite the snowflakes that fell silently from the sky. As agreed upon, Anatoly grasped his copy of *The Three Musketeers* to his chest.

Ten minutes passed. A lean young man with a slight limp whose face was almost completely obscured by a thick woolen scarf approached him. When he was very close, Anatoly heard him whisper one word. "Come." Anatoly hesitated for one second before following in the stranger's footsteps, in an attempt not to attract the attention of any potential shadowers. The trip through the streets was short. After a few turns, right and left, in the streets, quiet now at this evening hour, the stranger halted. He did not turn around to see if Anatoly was following him; the rustle of his footsteps told him that his "client" was still behind him. The lean young man disappeared into an apartment building with Anatoly close behind him. The two walked through the dimness. Anatoly could hear that the young man's footsteps were much less hesitant than his own. It seemed, then, that this was not the first time he had been here in this secret gathering place.

They walked slowly up a set of dark stone stairs. Anatoly kept close to the young man; he could hear his quiet breathing. The young man stopped at one of the doors and knocked lightly. It seemed to Anatoly that there was a pattern to his knocks, some kind of agreed-upon signal. The door opened. A dim yellow light illuminated the darkness of the hallway for one moment. The two figures disappeared into the apartment and the door was shut behind them.

Anatoly, nervous and agitated, looked around him. He immediately noticed the bearded man who had so angrily rejected him in the synagogue in Archipova Street when he, Anatoly, had asked him to teach him about Judaism. Their eyes met for a moment. Anatoly noticed that the man was looking at him nonchalantly, without giving any sign of having met before, though they had, in fact, spoken just yesterday. Despite his air of nonrecognition, Anatoly suspected that it was this bearded man who had sent the stranger who had spoken to him on the subway, and it was through his doing that Anatoly was now here at this secret gathering. Perhaps — But the man, in any case, was not giving any sign of being connected to the incident.

Anatoly scanned the others crowded around the table. He did not recognize any of them. Most of them were young women and men of college age or older. No one paid him any special attention. He saw an empty seat and hesitantly took it.

One of the participants announced loudly: "Anyone under the age of 18 is asked to leave this room. The law forbids him to listen to a Torah class."

Anatoly was confused; he didn't understand the announcement. He was surprised to see the others grinning at the strange declaration. Luckily he was already 20 years old; this request — or command? — had nothing to do with him. But he did not dare ask what it meant. (Later, he was to learn that Soviet law forbade teaching religion to young people below this age. The declaration was made out loud because of their certainty that the KGB was listening in on whatever happened in this apartment.)

Anatoly leaned back quietly in his chair and waited tensely for what would happen. At the head of the table sat a gray-bearded Jew whose eyes radiated warmth and good feeling. This was no Russian, of that Anatoly was certain. He seemed liberated, somehow, with no sign of stress on his face or in the way he held himself. The dress too, a dark suit and well-pressed white shirt with a matching tie, seemed to point to his originating outside the boundaries of Russia. How had he come here? Who was he? Anatoly did not dare ask anyone sitting around him.

The stranger at the head of the table held a book in his hands. He opened it and, even as he leafed through it, he began to speak quietly. He spoke in English, a language that Anatoly did not understand at all. After a few sentences the bearded man from the synagogue translated the stranger's words into colloquial Russian. Anatoly tried to listen to the translation. This stranger, it seemed to him, was speaking of one called Avraham, leader of the Jewish people. Anatoly had never heard of him: Who was he? What was he? When did he live? What had he accomplished? What did it mean, head of the ancient nation? Was he like Genghis Khan, or what? In any case, he listened attentively to what was being said.

Anatoly did not know how much time had passed from the beginning of the class. It seemed only minutes. Suddenly they could hear harsh knocks on the door.

Silence fell. The book in the stranger's hands instantly disappeared. Anatoly grew pale.

21

J eff clutched the receiver in the phone booth, making certain no one was nearby. When he did not get through to his father he felt a surge of impatience. His father's phone wasn't busy. If so, why didn't he answer? Nervously he shifted his weight from one foot to the other; his eyes darted back and forth, as if looking to see if anyone noticed his agitation. Finally, the ringing stopped. His tension increasing, he waited another moment until he heard "Hello" on the other side of the line.

"Abba, it's me, Jeff! I—"

His father cut him off, not letting him finish his apology.

"What's the matter with you, Jeff? What's the reason for such behavior? I'm trying to understand. And you—"

Jeff, his anxiety increasing, did not wait for his father to finish the lecture. Instead, he tried to halt the flow of words.

"Abba, let me explain. Don't be angry."

"*Nu,* so explain."

His father's voice was furious. Jeff hoped he would be able to calm him down.

"Please, just hear me out to the end and I'll explain."

"*Nu.*" His father was losing his temper.

"You have to understand, I just came back from Russia."

"*Nu.*"

"I tried to find the street that Grandfather mentioned."

"*Nu.*"

"*Nu,*" Jeff repeated his father's war cry, feeling increasingly exhausted. "Don't you understand? Someone there was interested in my interest! It's Russia, have you forgotten? Russia of Brezhnev and Andropov: in short, of the KGB."

There was a short silence on the other end of the line. Jeff again shifted his weight from one foot to the other, moving the receiver from his right hand to his left. His father's quiet voice came through clearly, the anxiety it contained was evident.

"What's that? They harassed you? They put you in prison?"

"No."

"*Nu,* so what happened?"

"What happened? They know that I'm interested. That's enough. That's enough in the Moscow that I saw for the first time in my life."

"How do you know?"

"I'm certain of it."

"Why?"

"In Russia you can smell these things. I smelled it. Besides, the way my business negotiations ended convinced me completely. The KGB suddenly got involved in the deal and pressured them to finish it off quickly. That made me even more suspicious."

A short, trans-Atlantic silence.

"Jeff," his father was interested, "I think I understand. You've come back from Moscow very tense. Okay. But that's a reason to hang up on your father?"

"No. Heaven forbid. That's not a reason. You're right, not because of that! But what if you suspect, if you're almost certain, that they are listening in on you? Then you do hang up! Do you understand me?"

Jeff's father burst out into hearty laughter that could be clearly heard in Boro Park. Jeff could hear the edge of hysteria in the laughter. "It seems, Jeff, that your grandfather is contagious. He also thinks the KGB is listening in on him! Two days in Moscow and already— What's wrong with you, Jeff?"

Jeff was quiet for a second, trying to figure out what to tell his father. Maybe he was right. It was strange to believe that the KGB, busy with global espionage throughout the world in its goal to overshadow the United States, would take the time to care about him, little Jeff Handler of Flatbush. On the other hand, a superpower as paranoid as the USSR, nervous about every independent statement made by each and every one of its citizens, would certainly keep an eye on every foreigner in its borders, particularly if the foreigner showed interest in things he should have nothing to do with. Jeff knew he could not make his father understand, not in a call from a phone booth on a Boro Park street. And yet he tried.

"Look, Father," he spoke slowly, careful of every word, "maybe it's the influence of my first encounter with Moscow. It's a city of fear, of suspicions. A city where one man doesn't believe the other. A wife doesn't believe her husband, a parent his children. Believe me, all the stories that they told us seem to be true, even though nothing happened to me. But the atmosphere itself is fraught with it. Everyone walks quietly there, like embalmed mummies. So give me a few days to calm down. Understand my fears that my phone line is being tapped. For that reason, and that reason only, I hung up on you. By the way, I am not talking to you from my home."

Jeff could not tell if his father had accepted his explanation.

"Okay, so let it be like that. In any case, let's get to the important matter. What have you done to your grandfather? You've destroyed him completely. I'm afraid—"

Jeff was once again attacked by a wave of impatience. "And what could I have done? Why am I to blame? He asked me to carry out a completely impossible mission. Until I got to Moscow I didn't realize just how impossible it was. Over there they know every step you take. Did you know that? I had an escort from Intourist; I'm certain that he was a KGB informer as well. You should have seen his eyes when I asked him about the street where Grandfather had left the *tefillin*."

"I'm not arguing with you. I've never been to Moscow; I don't know what it's like. But you didn't have to be so harsh with him. You could have left him a bit of hope. It was a little cruel of you."

Jeff took a deep breath. "Abba, I know, but please try to understand: I am not returning to Russia! Period. I thought Grandfather should know that as soon as possible. I don't want him bothering me morning and night, demanding that I go back. Can you understand me?"

"I understand you, but I don't agree. Besides, don't be so sure. Life is full of surprises."

Jeff smiled to himself. "Maybe, but not in this. Never!"

"At least say: *Bli neder*."

Jeff hesitated for a minute. He bit his lip and then, despite himself, he whispered, "*Bli neder*."

Yuri Primakov noticed Igor Grasimov from a distance. Igor looked strange, leaning against the building where Yuri lived. It seemed that he was waiting for someone, Yuri thought. Waiting for him? Who else did he know in this area? Yuri began approaching him eagerly. Igor still could not see him. He walked down the unlit road, where no streetlight shone. (It was two weeks since they had burned out, and the city had not yet changed them. Nor had they replaced those that had been stolen.) He would not call him, Yuri decided; better to surprise him. But now Igor lifted his head, listening; it seemed he had heard Yuri's footsteps after all. Yuri stopped. He was feeling good, this minute, feeling mischievous. He decided to circle the building and sneak up behind Igor, giving him a good shock. He would enjoy seeing his friend's reaction. Maybe he would even call out for the police! It was always fun to scare someone for no good reason.

Yuri had not known Igor for very long, only a few weeks, since the secret meeting of the students held outside the city. Sometimes they would return home together, exchanging a few words, a few stories, hinting and whispering to each other of their occasional gatherings.

Friends? Not particularly, but they did like each other. Igor seemed to Yuri somewhat introverted; he had never gotten him to really speak out. Yuri had not managed to find out what his father did, though he, Yuri, had proudly told him of his own father at their second meeting. His father was a pilot in Aeroflot, who had visited many of the cities of western Europe, and his tales of the decadence — a Communist term — of places like London had made a great impression on Igor. He had dreamed that Moscow, too, would take on some of that decadence, with things to buy, people laughing freely ... Yet Igor always remained silent when it came his turn to talk about his parents. Yuri did not push him: One never knew why someone was concealing his family's identity.

Yuri decided to skip his prank; instead he walked straight towards Igor, who was beginning to feel nervous at the sound of approaching footsteps.

"Igor? What are you doing here?" Yuri cried.

Igor smiled, but immediately grew serious. "I'm glad to see you."

Yuri peered into his friend's face curiously. "So what's the occasion?" he asked, surprised that he had finally come to his house, and at night no less.

Igor leaned against a wall. "There's a little problem I want you to know about."

Yuri came a bit closer. He ran the fingers of his right hand through his thick dark hair.

"What's it about, Igor?"

Yuri noticed that Igor was breathing deeply, breath after breath. The thought flashed through his mind: *This boy is worried about something.* By the dim yellow light of the bulb that shone from a first-floor apartment it seemed that he could see his friend's lower lip trembling slightly.

Igor tried to smile, but it was obviously forced.

"Don't panic, but it seems they know about us."

Yuri's heart skipped a beat. Perhaps he paled a little too; he wasn't certain himself.

"Who is 'they'? And what do they know? Explain!"

"You don't know who 'they' are? The Cometee. The KGB."

"And what do they know?"

"About our meetings."

Yuri breathed deeply. "And that's all? What did you think? That they didn't know about us? Then you obviously don't know anything at all about them! They are everywhere. I am certain that their spies are among the students who come to our meetings. Informers. The point is that we are not breaking any laws. That probably infuriates them to no end. Despite everything, it is not Stalinist Russia today."

Igor remained silent for some time. He pulled himself away from the wall and straightened up.

"They photographed me. There are pictures!"

"Oh wow," Yuri said admiringly. "Can I get a copy? Did you come out good?"

"Stop making fun of me," Igor fumed. "That doesn't scare you? No? I don't believe you!"

Yuri burst out laughing, but Igor did not believe that he found anything funny. It seemed to Igor that Yuri was trying to conceal his confusion, perhaps even his fear.

Yuri scowled. "You don't understand! It really doesn't scare me! It's that simple. It doesn't scare any of us, any of our group. We get them angry, we know that. But we will only defeat the KGB's dictatorship if we are without fear. Andrei Sakharov is our model."

Igor did not answer. He knew his father and his father's colleagues well. They would stop at nothing to destroy the group, shatter it, bring it down. Yes, they would work within the law. But the law was flexible; both those opposing the regime and those supporting it used it with skill and dexterity.

Yuri suddenly moved closer to Igor. He grabbed him by the lapels, his eyes flashing: "How do you know that they know, huh?"

Igor was frightened. Yuri's eyes held a frenzied and suspicious look.

"Talk." The command was firm. "Talk already."

And here Igor made the worst mistake of his life.

"My father told me."

Yuri was shocked. His grip weakened. "Who? Your father?"

Igor realized that he had made a terrible mistake. He tried to turn things back. "It's not important. I know that they have pictures."

"No, my friend. You said, 'my father.' I heard you. Tell me, what does your father do? You think I haven't noticed that every time I ask you that question, you weasel out of answering it?"

"Yuri, let me alone. I wanted you to know, so you would be careful. What's the difference who said it; I know it, that's all."

"Too late, my friend. Too late. What does your father do? Is he in the KGB?"

Igor did not answer. Yuri repeated the question, all the while tightening his grip on the jacket, and even clutching at his chest.

"He's in the Cometee? Yes or no!"

Igor maintained his stony silence. But Yuri could see the spark of fear in his eyes.

"I understand, Igor. You're an agitator! He sent you after us to spy on us, right?"

"If I were a spy, would I have come here to tell you? Is that what you think?"

The corners of Yuri's mouth went up in a wicked smile. He was taller and stronger than Igor. He could feel his friend squirming and wriggling in his strong grasp.

"That's true. You're right," he hissed. "True, you're not a spy. But if your father is in the KGB, you must be a Jew! All the KGB agents are Jews! All the true enemies of the Russian nation are Jews!"

Igor had never before seen such a look of pure hatred as Yuri's eyes projected, at that moment that they stood together, just the two of them, in the dark. He felt a kind of fear that he had never before experienced. He lowered his eyes; he could not bear the look of one who until that moment he had considered a friend. Suddenly he felt a terrible blow to his back. Yuri pushed him harshly towards the wall of the house. Then he took his hands off him, swiftly turned to the lobby, and disappeared inside.

"Have you got news for me?"

Dimitri Grasimov whispered the brief words into the receiver. The sour look on his face indicated that the news he was waiting to hear had not arrived. But there was one small thread to hold onto in the information given to him by the top department of the KGB, the one responsible for foreign espionage.

The man on the other end said: "We're still shadowing him. It seems that he's afraid of something. He cut off a conversation that he received from outside the country."

Grasimov moved alertly in his chair.

"Why?" he asked with interest.

"The voice spoke of a particular mission in Moscow."

Dimitri felt his curiosity grow sharper. "Very interesting. Did you hear what the mission was?"

"No, no. I told you that he hurried to cut off the conversation. He left the house and continued the conversation from a public phone in another neighborhood."

"That means, you don't know what the two of them spoke about?"

"No."

"What else?"

"That's it."

Grasimov was silent for a long moment. Finally, he muttered, "Continue to follow and listen. Patience usually pays off. Bring me results, and quickly. Understand?"

"Comrade Colonel, there's one more detail they gave us."

"What?"

"The man we're following screamed into the phone that he will never return to Russia!"

Grasimov was surprised. He reacted quickly.

"That's not good. He must return."

22

eff returned to his house feeling somewhat easier in mind. He hoped that his father had understood the clear message he had tried to give regarding the impossible mission. Jeff hoped, also, that his father would manage to calm Grandfather down.

"Where did you rush off to?" Miriam greeted him. She was still shaken from her husband's hasty exit from the house, and from his shouts when she had tried to pick up the phone.

"I went to make a phone call," he answered casually, as he trod heavily up the stairs going to the house's second floor.

"Maybe you can come down and explain what's going on." She sat down in the living room and waited for a response. She was certainly impatient. She was not pleased with her husband's strange mood, his high-strung reactions. She did not know what to think, and every effort she made to understand the reason for his behavior resulted in a dead end.

Jeff stopped in the middle of the stairway. His wife's demanding voice had brought him to a halt. Surrendering, he turned around and slowly descended. She stared wordlessly at him, slightly tense in anticipation of his revelations that would, perhaps, help solve the complicated puzzle of his behavior since his return from Moscow.

Jeff walked over to where his wife was sitting. There was a half smile on his lips. "Come, let's go for a ride. We'll drive around and talk."

She lifted an eyebrow. "Why?"

Jeff was adamant. "What difference does it make?"

His voice had a demanding quality to it. She stood up, confused by the sudden request.

"You were about to go to sleep. Suddenly you want to go out?"

Jeff winked. "It happens, no? I changed my mind."

There was something very odd about that wink. But she decided to go with him. The two wordlessly entered the car. Jeff started the engine and sped away. A car passed and he jammed on the brakes; the two passengers lurched forward.

"What's wrong with you today?" she asked with increasing surprise, as she watched his aggressive driving.

Jeff gave a broad grin. "Now I'm fine; at least I hope so. Give me another day or two and I'll get back to being completely sane."

Miriam was quiet. Her fingers gently rapped on the car window. When they were speeding down Ocean Parkway she turned to him.

"Are you ready to explain the meaning of all this now?"

"It's all connected with Russia," came the laconic reply. His eyes were concentrating on the traffic flowing around him.

"That's obvious," she said impatiently. "But connected in what way? Haven't you come home again and that's all?

"That's the one point that I'm not sure of," he answered quietly.

She repeated her request more emphatically. "Are you ready to talk?"

Jeff was ready. He briefly told her of all his fears, of the feeling that the Soviets were trying to investigate who he was because of his unusual interest in some far-fetched Moscow street. He was not certain but he felt by some instinct that they were listening in on his conversations. Maybe they were even following him in order to know who he was, if he was something other than a small-time diamond merchant. For that reason he had wished to speak with his grandfather and father out of the house, on a public phone. To tell them unequivocally that he was not returning to Moscow and that the attempt to find the *tefillin* was, in his eyes, a fruitless one.

She listened for a long while as he detailed all the events that had occurred during those two days in Moscow. The visit to the *shul*; the suffocating feeling in the city; his escort, Gregory, who had, it seemed, reported on his every footstep to the KGB; the *gabbai* in the *shul*; the frozen faces of the city residents; the obstinacy of the bureaucrats in the diamonds department who suddenly, after receiving orders from the KGB, rushed to finish off the business to his complete satisfaction. Everything was suspicious.

Miriam listened quietly. Finally, she roused herself. "And that's why you wanted to leave the house?"

He nodded his head in assent.

"You mean to say that they are listening in on your telephone conversations?"

Jeff nodded again and said, "I don't know. It could be. I suspect it."

She entwined her fingers. "It's frightening, no?"

"I agree."

She shuddered. "And maybe this car, the one we're riding in, is also bugged?"

"Maybe. Perhaps."

She shook her head back and forth like one trying to cast away a nightmare.

"And maybe it's all your imagination? Craziness of your overactive brain?"

Jeff agreed. "That's also possible."

She gave him a penetrating look. Without their having realized it, they had reached the Brooklyn Bridge. They sped through the streets of Lower Manhattan, in the shadow of its skyscrapers, whose upper floors were hardly visible in the mist drifting off the river.

"That's what Communist Russia does to a person in two days."

Jeff started to laugh. "I don't know. As I said, I hope that in another day or two it'll all pass."

They drove aimlessly through the streets of Manhattan for a little longer and then turned back home. When they reached Flatbush, Jeff pulled up to the Mirrer Yeshivah and went inside to *daven Ma'ariv*. His wife sat and waited for him in the car.

The congregation was in the middle of *Krias Shema* when he entered the large room. He hurried to catch up to the rest. When he had finished *Shemoneh Esrei* and lifted his eyes from the *siddur* he noticed, much to his consternation, a bearded man staring at him with overt interest. Jeff recognized him immediately; it was the same young Russian who had tried to give him a pair of *tefillin* before his flight to Moscow. Now the man was standing not far from him, giving him the once-over, while speaking earnestly to a man standing near the bookshelf. Jeff could clearly sense that they were talking about him. The Russian pointed a finger at him, and the other man seemed to explain something, his eyes also on Jeff.

Jeff felt a twinge of fear. He hurried out of the *beis midrash* and quickly went into his car.

"I thought it was all behind me," he whispered, still breathing heavily from the flight down the stairs. "It seems I was wrong."

Miriam awoke from her thoughts. "Has something happened?" she asked anxiously.

"I don't know. But something disturbed me during *davening*."

Two days later the phone call came.

Igor was dismayed. He stood alone in the darkness, leaning on the wall where his friend Yuri had pushed him. In those first seconds his brain could not absorb what had happened. There was no one to be seen, neither near the building nor in the main street nearby. From the adjoining houses, too, no sound could be heard, though it was still relatively early. The residents of Moscow do not like to make noise, and they shut themselves silently in their homes.

Igor lifted his eyes towards the fourth floor, to the windows of

Yuri's apartment. It seemed to him that he could make out Yuri's head swiftly going back into the house. His friend, it seemed, wanted to know what he, Igor, was doing.

Igor understood that he should get out of there as fast as possible. There was the clear danger that in a short time a group of friends would heed Yuri's call and give Igor a sound thrashing. Infiltrators were particularly hated by student groups longing to taste a little freedom. He had heard of several instances of their falling upon a suspected informer, covering his face with a bag, and beating him into unconsciousness. Igor knew that as far as his friend went, it was too late. He would not change: He had denounced Igor as an agitator, a KGB informer, and, worse, a Jew. That last thought shot through his heart like a flame.

He pulled himself away and hurried off to the main street that led to the nearby Metro station. He did not pass anyone along the way. A lone automobile drove on the road. It slowed down as it passed him, and its passengers stared. Igor walked with his head held high and, in a show of courage, ignored them. The car sped up and disappeared, and Igor's heartbeat returned to normal.

A half-hour's walk brought him to an intersection. Across the street he noticed the entrance to a park. It was dark; the only sound was the whistle of the wind through the leaves of the tall trees. In an instantaneous decision he turned around, crossed the street, and entered the silent blackness. He groped through the darkness towards a bench and then fell down weakly upon it. He wanted to be alone with himself, with the frenzied thoughts flying through his tortured brain. Igor suddenly felt something wet on his face. His hands brushed across his cheeks, trying to wipe away the falling tears.

Igor did not know how much time he sat there, doing nothing, on the bench in the darkened park. He also did not remember exactly when he decided to stand up again and be on his way. His full consciousness returned, from the misty vagueness that engulfed him, only when he found himself opening the door of his home; suddenly he was standing at the threshold, unsure of whether or not to enter.

His father was the first to notice him. The expression on his face, which had been rock hard and angry at first, changed, much to Igor's shock, to something heartfelt and pleasant. This was a surprise. This strange amiability of his father frightened him more than if he had come after him with a whip.

"Why don't you come in?" He heard his father's voice, artificially gentle.

"Dimitri," Igor heard the voice from the bedroom. "Who's there?" It was his mother.

Dimitri smiled. "Who would I be welcoming, if not our long-lost son?"

"I'm coming," came the muffled words.

At the sound of his mother's voice Igor overcame his hesitation and walked into the apartment. His suspicions of his father did not dissipate, but he had confidence in his mother. He gently closed the door behind him and waited for what would happen next.

His mother appeared in the room, her clothing disheveled. One could see that she had already gone to bed.

Without a moment's hesitation she lashed out furiously. "Where have you been? Where did you go? You think you can just disappear without telling us where?"

Igor realized he should not answer. Whatever he would say would simply infuriate her even more — and infuriate his father as well. Better to let them get out all their anger. That would help calm them down; afterward, he would figure out how to discuss the situation and appease them somewhat.

His father's behavior continued to worry him. Dimitri picked up his large heavy hand and waved his wife into silence.

"Igor's back! Mother, prepare something to eat, to drink. It's been quite a while since you've eaten, right?"

What did his father want from him? Igor approached the simple wooden table that stood in the middle of the room and chose a chair to sit upon. Silence reigned. His mother returned from the kitchen with a steaming cup of coffee and some dry biscuits.

"Do you want to eat?" Her voice, too, grew gentler, in view of the strange patience that Igor's father was displaying.

"No," he answered.

His mother wiped her hands on a towel that she was holding. "Oh, if you're not hungry, then you must have eaten."

Igor hurried to respond. He was pleased that they were conversing. He felt a tremendous need to unload the burden, to share the events of the past few hours.

"No, I didn't eat anywhere. I'm simply not hungry."

His head hung down a little and his fingers pressed the edge of the table.

Dimitri Grasimov bent a little towards him. His mother, too, sat down, not removing her eyes from her son.

"Look, Igor," his father began, "I don't want to talk about what happened. I'm more interested in the future. The damage that you've caused both me and yourself is enormous. The fact that in the archives of the Second Department of the Cometee lies a picture of you among a group of students who are no doubt enemies of the regime can bring upon us terrible problems. We've got to repair the damage immediately! Do you understand?"

Igor did not reply. His father, it seemed, had something planned. He listened to his father's voice continue to speak.

"It's not only your behavior that I am referring to, it's the behavior of the other students who are doing the same foolish things. I, and my colleagues in the KGB, won't turn a blind eye to such doings. But before we do that which the law allows us to do to these students we try to explain to them, understand? To show them how they've erred. Understand?"

Igor kept his face carefully expressionless. His head remained bent; that way, his father could not look him in the eyes.

"Besides that, Igor, we allow them — that is we *demand* of them — that they repair the damage of their behavior. We give them the opportunity to prove their loyalty to the socialist community, to the Russian nation. Understand?"

Igor understood. He understood all too well where this was leading, but he chose not to display any indication of comprehension.

"Loyalty, Igor. That's what you have to prove now. Otherwise I don't know what will happen to us. To me and to you. You are the son of a KGB officer, did you know that? And there in the hallways of Lubianka there is no mercy. One day I may have to pay a terrible price because of you. Do you want that?"

This was the first time that Igor reacted. He shook his head in dissent. His father saw it as a good sign.

His mother stood up and announced, "I'm going to prepare something to eat."

Without waiting for a response she disappeared into the small kitchen.

His father continued the monologue. He believed at that moment that his gentle approach would work. "Understand, Igor, I urgently need your help. Igor. Do you hear me? I need your help. I beg you to give me a full and detailed report on the meeting that was photographed. I want names, exact addresses, the topics discussed, and who said what at the meeting."

Igor did not hurry to answer.

His father whispered, "If you give me that report I will be able to clear myself and you in my superiors' eyes. Do you understand? Sit down and write. First eat something."

Igor lifted his head. "I can't do it."

In the blink of an eye the harshness returned to his father's face.

"That means that you want to bring tragedy upon yourself and your father?"

"No. Of course not!" Igor said vehemently. "I've already brought trouble onto myself, but the report you're asking for will hasten my death."

Dimitri straightened up. "What does that mean?"

Igor's voice trembled. "They suspect that I'm a troublemaker, an informer. They found out that my father is a KGB agent. Every word that I tell you will prove to them that they're right. And they— they— they already killed one of our members on such suspicions."

Grasimov did not answer. He sat, lost in thought.

"And something even worse happened."

"What?"

"They found out that I'm a Jew. A dirty Jew, of course."

Again, Dimitri did not answer. His expressionless eyes inspected Igor's face.

"Father?"

"What?"

"What does that mean?"

"What does what mean?"

"What does it mean, that we're Jews?"

23

J eff heard the nagging ring of the phone. He was already out the door, on his way to his office in Manhattan. He hesitated for a moment; then, for no real reason, he reached with a hesitant hand for the receiver.

"Hi," he said weakly.

"Mr. Jeff Handler?"

The voice was official and seemed somewhat disembodied. Jeff tried to catch the trace of an accent: Russian, perhaps? But no. The man was American in every syllable. Jeff breathed just a little easier.

"Yes?" he said briefly.

"I would be happy if we could meet. Is it possible?" The voice was soft.

"With whom am I speaking?"

It was not difficult to arouse Jeff's suspicions.

"If we meet you will know, Mr. Handler."

The suspicions grew.

"I would be happier to know right now. I don't like meeting with anyone, without knowing beforehand just who that person is."

A light silence reigned on the line, followed by the voice.

"You are very correct, mister, but that is true of a normal conversation. Not an abnormal one. And I can't tell you. Try to understand me."

"I'm not really interested."

"We're talking about a matter of a mitzvah. Sometimes sacrifice is demanded of a Jew."

Jeff was silent. He did not know what to say. Suddenly the conversation had taken a Jewish turn. Was this a trap? He had once read that the Soviets planted spies in the United States, after they had undergone thorough training and had been changed into full-fledged Americans. Then—maybe—perhaps they turned some of them into observant Jews? For some reason the image of the student who had tried to give him *tefillin* prior to his trip suddenly flashed into his mind, the same young man he had met in the auditorium of Mirrer Yeshivah only a few days ago.

Finally he answered, "If you're talking about sacrifice, mister, I am demanding it of you. What is your name? Who are you?"

Jeff could hear the laughter on the other side of the phone.

"You're a hard case, Mr. Handler. But it seems to me that the reason I don't want to give my name over the phone is the same reason that you are suspicious."

"What do you mean?"

"The KGB," came the answer.

And before Jeff could answer he continued. "At the very least I understand you and your suspicions. I will visit you in your office."

He hung up.

Jeff's first reaction was the hurried decision not to go to the city that day. But he immediately realized that this was a foolish idea. If a person was determined to meet with him, he could reach him in Manhattan, or in any other place, the next day. Jeff turned resolutely towards the door. He reminded himself that he was in New York, the free and vibrant city. He would fling these nonsensical fears out of his heart. But he was not certain that he would be all that successful.

⚜

"There's news."

Dimitri Grasimov sat in his office, his face stern. He thought endlessly of how to recruit his son, Igor, for the service of the KGB, in an effort to erase the stain of humiliation that now besmirched him.

"News? From New York, I presume."

"Mr. Jeff Handler has no connection to the CIA, nor to any of the other covert agencies in the U.S."

"Verified?"

"There were no suspicious calls, either to or from his home."

"That's obvious. The man is careful. We know that he traveled from Flatbush to Boro Park in order to speak on the phone."

"That's right. But from then on no suspicious activity has been noted. He leaves in the morning to a local synagogue for prayers, returns home for breakfast, leaves to his office on 47th Street in Manhattan, returns home. A normal life with no irregularities."

"And in the office itself?"

"We're listening to his conversations. Nothing unusual. And 'Give Red,' our man in the CIA, couldn't find any connection or business with Jeff Handler."

Dimitri listened silently, his face veiled, to the terse update. He kept his peace, leaving the agent on the other side waiting tensely. The affair still seemed somewhat odd. The earlier report had noted with confidence certain activities that the man planned on doing in the USSR, yet now the file seemed clean. Handler was not connected with any subversive group. If so, now what?

"That's it?"

"One more thing."

"Speak."

"Someone who refused to be identified wanted to meet him."

"Yes."

"Handler tried to get out of it as long as he wouldn't identify himself."

Dimitri listened with growing interest.

"And—"

"The anonymous stranger explained that he couldn't identify himself because of a mutual fear that they shared."

"Fear of whom?"

"Fear of the KGB."

Dimitri did not answer. It could be that this last piece of information would finally get them somewhere. At last, he responded briefly.

"They made up a meeting place?"

"He said he would go to Handler's office in Manhattan."

"See to it that men are there. Understood?"

"Yes, Comrade."

The conversation ended.

The banging on the door grew louder. So did the yells: "Militia!" The Moscow police!

The knocks sounded firmer, more impatient. None of those present stood up to open the door. Anatoly Dobrovitz, for whom this was the first encounter with the law that forbade subversive activities, trembled with fear. His frightened eyes wandered to the faces of those sitting around the table. To his surprise no one showed any sign of fear or panic. They sat quietly, awaiting events without moving. Anatoly could not understand such quiescence. Maybe they were used to it? But he? Why had he come here at all? Why had he gone this route?

Finally the elderly owner of the apartment opened the door with an abrupt movement. She stood in the entranceway, blocking the policemen who had arrived in the company of agents of the secret police. She immediately opened her mouth with a flood of harsh words:

"I was in Hitler's camps," she screamed, enraged. "The Fascists killed my entire family. The people sitting here are my only grandchildren. Hitler didn't kill me, and you won't succeed in killing me either."

The policemen were dumbfounded. They looked shamefacedly at this ancient, determined *babushka* and retreated. Anatoly could not believe what he was seeing. Grinning in embarrassment the policemen left the apartment, waiting in the lobby for their victims. There, outside, under cover of dark, it would be easier to deal with them.

After the door had closed and the sound of their footsteps had ceased, the participants stood up from their places. They quickly climbed onto the roof, where an escape route had been prepared for use when the police came to search the apartment. The escape route brought them to the building's other entrance; without giving the sinister black Volga automobiles parked nearby a second glance, the participants walked indifferently back to their homes.

Anatoly, too, sneaked out via the roof. One of the participants who was following behind him noticed his terror. He whispered to him, "We had luck this time! Our *babushka* is a brave woman. It's not always like this, my young friend. You have to be make sacrifices and be strong, if you want to rediscover your Jewishness."

Anatoly did not answer. He walked slowly down the stairway of the building's other entrance, went into the street and disappeared, like a leaf in the wind, sheltered by the darkness of night.

Jeff reached 47th Street at 10 o'clock. He parked in the underground garage and took the elevator to the floor where the offices of Diamond Enterprises Inc. were housed. He knocked lightly on the glass entrance door and greeted the receptionist with a wave of the hand.

"Hi, Jeff," she said. "The boss asked me to tell you that you should go into his office as soon as you arrive. The merchandise from Russia came to the office last night, right after you left."

"Oh," Jeff said, feeling himself grow alert. "That's really good news."

Jeff hurried to his boss's office. Mr. Northfeld was leaning over his desk, examining the small sparkling stones that were scattered on its surface. A fluorescent lamp illuminated the desk top, giving the gems an extra sparkle. In Northfeld's left eye was a jeweler's loupe, a kind of magnifying glass; in his hand he held tweezers with which he moved around the stones during this first inspection.

Quietly, and with a feeling of enjoyment, Jeff watched his boss handle the highly polished diamonds. The merchandise was, indeed, high quality — and cheap, too. Northfeld lifted his head and nodded a greeting. Jeff pulled a chair over towards the desk, sat down and, elbows propped on the desk, continued to gaze at the boss.

"Nice merchandise," Northfeld said casually. Jeff did not answer.

"You did a good job, Jeff."

Jeff stuck to his silence.

"From the letter that came with the package," Northfeld continued, not moving his eyes from the desk, "it seems that they want to keep in contact with us."

Jeff gave a mocking laugh. "It seems you're trying to tell me something."

Northfeld lifted his head, put down the tweezers and pulled the loupe out of his eye. He smiled. "Jeff, why are you so nervous? I just told you that they want to stay in touch with us, that our agents will continue to go to Moscow. That's all."

Jeff pursed his lips in disbelief. "That's all? Really, that's all? If so, I'm satisfied."

Northfeld burst out into laughter. "You're a sharp fellow, Jeff. It seems that they want you to come."

Jeff's face grew serious and tight. "How do you know?"

"This morning I sent a list of our salesmen to Intourist. They refused to send their names over to the consulate in Washington for a visa."

Jeff did not answer immediately. He tried to analyze this suspicious news logically. Something told him that the refusal to grant visas was directly connected to him.

"Did they give you a reason for the refusal?"

Northfeld dismissed his question with a wave. "Some formality. Security checks for candidates for visas take a long time and they haven't the time or money to check out your colleagues and their relationship to the USSR. I just know what they told me. Nothing serious."

Jeff would not let it go. "Okay, but they want to keep in contact with us."

"Yes, absolutely."

Jeff pretended not to know what was to follow. "*Nu*, so how are you going to do it?"

Northfeld's voice was slightly amused. "With the help of the only one who's already been cleared by them. The one who already visited them in Moscow. The one who already worked out a successful deal."

Northfeld was silent for a moment, and then asked, "Perhaps you know him, the man whom the Russians want to take care of our business?"

Jeff answered quickly and loudly. "I know him, but the man doesn't want to go to Moscow. Is that clear?"

Northfeld held his temper in check. "Don't scream at me, please. Keep your voice down. I haven't demanded anything of you. You asked me what the situation was and I told you. What's going on here?"

Jeff felt that he had gone too far. "I'm sorry. I didn't mean anything by it."

Northfeld had needed the apology. It chipped away a bit at Jeff's iron determination and obstinacy. Jeff would be more patient and understanding of the company's needs now. Northfeld, who desperately wanted Jeff to travel, at least one more time, to Moscow, decided to work on his feelings of guilt.

"Look, Jeff, I can't understand your hesitation to help our company's interests."

Jeff tried to avoid the guilt. "But—"

Northfeld silenced him quickly. "No, no, Jeff, don't answer me. Let me speak. I said that this opposition of yours to our company's development, in a way that only you can help, is odd. But what can I do? A man has a right to his opinion."

Northfeld took a deep breath. Jeff kept his peace. He knew that his boss had not yet finished.

"And because that is the situation, and the Soviet regime isn't prepared to give visas to any of our other employees, I've informed them that we are cutting our contact with them."

Jeff was stymied. His boss had backed him into a corner. He had, in this back-handed way, saddled him with the blame for the company's future losses.

"And there's nothing to be done?" Jeff said weakly.

Northfeld felt a growing elation. "Of course there's something to be done. But you don't want to do it!"

"And besides me, there's no one else?"

"Don't you see, the Russians refuse to give anyone else a visa, and that's it."

The boss was putting this pressure, carefully camouflaged, on him. It seemed to Jeff that Northfeld was not playing fair. How could he, Jeff, explain the reason for his refusal to revisit Moscow? Still, his boss could give his loyal employee a little credit. If so, why was he pushing him so? Why was he burdening him with guilt, with the feeling that the company would collapse because of him?

The phone on Northfeld's desk buzzed with an internal call. Northfeld picked up the receiver with a casual movement and listened for a moment. His face showed surprise and he handed the receiver to Jeff.

"It's for you."

"Yes?" Jeff whispered.

"Jeff." It was the voice of the receptionist. "Someone is waiting for you. He says you have a meeting set up."

Jeff trembled in anger. The unknown man's lie infuriated him. But he kept his outward composure. Instead, he asked, "What does he look like? Jewish? Non-Jew? Black? White?"

"A Jew, Jeff. A religious Jew. Wearing a hat, not a *yarmulke*. What should I tell him?"

Jeff hesitated. On the one hand, perhaps he should send him away. Jeff had no desire to meet with him. On the other hand, he was curious to know what he had to say. This, despite an inner voice that whispered to him that no good could come out of this encounter.

"What should I tell him? He's standing here waiting."

While Jeff was still mulling over his answer, a young man with a basket filled with sandwiches walked out of the elevator and pushed open the glass doors of the office. He offered his wares to both the receptionist and the stranger who was waiting for Jeff. Both gave him an indifferent refusal. He smiled politely and turned away. The two of them, the secretary and the stranger, did not notice the slight "click" of the miniature camera secreted in the young man's watch. He had photographed the stranger.

The receptionist heard Jeff's voice.

"What did you say? He's waiting?"

"Yes."

"Let him wait until I've finished here with the boss, and then I'll come out to him."

24

Jeff finally left Northfeld's office and turned to meet his uninvited guest. Jeff walked towards him with unhurried steps. He saw him sitting in an armchair in the waiting area next to the receptionist. Jeff did not recognize him. The man was wearing a dark suit with a yellow and brown tie. The stranger had not yet noticed Jeff's approach. He was deep in a small book that he held in his hands; perhaps a *Tehillim*, perhaps a *Mishnayos*. He wore a black hat on his head; sunglasses hid his eyes.

The stranger suddenly lifted his head and saw Jeff coming closer. He closed the book, jumped out of the chair, and stood up to his full, imposing height. With a swift gesture he removed the sunglasses and gave a broad smile.

The tension that accompanied Jeff throughout his walk down the long corridor dissipated at once. He burst out into a liberating, satisfying laugh.

"Yossel!" He enthusiastically called out. Yossel, that is Yosef, was Joe Hausbinder, a friend of Jeff Handler's from his days in the Lakewood Yeshivah.

Jeff pumped the hand that his friend stretched out towards him.

But with all the joy of reunion after years of separation, he did not allow himself to lose sight of the main issue. Jeff's left arm swung over his friend's broad back, and they walked slowly towards Jeff's office. They sat down, exchanging cautious glances, each examining the other.

A secretary walked in. "Would you like to drink something? Cold or hot?"

After a pause Joe answered, "Hot."

The next inevitable question: "Coffee or tea?"

"Coffee," came the casual reply.

The secretary asked Jeff with a simple nod of her head.

"Bring two coffees please."

The door closed behind her. Jeff got right to the point.

"What's this all about, Yossel?"

"What do you mean?" Joe parried the question. "I'm not allowed to visit a friend?"

Jeff was not interested in jokes. He answered impatiently. "You know exactly what I mean. Secret meetings. The KGB and all the rest of your foolishness on the phone."

Joe laughed heartily. He looked mischievously at his tense friend.

"Look, Jeff, I really have come to you on a matter of importance. It has something to do with your trip to Russia."

Jeff interrupted him angrily. "We haven't met each other for years and you already know that I've been to Russia? Are you following me?"

Joe was silent for a minute, slowly picking up the coffee that the secretary had just brought in. He wanted to give his friend a chance to cool down.

"I'm not following you. But I found out that you are traveling."

"Not 'are traveling.' I have traveled. How did you find out?"

Joe dismissed the question with a wave of the hand. "It's not important. Really, it's not. The important thing is what next."

Jeff, increasingly uncomfortable, shifted in his chair.

"It's important to me. And as for me, there is no 'next'."

His voice was firm and determined. Joe stared at him, surprised, trying to figure out what his friend was going through to make him act so strange. But Joe had come here for a purpose; he kept his voice smooth as butter.

"Okay, okay, I'll tell you how I know. But only on the condition that you be patient and let me finish my piece. Okay?"

Jeff felt a little distressed by his impatient behavior. His friend, after all, was not to blame for the hidden pressure that Northfeld was putting on him. Though he wanted to explain to his friend the reason for his angry mood, he realized that it would be better not to do so; particularly since this conversation had something to do with his travels to Russia.

Joe stood up and turned to Jeff.

"Come and let's go out. We'll go to a restaurant and speak there."

Jeff lay startled eyes upon him. "What's wrong with my office?"

Joe was friendly. "Your office is fine. Absolutely fine, but it would be better to speak on this particular topic outside, among others."

Jeff gave a bitter laugh. He understood. "Listening in, right?"

Yossel met his glance squarely. "Listening in? It's not certain. Ninety percent certain they're not. But then again — they may be."

They sat across from each other in the small restaurant, *The Diamond Dairy*, located on the second floor of one of the buildings on 47th Street. No one gave them a second glance. They did not warrant any special attention: They resembled most of the other diners, with their religious mode of dress. This was a luncheonette favored by the 47th Street diamond dealers for a quick chat over a cup of coffee or a good meal. A place where Yossel — Joe — felt comfortable.

"You're right, Jeff, the topic is Russia. And your upcoming trip there."

Jeff bit his lips. Joe hastily continued. "You promised to be patient and hear me out to the end, right?"

Jeff did not answer.

"Listen, Jeff. You remember that a student came to you before your trip to Russia and asked you to bring a pair of *tefillin* to a certain address there?"

Jeff remembered.

"You were right in refusing."

"Why?" Jeff blurted out the question in an unnatural voice.

"Because how could you be certain it wasn't a Soviet provocation?"

"That's right."

"And that's why I just said that you were right."

Again, Jeff did not reply.

"But you should know, Jeff, that the young man is absolutely okay. He's a Russian who became religious there. Do you hear? There, in Communist Russia, in the KGB's Moscow, he became a *ba'al teshuvah*! Get it? He managed to escape via Finland and to reach the United States. It was he who revealed to us one of the most incredible dramas going on in the world today: Beneath the eye of Brezhnev, leader of the USSR, and Yuri Andropov, the head of the KGB, young Jews are learning Torah, becoming observant, doing mitzvos. Do you get it?"

Jeff was surprised but curious. With that, though, he kept his features frozen, suspicious of just where this conversation was headed. But he did interpose a question.

"What does that mean: *ba'alei teshuvah*? How can it be? Do you know what Moscow is?"

"That's just it!" Joe said eagerly. "That's the miracle of it! The wonder!"

Jeff was silent. He suddenly remembered the bearded young man sitting in the synagogue in Moscow learning, despite the eyes of the KGB agents standing like robots at the doorway. He remembered how he had watched the young man when he had pushed away, for some reason, another disheveled youth who had spoken to him for a short while.

He realized that he had not paid the bearded man the proper attention. Perhaps he was one of these *ba'alei teshuvah* that his friend from Lakewood was speaking of. He felt a slight shiver down his spine. What? Could it truly be there was a *ba'al teshuvah* there in the synagogue, on Archipova Street in Moscow? Impossible. But if not, where had he come from? Jeff felt his head swim.

"Listen, Yossel, to what I'm telling you. There are no *ba'alei teshuvah* in Moscow! Period."

Joe's eyes showed their surprise. "Why not? How do you know?"

"*Ba'alei teshuvah* don't sprout up in the air, my dear friend. They have to learn from someone. And they have to see what a religious person looks like, and what mitzvah observance means. Who showed them what a pair of *tefillin* is? Or a Jewish Shabbos? *Kashrus?* Family purity? And all of it? What are you talking about? Go visit there for one day and you'll see it's impossible. Why are you laughing, Yossel?"

Yossel was, indeed, laughing. But not a laughter of mockery. He laughed at having so shocked his friend with the news of the existence of a Jewish underground battling for Torah learning and mitzvah observance in the middle of Moscow, not far from Red Square and the Kremlin.

"And if I prove to you that it really does exist, will you cooperate?"

A red light went on in Jeff's head.

"What kind of cooperation are you suddenly talking about?"

Joe repeated his words carefully, emphasizing each one.

"If I can prove to you that there is a revolution truly beginning in Moscow, a Jewish revolution, will you cooperate with me?"

Suddenly Joe leaned forward towards Jeff and hissed, "Sit quietly. Don't look towards the door."

Jeff felt a stab of fear. "What's happening?"

"Keep talking in a natural manner, do you hear? One of them is standing there. I already recognize them, here in New York also."

Jeff was stunned. "You're scaring me. Why have you come to meet with me?"

"Don't panic so much, Jeff. I asked you not to look towards the door, that's all. The KGB doesn't like our activities. They follow us. That's all. They can't harm us. Look, he's found me."

Jeff had had his fill of this convoluted conversation. "Yossel, let me go. I want to go back to work. I simply don't understand what you want from me. I don't need any more stress. I've had enough, those two days in Moscow. Enough!"

Jeff decided to stand up, but Joe grabbed him by the hand.

"Sit down!"

For some reason Jeff obeyed the command. He was furious with himself for his weakness. He remembered his grandfather's commands, the ones that had sent him on his trip to Moscow.

Joe began to speak hurriedly. He understood that he had to reveal everything, and quickly. He cast a glance towards the door. The stranger, who didn't fit in with the rest of the diners in the small luncheonette, had disappeared. Joe took a deep breath and sighed slightly, a sigh of relief.

"Look, the *teshuvah* movement in Moscow is a fact. How did it happen and how did it develop? That's an incomparably exciting story."

"You mean the activities of Chabad?"

"No. What Chabad does is well known and praiseworthy, and it's been involved in underground activities for many years. But I'm talking about a completely different route. Does the Soviet regime know exactly what's happening? I don't know. I suspect they do. But the people in Moscow with whom we're in contact—"

"The people? Contact? Who are these 'people'? And how do you keep in touch?"

"I hear your question. Now listen. We're a group of *bnei Torah* who've decided to help the young Jews of Moscow, Leningrad, Kiev, Odessa, Vilna, Riga, and other places, to live a Jewish life under the harsh conditions of the KGB dictatorship. We're obligated to help Jews who want to return to Yiddishkeit! We can't just stand by!"

"And how do you help?"

"With the help of Jews such as you. With the help of people who travel for business or as tourists to the USSR. Their American passport protects them, understand?"

Jeff was quiet. He felt trapped. He quietly waited to hear what would come next.

"Men come from the United States and learn with the members of this Jewish underground for a week or two. They come as tourists, as businessmen. They sneak into private apartments all through the city, each time a different place, give a *shiur*, teach them how to observe mitzvos, and then rush to leave the USSR."

Jeff rubbed his hands together nervously. "Isn't it dangerous?"

"Of course it's dangerous! Who told you it wasn't dangerous?"

"But—" Jeff couldn't manage to finish his protest.

"Wait a minute, Jeff, just a minute. A little patience. Don't you think that sometimes a little sacrifice is demanded of us? If you would hear of the self-sacrifice of these boys and girls in Moscow in order to observe mitzvos you would feel you can't stay out of it. I promise you. You'll suddenly feel that you're fulfilling a mission."

Jeff's heart pounded in his chest. Where did they want him to go?

"So don't tell me, okay?"

Joe opened wide, shocked eyes at him. "That's it? You go into business to make money and forget everything you've learned in yeshivah? Jeff, I don't think I know you!"

Jeff shifted his weight. He felt as if he was suffocating, that he was powerless.

"I understand that you want me to travel to Moscow. Right?"

"Right."

"Hillel the Elder taught us, 'What is repulsive to you don't give to your friend.' Why don't you go first! And then we'll see what you say. Even without meeting someone from the secret police you feel threatened every second that you walk on the Moscow streets. You go there!"

Jeff, angry, turned his head towards the other diners, who were conducting serene discussions, laughing, unburdened. He could not meet the eyes of his former friend. Not at that moment.

"Jeff." He heard his friend's soft voice.

"What?"

"I've been to Moscow already."

Their gazes crossed. Jeff's eyes showed his surprise.

"I was there twice."

Quietly they stared at each other. Joe continued. "The first time, they called me in for an examination. The fine, pleasant boys from the KGB. No, they didn't hurt me. Heaven forbid. But I heard that one of the participants in my class, a young Russian man, a student in nuclear physics, disappeared."

He took a deep breath.

"They warned me most firmly not to dare visit a private citizen's home to teach Judaism."

Joe lapsed into silence. Then he spoke again. "It was a tough conversation, polite but firm and very, very frightening."

Joe played with his coffee cup and sipped the last few drops. "And then— I went a second time. I gave three *shiurim*. Two in Moscow and one in Leningrad. Seventeen young men and women took part in a class given each week in a different Moscow apartment. Twenty-two came to the class in Leningrad."

Silence fell between them. Joe's revelation had shocked Jeff. He sat, dumbfounded, his face expressionless, not knowing how to react.

Joe stood up. He gave a weak handshake to Jeff and said, his voice disappointed, "I'm sorry that I bothered you, Jeff. Really sorry."

Jeff did not answer. His eyes followed his friend as he slowly left the small restaurant.

At one of the more distant tables a well-dressed man slowly folded up his copy of *The New York Times* that he had been reading. He left a tip on the table and turned, also, towards the exit door.

25

natoly did not run. He forced himself to walk calmly, serenely, through the dark, frigid streets, not to draw any attention to himself. Despite his best intentions, though, he felt himself hurrying. The streets were deserted and not even an automobile passed by on the silent road. Suddenly he heard a car approach behind him, slowing down as it passed near him. Despite his racing heart Anatoly managed not to turn around towards the car. The vehicle didn't stop; it continued to make slow progress up the street until it disappeared. He gave a silent sigh of relief.

Anatoly reached the steps that led down to the nearest Metro station. Only a few people waited quietly for the train. Anatoly maintained a frigid aloofness. He did not glance around at all. He stepped into a train that pulled up a few minutes later, and sat down. He got off after a few stops and began to walk towards his house on Krasno Bogatirski Street.

In the distance, near the local pub that was still open at that hour, he could see a group of young people. They were leaning against a tree, not saying a word. He didn't notice the black Cheka parked nearby. Then he halted. In his past life, he had never been afraid of the bullies and gangs who had, with the weakening of the regime, begun to operate in the streets. But tonight, after his first encounter with the secret police at the *babushka's* home, he had changed. He bit his lip and proceeded, his caution growing as he approached.

A few steps separated him from them. Only now did he see the Cheka automobile, its engine humming in low gear. He saw, also, that they were dressed in black leather and that their hair was cut in street-gang fashion.

Suddenly, without warning, he felt a brutal kick in his neck. Instinctively he turned around to face his attacker. Not fast enough: one of the punks left his place near the tree and tripped him, leaving him lying on the ground. He could hear the wild laughter of the hoodlums enjoying the situation. His back ached; his face burned. He realized that he was in serious trouble. Should he even bother getting up? The punks would only throw him right back down onto the cold concrete. They didn't seem drunk, even though they were pretending to be. With his left hand he rubbed his chin. It was wet. Blood? Undoubtedly, blood.

In a frightened voice he asked, "What have I done to you? What do you want from me?"

The gang broke out in raucous laughter. One of the gang came closer to him and put his black-booted leg upon him, pushing down viciously. Anatoly felt his breath coming harder. Who knew how long he could last? The man repeated Anatoly's question in a whining voice: "What have I done to you? What do you want from me?"

Anatoly was convinced his end was near. At that moment he hated himself. Because of his furious anger at the university for having rejected him as a Jew, had he put himself onto this doomed path? His war of words with his mother; his demonstrative visit to the synagogue on Archipova Street. He had ignored the KGB agent's warnings and had covertly attended an underground class that had been broken up by the militia, in conjunction with the secret police. And now, because he had been outside at such late hours, he had fallen into the hands of these stupid bullies.

The hoodlum took his boot off Anatoly's chest. "Get up!" he commanded.

With great effort Anatoly got to his feet. As he got up he became a ball within the hands of the gang: One roughly grabbed the ends of his jacket and pushed him into the arms of another, who quickly pushed him with all his strength toward a third. On and on— His head spun and in only a few minutes he collapsed on the ground, completely drained of strength.

"That's it, you filthy Jew," one of his attackers hissed. "Did you think we didn't know where you were going?"

Anatoly did not react. Silence was his last and only defense in this unequal battle. These thugs were clearly on a mission. That fact was clear; otherwise, how would they have known that he was a Jew?

The brutal voice could be heard once again: "Maybe now you'll remember that we've warned you."

One last kick sent a wave of nausea through him, and then suddenly, swiftly, the bullies were gone, disappearing into their Cheka. There was the sound of an engine's roar and the car vanished into the darkness.

When the last echoes of their voices had died down and silence reigned once again on the dark street, Anatoly pulled his aching bones together, rose heavily from the sidewalk, and limped home. *You have to make sacrifices and be strong, if you want to rediscover your Jewishness,* the stranger had whispered to him, the one whom he had met in the *babushka's* house as they had fled on the rooftops from the KGB. Anatoly did not know much about sacrifice, about this Jewishness he was to rediscover, but he had learned well now the lesson of being strong.

He dragged himself home. Fortunately, his mother was already asleep. He tiptoed to the small bathroom, washed himself off and cleaned his clothing. He examined his injured chin and put a moist rag on the wound. With some difficulty he got his aching body to bed. He fell weakly into it, with no strength left, without bothering to undress. For many long hours he lay there, unmoving in the darkness, in the deep silence of night, without managing to fall asleep.

Jeff returned to his office and retreated to his room. He tried to work, but it was too difficult. He pulled out some packages of diamonds from his safe and scattered them on his desk, but he could not sort through them. He was angry that his friend's words had so deeply disturbed him. He suspected that Joe had succeeded in putting a crack into his iron-clad decision not to return to the city of Andropov and Brezhnev. The fact that his friend Joe had actually traveled to Moscow, not on business but specifically for underground activities — and Jeff tended to believe his story — with the sole purpose of teaching Torah, confused him. Here was a living, brave example of the obligation to learn and to teach. He knew the difference between teaching in a yeshivah in Boro Park, Williamsburg, or Jerusalem and teaching a group of young people, thirsty for Torah learning, under the noses of the KGB. A spark of adventure flashed for a moment within him, a spark that Jeff took care to extinguish with a sharp wave of the hand, like one shooing away a bothersome fly.

The telephone gave a low ring. An internal call. Jeff put on the speaker. He heard the secretary's voice.

"Jeff, the boss is on the line. Do you want to speak with him?"

"No. Absolutely not, I don't want to. But put him through anyway."

The boss was already on the line. "Hi, Jeff." Mr. Northfeld's voice was warm and inviting.

"Yes," Jeff answered, controlled.

"Listen, Jeff, Intourist has rejected another candidate. I was talking with Eddie Heisler. He doesn't work for us, but you must know him. He's an agent. No? Interesting. He's been here often. I offered him the trip. He was actually excited about it, but over there they were less excited by the idea."

"Yes," Jeff answered, trying to be courteous. The information simply didn't interest him.

"Jeff." His boss's voice hesitated slightly.

"Yes?" This time, there was just a tinge of curiosity in his reply.

"The people at Intourist mentioned you by name. They wanted to know why you weren't the candidate for the next trip."

Silence. Finally, Jeff burst out. "It seems that someone in Moscow is interested in my returning. I told you that already."

"Why do you think so?"

"Don't you see it too, Mr. Northfeld?"

Jeff was angry. After a moment's silence Northfeld asked, "Did you do something there to make them interested specifically in you?"

With an effort Jeff controlled himself.

"You asked me that yesterday. Has Intourist told you something?"

"No, no, they didn't say anything. I see that my questions are upsetting you. In any case I wanted you to know the situation, the situation within the company, regarding the matter—"

After a moment's delay he added, "And my own opinion also, Jeff. Bye."

The line went dead. Jeff replaced the receiver and whispered to himself, "The pressure is starting."

He bit his bottom lip and determined even more not to give in, if only to prove to his boss that he was no wimp. The Intourist determination that he and he alone come only deepened his belief that his suspicions were well founded. Someone in that city remembered him and was interested, it seemed, in asking him some questions. And here, within his iron-clad decision, suddenly came, in an increasingly powerful flow, thoughts of his friend from Lakewood days, and his words of *mussar* to him.

The next few hours passed fruitlessly. He sat by his table, not moving, deep within his own thoughts. The heavy silence in the room when the window was shut, keeping out the endless noise of the traffic in the street below, added to the feeling of oppressiveness. Jeff had no idea how much time had passed when suddenly the hum of his phone broke the silence.

"Yes."

Again, it was the secretary.

"Hi, Jeff. Your wife's on the line."

Jeff took a deep breath. His wife never called, except in the most urgent situations. What could she possibly want?

"Put her on, please."

"Jeff?" He could hear her voice.

"Yes?"

"Hi. How are you doing?"

He responded with questions of his own. "What's happened? Why are you calling in the middle of the day?"

"First of all, it's not midday anymore. It's late afternoon."

"Okay. But why are you calling?"

"Your father called from Israel."

Jeff suddenly felt a suffocating mass jump from his heart to his choking throat. A spontaneous scream almost burst out of him: What has happened? But somehow he managed to control himself, and simply said one word, coolly and with feigned indifference. "Yes?"

"Your father asked me to tell you that your grandfather is sick. He's in Tel Hashomer Hospital."

The headache landed onto Jeff with a thud. The terrible throbbing began in his left temple, covering a good portion of his forehead, and pressed onto his eyes. He burst out furiously: "Another try at pressuring me? Not interested!"

Miriam was astounded. "What's wrong with you, Jeff? Your father is worried about Grandfather's condition. He wanted you to know about it. What's happened to you?"

Jeff recovered swiftly. "Sorry. Nothing happened."

"Who's pressuring you?"

"Really, it's nothing. Leave it alone. It's nothing at all."

Miriam realized that he was hiding something, but did not want to push him too hard. She simply said, "I think you should call him to show you're concerned. Don't you agree?"

"Yes, absolutely. I'll come home right after *Ma'ariv* and call. You know that I try not to make personal calls from the office."

"Okay. Bye. And I hope he gets well soon."

"Amen."

The conversation came to an end.

Jeff exhaustedly stood up. His workday was finished. He felt he had to rest a little and organize his thoughts. He put all the merchandise into the safe, locked it with a firm gesture, and left the office. He hurried to his car, parked in the underground lot, and headed towards Flatbush. For some reason the ride was smoother than usual; in a short while he was already at home. A cup of coffee wouldn't hurt; maybe it would even make him feel better.

But as he was about to turn off the engine in his driveway he changed his mind. He turned the car around and headed towards the Mirrer Yeshivah a few blocks away. He walked into the *beis midrash,* looking for the Russian student.

26

J eff stood at the doorway of the *beis midrash,* alive with the sound of men learning by themselves or with *chavrusos.* His eyes skimmed over the large room, searching for the young Russian man. He wasn't certain he was actually a student here, but since he had seen him *davening Ma'ariv* in this *beis midrash,* there certainly was a chance that he would meet him again, particularly because *Ma'ariv* was to begin shortly.

Jeff hesitantly stepped into the *beis midrash.* Some of the men lifted their heads toward the stranger wandering through the aisles between the benches, his eyes searching row after row.

A young man leaning on a *shtender* not far from where Jeff stood lifted his head suddenly and looked at Jeff. He stood up and approached him.

"Are you looking for someone?" he asked softly. It was apparent that he was trying to help.

"Yes, a Russian."

The young man grinned.

"*Baruch Hashem* there are several young men from Russia learning in yeshivah here. Do you know his name?"

Jeff got the message. It seemed that his friend, Joe Hausbinder, was right. Something was happening among the young people of Russia, if several had already arrived to learn in America.

"No," he said hastily. "I don't know it. He has a short black beard, and he's not particularly tall."

The young man made an effort to figure out who the student could be. Finally he held out his arms out in a gesture that indicated he did not know. Jeff thanked him with a nod and with a weak smile turned towards the end of the auditorium, near the bookcases. He would glance through a *sefer*, he decided, until it was time for *Ma'ariv*.

The prayers were already over and the Russian young man had not appeared. Jeff returned home. He knew that a difficult conversation with his father in Israel awaited him.

"Hi," he called to his wife as he walked into the house.

"Hi. I'm coming right down." He could hear her voice coming from the second floor, together with the merry sound of his youngsters refusing to go to sleep.

Jeff suddenly felt a strong urge to see his children. He raced up the stairs. He had just entered the room when his three children jumped upon him with joyful cries of "Daddy, Daddy!"

Strange, thought Jeff, as he patted, hugged, and kissed the children. *What are these strange feelings that I'm experiencing now?* He felt almost as if he were parting from them, an odd, disturbing emotion. The thought passed through his head, quick as a shooting star: *Am I going to travel there?*

His eyes met those of his wife. Her eyes, too, were not tranquil. In order to cover her confusion she gave him the latest news.

"Your father called again."

"What's the situation?" he whispered in response.

"I understand that it's not good. Your grandfather is in intensive care. He needs *rachamei Shamayim*."

Jeff was silent. For some reason even the children grew serious and went quietly to their beds. After a moment's thought, he blurted out, "And he blames me, naturally, because I didn't want to go to Russia. That's why it happened."

His wife, annoyed, put out the light in the children's room and turned toward the stairway that led downstairs. Jeff followed behind her.

"Your father didn't say a word. Why do you immediately think that they're blaming you?"

Jeff did not reply. He himself did not know why he had blurted out the sentence. He had no proof of his claim. Despite that, he could not avoid the feeling that even without words the guilt was being placed upon him, because of his firm declaration that he would not go to Moscow to search for the *tefillin*.

Jeff and his wife reached the ground floor. Miriam went to the kitchen to prepare dinner; Jeff turned toward the living room to call his father. Despite his fear of wiretaps Jeff decided to make the call from home. He picked up the receiver and began to dial. Suddenly he heard the doorbell ring. Jeff put the receiver down and listened. The ring of the bell was long and harsh.

Anatoly finally managed to fall asleep at dawn, when the difficult thoughts attacking his spirit finally quieted down. Even so his slumber was uneasy, with the nightmare of the evening's events still disturbing him. In his short, confused dreams he could still feel the burning humiliation he had suffered at the hands of those who had beaten him.

A sharp pain in his forehead finally awakened him. The terrible pain brought him right back to the events of his difficult night. He rose wearily from his bed, put a banned American record on his ancient stereo and, after eating something he had found in the kitchen, went in search of something to do. The pile of books stacked near his bed did not interest him. His thoughts drifted to the strange meeting he had taken part in the previous evening. He had barely understood what the visitor from America had been talking about; as a result, his eyes had wandered to the participants sitting around the narrow table. Anatoly had noticed that the vast majority of them were young men and women, probably students. He did not know any of them, though it was certainly possible he had met them before. He noticed the lines of firmness and determination etched upon all of their faces, as if to say: We are in the struggle, and that is why we are here. He was particularly taken by the intense concentration with which they listened to the speaker, who had lectured in English, then translated each paragraph into Russian.

The speaker, too, aroused his curiosity and interest. This was the first time that he had met a Jew from the Western world up close, and a religious Jew at that, a theologian! Anatoly noticed that the man had been carefully dressed in a good suit; his beard was trimmed and his handsome red tie hung neatly from his neck to his belt. The lecturer spoke calmly, and Anatoly tried, by staring closely at him and following his every move, to understand the life of Jews outside of the Iron Curtain. It was hard for him to imagine, but the man's tranquility held him riveted.

The stereo grew silent. Anatoly awoke from his reverie and slowly chose another record. The man had spoken, he remembered, of the nation of Israel, of the Torah that it possessed, of the laws specific to Jews. He mentioned the great war of the fascist Nazis and the Jews they had murdered. He had discussed Babi Yar. But Anatoly, despite the simultaneous translation, had found it hard to understand the connection between everything the guest from America had touched upon.

Anatoly's hand occasionally stroked his aching chin. The pains in his back and feet were also not particularly pleasant. Without warning a powerful surge of anger passed through him. He flung the cup that he was holding in his hand at the wall opposite him. The force of the blow ripped the faded wallpaper a little, but the cup remained intact and unbroken. It rolled about on the floor and finally came to a stop, looking desolate and ashamed, in a corner of the room.

Anatoly calmed down. The fury that he had felt against his attackers melted with the flinging of the cup, as if through it he had avenged himself for the humiliation. Now he sat at the edge of his bed, slightly tense but contemplative and serious, able to make a careful reckoning of all that was happening to him. In reality, from the moment that he had decided to rebel against Soviet society because it had refused him entry to the university, he had been endlessly examining himself to see if he was acting properly. He had been full of doubts about the risky course he had been taking, because of the dangers of the long arm of the Party and the KGB that protected it, ensuring that all toed the socialist line. Last night's blows were merely a concrete symbol of the danger in which he found himself; an ominous symbol. And yet he could not ignore the feeling of liberation that he had enjoyed when joining with covert forces, in opposition to the ways prescribed by the regime and the Party, or the possibility given to him to think his own thoughts. And last night, at the secret meeting that was cut off by the appearance of the militia, he had noticed a brand new emotion within him: a feeling of belonging. True, he had not understood much of what the lecturer had said. But what he did understand was that at that moment he had become joined with the Jewish nation, oppressed and downtrodden, but still a great people. And they were his people.

Anatoly stood up. He tensed his limbs and got the blood flowing. New energies pulsed through his muscles. Right now he knew that the feeling of belonging that had begun to beat within his heart last night would overcome all the blows and dangers along the way. He pulled on his leather jacket and decided to go to the synagogue on Archipova. Perhaps he would meet the bearded man there again. This time he would speak differently to him, now that he had seen Anatoly last night at the home of the *babushka*.

Jeff hurried to the door and opened it. He was totally surprised: The young Russian stood there.

"Good evening," the young man said courteously, in a slightly amenable tone. "May I come in?"

Jeff, shocked, didn't answer, but he opened the door wide and with his right hand gestured toward the living room. The Russian entered with small steps, his hands crossed on his chest and his body stooped slightly. Jeff followed him attentively, staring curiously at him as he seated himself on the couch — actually, it was on the edge of the couch, as if doing something he shouldn't. Clearly, the young man was tense.

Jeff sat down across from him, on his favorite leather recliner. He looked at his guest, waiting for him to speak. And the Russian did, indeed, begin.

"I heard that you were looking for me."

"That's right. How did you find out?"

"They told me in yeshivah. I was late for *Ma'ariv*."

Jeff wasn't satisfied. "I understand. But how did they know that I was looking for you? They don't know who I am."

"True, they didn't know."

Jeff didn't understand.

"So how did you know?"

The young Russian shrugged. "I guessed."

Jeff lifted a skeptical eyebrow. "You guessed?"

"That's right." The Russian's gaze was straightforward and open.

"How did you guess?"

The Russian was silent. His eyes remained as clear as they had been, but now Jeff could see a spark of mystery within them. The Russian lowered his eyes, and Jeff's curiosity remained unsatisfied. After a minute of heavy silence the Russian added, "And that's why I've come."

Now it was Jeff's turn to take the conversation into his hands.

"Well, you're right. I was looking for you."

Jeff pulled a Marlboro out of a cigarette case lying on the mahogany table that stood near him. He bent forward and offered one to the Russian, who refused.

"I don't smoke."

When the smoke rings drifting out of Jeff's mouth had finally reached the ceiling, Jeff began a hailstorm of questions:

"You're from Russia?"

"Yes."

"From where?"

"Moscow."

"The city itself?"

"Yes, the city itself."

"Do you perhaps know a street by the name of Krasno Bogatirski?"

The Russian wrinkled his brow. His answer came slowly and with emphasis. "Krasno Bogatirski? No. I haven't heard of it. Why do you want to know?"

Jeff waved the question off. "Nothing, just asking."

Jeff clearly saw the young Russian's suspicious look and hastened on to a new topic.

"What's your name?"

"Boris. Today Shmuel Boris Yeruslavski."

Jeff was silent. He looked for the right words to open the conversation. He took a deep drag on what was left of the cigarette in his hand; his eyes wandered aimlessly from one point to the other on the wall across from him.

The Russian broke the silence. "Why were you looking for me?"

"Hmm. How can I say this?"

Jeff's wife suddenly came in from the kitchen. In her hands was a tray bearing a pot of boiling water, two cups, a small milk container, tea bags, coffee, and a sugar holder. Without a word she put the tray down on the small living room table that stood between the sofa and the recliner. She went back to the kitchen and after a few moments returned with a tray of cake.

"Sit down. Stay here, I want you to hear this too," Jeff whispered to her. She sat down on a chair a short distance away from the men and listened quietly as her husband suddenly shot out the direct question:

"Tell me, Boris or Shmuel, whatever you like — do you work for the KGB?"

Igor decided not to back down. He could clearly see the confusion of his father, the KGB agent, when he had asked him the direct question: "What does it mean, that we're Jews?" His father's hesitation gave Igor strength; he felt a process of liberation from his subjugation of the spirit.

"Do you have an answer for me?" he challenged his father, who sat by his desk, unmoving.

Dimitri Grasimov looked at his son with blank eyes. Igor's question had no answer and any answer there was did not particularly interest Dimitri. His brain whirled, searching for a way to get his son to contribute to his plans for clearing his name, plans so necessary at this time. Dimitri continued to speak pleasantly, before he would be forced to take a firmer line with his wayward son. One thing was certain: This could go no further.

"Look, Igor, in our Soviet regime the word 'Jew' has no meaning. We continue to build here the homeland of man, of the Soviet worker, the peace-loving Soviet citizen who is prepared to make great sacrifices for peace—"

"The invasion of Afghanistan, for instance."

Dimitri, offended by his son's sarcasm, felt his face redden with increasing anger.

"Are you prepared to keep your mouth shut while I'm talking?"

He stood up in a threatening movement. Igor sensed his mother appear behind his back from the other room. She always knew when to turn up in order to cool down Dimitri's fury. This time, though, he would not be appeased:

"Don't forget, I am an officer in the Cometee! I won't have mercy even on my own son if things come to such a pass! Colleagues of mine send their sons who misbehave to mental hospitals for medical treatment. I believe that you, too, are mentally ill."

Igor did not know what had come over him. For the first time he felt his fear of his father disappear. The wild and violent words of his friend yesterday, when Igor had told him that he was Jewish, had released some dormant, coiled spring in his heart; a spring whose very existence he had never suspected. Yesterday he had stood before his destiny, as a Jew. He felt that he could not let the matter go. Away with all the nonsense that his father proclaimed, of the fair and just society in which all men were equals, a society of labor, a society of equality where nationalism had no place, etc. — all the nonsense that he had heard all through the years in various schools and in the Komosol youth movement. All these empty slogans had been shattered yesterday near the wall where his good friend had struck him, spitting the word "Jew" into his face with foam on his lips, murder in his eyes, and hatred in his heart.

Igor answered quietly, in a voice that could barely be heard.

"You know what, Father, I won't destroy your progress at work. I'll disappear. I'll simply disappear out of your life. You can tell everyone that you've put me into an insane asylum. They'll promote you because of your sacrifice for everything you say you believe in. Even your salary will rise, and who knows what else? And me, you will never see again."

He took a few steps towards his father.

"And I will not rest until I've gotten the answer: What is a Jew? Do you understand?"

The last words came out of his mouth as a scream, like a man suddenly sustaining a mortal wound. Dimitri lost all control and tried to grab him, but Igor managed to avoid his grasping hands. He flew towards the doorway, burst through it, and disappeared into the darkness of the Soviet night that hung over Moscow — like a balled fist.

As he raced away he could hear his mother's screams, the screams of a desperate animal:

"Igor, don't go! Igor, don't be afraid of Father. IGOR!"

27

Boris, or, to use his Hebrew name, Shmuel, wasn't offended by Jeff's blunt question. Jeff did not see any indication of confusion in the face of his surprising challenge. Nor was Boris in any rush to reply. His eyes glimmered in a questioning gaze. Finally he said, "And if I'm not a KGB agent, how can I convince you of that, Mr. Handler?"

In fact Jeff did not know how he could be persuaded. Wasn't it obvious to him that Boris would deny all connection with the multitentacled organization? Since he had returned from Moscow Jeff had felt this strange feeling coming over him, causing him to suspect that Soviet spies were following him. He knew that he was exaggerating, but certain inexplicable events had raised the suspicions within him. He answered casually, as if admitting his culpability. "You're right, Boris."

"Shmuel," he hurried to correct him.

"Shmuel, let it be Shmuel. You know that I was in Moscow for a few days and there I felt this phenomenon of every man suspecting his friend."

"That's true. I know."

Jeff laughed.

"So I guess I've become a bit Russian myself. I caught it from them. I am suspicious of every Russian who speaks with me."

Shmuel did not laugh. *It seems*, the thought raced through Jeff's mind, *as though in Russia even laughter was forbidden.* Boris/Shmuel slowly poured himself a cup of coffee with a slow movement. He sweetened it with sugar, said the blessing of *Shehakol* with great concentration, enunciating every word, and took a sip. Somehow, the *berachah* relieved Jeff's suspicion and anxiety somewhat.

Jeff asked, "If you're from Moscow, how did you become observant?"

Boris took a deep breath.

"You obviously weren't really in Moscow, if you haven't heard about my friends there."

"I was in Moscow and didn't hear. Moscow is a big place."

"Yes, Moscow is large, but not Jewish Moscow. Were you in the synagogue in Archipova?"

"Yes I was."

"*Nu?*"

"What, *nu*? I met a few old men there and one, who introduced himself as the *gabbai*, didn't let me speak with the others."

A bitter smile appeared on Boris's face.

"Oh, him? He's a KGB agent."

After a moment's silence and a few sips of coffee he asked, "And you didn't see in the corner near the table a young bearded man learning Torah?"

Jeff remembered.

"Yes, yes, of course I saw. It was amazing. Until that moment I knew that Torah study was prohibited, particularly in Moscow, particularly for the young."

Boris seemed to awaken from a dream. "You saw him." His voice held a tremor of emotion. "If so, you saw it all!"

"What does that mean: I saw it all?"

"My friends! The *teshuvah* movement of Moscow's Jewish young people learning Torah secretly, keeping the mitzvos underground, not just observing them but sacrificing for them!"

Jeff grew defensive. "But I only saw one with a beard."

"Yes. But he is our leader, the leader who can do all, our rabbi. Even the KGB didn't manage to break him."

Jeff did not answer. He and his wife exchanged swift glances.

"I saw," Jeff said with obvious hesitation, "the opposite, actually. I saw how a young man who entered the *beis midrash* approached him, asked him questions about learning about Judaism, and the bearded man answered him quite rudely. He very firmly pushed him away."

Boris put the cup of coffee down upon the table.

"Impossible."

Jeff poured himself a cup and sipped it slowly.

"That's what I saw with my own eyes, Shmuel."

Shmuel was adamant. "I am certain that your eyes didn't see everything. The eyes of a Jew in Moscow are not those of a young Jew in New York."

After a short silence he added, "And I, Boris, today know both types of eyes."

Jeff did not really want to get into an argument with the Jewish youth about what eyes could see or not. He was more curious to know what had brought the Russian to his house. True, Jeff had been looking for him during *Ma'ariv* at Mirrer Yeshivah but it was obvious that the man was trying to sell him something.

Boris continued. "I am certain, Mr. Handler, that the bearded man — I won't tell you his name — took care of the young man who approached him. It's not possible that he left him on his own. Perhaps there were some KGB agents standing there at the time and because of that he didn't want to speak with the young man. I don't know. But believe me: He didn't abandon him. Do you believe me, Mr. Handler?"

Jeff decided to cut the meeting short. He gave his watch a swift glance. It was 8:10.

"Let's get down to business," he said in purposeful tones. "What's brought you here to me? What do you want to tell me?"

"This topic."

"What topic?"

"The topic of Moscow's *ba'alei teshuvah*. Last time, when you traveled to Moscow, you didn't want to take a pair of *tefillin* with you. I hope that next time you travel, and from what I understand that may be in the near future, you will agree to take the *tefillin* for my brother."

Jeff's fury erupted all at once. Another person getting involved in his personal battle against a trip to Moscow? He wriggled uncomfortably in his recliner and instinctively glanced at his wife, who declared firmly. "My husband will not travel there again. It's too dangerous for him."

Her firmness surprised Boris, and he asked hesitantly, "Why should it be dangerous?"

"It's dangerous," she repeated without further explanation.

"Why do you think that I am about to return to Moscow?" asked Jeff.

Boris gave a broad smile. "I know," he answered in a soft and quiet voice, his face wearing a mysterious cast. Jeff's suspicions of the man were aroused anew. With some difficulty he controlled his temper, that was ready to explode. His wife stood up and hurried to the kitchen, like one needing some activity as therapy, returning with cups full of multihued ice cream.

Jeff would not give in. "Why, sir, do you think that I will be traveling to Russia again in the near future? You must answer me."

Jeff was firm and serious in his demand; Boris could feel it.

"Your friend, Joe Hausbinder, told me."

Jeff was taken aback. "Joe Hausbinder? What do you have to do with him?"

"We're friends and we work together."

"Work at what?"

"At what I'd like to talk to you about right now."

"Okay, but he told you I was going to Russia? To Moscow? I don't understand." Jeff was upset. "I told him plainly that I wouldn't go and I wasn't preparing any trip."

Boris smiled again. "Yes, he told me. But he added that everyone refuses at the beginning, and then they go. So he figures you will too."

Jeff's fingers drummed nervously on his leg. "My friend Joe," he said, "is certainly a smart man, but this time he's mistaken. Absolutely mistaken."

Boris did not answer, he just lowered his eyes. He did not want to infuriate his host any longer with a look that clearly said, "But I know that you will be going."

After a short silence Jeff asked, "By the way, did Joe send you to me?"

"No. You looked for me in Mirrer Yeshivah, so I came."

"Okay, what do you want from me?"

For a considerable length of time Boris told the story of his life. In his heavily accented English he told of the adventures he'd undergone from the time he had awoken, early one Moscow morning, to face a sharp internal pressure that forced him to search for the answer to the question of what it meant to be a Jew. No, he had never felt the lash of anti-Semitism. All his friends in high school and college, where he was studying electrical engineering, knew that he was "Yevrei" but he'd never seen anything strange in their behavior toward him. He knew that anti-Semitism existed but had never encountered any.

Yet one day it happened. He heard about a forceful demonstration of Georgian Jews at the Presidential Palace in which they had vociferously demanded, in a way that brooked no misunderstanding: Let my people go. How had he heard of it, when there was no publicity in the newspapers? A Jewish friend, a student in the nautical engineering department, had whispered the news to him as they walked home together one evening. The Jewish student had described to him how they had entered the palace during an official presidential reception for foreign guests, how they had sat down on the ground and had begun to read the Torah portion that speaks of Moshe's demand: Let My people go so that they shall serve Me. He told him how the demonstrators had reveled in the confusion and inability of the KGB to respond immediately to the odd situation forced upon them by the Georgian Jews. The KGB agents could not forcibly remove the demonstrators from the hall, not in front of all the foreign diplomats wandering in and out.

Boris remembered how he had felt at that moment: Something in his heart had changed; the story had transformed him. And he began to wonder about the concept of being a Jew.

One day he noticed that one of the students in his department, a Jew like himself, a good friend, was spending too much time near the blackboard. Most of the students weren't in the classroom at that time, and the lecturer, too, was absent. His friend stood by the board, acting as if he were drawing what looked to be engineering symbols, but the chalk remained on the desk and not in his hand. Boris told how he approached him and saw him whispering to himself. Boris was certain that the young man had lost his mind. But with a smile his friend gestured to Boris that he should wait for a few minutes.

Boris waited, and the friend eventually explained to him that he had been *davening* the *Shemoneh Esrei* prayer of *Minchah*, because he was afraid that he wouldn't have time before sunset. His friend begged him not to let on to anyone, as it could be dangerous. Boris told Jeff and his wife that at the time he didn't understand what his friend was talking about. What was it, to pray? What was the meaning of *Shemoneh Esreh* and the importance of sunset? But since they were good friends he was interested in what he was talking about, and they discussed it many times.

At the beginning, despite their camaraderie, his friend remained distant, and explained things with great restraint and hesitation. Boris felt the little he heard of Judaism tugging at his heart, but his friend could not satisfy his thirst. Months passed before his friend revealed to him, a little at a time, step by step, the existence of groups of students covertly learning about Judaism, of young people doing their all to observe mitzvos to the best of their ability, given the possibilities open to them. Finally he told him about the bearded man who had rebelled against society's conventions, first because of anti-Semitism he had encountered in college and the army, later because he had recognized the truth of Judaism, to the point where he was prepared to give his life for it by organizing groups to provoke the regime of the KGB.

Jeff and his wife listened with rapt interest to Boris's story. They tried not to ask irrelevant questions, only what was needed to gain a better understanding of the topic. They also did their best not to be infected by the growing fervor and enthusiasm of the Russian narrator.

Shmuel described to them the covert meetings, how word was passed from one to the other, the attempts to slip out of the traps set by the KGB, who continually followed them, and their efforts to observe mitzvos under the KGB agents' noses — not even giving up on praying *Minchah* in a college classroom. Boris also told of summer camps that the bearded man had set up far from Moscow, far from the scrutiny of KGB agents, in *dachas* — summer houses — set up in the forests. Here, in what were ostensibly vacation resorts, they conducted seminars on many topics. Here, too, representatives of the regime would appear occasionally, imprisoning some of the participants, sending the rest back home with stern warnings.

Boris spoke, with increasing warmth, of Jews hoarding flour in order to bake matzahs in home ovens, distributing them afterwards to the many young people who had chosen not to eat *chametz;* of *sedarim* conducted secretly, as in the time of the Inquisition; how they celebrated *bris milah* and even ritually slaughtered kosher meat. All the activities that in New York were no big deal, in Moscow, in Leningrad, in Riga, and Vilna and other cities were functions of massive efforts and perpetual battles against all those who would stop them — including their own Communist parents.

Boris spoke particularly of the brave American Jews, of rabbis and businessmen who traveled to Moscow under any pretense, endangering themselves by attending the covert evening meetings in order to give a lesson in the weekly Torah portion, to tell the history of the Jewish people, to teach Mishnah or Halachah, or to give a class in Jewish ethics. Not infrequently, Boris reported, the Cometee agents would burst in on such a lesson, terrorizing the participants. Often these guest lecturers would be deported from Russia the very next day, with a stern warning never to return or to involve themselves in anti-Soviet activities. Yet there were those who did return, and they returned bravely, waving their American passports as some kind of protective shield.

Boris gave a small, miserly smile. "You don't know, Mr. Handler, what important missions these Americans undertook when they arrived. Suddenly we felt we weren't alone. We were given the strength to continue in our approach to Torah life. It makes us feel that our fellow Jews in the United States haven't abandoned us and that their hearts beat together with ours."

Boris sat for a long while, describing the Moscow *teshuvah* movement. Suddenly the clock gave twelve beeps, signaling midnight. He stood up from his place.

"I apologize for having stolen so much of your time. I feel it's my mission to tell our American brethren of what is happening to us. Maybe that's why I succeeded in escaping."

Jeff, too, stood up. His face did not reveal a trace of what he was feeling in his heart.

"No, no, it's all right," he said.

"It was actually very interesting, very moving," his wife added.

The two escorted him to the door. The silence, the quiet of midnight, fell upon the house after she had locked the door. Jeff and his wife did not exchange a word. Jeff poured himself another cup of coffee.

Suddenly his wife, already going up to their room, called down to him. "Jeff, we completely forgot, you've got to call your father."

"Yes, I did forget. I'm coming up; I'll call from there. It's 7 o'clock in the morning in Ramat Gan, so that's okay: Abba will still be in the house before *Shacharis*."

Jeff climbed the stairs and sat down to make the call. As he dialed, the tension grew in his heart, along with the fear of what news he would hear from Israel.

"Hello, Abba, good morning, what's happening?"

His father sighed. "It doesn't sound too good."

"What does that mean?"

"Grandfather is in intensive care, heart trouble. He doesn't seem to have the will to fight for his life."

Jeff was quiet. His mind was feverishly at work; the thoughts raced wildly through his head.

"Is it — because of me?"

His father was quick to reply. "Look, everything is from Heaven. What do I know? Maybe. Maybe it had some influence, but don't blame yourself too much."

Jeff was quiet again, this time for quite a while.

"Abba."

"Yes?"

His father could clearly hear Jeff's breaths coming fast, labored. His wife, too, noticed that her husband was undergoing some kind of metamorphosis and she watched him, fascinated. She saw that he was gripping the receiver tightly in his clenched hand.

"Abba?"

"Yes."

"Look, Abba, if you whisper to Grandfather that I will go to Moscow again, that I will try once more, do you think that might help?"

His father, shocked, did not reply at once. "Do I know? Maybe. Actually, I think so. Yes, that's right. He was a little disappointed after speaking with you. I think that it will truly have some influence on him."

Jeff was still holding onto the receiver. He threw a frightened, swift glance towards his wife. She walked towards him and waited impatiently for what would happen next.

"Abba?"

"Yes?"

"Then tell him that I'll go, I'll go soon, maybe even next week. Tell him that I'll give it one more try, okay?"

Jeff heard his father's tremulous voice.

"I'll tell him; of course I'll tell him. Maybe even this morning. Thanks, Jeff. And good night."

His father hung up. Jeff stood opposite his wife, trembling. His face was pale in the cold clear light of the fluorescent lamp.

"Abba was very moved," he said, trying to break the tension.

"Yes," she said evenly.

"I've decided to go."

She looked at him and said, "Jeff?"

"What?"

"This time, I'm going with you."

Jeff's eyes opened wide. She quickly added, "Don't worry, there'll be a reason for it. Maybe I can give a lesson to the women. Who knows?"

Jeff did not answer.

natoly arrived at the synagogue at 7:30 in the morning. When he reached the narrow street leading to the entrance of the imposing building he noticed a black Cheka automobile parked not far from the wide stairs that led up to the synagogue facade. He halted for a minute. Then he took a deep breath and decided to pass by without giving it any notice. From the corner of his eyes he saw that two KGB agents were sitting inside, one speaking into a two-way radio, the other tightly gripping the steering wheel. Anatoly knew that it wasn't for his sake that they were sitting there watching the synagogue. No one knew that he had decided this morning to come to Archipova. And yet he could not be quite sure. He wondered if these two had taken part yesterday in the "inaugural ceremony" near his home. If so —

Anatoly passed the car and with slow, confident steps climbed the wide stone stairway. He disappeared behind the wooden door into the building. The entranceway was dim, giving it a dismal and gloomy atmosphere. Anatoly opened the door to the synagogue itself. Inside he saw a number of people bent over their *siddurim* in various corners of the room. His eyes fell upon the bearded man sitting at the same place that he had been in before, next to a wide low table. Near the entrance stood the same non-Jew who had accosted him on the street after his first visit in order to warn him. He was standing motionless, his sturdy arms crossed on his chest. He wore dark sunglasses that concealed his eyes and made his upright bearing seem somehow more threatening. Anatoly tried to ignore him completely and walked directly to where the bearded man was sitting. The man was bent over an oversized book that was open before him; he made no sign of having noticed the stranger who sat down next to him.

Anatoly sat without moving, without opening his mouth. His eyes were riveted upon the face of the bearded man sitting opposite him. Occasionally he tried to glance into the open book that seemed to have captured the man's interest so completely, but he did not understand what was written there. After about a quarter of an hour in which absolutely nothing happened the bearded man lifted his head, gave Anatoly a swift glance, but made no sign of having ever seen him before. He lowered his gaze and peered firmly between the lines of the book, without saying a word.

Anatoly was offended. He could not understand this infuriating behavior. With all that, he continued to sit motionless, hoping that the thick wall of ice would shatter. On his way to the synagogue an hour earlier he had resolved to speak with the bearded man, no matter what. Whatever the price, he would set forth before him his problem and force him to solve it. Anatoly realized that he had reached his final destination. He had no desire to return to his mother's house. He urgently needed a home, a shelter, friends, particularly since he had already been marked by the KGB. Some sixth sense told him that the bearded man held the keys, the solution to his problem. The man radiated serenity, leadership, and the authority of a person who knows how to get what he wants.

His utter disregard of Anatoly lasted way too long for Anatoly's taste. Because of a fear of the frigid reaction he had had last time, Anatoly was loath to begin the conversation. He sat quietly and waited with patience that grew thinner and thinner. The bearded man showed no sign of changing his approach. He was immersed in his studies. Occasionally he would walk to the bookshelf, which contained two or three tattered old volumes, and pull one out. An inner voice told Anatoly that the bearded man was not really paying attention to their contents. Anatoly watched his every move. The bearded man placed the books on the table in front of him, in the empty space between him and Anatoly. With a strange movement he lifted all the books and looked at what was beneath them; then, he placed them back on the table. All through this he did not look at Anatoly at all.

After these activities the bearded man returned to his learning, as if nothing at all had occurred. Anatoly noticed that the man was constantly writing in a notebook that was open in front of him. As he learned he swayed in his place, one hand gently stroking his beard. Anatoly had never seen someone learn in what seemed such a nervous manner; this, despite the air of serenity and peace that the bearded man gave off in his impressive appearance.

Anatoly felt a touch of bitterness in this strange relationship. After all, he wasn't a complete stranger to the man, in the classic sense of the word. Hadn't he met him last night in the *babushka's* home? Didn't he warrant just one friendly word? A drop of notice?

Anatoly realized that the man watching by the entrance door was scrutinizing them with penetrating eyes. The moment Anatoly's gaze fell upon him, the man looked hurriedly at someone else. *Maybe,* the thought flashed through his mind, *maybe that's the reason — those KGB eyes — that the bearded man is ignoring me.*

Anatoly decided to get up and continue his aimless wanderings through the city's streets until he had figured out what he should do. At that moment the bearded man stood up and left the synagogue, not looking around him at all. Anatoly was bewildered by the swiftness with which the man had anticipated his move. It seemed to Anatoly that he had heard the man whisper, in a voice that was no voice: "Stay." In any case he stayed, not moving from his seat. Then he began to touch the holy books lying there before him on the table. This was the first time in his life that he had touched a Jewish book. Carefully, with awe and respect, he pulled the large book toward him. He felt that with this he was connecting himself to something ancient, something that mysteriously belonged to him. The bearded man, Anatoly realized, had risen swiftly, leaving the book open. It seemed strange to him. Anatoly looked into the book. He did not understand what was written; the Hebrew letters were completely unfamiliar.

Upon the large book (much later he was to learn that it was a Gemara) lay the notebook in which the bearded man had so diligently written — a notebook that contained writing in the Russian language. With one clear look he saw the words written on the left-hand page:

To the young man —

Tonight at 9 at 23 Moscovaskaya Street. Stand there quietly and follow whoever calls you. There I hope we will be able to speak a little. Go to the first pages in this notebook. There you will see Russian letters next to Hebrew ones. Study it a little as a way of beginning Hebrew lessons. Then slowly close the book leaving the notebook inside, after you have carefully torn out the page you are reading now. Rip it into tiny pieces, but don't let the man standing by the door see what you are doing.

One other thing, my friend. Beneath the second book you will find an envelope containing some rubles. They are yours to buy food with.

I will see you later.

With some difficulty Anatoly controlled his emotions. A wave of warmth engulfed him, and tears of happiness almost fell from his eyes. He suddenly felt that he meant something to this bearded man. How had he known and understood that Anatoly had to find something to eat?

Anatoly worked slowly and with caution. Occasionally he gave a swift, short glance toward the agent who still stood at his post, despite the fact that the last of the men praying had left the synagogue. Anatoly tore out the page with the letter that had been written for him. After each tiny rip, that in the absolute silence of the synagogue sounded like the sound of a power saw, he would stop for a second, in order to persuade himself that no one was paying attention. The procedure took more than ten minutes, with several long breaks. He folded the ripped-out page and put it casually in his pocket. There, he felt, it would be easier for him to rip it into tiny pieces. He would then throw the scraps out in the street, each piece separately. With his right hand he managed to pull out the envelope that contained the rubles that the bearded man had left him, in his generosity, while ostensibly closing the book with his left. After he had succeeded in these two maneuvers he leafed through the pages of the notebooks, growing almost tipsy from the sight of the Hebrew letters printed neatly next to the Cyrillic characters. He looked at the carefully drawn letters for some time, comparing them to their Russian counterparts. They were hard to understand. As he worked, his hand, jammed in his pocket, slowly tore the paper stuffed in there to bits.

Anatoly did not know how much time had passed, but he suddenly felt a heavy hand on his shoulder. He heard the harsh tones asking him clearly: "What do you have, my young friend, in your pocket?"

Jeff arrived in his office at the usual time.

"Hi, is Mr. Northfeld here yet?" he called to the secretary as he walked towards his boss's office, not even waiting for her reply. She looked at him in astonishment and shouted to his retreating back, "Yes, he's here!"

Jeff couldn't hear her answer, as he was already knocking on Northfeld's door, and then walked in without waiting for an invitation.

"Good morning," he called into the emptiness of the large office.

"Hi, Jeff, how are you?" Northfeld cried out in surprise.

Jeff noticed that his boss seemed to be in a good mood today. Jeff walked slowly into the luxuriously appointed room and approached his superior's desk.

Mr. Northfeld sat, his fingers intertwined, his elbows on his desk.

"Something new, Jeff? You look a little anxious."

Jeff raised an eyebrow. "Me? Anxious?"

Northfeld retreated a little. "Okay, not anxious. How shall I put it? Stressed out. Am I right?"

Jeff saw no reason to deny the obvious. "Maybe you are right, just a little."

Northfeld laughed. "I'm glad we finally understand each other."

Now it was Jeff's turn. "I think that we really do understand each other."

Northfeld felt that some kind of declaration was in the offing, but Jeff merely smiled. Northfeld untwined his fingers and pointed one at Jeff.

"Let me guess what you're talking about."

"Okay."

"I think, Jeff, that you've come to tell me that you have changed your mind on your refusal to go to Moscow. Am I right?"

Jeff laughed loudly. "This time you are right, 100 percent!"

"Great! I congratulate you. But what happened to make you decide?" Northfeld asked, interested.

"Nothing happened. I decided. That's all."

Northfeld leaned back in his executive armchair and looked deep into Jeff's eyes. He did not believe that nothing had happened. He stretched for a moment, like a person who has attained a hard-fought goal, and then returned to his normal posture: back straight, head slightly bent forward. "You understand that I'm thrilled with your decision. However, it's difficult for me to understand why all of our requests to Intourist on behalf of our other employees were rejected. They only wanted you. Why? What's the secret?"

Jeff's face hardened somewhat. He bit his lower lip as the anger tore through his heart. Jeff knew quite well why the Russians wanted him back. *But why does the boss have to mention it to me right now? To dampen my spirits?*

Jeff answered quickly. "I also don't know why. Maybe I made a good impression on them. I don't know. But what really happened is that this time my wife is going to go with me. I want to go for one to two weeks."

Now Northfeld was really surprised. "Oh my! So we're talking about a state visit!"

"Why not?" Jeff answered shortly. "If I'm already there I want to get to know the city. My wife is also interested in peeking behind the Iron Curtain. To walk through Red Square and feel she's touching a piece of history. To know Moscow. It really makes one curious."

Jeff knew well that the only tourist site that interested him was a street called Krasno Bogatirski. But that fact could not be shared with his boss.

"And the dangers? The fears?" His boss asked.

"The dangers and fears exist, it's true, but American citizens usually return unharmed. There's a lot of courtesy and respect there for our American passport. That's what you told me when you tried to convince me yesterday, right?"

Northfeld did not respond; he merely chuckled lightly.

"I'd like my wife's visa request go through the office as well. I hope there won't be any problems with it."

"Okay, I'm convinced," Northfeld answered cordially.

The two men stood up and shook hands. Then Jeff said, "I have some errands to take care of. I'll be back in an hour or two."

Jeff rode back to Boro Park, parking on the corner of 16th Avenue and 59th Street. His wife was waiting for him there. They turned together towards a house whose address the Russian had scribbled on a business card that he had put on the table before leaving their house.

"The news is good, Comrade."

Dimitri Grasimov lifted his weary, ashen face and looked at the man standing straight before him at the entrance to his office.

"Close the door," Grasimov commanded.

The young officer followed the order instantly and took a place near the doorway, his posture still straight and disciplined.

"Now, what's the good news?"

"The tall thin American is returning to us in a few days."

A surprised smile lit up Grasimov's eyes.

"What happened? Wasn't it clear that he wasn't coming?"

"We don't know what happened. Maybe our demand that Intourist refuse a visa to anyone in the office except Mr. Jeff Handler did its work. We're not sure."

Grasimov did not answer. He thought about the significance of the news. Maybe this time he would successfully figure out the American's interest in Krasno Bogatirski Street.

With a nod of the head he motioned to the young KGB officer to continue.

"He isn't coming alone, sir."

Grasimov's narrow eyes widened; a spark of curiosity glowed from within.

"What does that mean: not alone?"

"He's coming with his wife."

"Ahh." Grasimov made some meaningless noise. The officer ignored his superior's reaction and continued.

"They requested a two-week visa, for the purpose of tourism."

"A visa for outside Moscow as well?" Grasimov asked.

"No. Just Moscow and its environs."

Grasimov gave an evil laugh. The young man, it seemed, was fixated on that street, the one he had searched for during his previous visit. But now, Grasimov hoped, he would unearth the secret of what the American was searching for on Krasno Bogatirski.

From within the fog of his thoughts he heard another sentence from the reporting officer.

"He and his wife visited in Boro Park. On 59th Street. They visited THEM!"

Grasimov awoke from his reverie and said alertly, "Now this is really interesting. Absolutely, it works with my plans. When are they supposed to arrive?"

Grasimov realized he had asked this last question impatiently, as if he were already looking forward to the moment that he would meet a long-lost friend who had traveled from far, far away.

"He and his wife have reservations from Vienna on Austria Airlines flight #601 to Moscow, in two days."

Grasimov rubbed his hands together in obvious delight.

"That's good. That's very good."

The startled KGB officer politely smiled back.

29

Jeff and his wife stood on the sidewalk and looked with interest at the house that they were to enter. A typical Brooklyn home: three floors, dark red roof, small garden in the back, stairs leading to a wooden doorway with glass windows. Heavy drapes concealed all that went on inside. The house was enveloped in silence; nothing was going on around it. No one went in and no one went out. There was no car parked in the driveway at the front of the house.

Jeff glanced for a split second at his wife. It seemed that she, like he, was a little tense. They did not know what awaited them behind the facade of the silent house.

"Come on," Jeff said out loud, in an almost overt effort to break the increasing tension.

He motioned to his wife to ring the bell. They could clearly hear its shrill sound. After a long minute the door was opened wide. A young pleasant-faced woman asked them what they wanted. The question confused them: They were not sure how to describe their reason for coming. Jeff did not know which words he should use, which he should avoid.

"We are traveling to Russia in another week," he said in a hesitant voice.

The young woman's face grew serious. She gave the couple standing frozen in front of her a careful scrutiny, looking them up and down from head to toe. Jeff tried to guess, from the expression in her eyes, what she thought of them.

Finally she asked shortly, "So what?"

"So we've come."

She did not take her eyes off them. She could clearly see that the couple standing before her met the criteria of a religious man and woman, both from their dress and their bearing.

Finally she asked, "Do I understand you correctly?"

"I hope so," Jeff answered quickly, not certain if he was saying the right thing. He realized that from this moment on he was entering the mysterious world of hints and nuances, where one did not spell out directly and clearly what one meant. The effort needed to understand and reply in such terms, he knew, was great.

"What's your name?" the woman asked, still not letting them in.

"Jeff Handler. And this is my wife, Miriam. We live in Flatbush, and we have three young children. I'm a diamond merchant, and my wife is a homemaker, a graduate of Bais Yaakov."

The woman showed no reaction to the detailed information that Jeff was pouring out for her.

"I understand," she said. "Who sent you here?"

"Joe Hausbinder," he answered shortly. He felt he had laid all his cards on the table, leaving nothing more for their discussion.

The young woman's face showed complete surprise. "Strange," she said, "but in any case, please come in."

The Handlers walked hesitantly towards the door. At the threshold Jeff got the courage to ask, "What's strange about Joe Hausbinder?"

The woman laughed loudly. "There's nothing strange about Joe Hausbinder, except for the fact that I'm his wife. What's strange is that he didn't tell me to expect you here."

"He didn't know that he was sending me," Jeff admitted.

Joe's wife sent him a swift, surprised glance. They entered the house following their hostess. Miriam closed the door behind her. The mess that was obvious even in the entrance hall bothered her, but she ignored her feelings in anticipation of what awaited them.

Jeff felt obliged to apologize and explain himself. "I hope you understood what I said. He didn't exactly send me, but he caused me to come."

Mrs. Hausbinder smiled in comprehension. She didn't ask for further explanations. She knew her husband and his ways of operating, and therefore this didn't seem unusual to her.

"Please come in," she motioned to them to enter the living room.

The scene that appeared before their eyes was astonishing. The place was in complete disarray. It looked like a room that had undergone a violent police search or one whose owners were just about to move out. All kinds of different objects were piled up everywhere in total confusion: clothing, foodstuffs, leather suitcases large and small. On the table in the middle of the living room Jeff could make out piles of yellow cheese lying not far from dozens of packaged salamis. Two expensive cameras, a Nikon 30 and a Minolta 900, vied for top honors on a mountain of cookie boxes and containers of Osem and Manischewitz powdered soups. A luxurious fur coat hung from the back of one chair; the others were covered with men's jackets, three to four on each chair. Pairs of *tzitzis, yarmulkes,* sets of *tefillin, Chumashim, siddurim,* and other books whose names Jeff could not make out from where he was standing lay both on the table and on nearby chairs. Silently, and with their eyes expressing deep surprise, Jeff and his wife examined the hodgepodge. The hostess, standing in a corner of the living room, followed them with a scrutinizing gaze as they took their tour of her topsy-turvy kingdom.

"Are you moving?" Jeff asked quietly.

"We don't live here at all," came the swift reply.

"Why so much food?" Jeff's wife asked, fascinated.

"Come, let's go into the kitchen. We'll talk there. Maybe we can even find some empty chairs.

"You are at the center for missions to Russia," she said, after they had sat down. "From this center we prepare and train the people who are about to travel for us to Russia."

"You buy them all this food?" Jeff's wife interrupted. For some reason, the vast quantities of food had caught her attention.

"I'll explain everything soon."

The sound of a key being turned in the lock ended the conversation before it had really begun. After a few seconds Joe Hausbinder appeared at the door to the kitchen.

"Jeff!" he called out excitedly at the sight of Jeff and his wife.

Jeff merely nodded weakly, forcing his lips into a feeble, almost forced, smile. Joe pulled up a chair and sat down not far from him, encouraging his wife, with a motion of his hand, to continue speaking. She proceeded willingly:

"The missions are absolutely secret," she explained. "We have to train the men properly so that they don't get involved with the KGB, which follows them from place to place."

Jeff and his wife exchanged a swift glance, but held their peace.

"The men who go out on our behalf are the liaison with the world of the refuseniks in the USSR, particularly those who have become newly observant. These people are particularly persecuted by the regime. The KGB usually sees to it that these men and women lose their livelihood, are fired from their jobs. In order to eat they are forced to take menial, demeaning work, cleaning streets, parks, public toilets, or working in the city dump. Look, we're talking about highly intelligent people, mathematicians, physicists, engineers, even doctors. The morning after they've given in their request for an exit visa and their desire to go to Israel becomes known, or if they are caught keeping the mitzvos, they find themselves in the street, with almost no source of income."

"And the food is for them?" Jeff's wife returned to the large quantities of food in the living room.

"Yes, the food is for them."

"Is that legal under Soviet law?"

"Is what legal?"

"To bring them food in such quantities."

"No. Of course it's forbidden. It's a simple matter of smuggling so that Jews who need it will have something to eat, particularly those who need kosher food. From the time they take it upon themselves to eat only kosher, months can pass before they get a morsel of meat. It's a real sacrifice."

Jeff's wife moved uncomfortably in her chair. "Yes, I understand. Sacrifice. But bringing foodstuffs is smuggling?" Her voice took on an anxious tone. "We're being asked to smuggle food, to break Soviet law?"

Joe Hausbinder broke into the conversation.

"Yes. To smuggle kosher food in for hungry Jews. Yes!"

The words were said with decision and firmness.

"And if Customs finds us smuggling?"

Joe laughed. "It's not 'if.' They will certainly catch you; the Customs inspections there are very serious."

Jeff and his wife once again exchanged tense glances. A spark of anxiety flashed in their eyes.

Jeff asked: "I don't understand. If Customs will discover the smuggling in any event, as you say, why bother trying to smuggle anything in?"

"That's it, Jeff. That's why you're here," Hausbinder gave a small smile and continued his explanation in a quiet voice. "Here we teach you how to smuggle. It's a course for smugglers."

Jeff cut him off. "But you said that Customs there always opens all luggage. That they carefully check the contents, and if so —"

Jeff's discomfort was obvious.

"Calm down, Jeff. We will explain to you how to smuggle to Russia in a manner that they will see everything and understand nothing."

"And it's not dangerous?"

"Did someone say it wasn't dangerous? Since when do you get a difficult mitzvah easily, without risks?"

"And we're to smuggle *tefillin* in too, *mezuzos,* and all the other things we saw in the living room?"

Joe looked wonderingly at Jeff, as if he couldn't comprehend why Jeff did not understand something so self-evident. "Of course; what's the question? The people there are awaiting them even more than they wait for food. I admit that this, too, is dangerous. Even more. You've got to know it all before you go out there."

Jeff found breathing difficult. Outside, a passing automobile honked its horn loudly. To Jeff's ears, it sounded like a warning siren.

"Okay, go on," he said after a short silence. It seemed to Joe that Jeff's voice held a note of despair, as one sentenced to death. He sounded like a man accepting a horrific fate.

Joe stood up and approached Jeff. He put a friendly hand on his shoulder and said, including Jeff's wife in his words, "Maybe it's not fair of me to be frightening you so much. I feel a need from the outset to emphasize the dangers arising from this mission to fulfill this mitzvah. And it is for certain an unmatched mitzvah."

He removed his hand from Jeff's shoulder and continued. "And with all this, I want you to know that our representatives are constantly going to Russia. All the time! In about half an hour the *mashgiach* of one of America's best-known yeshivos will be coming here. He's not a young man and he is well aware of the risks and dangers of his trip. But you should see his enthusiasm for the coming journey."

"Why?" Jeff regretted the question as soon as it came out, unguarded, from his lips.

"You ask why? 'When,' this *mashgiach* asked me, 'will I be given the opportunity to teach Jews under conditions of self-sacrifice? To come to a well-run yeshivah in a neighborhood in New York, to speak words of *mussar* and *yiras Shamayim* with young students living in peace and tranquility, that takes wisdom? If I manage to get into Russia,' he said to me during our first meeting, 'if I manage to teach even the tiniest group how to *daven*, or bring to them a bit of the love of Torah, in my eyes that's worth more than all the Torah I teach here in the United States, under a kind government that allows us, thank G-d, to learn Torah in peace and security.' The *mashgiach* told me this just one week ago. You should have seen, Jeff, how he grabbed my arm and held onto it as he said, so fervently, 'Torah learned in difficult situations, with sacrifice, that is Torah that is ours eternally. When have I merited such a thing?' he asked me. 'Maybe after a week in Russia I will have merited to learn and teach such Torah.' Do you understand, Jeff?"

"I understand, I understand," Jeff answered impatiently.

Joe's wife interrupted, looking past Jeff. "And the woman has an enormous task when she accompanies her husband into the lair of the KGB."

Jeff did not respond. His head was raised towards the kitchen ceiling, and his eyes rested upon the round fluorescent lamp that emitted its harsh white light. The bulb suddenly began to flicker. Perhaps it was answering the thumping of Jeff's heart. He longed to be home in Flatbush, his three young children around him. Suddenly he thought: *If my wife is going with me, where will the children stay?* He couldn't take them with him. *Someone has to stay behind in case we don't get back.* He cast away the dismal thought with a shake of his head, but it remained with him in the dim recesses of his mind.

"Tell him, Joe, how many people have already gone on our behalf to Russia."

"Two hundred have already gone out. And we're constantly sending out more," Joe answered in a quieter tone. "We need a lot of people, because we don't usually send someone twice. That's dangerous. He's too likely to have been marked by the KGB. The underground lessons given in concealed apartments in various cities in the USSR are against Soviet law, which forbids religious activity. And if he gets caught in the act there is the danger of imprisonment and investigations. We want to avoid that. We have our methods in dealing with the secret police. We'll explain it all to you. You'll spend a week in Russia: a few days in Moscow, then Kishinev and Leningrad. You give a few lessons in each place, every one carefully scheduled, and then get out of the country. And that's it. With all the fear and terror that the KGB places upon the entire nation, and the refuseniks in particular, they are still a little slow in their reactions."

Jeff bit his lower lip.

"Have there been instances of imprisonment, interrogations, and other unpleasantries?"

Joe glanced at his wife, as if looking for her support in the reply he was forced to make.

"There were, but not too bad. They were isolated instances."

Jeff straightened up and crossed his arms on his chest. "Here in America it wasn't too bad, when your messenger got caught."

Joe's face tightened. "You're insulting me, Jeff. You don't have to go. I didn't force you to come here for training. Look, even my wife didn't know that you were coming. You've come here of your own free will."

After a moment's tense silence: "And you can certainly leave here of your own free will. You're not obligated, Jeff. Really, no obligation. I won't be angry with you, honestly. We'll stay friends. It's forbidden to be angry at someone whose fear is stronger than all other factors."

A leaden, uncomfortable quiet fell on the small kitchen. The two couples took great pains to avoid each other's eyes. Their perplexity sat heavily upon them, giving them the feeling of suffocating.

Joe was the first to break the uncomfortable silence. "You're traveling with an American passport, Jeff. You're much safer than you believe. They won't do anything to you. At worst they'll deport you, if they don't like you. Isn't that worth such a sacrifice for *Am Yisrael*?"

Joe felt the need to say this, in order to justify himself in Jeff's eyes, to assure him that they did not routinely send messengers into danger. A holder of an Israeli passport, for instance, would never be sent.

Jeff's knees began to shake involuntarily. He was nervous. Without raising his eyes towards his friend from the past Jeff whispered, "Can I smoke?"

30

natoly began to shake uncontrollably. The suddenness of the hand landing on his shoulder aroused all his fears, awakened a terror that could be clearly seen in his eyes. Before him stood the robust man who had been posted at the entrance to the synagogue.

Anatoly tried desperately to control himself and put a calmer look on his face.

"What do you have in your pocket, young man?"

Anatoly pulled his hand out of the pocket and showed that there was nothing there. The man laughed, a frigid laugh. Without raising his voice he said, "I saw everything, kid. Take the paper out of your pocket."

Anatoly did not respond. He showed no inclination to hand over the torn scraps of paper into the hands of the KGB agent.

The man thus far showed no signs of getting ready for action. He stared silently at Anatoly standing opposite him. Anatoly himself accepted his fate — he was in deep trouble with the secret police — and the acceptance itself offered him a little tranquility, like the feeling a person gets after his verdict has been announced.

The KGB agent stepped toward Anatoly. "You returned to the synagogue, even though you'd been warned. Parasite! I imagine that two nights ago you enjoyed yourself there, not far from your house. You look like an intelligent sort of fellow. What's happened to you?"

Anatoly felt nothing. He understood what the man was hinting at and, without bothering to control himself, asked, "Were you one of the people who hit me?"

The man laughed loudly, as if he had just heard a good joke.

"Did someone hit you? Where? Why do you think I hit you? Do I look so frightening?"

Anatoly answered seriously, without a hint of a smile. "No. The comrade doesn't look frightening at all. Not at all."

It seemed the man was satisfied with the answer. Anatoly quickly asked, "Can I go now?"

The KGB man's face took on a fearfully serious cast. "Are you laughing at me? You don't have much experience with us, it seems."

Anatoly realized he had gone too far. The agent was quiet for a second and then continued. "I've asked you for the paper in your pocket, the one you took from the table. I'm not naive, kid."

And suddenly a blood-curdling shout rent the air of the entire deserted synagogue. "Now!"

The threatening echo bounced off the walls of the sanctuary and reached Anatoly's ears in wave after wave. The man's hand was stretched out towards him, his palm almost touching his face.

Another short hesitation and Anatoly surrendered. He felt he had reached the end of the road. He put his hand into his pocket. His nervous fingers tore the creased paper a few more times before he pulled out the shreds and placed them, his hands trembling and hesitant, into the outstretched hands of the terrifying government agent.

The agent took the ripped piece of paper and looked at it for a moment with great satisfaction. His superiors in the First Department of Lubianka would be pleased. Perhaps he had gotten incriminating evidence against the bearded man. He certainly hoped so. He sat down, spread the ripped pieces of paper on the wooden table, and began to try and put them together. Each second he put another piece in place, trying endlessly to reconstruct it. His curiosity to know what the note contained kept him at it. After 15 minutes of effort it was ready. He slowly read the incriminating words:

To the young man —

Tonight at 9 at Moscovaskaya Street 23. Stand there quietly and follow whoever calls you. There I hope we will be able to speak a little. Go to the first pages in this notebook. There you will see Russian letters next to Hebrew ones. Study it a little as a way of beginning Hebrew lessons. Then slowly close the book, leaving the notebook inside, after you have carefully torn out the page you are reading now. Rip it into tiny pieces, but don't let the man standing by the door see what you are doing.

One other thing, my friend. Beneath the second book you will find an envelope containing some rubles. They are yours to buy food with.

I will see you later.

The agent, Yuri by name, was very pleased with himself. Here, he was finally bringing something substantial back to his superiors: clear evidence of religious activity on the part of the bearded man. Yuri lifted his eyes, ready to hurl his guilt into the face of the young man whom he had captured. Suddenly he opened his eyes wide with shock, and jumped from his place in absolute consternation.

The boy was gone!

Surprise quickly turned into fury. With increasing wrath he searched for him, his gaze running over the entire synagogue. But the synagogue was empty. The young man had, apparently, taken the opportunity of disappearing while Yuri had been busy putting together the ripped pieces of paper. The scoundrel! Yuri stamped his foot in boundless rage, balled the fingers of his right hand into a fist, and hurled it with a powerful blow into his left palm, as he hissed between clenched teeth: "I'll get him yet, that thief."

He put his mouth to the miniature microphone that was attached to the lapel of his coat and whispered into it. "A young man whom I caught in suspicious activity in the synagogue has escaped from me.

It happened in the past 10 minutes. Description: black leather jacket, curly black hair. American baseball cap, its visor worn backwards. Average height, somewhat swarthy complexion. Pants? I don't remember the color."

Several cars that had been parked near Dzerzhinski Square began to move.

Jeff lit himself a cigarette with a trembling hand. Without asking permission he turned towards the exit door.

"I'm going to get a bit of air," he said apologetically to his friend Joe. Joe was patient and forthcoming. "Sure, make yourself comfortable."

Miriam watched her husband, a little concerned. She stood up and followed him out. As he opened the door he found a bearded man in his 40's was standing on the doorstep. Jeff was surprised at first. He did not recognize the man, but he looked like a *ben Torah*.

From behind him he could hear the voice of his friend Joe.

"Oh, welcome, Rabbi Blasbolt. *Kumt arein*, come in," he said in Yiddish. "Jeff, this is Rabbi Aryeh Blasbolt. He's a *mashgiach* in a yeshivah in Far Rockaway, and he's going out on a mission for us today to Moscow."

Jeff, confused, shook the man's hand and introduced himself. "Yisrael Yaakov Handler."

The rabbi answered courteously, speaking in Yiddish, "Pleased to meet you."

Jeff darted out into the fresh air while Rabbi Blasbolt was still going in. Jeff's wife followed him.

"What's the matter, Jeff?"

"I don't know. I think that it's not for me, all this business."

He took a deep drag on the cigarette in his hand. As they strolled together down the street, almost deserted at this hour, he said quietly, "The truth? I'm paralyzed with fear."

"Jeff." He heard Miriam's gentle voice.

"What?"

"It doesn't suit you."

Jeff stopped. He threw his cigarette butt down onto the sidewalk, stubbed it out with his shoe, and kicked the remains into the street.

"What doesn't suit me?"

"This fear."

"You weren't there, so you can talk!"

"That's true. But people go and come back, thank G-d. Didn't you hear? Two hundred people already! They've sent two hundred people!"

Jeff turned towards his wife and gave her a piercing look.

"What's happened to you that you're suddenly so enthusiastic?"

"Do you really want to know?"

"Yes."

"I'm ashamed."

Jeff raised his eyebrows. "Ashamed of who? Of what?"

"I'm ashamed because of those young Jewish heroes, in Moscow, in Leningrad, in Kishinev, and all those other places. I'm ashamed because of their sacrifice for Yiddishkeit, for the observance of mitzvos. What are we? We live quietly and peacefully in Flatbush, trying to keep Shabbos and mitzvos. We do what's comfortable, don't exert ourselves unduly. Very good, but do we know anything at all about sacrifice?"

Jeff interrupted her. "So we don't. So what?"

His wife was very worked up. "What do you mean, 'so what'? At least let us have the self-sacrifice to help these Jews when they ask us for it! It's dangerous, it seems, but not a life-and-death situation."

Jeff did not answer. He resumed his slow walk. They reached the corner of 15th Avenue and stopped there.

"Jeff," she called.

"What?"

"It doesn't seem strange to you, this chain of events leading to your trip? I think that it's not just a coincidence. Heaven wants something from you. Suddenly they ask you to buy diamonds from the Russians. Suddenly your grandfather wakes up with some story of holy *tefillin* hidden in Moscow. Suddenly a Russian student turns up and asks you to give a pair of *tefillin* to someone in Moscow. A friend of yours from yeshivah somehow hears that you were in Russia and came back, and he speaks with you. You think you went to buy diamonds for profit, for the business. It seems to you that in addition you have the opportunity to take on a mission whose point is the mitzvah of honoring your father. And suddenly it becomes clear that what is really demanded of you is the holy mission of teaching Torah to young Jews whose parents are dedicated Communists."

Miriam's emotions threatened to engulf her. She felt it was time to stop speaking; she had said enough. Perhaps too much. Now she waited for his answer, but he said nothing. His steps had grown smaller, more hesitant.

"Jeff!"

"What?"

"Be honest. I ask you again: Don't you feel a little ashamed? You've heard how they are so careful with the observance of mitzvos, in the midst of great danger. You've heard how they won't give up even a tiny aspect of Halachah. And us? Don't we cheat sometimes? Isn't that enough to make you embarrassed? Tell the truth!"

"Y—yes." He finally managed to make the declaration demanded of him.

"And so? What's the conclusion?"

Jeff didn't answer. Instead, he turned around and began to walk in the opposite direction, towards the house that he had left a quarter of an hour before. Miriam followed him. He was confused; he had seen his wife in a completely new light. Where did this courage suddenly come from? He heard her say, as she tried to keep up with the brisk pace he was suddenly setting, "Don't worry. 'Those who trust in G-d will be given strength.'"

Igor ran. He ran in the blackness through the quiet streets of his neighborhood, now engulfed in the silence of night. He had no idea how much time passed as he ran, ran without stopping. Finally he came to a halt on a dark street. Exhausted, with no strength left, he leaned on a fence surrounding a house whose windows showed no trace of light. In the distance a dog howled angrily; after a moment even it fell silent. Igor's breath came in wild gasps, swiftly, as his strained lungs begged for oxygen. He stood there for half an hour, in absolute darkness, until his breath returned to normal. Only then did he begin to feel how miserable he was, how trapped, without a way out. The tears flowed; he didn't even try to stem them.

Igor's thoughts were obsessed with his father. It was clear to him that he could never play games with him, the frightening KGB agent. No game of hide-and-seek. His father would find him. He would get him eventually. His agents would do everything under his unequivocal command to find out where Igor was hiding. Igor knew clearly that his fate would be bitter. It was doubtful if even his mother could protect him, as she had done in the past so many times, in the face of his father's wild fury. His fate was sealed; he knew that absolutely.

Igor sat down on the ground. On the other hand, he could not ignore the crisis of identity which he was now facing. The anti-Semitism that had hurled its balled fists at him gave him no rest. He was living with lies, with people afraid to lose their salaries and their positions, who preferred holding their peace to having a dialogue with the truth that kept seeping through the ever-widening cracks. That was the way of the Soviet regime. From Brezhnev and his cronies in the Politburo, from the terror-inspiring Andropov of the KGB, there was fear and suspicion between men, fear fanned by men of the Cometee. Men like his father. So what could one do?

The hum of a motor broke into the thick silence. At first it came from far away. Igor picked up his head. He was certain that the automobile would soon appear in this temporary refuge of his. He jumped up, looking for a better hiding place. But there was not enough time. The car burst into the street and he was trapped within the beams of its headlights. Despite the blinding lights Igor could see that it was a taxi. Without hesitating he lifted his hand and hailed it.

The driver saw the young man standing by himself in the depths of the night. Igor ignored his searching glance and said, "I want the Chepekau." He was using the popular term for the Soviet's Park for Culture and Recreation, *Tzentralni Park Kolturei i Ohtdicha.*

Without awaiting a reply Igor opened the door to the cab and jumped inside. The taxi went on its way without the driver asking unnecessary questions. Nothing mattered to Igor at that moment. He had only one goal: to get as far as he could from his home. The chances that the driver was a KGB informer were high. Igor knew that the odds were that the driver would report to his superior officers about a midnight ride of a young, frightened man.

Igor's sleep was restless, and more than once he awoke in a panic. The third time he felt something strange touching his feet and hands and patting his face. He shuddered upon the park bench where he had been lying and saw a wolfhound walking stealthily away into the woods of the park. The uninvited guest took away from him any last desire to go back to sleep. But the demands of human physiology were too great for him: He was deathly tired and his eyelids finally closed, against his will.

He awoke with dawn. His body trembled in the cold Moscow morning. The month of November heralds the approach of the Russian winter. He jumped up and down trying to warm himself up just a little. Suddenly he remembered why he was here. His limbs felt weak and he collapsed on the bench, his breath shallow and coming in quick gasps. Hunger began to make itself felt in his stomach.

Thoughts flew wildly through his brain. He could hear the questions echoing endlessly: What to do? Where to flee? He didn't know, he truly didn't, where he could turn.

Suddenly, strangely, an odd thought flashed into his head: Archipova. Igor flinched before the idea that appeared in his mind like a shooting star. The name of the Jewish synagogue was a frightening one even among the radical students, the dissidents whom he had decided to join. Archipova was the gathering place of the Jews, the refuseniks, the ones shunned by government and society. These were the ones who joined a lost cause publicly because they had nothing more to lose. They were exposed there to great danger. Igor had often heard from his father of the complete surveillance on the place. His father's men, and the agents who worked under Malenkov in the First Department, knew everything about everyone who dared turn up there. More than one had been arrested and tortured. Even after a subsequent release, the victim remembered well the lesson he had learned in the cellars of Lubianka. It was the tallest building in the capital, a student had once told Igor: Even from the basement one could see Siberia.

Dimitri had told him of Archipova with glee and satisfaction. Even as an unschooled youngster Igor had been repulsed by his father's cruel enjoyment.

He remembered one more thing, something he had picked up from the hints his father had given during a conversation with one of his officers. The First Department, that was responsible for internal security, included surveillance on Jewish refuseniks. His father had hinted that the battle with them was very difficult because imprisonment of one of them led to immediate publicity throughout the world via their links with foreign journalists who worked in Moscow.

Archipova! That was the way! There, at least, even if he was captured by the agents of the Cometee he wouldn't just disappear. There would be someone in the world who would protest. Maybe he would get onto Reuters or AP! There was a chance! The burning humiliation of *"zhid"* that his anti-Semitic friend had flung at him would bring him today to the threshold of the synagogue! What irony!

Igor left the park, rubbing his limbs with his hands to warm them from the sharp cold. A taxi stopped next to him without him hailing it. For a moment he wanted to enter, but he immediately changed his mind. Who knew who the driver would be? Perhaps this one had come after hearing the report of his earlier cab driver. And if he was planning on going to the synagogue on Archipova Street, did he really need the driver of a suspicious taxi with connections to the KGB to know his destination?

Igor motioned to him that he wasn't interested. He walked to the

Kropotinskyka subway station and boarded a train which was still fairly empty. He hoped that no one would pay attention to him as he got off at the Ploshad Nagina station, from there to walk to Archipova Street.

Standing on the other side of the street, opposite the imposing entranceway of the synagogue, he stared at the white marble pillars rising up to the ceiling; he was thunderstruck by what he saw.

31

The KGB agent was completely intent on putting together the
scraps of paper he had wrested from Anatoly. The agent leaned
over the table, moving pieces of paper back and forth as he
pieced together the incriminating jigsaw puzzle. Anatoly hoped
that he wouldn't notice anything else going on around him.
Perhaps there would be a chance to escape. He would try it.

He took one step backwards and no more, his eyes fixed upon the
heavyset figure sitting by the table. No reaction. Anatoly took still another step, and another, until, after some moments had passed, he
stood near the doorway. The KGB agent did not lift his head. Like a
young child he was absolutely immersed in the puzzle created from
torn scraps of paper.

Anatoly grabbed the doorknob tightly. Tensely he gathered the last
vestiges of daring left in him. He knew well: to flee from the bullies of
the regime and then be recaptured would only make his bitter lot
even worse. These people did not like those who provoked them.
With all that, he carefully opened the door. With tiny hesitant footsteps he walked out, closing the door behind him with incredible
caution. Then he broke into a wild run. He took the steps leading out

of the building's side door in several leaps, galloped down the wide stairway in front of the building, and raced down the street towards the nearest Metro station. He hoped to escape anywhere, into one of Moscow's neighborhoods; the further from the danger zone the better. As he fled a thought flitted through his brain: How could he warn the bearded man of the pending danger? He didn't know his name or address, didn't have any idea of how to contact him.

Anatoly ran. Suddenly he heard a voice calling to him. "Anatoly! Anatoly Dobrovitz!"

For a moment he froze in place. No, it wasn't the man who had wrested the torn pieces of paper away from him. It couldn't be: That man did not even know his name. To his good fortune, the KGB agent had forgotten to ask him that all important question. If so, who could it be? Who knew him around here? What disturbed him most was that the voice was familiar. Shouldn't he continue running? Why had he stopped?

The voice grew closer. "Anatoly, wait a minute."

He did not dare turn around; a paralyzing fear would not allow him to. There was only the tiniest of delays and suddenly, before him, stood Igor, Igor Grasimov, whom he had met at registration for the university. They had sat together on a bench in the waiting room and, in a short conversation, had felt some kind of bond between them.

Anatoly, surprised, called out, "Igor!"

Igor did not answer. His eyes looked deeply into Anatoly's brown ones.

"What are you doing here, in this neighborhood?" Anatoly asked quickly.

"And what are you doing here?"

"That's none of your business," Anatoly answered impatiently, with a touch of anger. Some inner voice warned him of a possible trap.

"I'm in a rush," he blurted out, resuming his run up the street, upset with himself for having stopped.

Igor would not let go. He ran after him, grabbed him by the jacket. "Wait a minute," he said loudly.

Anatoly did not answer. With a sharp gesture he pulled away from

Igor and continued his flight. Igor ran after him, catching up to him when he reached the main street. Igor stood in front of him, grabbed Anatoly by the lapels of his black leather jacket, and hurled the words at him. "Why are you running like a maniac? Can't I say one word to you? Maybe I'm just as upset as you are!"

Anatoly tried to pull himself away. "I don't understand what you mean."

Igor would not let go of the lapels. "Maybe you really don't understand. That's what I want to figure out."

The two looked like wrestlers. People passing them by studiously ignored them even though they clearly saw what was going on.

"Leave me alone!" Anatoly hissed.

With a blow to Igor's arm Anatoly managed to extricate his lapel from his powerful grip. But freedom was his for just a short moment; Igor returned and grabbed him again, holding on like a drowning man. He shoved Anatoly onto the rough stone wall of a nearby corner house. Igor was furious with Anatoly. Right now he, Igor, needed someone who would listen to him, hear what he had to say. Here, miraculously and surprisingly, someone who might be able to serve as a listening ear had turned up. Igor knew that he would not let up until he had figured out what Anatoly was doing in the synagogue that he, Igor, had turned to this morning.

"I honestly don't understand what you mean," Anatoly panted. "Now leave me alone! I've got to get away from here, and quick. Get it?"

The last words came out as a scream.

"Are you running away from someone?"

"That's none of your business! I'm telling you a third time: Leave me alone!"

"I'll leave you, Anatoly, but tell me something first: What were you doing in the synagogue? Are you a Jew?"

Anatoly's eyes gave off sparks of fire; this young man seemed very suspicious to him.

"That's none of your business either. Leave me alone! I don't want to know you. Understand?"

Igor decided to cash in all his chips. He said quietly, almost in a whisper, so that the few passers-by couldn't hear, "You're a Jew, Anatoly? I — I — How can I say this? I am a Jew also. I was on my way to the synagogue. I can't talk about it here. Do you understand?"

Anatoly gave up the battle. He felt that the young man he had met by chance was in trouble. His arms, his entire body relaxed. Igor, in response, took his hands off Anatoly's coat. The two stood facing each other, panting, their breaths rising and falling in labored rhythm from the effort. Their gazes crossed, both curious, both still tinged with suspicion. Suddenly Anatoly noticed a Cheka automobile cruising by slowly, its occupants staring at the two young men standing on the corner. KGB. The frightening thought flickered through Anatoly's brain. He bent over a little to try and conceal himself behind Igor.

"What's going on?" Igor asked nervously.

"Nothing. Don't move. Don't turn around. Stand exactly where you are and continue talking."

"Is someone looking for you?" Igor asked curiously.

"Just continue speaking with me normally and don't ask stupid questions, okay?"

Igor felt Anatoly's fear, and yet he listened to his instructions. He didn't move. Then he heard Anatoly's confession.

"Yes, I'm a Jew. If you must know."

"I didn't know."

"And you? Are you, Igor, really — Jewish?"

The automobile had disappeared without stopping. Anatoly took a deep breath and straightened up a little. He didn't know if they had been after him or if he had imagined the whole thing.

Igor didn't answer his question. Anatoly wondered why.

"I want to speak to you," Igor said. It seemed to Anatoly that there was a trace of pleading in his voice.

Anatoly did not rush to answer. He straightened his jacket, which had become crumpled during their struggle.

"Okay, but where? Here it's impossible to talk. I am in danger while standing here."

"You name the place."

Anatoly thought for a minute. "What about Chepekau Park?"

"Impossible!" Igor replied firmly. He was certain that his father, there in KGB headquarters, already knew that his son had spent the night on one of the benches in that lovely park. Anatoly, hearing the decisive negative, wondered what was behind it. His suspicion of Igor had not yet dissipated.

Jeff and his wife returned to the house with unhurried steps. Jeff opened the door, which hadn't been locked, without ringing the bell. The tumult going on in the living room enveloped them even in the hallway. They did not enter, in order not to disturb anyone, and also so that they could see what was going on, spectators on the sidelines. Joe noticed them from the corner of his eye, but did not acknowledge their presence. He was busy. His wife, too. And R' Aryeh Blasbolt as well, as he hurtled around the living room like one possessed.

Three large suitcases lay open on the couch. They were quickly being filled with some of the items that loaded down the table, covered the chairs, and were piled on the carpet.

"R' Aryeh," Joe called to his guest, who had opened a package of *sefarim* that were placed on the floor in a corner of the room, "does the Rav remember what he must tell the suspicious Customs official, if he's a bit too interested in why the Rav is bringing so much salami and yellow cheese?"

The rabbi did not put down the *sefer* in his hand, but continued looking through it as he laughed, "Of course, of course, don't worry. I'm not traveling alone, you know; *Hakadosh Baruch Hu* is going with me. 'Even if I walk in the valley of the shadow of death I shall not fear evil, because You are with me.'"

Joe took a deep breath. This kind of answer, which he was used to receiving, was absolutely true. But still, it did not provide him with practical advice on how to respond correctly when facing the suspicious Soviet machine. A wrong answer could be dangerous.

Joe continued with his questions. "And what about the *sefarim*? A tourist coming for a week needs so many books? What will you say?"

"It's okay, Reb Yossel," R' Aryeh returned. "Stop worrying." He began to spread a set of *Chumashim* among the three suitcases.

"R' Aryeh, they're very suspicious, these Russians. They're less afraid of the salami than of the *sefarim*: Forbidden literature makes them shudder, R' Aryeh."

"We've already discussed what I should say to them."

"That's true. But remember," he warned, "you have to keep a calm face. Don't get confused, don't show signs of nervousness, fear, or anxiety. Answer their questions naturally."

R' Aryeh lifted his head. "Against fear, Reb Yossel, we have *Sefer Tehillim*, and —"

R' Aryeh stopped short in midsentence. He held a *sefer* in his hand, one he had pulled out from the pile destined to travel with him to Russia.

"Oh!" he cried in wonder. "*Meshech Chochmah on the Torah!* To Russia?! Who needs it there?"

Joe's eyes sparkled. "It's by special order from them! It's true, it's unbelievable, there are those there who can already learn a page of Gemara. The Rav will give a *shiur* in Gemara. They are learning *Perek HaMafkid.*"

Jeff, still standing in the entrance hall, could no longer contain himself. "But how in the world do they know about the existence of a *sefer* such as *Meshech Chochmah*?"

All eyes turned to Jeff.

"Oh, Jeff, welcome back," Joe said.

"We've been watching your preparations."

"Nice."

"But," Jeff repeated his question, "How is it that in Moscow they know about a *sefer* called *Meshech Chochmah* by R' Meir Simchah of Dvinsk? That's astounding!"

"R' Aryeh," Joe said tranquilly, "is going to Leningrad tonight. And you're going to Moscow tomorrow."

He looked, perceivingly, at Jeff's face. To his joy he found no trace of resistance, surprise, or confusion. *This man is ready to go*, the thought flitted through his mind. He continued, "The group in Leningrad, Grisha Wasserman's group, is making a lot of progress in study and mitzvah observance. Their sacrifice is truly amazing. One of the *rabbanim* who visited Leningrad last month mentioned a *"vort"* on the *parashah* from this *sefer.* They liked the explanation, and one of the students asked for the book."

"How did he let you know?" Jeff asked, interested.

"They have their methods." He would say no more.

In the meantime R' Aryeh's bags had been packed. With great effort the three men managed to compress everything within the zipped bag's confines. One of the overstuffed pieces of luggage nearly tore. The bags were carried to a van parked in the driveway. Joe, always energetic, ran towards the driver's seat, while R' Aryeh sat down next to him. Joe pumped Jeff's hand as he spoke. "I'm taking R' Aryeh to the airport. He's leaving in four hours for Vienna, and from there to Leningrad. Tomorrow, at this time, I'll be glad to see you here in my house. Bring all your personal belongings and we'll organize the delivery to Moscow. It's worth it," he added with a grin before disappearing into the car, "when else would you get to have me drive you to your flight?"

The car roared away, and after a few minutes disappeared around the corner, on its way to JFK Airport.

Dimitri Grasimov read the note that his agent Yuri, assigned that morning to his post at the city's Great Synagogue, had brought to him. *This business of pasting it together undoubtedly took him a lot of time,* he thought. *He deserves some kind of compliment on his faithfulness and diligence.* A second thought immediately followed the first. *No, it will go to his head. He'll ask for a raise in his miserable salary, transfer to another post, who knows what else? It's bad for people to know you're pleased with them. Better for them to have doubts about their standing and what their superiors think of them. They'll work harder that way.*

He looked at Yuri, who was standing in front of him, his eyes silently pleading for a favorable word. But Dimitri's thoughts were already far away. Where could Igor be now?

Grasimov read the note a second time. He was pleased. This was the first time he had found clear proof that the bearded man was committing anti-Soviet activity. It would be a good idea to get his hands on the young man who had escaped from the synagogue, to check whether he was under the age of 18. Maybe this time they would succeed in sending that brazen bearded man for a short visit to the heart of Mother Russia — to distant Siberia.

Grasimov leaned back in his wooden chair and crossed his arms behind his neck.

"How did the young parasite manage to get away?" He shot the question at Yuri.

Yuri swallowed hard in obvious disappointment. All his efforts at uncovering and piecing together the incriminating note hadn't earned him even one word of praise. That fact took away his presence of mind, leaving him without the possibility of figuring out an answer that would satisfy his superior officer. He gave a reply that was absolutely forbidden. 'I don't know.' "

Grasimov jumped up from his seat and screamed, "What does that mean: 'I don't know!'"

But before he received an answer to his savage shout he sat down again and closed his eyes. Igor! His image once again appeared in his mind. Would he, Dimitri, have a better answer than "I don't know" when Malenkov or one of the other animals filling this building asked him how it was that he hadn't known that his son was hanging around with enemies of the state? How was he different from Yuri who stood here before him, shaking like a leaf?

Like a chameleon transforming, Grasimov changed into something else entirely. His body grew slack and his anger melted away. He sat tranquilly, his hands resting on his desk. He gave Yuri a broad smile.

"I must say, you've done well. Your diligence in your task and the document you brought as a result are worthy of note, Yuri."

Yuri stood, baffled. The sharp, sudden metamorphosis filled him with fear. Who knew what lay behind that false smile? He had been an eyewitness to interrogations of suspects in this place. He had seen how the expressions on the interrogators' faces could change from cruel fury to loving smiles. Yuri felt a shudder go up his spine. "I really don't know where the kid disappeared," he said, his voice beseeching. "I was completely involved in putting together the pieces. He took advantage of my concentration in order to run away."

Grasimov gave a hearty laugh. Yuri had never before seen such a sight.

"Relax, my boy. The parasite ran away; it happens. It happens to your colleagues, too; they often lose the person whom they're following. But such an incriminating document hasn't fallen into my hands in a long while. So relax."

After a moment he added, "Tonight, we'll go and meet them in the apartment they mentioned in the note. You'll come also in order to identify them. I hope this will help put an end to these hooligans' games."

"*Spasibo,*" Yuri whispered.

Grasimov motioned him out. The next hour was dedicated to planning the raid that was to take place that night on the apartment on Moscovaskaya Street 23.

32

natoly scrutinized for a long while. Igor's face a prolonged scrutiny. Finally, he asked, "Krimsky Bridge?"

"*Nyet.*" Again, Igor was adamant.

"Why?"

"Too far. Also, at this hour traffic is very light there. We'll be noticed."

Anatoly tried his luck again. "Red Square?"

"That's better. A visit to the mausoleum where Lenin's body is embalmed might lift our spirits a little. It will do me good to say goodbye to his socialism, embalmed or not."

Anatoly heard those last words of Igor's, but he still suspected the possibility of provocation. His heart simply would not let him believe that Igor honestly meant what he said. Yet he agreed to the suggestion: "Fine. We'll separate now and meet at the mausoleum in half an hour. Better not to go together."

The two separated without another word. Half an hour later, they met as planned. Quietly they looked at the long line that had gathered at the entrance, at the many people waiting for the privilege of taking a quick peek at the body of the leader who was one of the main symbols of the Communist revolution. On the way Igor had stopped at a store to buy two *bobliks,* a kind of Russian bagel; now, he handed one to Anatoly. Anatoly, starving, thanked him with a sparkle in his eyes but didn't say anything. The two hurriedly gulped down their bagels, both remembering that they had not eaten anything since the day before.

They wandered about the square a little, not exchanging a word. There were too many listening ears around them, too many Soviet citizens about. Finally the two approached the walls of the Kremlin and found a place to sit far away from anyone else. Still, out of some deep instinct, when they began to speak after an extended silence they kept their voices hushed.

Anatoly was the first to whisper, "They wouldn't take me into the university."

Igor showed his curiosity. "Why?"

Anatoly did not rush to answer. He still wondered if he was doing the right thing in revealing all that he was feeling to someone he hardly knew. But some kind of inescapable internal pressure was forcing him, making his decisions. He hoped he would not live to regret it.

"Because I am a Jew!"

"Impossible."

"What, impossible? That I'm a Jew?"

"No. It's impossible that you weren't accepted because of your Jewishness."

Anatoly felt a stab of discomfort. "How do you know it's impossible? Am I a liar?"

Igor realized that he owed him an apology. But he held himself back. "Did they tell you so specifically?"

"No. But it was made quite clear."

"That's not enough."

Anatoly gave a bitter laugh. "If you really were Jewish, Igor, you wouldn't have answered me like this. Besides, one of the professors gave me a really broad hint."

The two fell silent. A few people were passing by; they had to be careful. They returned their attention to the last crumbs of bagel still held in their hands.

"It's good, you know?"

"I bought the most expensive ones; seven kopeks a piece."

The strangers passed. They hadn't even spared a glance at the two young men eating bagels and drinking lightly flavored mineral water (another four kopeks each).

Anatoly could not relax. He stood up. "Let's get out of here. I think I know one of the men who just passed us, and I'm afraid of being recognized."

Igor rose, clearly against his will. The two began to walk towards the large government department store, Gum, housed across from the Kremlin walls on the other side of Red Square. Anatoly, in an act of carelessness, turned his head back, curious to see if the man who had passed them by was, indeed, someone he recognized. And just at that moment the thing he was afraid of came to pass: The man, too, turned his head, and despite the distance between the two their eyes met for a moment. Anatoly could not remember, though, where he had seen the man before.

"Let's hurry up," he said, his heart pounding wildly.

"Why? Has something happened?"

"No. But still, hurry up."

They quickened their steps.

"You know, Anatoly, something did happen."

Anatoly did not slow down. "What do you mean?" he asked.

"You seem to doubt that I'm a Jew."

The blunt sentence was a clear challenge. They were now standing at the entrance to the huge department store. Anatoly, almost against his will, stopped and whispered, "You don't understand my suspicions? Is this Moscow or not? KGB or no KGB?"

Igor hesitated. He thought of his father, member of the Cometee. Finally, he agreed. "You're right, at least a little bit."

They entered the department store. There were few shoppers within, and even fewer wares to buy. They wandered through poorly stocked aisles, picked up items here and there, and in the meantime shared their histories. The two revealed to each other the distress each had felt when discovering the difficult fact — that he was a Jew; the hurt each had felt because of the lack of meaning that this fact had for him; the anger against the purposelessness of the suffering that this fact had engendered. Anatoly focused in on the anguish and hurt he had undergone when rejected by the university, while Igor grieved over the rejection by his student friends as soon as they discovered that he was a Jew.

Anatoly heard from Igor the story of how he had run away from home. Igor, though, still didn't dare reveal his father's identity to his friend. Anatoly then described his difficulties with his widowed mother, that fanatically loyal Communist. But he, too, kept a secret, carefully omitting any mention of his joining up with the Jews learning Torah underground in Moscow. Many thick walls were dismantled between the two young men, but there were still massive barriers between them that remained to be breached.

The two young people felt it was time to leave the store. A few of the employees, with nothing to do, had begun following them with suspicious eyes. Igor and Anatoly walked slowly towards the exit door. A few moments later they were outside in the clear cold air of Red Square. The line into the brown building of the mausoleum was unusually short; the number of people in the square had diminished before the winter chill that had begun to send the mercury in the thermometer plunging to below zero. The skies were leaden, and snowflakes drifted elegantly down from the gray clouds above. At first it was a light dusting, but soon the tiny white angels were doing their mysterious dance in every part of the air, and Red Square slowly turned white.

Because of this, because winter's sudden appearance had kept the number of passers-by down, Anatoly saw him.

"Igor."

"What?"

"Wait for me here. I'll be right back."

To Igor's astonishment, Anatoly broke out into a run, racing towards the mausoleum.

Jeff called his father from a public phone far from his Flatbush home.

"Hi, Abba, how's Grandfather?"

"Baruch Hashem, day by day. He still needs much mercy from Above. His condition, according to the doctors, is stable. But he's still under strict supervision in intensive care."

"Thank G-d. Tell me, Abba, did you whisper to him that I'm going to Russia for a second trip?"

"Yes."

"How did he react?"

"It's hard to know; it seemed that he was excited by the news."

"So tell him that I'm going and this time I'll do my best to try and find the *tefillin.* Everything else is in G-d's hands. Also, my wife, Miriam, is coming with me."

"What? What did you say? Miriam is going with you? Jeff, what's going on here?"

"What's the matter, Abba? I don't understand. She wants to come with me. I'm sure she can help me out a lot."

"But," his father cut him short, "it's dangerous! And what will you do with the kids? Don't tell me you're taking them along too!"

Jeff smiled bitterly in that phone booth so many thousands of miles away from Israel. He shifted his feet, now leaning on his left leg.

"I don't understand. For me it's not dangerous, but only for your daughter-in-law, the princess, for her it is?"

There was silence on the line for a few seconds. Finally, Jeff's father's voice came on weakly.

"I suppose you're right. But be careful."

"Okay, okay. The main thing is to give Grandfather hope that I haven't neglected the matter."

Jeff and his wife traveled the next day to JFK in Joe Hausbinder's Plymouth van: silver, with tinted windows. The six large, overstuffed suitcases were squeezed into it. Joe's wife waved them off, shouting as they left, "Good luck, have a safe trip. Get back safely, *b'ezras Hashem.*"

The Handlers sat, a bit crowded, in the car, nervous and trying to control their unruly thoughts. They did manage a slight smile for Mrs. Hausbinder from the open window of the van. The further they got from their own neighborhood, the more they felt a sense of oppression weighing them down. The little ones had been left in the care of Miriam's oldest sister, who had registered shock and amazement at her sister's decision to enter the jaws of the lion. "Of all the beautiful places in the world — you have to go there?" she had said aloud, within earshot of the Handler children, who had gazed at their mother and their aunt with big, wondering eyes. "You, the well-known coward who was afraid to take a long hike on Mount Kisco, are suddenly going to Moscow? What's come over you?" But Miriam did not respond. Her sister had tossed one more sentence at her: "Think it over." "It's okay," Miriam had answered. She quickly kissed her children and raced swiftly out of her sister's house to their car, which Jeff later parked in Boro Park near the Hausbinder home.

Now, on the road to the airport, she followed her sister's advice to think it over. Had she really given enough thought to this Moscow adventure? She rubbed her hands together, bit her lip, and lifted her head in a swift sharp movement. Her eyes, she knew, shone with the glint of determination. From out of the corner of her eye she squinted toward her husband sitting next to her, trying to decipher his emotions at this moment. She didn't see any trace of nervousness on his face. He was, though, contemplative, sitting quietly and occasionally closing his eyes. Joe drove silently, his hand steady on the wheel.

After about 40 minutes they reached Pan Am's giant terminal. The flight was scheduled to take off in two hours. Destination: Austria. From there they would take a direct flight to Moscow.

Joe stopped the car in front of the entranceway. He jumped out to find a baggage cart, leaving the Handlers standing silently next to the van. Jeff helped Joe load up the heavy luggage on the cart. On their way to the line at the check-in counters Joe glanced quickly at Jeff and his wife. He was reassured. They had not forgotten the cameras he had given them. They stopped before they reached the counter and Joe pulled out a handful of kopeks from his pocket and said, "With two kopeks you can call from any phone in Moscow. Remember, never call from the hotel; I don't have to repeat to you why not. Follow the rules when you call! On the way go over all the codes that you will use in your conversations. Understand?"

Jeff didn't answer. The ghost of a smile on his slightly pale lips indicated that he fully comprehended his instructions. Joe pulled a small plastic case from his pocket and handed it to Jeff.

"Here are the pictures. Even though you studied them in my house, I've decided you should go over them again a few times on your trip to Vienna. When you get to Vienna destroy them. Don't take them accidentally with you to Moscow. That would be a terrible mistake. Destroy them, together with the booklet." As he spoke Joe pulled out a typewritten booklet and handed it to Jeff.

"What's this?" Jeff asked.

Joe gave a broad grin. "Motivation. Read it. And as for the rest — all you need is *siyata d'Shemaya.*"

The smile still lit up his face. "And now, goodbye, have a good trip, and let the Creator help you out." The two shook hands warmly, a lengthy handshake, followed by a clap on the back. Joe nodded in Miriam's direction as he wished her good luck. "And please remember: you are messengers of G-d and of the Jewish people!"

An hour later Jeff and his wife took off for one of the longest, most fascinating trips they had ever experienced.

33

natoly consciously forced himself to stop running. He did not want to arouse the curiosity and attention of the people passing by in Red Square. And yet he hurried, frightened that the bearded man, whom he had suddenly noticed, would disappear into the crowd or onto one of the streets that stretched like tributaries out of the square. Anatoly had seen him as he walked near the exit gate of the square. Anatoly understood the dangers of his attempt to speak publicly with the bearded man, who was almost certainly under surveillance. And yet Anatoly did not stop. He had to report to him that the note that he had left for Anatoly on the table in the synagogue had fallen into the hands of the KGB.

Eventually he broke into a gentle dash. In his haste he wasn't careful, and he bumped into an elderly pedestrian, who almost fell. "Excuse me, I'm very sorry," Anatoly whispered hurriedly. That was all that was missing, the added attention that this incident would draw upon him. He grasped the old man by the shoulders in order to keep him from falling. The man, instead of reviling him for the unpleasantness, replied in a slightly confused tone, "It was nothing."

Finally, Anatoly reached the bearded man. He passed him by and whispered in a voice that only the two men could hear, "They took the letter from me."

The bearded man didn't break his stride, continuing to walk without favoring Anatoly with even a glance, despite the fact that from the corner of his eye he could see quite clearly who was speaking. Anatoly walked two paces in front of him. He could hear him whisper, "What letter?"

Anatoly bent down, as if to tie his shoelace. The bearded man passed him by and heard him whisper, "The letter you wrote in the notebook."

He stood up and again put a distance of two paces between them.

"I understand."

Anatoly waited for more, following behind him. They were already quite near the Lenin Museum, near Manzinia Square, when Anatoly dared asked the question to the open air. "What should I do? Come tonight?"

"No," the bearded man returned. "Tonight is canceled. Three days from now, in the same place."

The bearded man increased his pace, but Anatoly did not fall behind.

"I'm not alone."

"Meaning?"

"A friend of mine. A student."

"Loyal to you? Can he be trusted?"

"It seems so."

The bearded man stopped suddenly and whirled around toward Anatoly. If he was under surveillance, they had certainly noticed that he was talking with someone. But now it was important for him to stare directly into the eyes of the young man who had latched onto him.

The bearded man asked, "Loyal to you? Do you know who he is? Where he's from?"

"Yes. That is, I knew him while we were both at the university."

The bearded man was silent for a long minute. His face was a mask, his eyes piercing and direct.

"Bring him."

Anatoly believed that the proper moment had arrived.

"He's run away from home."

Silence.

Anatoly continued. "I, too, can't return home."

The bearded man understood exactly what was being said here. These two young men were turning to him with a request for sanctuary and refuge. It was terribly dangerous. He could not be certain if these two hadn't been planted by the KGB's Second Department; he wasn't sure if the paper had actually fallen into the KGB agent's hand, or if the young man hadn't handed it to him of his own free will, or — who knew?

Finally, he said, "In three hours sit in the reading room of the Lenin Library. It's not far from here."

The bearded man turned away and calmly continued walking, without saying goodbye.

Anatoly hurried back to Red Square. He reached the doorway of Gum, where he had left Igor. But Igor had vanished. Anatoly wandered through Red Square for about half an hour, but found no trace of him anywhere.

Takeoff was uneventful. They settled into their seats. Jeff closely observed passengers sitting in front, behind, and to the side of them. He felt good: They all looked like elderly Austrian retirees returning to Vienna after a visit to the United States. That was his impression, at least.

Shortly after takeoff they were served their kosher meals. When the steward dimmed the lights throughout the length of the aircraft and the few passengers curled up for their night's sleep, Jeff and his wife turned to the material that Joe had given them before they had boarded.

Jeff spread out a collage of photos wrapped in transparent plastic upon his knees, and the two of them looked quietly at the pictures, which they had already seen in Joe's house in Boro Park. The photos were numbered consecutively from right to left. Actually, the photos were all much the same: the gray facades of Soviet buildings, heavy and drab, as the background, and in each photo a picture of a sign from a bus stop. Jeff and his wife stared at the pictures for a good length of time, as if they were photos of enchanting scenery. After a moment Jeff began to point with one finger at picture after picture; with the fingers of his other hand he counted off: One, two, three... His wife alternated between looking at him and looking at the photos, nodding her head as a sign that she understood and comprehended what he meant. The two of them remembered the briefing that they had gotten at Joe's house in New York. There, sitting amidst the shambles in the living room, he had explained to them how to travel and reach the house of one of the best known of the refuseniks. Their route was shown to them in pictures in order that they could reach him without having to ask anyone for directions. Each picture showed one of the bus stops that would reach the man's home. The scene in the photo was the scene that would face them from the bus's right-hand window. They had to pass six bus stops, get off at the seventh, reach a tall building located behind two other buildings which were each just four stories high. The fourth floor of the tall, ten-story building was the home to G.B. — the fifth door to the left of the stairway. They knew him only by his initials; Joe wouldn't give them more information. If they would remember all the details they would be able to reach his house without any problem, and without having to ask for help from anyone. It was possible that they would arouse some suspicion, being so different from the rest of their surroundings. There was always the possibility, however small, of danger. But the danger would grow much stronger if they would start asking people passing by or neighbors for the address of someone who had been declared an enemy of the regime.

Jeff folded the photos. The couple exchanged weak, tense smiles and took deep breaths. During their stopover in Vienna they would study the pictures one last time before destroying them.

Afterwards both engrossed themselves in the "motivational" pamphlet, as Joe had called it when he had handed it to the Handlers.

Dimitri Grasimov enjoyed a moment of self-satisfaction. Tonight would be the night. Perhaps this time he would manage to get his hands on the bearded man. This "clericalism" that had suddenly arisen among many young people was spreading. For some reason, Grasimov's heart was pierced by the terrible suspicion that his son, too, was under its influence. The questions he had asked about his Jewishness hinted at a dangerous direction. He was not certain if Igor had made a connection with this particular group, but, like any epidemic, it could spread and contaminate him, too.

Grasimov knew well that Soviet law had tied their hands in the past years. Comrade Brezhnev, under pressure from the Western countries, had eased the rules of imprisonment and the regulations governing interrogations that had been in place during the grand old days of Comrade Stalin and the first years of Khrushchev. But it seemed to Grasimov that the confiscated note could make a good contribution and would allow him to place the heavy hand of the law — and the fist of the KGB — upon the leader of the group. To make things even simpler, perhaps Grasimov's men would manage to plant a few more pieces of incriminating evidence that would lead to the imprisonment of this bearded man, together with several other participants in his illegal activities.

If this succeeds, thought Grasimov, it would help in the matter of Igor as well, at the very least keeping him distant from these religious refuseniks and dissidents.

Grasimov closed his eyes in satisfaction. His hand groped on his desk for his cigarette case. Though his wandering hand didn't find it, he still did not open his eyes. It felt good like this. In his mind's eye he could see himself taking part in the night raid on the apartment on Moscovaskaya Street. It would be a liberating activity, helping him to rid himself of the burden of tension that had been building up since the appearance of the American and his strange inquiry about the location of Krasno Bogatirski Street (*Why does it bother me so much?*), and since the profound disagreement with his son.

At first Grasimov did not hear the knock on the door, he was so deep in his own thoughts. The second knock came, stronger this time.

"Yes?"

One of his men entered and placed on the desk a report that had just come in. Grasimov, his face expressionless and without greeting his agent, pulled the paper towards him and read:

"X left New York with his wife from JFK Airport. Pan Am Flight 184, destination: Vienna. From Vienna, Austrian Airlines, three hours after landing. Destination: Chermentyevo, Moscow. He didn't arrive at the airport by himself; he was escorted by 'the fox.' They have six heavy suitcases with them."

Grasimov turned over the paper, that was not addressed to anyone and bore no signature. He could not suppress a twinge of triumph. He managed to lure the strange American back to Moscow. An American, a Jew, and religious. Somehow, the incomprehensible, mysterious story of Jeff Handler was mixed up with the possibility of imprisoning the bearded man. In truth, he knew of no connection between the two. But the internal reflexes of a hardened interrogator whispered to him that the two events would somehow merge. It didn't really matter. If he would manage to unravel these two problems, his position, which had been badly damaged, would improve tremendously.

He lifted his telephone receiver. From the other end came one word. "Yes?"

"Please come in," Grasimov said laconically.

The man who entered, Yevgenyev, an incredibly loyal junior officer, always carried with him a cardboard file containing position papers, documents, newspaper clippings, and more. He well knew his superior, who always needed something — and woe to him if he could not supply it immediately.

Yevgenyev didn't say a word, waiting for Grasimov's orders. Grasimov ignored him for a moment; a display of sovereignty, authority, domination. He looked at the good news that lay on his desk for another minute. The junior officer maintained his silence and his rocklike bearing without blinking an eyelash.

Finally, in his goodness, Grasimov lifted his eyes and barked, "Oh," as if he had not known the man had entered, "Yevgenyev."

Yevgenyev tensed up, expectant.

"Yevgenyev, check who is on duty in Customs tomorrow evening."

"*Da*," he answered shortly.

"And tell the head of Customs in the airport that Colonel Dimitri

Grasimov of the Cometee asks that Ilitz Alexandrovitch, head of the shift, be present during customs inspections, particularly at the hour when the Austrian Airlines flight arrives from Vienna."

"*Da.*"

"And one more thing, Yevgenyev, let them particularly check the American citizen by the name of — one minute —"

Grasimov flipped through the papers that were piled haphazardly on his desk. Finally, he found what he was looking for.

"By the name of Jeff Handler. Will you remember the name?"

"*Da.*"

Grasimov fell silent, his eyes embedded onto the functionary standing so humbly before him.

"And let the inspection be tough, tough and very thorough. Understood?"

"*Da.*"

Grasimov's nod hinted to Yevgenyev that it was time to leave. The underling knew his boss well, recognized his hints and gestures. He turned and walked through the door.

34

I gor Grasimov stood in the doorway of the department store, waiting uneasily for Anatoly's return. Against his will his eyes strayed over Red Square, scanning the people walking there as if each were a potential threat to him. One of his father's friends or agents could notice him and then — The tall, dark red wall surrounding the Kremlin never left his consciousness. Here he felt he had finally found himself a friend upon whom he could rely in times of trouble — and the friend had disappeared. Again, he was alone. *Where is Anatoly?* The thoughts raced through his fevered brain. *Where did he suddenly go? Why did he run away without telling me who he wanted to meet or who he was escaping from? What will happen now?*

Igor felt his fearful thoughts sapping the last of his spirit. To dispel them he began to wander about. At first he entered the Gum department store, strolling about aimlessly, hoping to escape from the inquisitive stares (or what he thought were the inquisitive stares) of the passers-by. But he quickly came to regret his hasty decision, and hurried out of the large empty store, realizing that here he was even more exposed to the stares of the few salespeople, who stood about doing nothing.

Igor glanced at his watch. Ten minutes had passed and Anatoly hadn't returned. *Maybe, just maybe, this Anatoly is an agent? And maybe, just maybe, he, Igor, had revealed his secrets to him much too early?*

Igor began to walk slowly towards the other end of the square. From a distance he could see the large structure of the Russia Hotel. He turned and walked down the street that bordered upon the entire length of the Moscow River, to Moscovaskaya. At first he planned on crossing over the river via the Bolshoi Moscovertiski Musht Bridge, but he abandoned the idea and instead strolled along the river's edge. He didn't know where his legs would take him and what awaited him at the end of the road. Ultimately, he learned that he had been right to follow his instincts.

Jeff began to read the pamphlet. His wife dozed, her pamphlet fallen from her hands. Jeff moved the small overhead light to the left. The beam of light now fell directly on him and on the thin pamphlet held in his hand. With a slow and gentle movement he extinguished the reading light above his wife's head. The extra darkness made his own light seem even brighter.

At first he flipped through the pages, giving the contents a cursory look, but unable to sleep — a result of the tension that wouldn't leave him — he decided to read it from start to finish. If he'd get tired of it he also had brought a small volume of *Mishnayos* with him that would rescue him from loneliness, an insomniac among the sleeping, snoring masses around him.

Jeff didn't know how much time he had been reading quietly, completely enwrapped in the fascinating words dancing before him. Suddenly he blurted out, "Incredible. Really incredible."

His wife woke up, startled.

"What's the matter, Jeff?"

"Nothing. Go back to sleep."

But she could see his eyes dancing with admiration and satisfaction, and she wouldn't let up.

"Tell me what's got you so excited. Sleep? I've got plenty of time to waste on that later."

"Okay. The stories in this pamphlet are really amazing. We're traveling to a land of heroes, heroes with a sense of humor."

She whispered, in a voice that was neither a question nor a declaration: "And we're cowards."

Jeff gave her a swift, direct look. "No. Why do you think so?"

She didn't answer, understanding that she had somehow crossed an off-limits border.

"Forget it. Tell me what you read. I fell asleep before I hardly started reading, and I don't even know what it's about."

"Okay. This is a collection of stories describing the lives of the observant Jewish underground. Women and men. True heroes, believe me."

His wife sat up in her seat, by now completely awake. "Tell me," she said. "Tell me the story that got you so excited and made you wake me up."

"Sorry."

"Don't be. If the story is a good one, it'll be worth it. *Nu*, tell!"

Their conversation was held in whispers, in order not to awaken the dozing passengers around them. The hum of the motors also helped muffle their quiet voices.

Jeff shifted in his seat. "Once, KGB agents appeared in the apartment of one of the activists in the underground. The apartment's owner, a refusenik, knew that their primary goal was to instill fear. Two uniformed policemen entered, together with two young men in civilian clothes who were to serve as 'witnesses,' by Soviet law, to the 'criminal' activity that they would find in the house. Are you listening?"

"To every word. Go on."

"I thought you were asleep again."

"Go on already."

"Okay. The policemen and witnesses were joined by three truly dangerous men. KGB men. The policemen politely showed the apartment owner their search warrant. They were there to find anti-Russian literature. There was complete silence in the small apartment. The agents locked the apartment's door and disconnected the phone. Then they began a systematic search of the apartment.

"'You have children,' one of the investigators said politely, with a pleasant smile, to the young refusenik. 'We'll start the search in their room so that they can get to bed.'

"The three agents turned over the children's room. They checked every corner, went into every closet, took apart pieces of the floor. They finished their work in the children's room at 11 p.m. All through it, the people who were in the apartment sat, their mouths sealed.

"The investigators turned to the kitchen. They thrust a long, thin needle through every bag of sugar and rice. What do you think they were looking for?"

"Diamonds, probably. Or dollars. What do I know?"

"No. They were looking for anti-Russian writings. Letters asking how to put on *tefillin* or what is Shabbos."

"That's anti-Soviet writing?" Miriam asked resentfully.

"Now you know. That's the way it is. Finally," Jeff continued, "the investigators reached the living room. There they found 'treasures.' Absolutely, treasures. Underground periodicals, documents for a symposium on Judaism, and books. Books that would clearly incriminate the owner. The investigators left all the books in a pile on the table. The owner noticed that the book on the top was written by Israel's general prosecutor, Gideon Hausner, about Eichmann: *Six Million Accuse.*

"The apartment owner, this refusenik, turned to the KGB official and pointed to the book.

"'Do you want me to talk to the news agencies, to Reuters or AP, tomorrow, and explain to them that the KGB sees anti-Soviet activity in a book about the trial of one of the heads of the Nazi Fascists?'

"The investigator was puzzled. He wasn't used to this style and manner of speech from one whose house was being searched. 'No,' he replied, hurriedly replacing the book. It was indeed a small victory on the part of the refusenik against the great engine of the KGB.

"He didn't let up. 'But you're taking all of my books. Perhaps there are others among them that aren't anti-Soviet?'

"The investigator began to sweat. He wasn't used to dealing with such challenges. After speaking with his comrades he began to go through each book, one by one."

Miriam was getting impatient. "*Nu*, so what happened?"

"One minute. Let me finish. Where was I? Oh, yes, at 1 o'clock in the morning they finished their inspection and sat down in the small living room to prepare their report. Their faces glowed: They had managed to get their hands on some incriminating books.

"The report that the KGB agents are expected to prepare is quite unique. For example, when they confiscate a letter they write: 'Letter written on yellow paper with blue ink, size 3 x 5 cm.' They then write down the words with which the incriminating letter begins and the words with which it ends. They do this to every single letter that they confiscate.

"And so, my tired wife, I'm getting to the best part of the story. One of the refuseniks sitting quietly by the table watching what was going on suddenly took a piece of paper in his hand and scribbled a few words on it. He secretly passed it on to the owner of the apartment. The KGB agent noticed the movement and demanded the note, certain he had latched onto something hot. Of course, the refusenik handed him the note. The agent took it and added it to his report. And these were the words that he wrote to describe the note: 'White, lined paper, black ink, 5 x 12 cm.' Then he wrote the Russian words that had appeared on the paper: 'I believe, with complete faith, in the existence of the Creator, may He be blessed.'

"The apartment owner and his guest watched the agent as he wrote his report. It was very hard for them to keep from bursting out in laughter. Here was this atheist of a KGB agent in his official capacity writing those dreadful words: 'I believe in the existence of the Creator.'

"Are you listening to me?"

"Yes, yes, I'm listening," his wife answered. "I heard every word," she added.

"That's not a remarkable story of Jewish heroism? The ability to pull a practical joke against your enemies, in whose hands you've fallen?" Jeff tried to get a positive reaction from her. "I don't know about you, but I'm amazed."

"Of course, of course," she murmured reluctantly. Feeling that her husband was a little offended she began to speak, wanting to keep the conversation going.

"And we have to take part in such lessons?"

"You know we do."

"And if the KGB interrogators show up?"

Jeff felt a stab of impatience. Now was the time to strengthen his resolve through stories like these, not to fill himself with questions that would raise more and more doubts.

"So they'll come," he said in a voice laced with anger.

A stewardess passed by and politely motioned to them that they should lower their voices.

"Sorry," the two of them said at the same moment.

Miriam continued, "And it's so simple?"

"Maybe. If we keep our sense of humor, like those men did, we can overcome anything."

"Jeff!"

"Yes?"

"Do I have to go to those *shiurim* too? Can I just stay in the hotel?"

"What? Have you forgotten our cover story?"

Jeff felt impatient before his wife's sudden weakening. But he decided to try and break the tension a little.

"But don't forget the main reason for our mission."

"Yes, I remember. Your grandfather's *tefillin*."

"No," he laughed, "to buy diamonds."

"Oh, that. I forgot." She joined his laughter, and the tension diminished.

Jeff again grew absorbed in the pamphlet that had so moved him. The hum of the engines gave an appropriate musical background. By his watch it would be another six hours until they would reach Vienna. And from there — a direct flight to Moscow.

3̅5̅

gor leaned on the gate, his tired eyes, half closed, staring at the dark blue waters of the Moscow River as it flowed slowly by his feet. Behind him he could hear the hum of the few cars passing on Moscovaskaya. He did not dare turn around to face the street. His fear of someone recognizing him kept him back. Igor felt himself weaken, limb by limb, muscle by muscle. He knew that he could not go on like this much longer.

Suddenly he felt a body brush against him. He felt truly frightened, almost paralyzed. Who was it? The body rubbed against him again, giving off an unpleasant odor. Igor felt repelled, almost nauseated, and instinctively desired to flee. But he didn't; with great strength of character, he didn't. He must not show any fear, no matter who rubbed shoulders with him. The pungent smell of cheap alcohol that filled the air showed him that the man was drunk. But who was he?

"Ah," he could hear the throaty, hoarse voice. "A lovely Moscow day, no, *tovarish?*"

Igor didn't answer. The best thing for him to do would be to disappear. Gingerly he pushed the drunk aside, but with no success.

"What's my friend doing here? Oh, comrade, you're not working? Not studying?"

Igor kept quiet. His brain worked feverishly, searching for a means of getting away from this leech, who was adding anger to Igor's already overwrought emotions of fear and disquiet.

The drunkard continued: "Ah, surely you'll want to know why I'm not working. Why I'm not helping the homeland. Ha! Why aren't I productive? Huh? I was productive; oh, was I! You want to know, do you?"

In all honesty, Igor didn't want to know. All he wanted was for this creature to get away from him.

The drunkard spoke again. "I'll tell you anyway, even though you're pretending that you don't hear me, you young *tovarish*. It was your government — I'm not afraid of it! I'm not afraid of anyone! Not even Brezhnev — your Brezhnev! What can they do to me after that cursed war in Afghanistan? A Lau missile made a direct hit on my tank. A direct hit! Yes! Yes! I was burned over my entire body, and my left leg was gone forever! You don't believe me? Look!"

The drunk moved around, trying to show his wounds to Igor. But Igor refused to look. He was trembling uncontrollably; his entire being seemed to shake. Here was a man standing next to him, openly cursing the government. Perhaps he really was a disgruntled veteran of that cursed war. Or maybe he was another provocateur trying to set Igor up and trap him.

"Look, *tovarish*, if you don't believe me, see what your government has done to me, and how they finally just threw me to the dogs. No work, no means of living, no wife, no children."

The words sent a chill of horror through Igor. Suddenly he realized the full significance of his situation. Would he, like this poor drunk, be doomed forever to live under threat, in the shadow of fear, like an animal being hunted, like a prisoner who had broken out of jail? Would his efforts to ensure that he was not caught help him discover the Jewish identity that suddenly was disturbing him so? He realized that it was a lost cause, from the outset! No! He couldn't run away for much longer. Every Cheka that would pass on the street would cause him to jump out of his skin. Every passerby would be an object of suspicion. And what would he eat? Where would he sleep? Could he work? He would ultimately fall into their hands! For a short time he had had some hope; hope that flared when he had met Anatoly at the synagogue gate. Now that, too, had faded, faded quicker than he would have imagined possible. Igor suddenly felt that he might go mad; then his father, putting him into an asylum, would be proven right. He felt that he was going to give in. Rebellion left him, followed by an acceptance of a fate he could not escape. He reached a decision: He would return home. Let his father do whatever he wanted.

The drunk tried to explain something else to Igor, but Igor, distraught and impatient, pushed him away in disgust. It wasn't a powerful push, but it was enough to send an amputee off balance. The drunk swayed for a frightening moment and then, within seconds, lay sprawled on the ground.

Igor was terrified. People passing by, even cruising automobiles, might stop to see what had happened. His situation would worsen. Even the city militia might became interested in him, in his identity. Without thinking much, taking advantage of the fact that there was no one in the area, Igor hurriedly crossed the street and hailed a cab. If he could get away, he would be fine; drunks lying on street corners were not a rarity in the city of Moscow.

The taxi stopped. Igor quickly opened the door. And then, just as he hoped he could disappear within it, he heard a shout from the distance. "Igor! *Stoi!* Wait!"

Igor hesitated. Despite everything, the call brought him to a halt. He recognized Anatoly's voice. But in the last few hours spent wandering on the banks of the Moscow River, alone and desolate of spirit, he had lost his confidence in the youth who had disappeared so suddenly without explanation.

Finally, though, he decided to wait. He didn't get into the cab, giving the driver some sort of excuse and asking him to wait for him. Still he didn't turn around toward Anatoly, who approached him at a run. He stood straight, his back to the one calling him from afar.

Anatoly finally reached him, breathing heavily.

"Why'd you disappear on me?" he panted.

Igor, offended, replied, "I disappeared on you? It seems to me that it was you who disappeared on me!"

He tried to mimic Anatoly's tone for the last few words. Igor felt a surge of suppressed fury; Anatoly could sense his wrath, hidden behind the mockery of his imitation: "You disappeared on me!"

There was a moment of confused silence. Each looked at the other without confidence. The taxi driver shouted loudly, "Are you getting in or have you decided to stay here?"

Igor, without turning his head, called, "I'm going with you!"

Anatoly felt a stab of disappointment. He realized that his relationship with Igor had changed. The boy was going back; he had decided, evidently, not to deal with his situation.

"What a shame. I found a place where we both can hide," he whispered, a catch of despair in his voice.

Igor, his hand on the taxi's door handle, quickly responded. "But you didn't tell me where you disappeared to! What did you want me to think, when suddenly you raced away into the crowd?"

Anatoly looked all around. He walked closer to Igor and whispered to him, keeping one eye on the driver, who was watching with interest the sudden argument that had broken out between these two young men. "Try to understand, Igor, I didn't disappear. I suddenly saw the man — the one who could help us — passing by in the square. I ran after him so that he shouldn't get away. He's set up a meeting place in order to help arrange a hiding place for us. I went back to Gum and didn't find you. I've been looking for you for hours! I was worried about you!"

Igor softened a little. He pulled his left leg out of the cab. The driver responded immediately to his action. "Are you coming with me or not?"

Igor answered decidedly, "One minute, please, driver. I'm getting in."

Anatoly bit his lower lip. He knew that he was losing the battle for Igor's soul. And maybe, just maybe, there hadn't been any battle at all. Maybe this student, this Igor, had been sent to him as bait. In the meantime Igor, afraid that the driver would lose his patience and leave him, hastened to finish up the conversation:

"Look, Anatoly, the hours that I was alone allowed me to think a lot. They taught me where I really am, get it? I'm going home, Anatoly, do you understand? And whatever happens to me will happen. Okay?"

The suspicion that Anatoly was working for the KGB had not left Igor. He quickly entered the taxi. A moment before he had closed the door he heard Anatoly's voice.

"Anyway, if you change your mind you should know, the lesson won't take place tonight, but it will be in the same place three days from now."

Igor didn't answer. He turned to the driver.

"Dzerzhinski Square."

Anatoly heard the words — the infamous address of KGB headquarters — and shuddered. He could have kicked himself for having incautiously revealed the new schedule for the lesson, which had been put off because of fear of the secret police. At least he hadn't revealed to him whom he had been speaking with; nor had he told him of the meeting scheduled for 5 p.m. at the Lenin Library. Now he realized that he had to go deep underground. Who knew what Igor (if his name really was Igor) would report on him, there in KGB headquarters?

Pan Am's DC-9 aircraft landed in Vienna at noon. Jeff and his wife, a little tense, walked toward the transit passengers' lounge. In four hours they were scheduled to be on their way to Moscow. In the meantime, the couple searched for a quiet corner of the airport where they could rest a bit and dip into the stock of sandwiches they had brought with them from New York, enough to last them for their entire Moscow stay.

"If you don't mind," Jeff said to his wife after they had settled themselves down on a bench in a far corner of the airport, where only a few people passed by, "I'm going to take a nap." His face clearly showed his fatigue; he hadn't slept at all on the plane.

"Do you want to eat?" she asked, pulling out a sandwich wrapped in waxed paper.

"Later," he responded.

"And what about telling me the stories you read all night in the pamphlet?"

He leaned back in his chair. "Also later." The words came out as he began to doze lightly.

"Later" came about half an hour afterwards. Jeff suddenly awoke from his nap, slightly dazed.

"Where are we?" he asked.

His wife laughed. She chewed her sandwich slowly, with enjoyment.

"We're in Vienna, Jeff. Not yet in Moscow." The agitated look in Jeff's eyes subsided a little.

"Were you dreaming of Moscow?"

"Yes."

"What were you dreaming?"

"It's not important."

His wife persisted. "Yes, it is."

Jeff took one last yawn before awakening fully. This conversation completely dissolved the last tentacles of sleep that had him in its grasp.

"And I think," he said stubbornly, "that it's not important."

His wife took a deep breath and gave him a penetrating look. "Would you like me to guess?"

Jeff felt a little uncomfortable. "I asked you to forget it."

His wife ignored him. "I think you dreamed that the KGB had arrested you. Right?"

Jeff answered hesitantly, " Not exactly—that is—"

She knew that her guess had been correct. She cut him off. "At night you dream about the fears that you won't face during the day. That's right, isn't it, Jeff?"

He didn't answer. She continued.

"Maybe we should go back home, Jeff. It's not too late; we're not yet on the plane that will bring us to Red Square, to the Kremlin, to danger. We can still change our minds."

Jeff would have none of it. Clearly, he was getting a grip on his emotions. He stood up, as if trying to restore complete awareness, and shouted, "What are you talking about? Who's thinking about going home?"

Two black janitors washing the floors nearby were startled by the sudden shout. "Lower your voice, Jeff," his wife said to him. "Everyone doesn't have to hear that you're afraid to travel to Moscow."

Jeff sat down, offended and angry. He reached into his briefcase and pulled out the thin pamphlet that he had read through the night and thrust it in front of his wife.

"Listen, Miriam, I confess, I have some fears about this trip; I am, after all, just a person. But absolutely not, I have not given one thought to changing my mind. There are Jews sitting in Soviet prisons, under a tyranny that wants to destroy them spiritually, with all the means in its power. I am a free man, living in a free land, and if I have the power to help them, shouldn't I do it?"

His anger turned to laughter. "Actually, what's happening is that I'm giving you the same lecture you gave me in Flatbush."

"That's right," she said, as she cleaned up from her breakfast. After a moment she added, "Eat something, Jeff."

He thanked her, made a *berachah* and ate. After a few bites he heard her say, "And now it's story time. Tell me the stories that made you wake me up so many times last night."

Jeff nodded. He flipped through the pamphlet, looked at her and said, "First of all, I apologize for having disturbed you last night. But tell me, how would you have reacted to a boy like Viktor? The Russians imprisoned him for learning Hebrew and for his desire to know more about Judaism. In labor camp he circumcised himself — with a razor."

His wife flinched. "I don't believe it!"

"I do. Even though it's hard for us to imagine it, I believe it because the author of the pamphlet says at the beginning that he checked each story and verified it before publishing it.

"What's particularly interesting is that on the day of the *bris* he went out to work after bandaging himself up as best he could. The Russians couldn't dominate him! Incredible!"

After a moment's thought he added, "Listen. That's heroism that makes me ashamed, no?"

Miriam was silent, but her eyes showed her interest in hearing more.

"We're talking about a young man whose parents are faithful Communists. The Jewish spark began roaring to life."

Jeff did not stop talking. He spoke and spoke for a full hour. He spoke of the sacrifice of the Chabad *chassidim* for the observance of mitzvos through all the eras, even during the dark days of the Stalinist regime. He told her how, for instance, the hidden community of Leningrad organized the baking of matzahs. How a few activists traveled to Georgia in order to cut wheat and made sure that it did not get wet. How they ground the flour and flew it in sealed packages, right under the noses of the KGB. He told her of the blows that they had gotten when the KGB had discovered their activities, how their Communist parents had even thrown them out of their homes. He spoke of young people who dared to sing *zemiros* on Shabbos by open windows. How they endangered themselves by refusing to work on Shabbos. Of groups for the learning of Yiddishkeit that were opening in every place—

His wife suddenly glanced at her watch and came out of her trance. "Jeff, it's late. We'd better run to Gate 7 and wait for the announcement. You can continue telling me on the plane."

Jeff's enthusiasm cooled down. They quickly gathered together their luggage, as he responded to her words.

"Listen. From the minute we get on the plane, there is no further talk about this. We get on the plane and buckle our seat belts — and we're already in Russia. Got it?"

As they walked swiftly toward Gate 7, Jeff suddenly stopped. "Wait a minute."

She stopped, impatiently, and watched his hands nervously rummage inside the pack slung over his left shoulder. He pulled out the pictures that showed the path to their contact in Moscow.

"We forgot," he said. "We were supposed to look at them again and throw them out. It's a good thing that I remembered before we boarded."

Jeff and Miriam stood near one of the walls of the large airport lounge in order to avoid the flow of passengers. They studied picture after picture. Afterwards they tore each one into small pieces and scattered them among the garbage cans that dotted their path towards the gate.

Dimitri Grasimov sat in his office, slightly nervous. It was the tension that came with the feeling that he was encountering the unknown. The plans for the raid on the apartment in Moscovaskaya 23 were routine in the KGB's Second Department. He had wanted to be a part of it, to see for himself their success as they laid their hands on the bearded man. But then he would not be there to check out the mysterious American, Jeff Handler, as he landed in the airport. Dimitri did not plan on interrogating the man right away on his activities in Moscow. He intended just to look at him covertly as he underwent the tough customs investigation that Dimitri had arranged.

Dimitri called his home. His wife answered. Without greeting her or asking how she was doing, he barked out, like a military command: "I'll be late tonight. At the airport."

"Work?" she said, asking a question she did not usually dare.

"Yes, work," he said shortly.

Grasimov was ready to cut off the conversation.

"Dimitri?"

"Yes?"

She clearly felt the impatience in his voice.

"Igor called."

"What did he want?"

"He said he's coming home. He said he wanted to come to your office to speak with you, and they didn't let him in. They wanted to grab him, he said, under your orders. And he managed to get away from them. What's going on, Dimitri?"

Grasimov did not answer. Without another word he slowly put down the receiver, terminating the conversation.

36

ustrian Airlines' Boeing aircraft prepared for takeoff. Flight number 601, from Vienna to Moscow, was about to embark on its journey. Jeff and Miriam sat tensely, seat belted, awaiting the moment that they would leave the runway. Without even looking around Jeff sensed that there were few passengers; 20, perhaps 30 at most. Moscow, it seemed, was not drawing many visitors. After his first visit there, Jeff understood why. The plane's engines roared with increasing fury until, with a final burst of noise, the aircraft left the runway. Jeff glanced at his wife from the corner of his eye. He saw her clutching a picture of the three children they had left behind in New York.

The plane gained altitude. Beautiful Vienna disappeared behind them, left somewhere down below. The plane climbed over the cloud cover, straightened, and went serenely on its way. Stewardesses began to give out food. Jeff and his wife hardly exchanged a word. He murmured some chapters of *Tehillim* by heart, then opened a small *Mishnayos* that he had taken for the trip. He flipped lightly through it, reached a page whose corner had been folded down, and began to learn the third chapter in *Maseches Bechoros*. His wife, he noticed, was reciting chapter after chapter of *Tehillim* from her small *siddur*.

Jeff unbuckled his seat belt, stood up, and took a short tour of the plane. Yes, he had been right: There were few passengers. There were only two or three Russians; diplomats, perhaps, or consular officials on their way home. The others were Europeans, the majority obviously businessmen. The passengers spoke quietly among themselves or busied themselves with newspapers.

Jeff returned to his seat. Despite himself, he began one more time to go over the plans for communicating with the refusenik. With his eyes closed he repeated the names of the bus stations that he was to pass in order to get to the bearded man's home, if the man would ask him to. His thoughts wandered to the stories in the pamphlet that he had left behind in one of the garbage cans of Vienna's airport. He remembered the lovely story of how they had smuggled Gemaras into Leningrad, which had an active learning group. The Gemaras had been smuggled in by a group of non-Jewish Finns who often crossed the border in order to enjoy some vodka, avoiding Finnish laws against drinking. Joe Hausbinder's contacts had discovered this group and had given them the Gemaras. Throughout the entire bus ride the Finns sat and looked into the large books, as if they understood what they were reading. The customs officials didn't give a second glance to the book-bearing Finns.

It was also pleasant to remember how they learned in Leningrad with American lecturers. Members of the underground would buy tickets to the many museums which graced that fascinating city, and then take their American guests out to tour. The American rabbi would teach his tour guide Torah and Jewish law as they wandered from exhibit to exhibit.

Jeff's thoughts grew fuzzier as the fatigue of a sleepless night finally hit him. His eyes grew heavier; he slept.

The captain's voice on the loudspeaker broke the heavy silence in the cabin. Jeff awoke from a deep sleep to hear the announcement:

"Our honored passengers should be aware that we have just crossed the border and we are now in the airspace of the Union of Soviet Socialist Republics. Photography is now prohibited."

Jeff turned to his wife.

"Was I asleep?"

She picked up her head from the *Tehillim* in front of her and said, laughing, "You certainly were!"

He did not answer. He opened his *Mishnayos* once again, but the letters danced in front of his eyes; he simply could not concentrate. The captain's announcement had increased his feeling of disquiet.

Soon the passengers were asked to find their seats and buckle their seat belts. Slowly the plane descended towards Chermentyevo Airport. It was 6 p.m. Moscow time. Through the window they could see a heavy snowfall arrive to greet their plane.

The first thing that Miriam noticed upon landing was the vast number of uniformed soldiers carrying submachine guns who could be seen throughout the terminal and outside. Jeff and his wife stood in line for passport checks. After a few minutes they stood opposite two stern-faced officials sitting on high stools behind heavy-duty glass.

Jeff nervously pulled out their passports from a plastic holder. He placed them on the counter and pushed them through the small opening in the bullet-proof glass. The young official, who it appeared had not smiled since the day of his birth, inspected the passports carefully and scrupulously. He stared at Jeff and his wife, then back at their passport photos. He then took the entry visas of the Handlers, tore off the top for himself, and stapled the bottom half to the passports, returning them to Jeff through the same opening.

The Handlers had passed the first hurdle safely. From here they went to the place where the travelers' luggage was piled high, identified their own heavy suitcases, and took them for a customs inspection. Two blue-uniformed customs officials scrutinized them from head to toe and then, in passable English, politely asked them to open their bags. Jeff knew that this was the first serious test that they had to pass.

Jeff shot his first salvo in the frozen faces of the officials. "*Dobri vetzer,*" he said, wishing them a good evening.

Nothing. The two did not seem very impressed with the friendliness and the Russian language of the young American man. They answered matter-of-factly, in a tone which made their polite request sound like a command, "Open the suitcases."

The battle against the Communist regime had begun.

Dimitri Grasimov's spirits improved. It was a particularly cold night in Moscow, and through the snow hurling down on the city he could see, from his office window, the four Lada automobiles that would soon leave on their way for the raid that would have far-reaching consequences. At least, so he hoped. For this particular action they did not have to travel far to reach their destination of Moscovaskaya 23. Deployment around the building would follow standard procedure. They would stay a careful distance away in order not to rouse suspicion. They did not want a repeat of what had happened occasionally in the past, when participants in lessons in Hebrew and Judaism, always alert and suspicious of anything unusual, would turn away at the sight of KGB cars and not go to the apartment under surveillance. More than once Grasimov himself had seen a young Russian Jew hesitate before the building in which illegal activities were going on. The young Jew would look back and forth, and upon noticing out of the corner of his eye a car parked some distance from the house, he would continue on his way, as if he had merely come to the wrong address.

Tonight, it won't happen! Grasimov declared to himself. He had instructed his men to undertake surveillance from within an apartment close by. No one would dare refuse his men entrance. The ones who would actually break into the suspicious apartment would come in their cars at a late hour, after receiving a detailed report from the observers in the nearby apartment over their communication devices.

It was cold. Grasimov rubbed his hands together pleasurably. This might be his night. He might catch the bearded man red-handed, and perhaps he would watch the strange American from the sidelines as he underwent his customs inspection. And Igor? Ah, Igor, he, too, had returned home. Reason had prevailed and he had returned home. What should he, Dimitri, do about it?

Grasimov lifted the phone receiver.

"Colonel Malenkov."

"*Da?*"

"Don't be too tough on the others."

"Meaning?"

"The important one is the bearded one."

A short silence, then one word — a question, or possibly a demand.

"Meaning?"

"In order to shatter the counter-revolutionary activities of this group, I don't need a prison full of dissidents. Tomorrow the tumult will be brought to the attention of the American president. Only the bearded one is important."

"And he won't make a lot of noise?"

"It seems that this time he actively broke Soviet law. If so, it's another story. He can't scream at the world that we're persecuting him, that we're after him and he's absolutely guiltless."

"What are you referring to?"

Here, at this point, Grasimov took some revenge against Malenkov, the KGB officer who was constantly undermining his authority. He would not reveal to him the existence of the note that the bearded one had written, inviting someone to underground lessons in Judaism. Let Malenkov stew a little in his curiosity.

"One of my men will show him the incriminating evidence."

Grasimov, who was eager to reach the airport in order to examine the American, had been forced to give over the activities at Moscovaskaya Street into the hands of his sworn enemy, Malenkov, who was on duty that evening. But he, Grasimov, continued in charge of every detail of the raid itself. As such, it was he who briefed his men and instructed them as to how to act, not informing Malenkov of every detail of the operation.

He thrust his hand out toward the vodka bottle that had its usual place on his desk. No; he pulled away. Tonight he had to be totally sober. After a moment, he again grabbed the bottle standing so humbly by. He poured a cup of the drink and downed it in a gulp, enjoying its burning warmth as it slid down his throat. One cup won't hurt, he whispered to himself. On the contrary: In this biting cold, it might help.

Grasimov stood up and put on his coat and fur hat that bore the KGB logo upon it. He locked his office and with a jaunty step descended to the armored car that awaited him downstairs. The engine was already on, and the driver quickly concealed the newspaper he had been reading and waited for orders.

"Chermentyevo," Grasimov barked.

Igor sneaked into the house, opening the wooden door cautiously. But the squeak of the hinges alerted his mother in the kitchen.

"Igor!" she cried, her face alight. She walked over with hurried steps and kissed him on the cheek. Igor stood by, stolid, not returning the kiss.

"My Igor! Igorishe, where did you disappear to? Why did you run away? You broke my heart. Why?"

Her calloused hands stroked his blond hair; tears appeared in her eyes.

"Why don't you answer me, Igorchik?"

"I have nothing to say. I want to sleep."

His voice was cold and distant. His mother removed her hands, backed off, and gave him a searching look. Finally she said, her voice laced with a thread of harsh steel, "Okay, you want to sleep. So go to sleep."

Igor turned slowly toward his room. But his mother's voice stopped him, a voice much softer.

"Maybe you want to eat something? You probably haven't eaten for a while."

Igor stopped. Her question reminded him; he was, indeed, hungry. After a brief hesitation he turned around and quietly walked to the kitchen.

His mother wordlessly put bread on the table and hurried to cut some vegetables. She cracked open an egg and began to scramble it. Igor ate, his mother sitting across from him on a wooden stool. She leaned her head on the palm of her left hand and watched her only child as he ate his bread. *Who knows how long it's been since he's eaten,* she thought.

The meal worked its magic. With a great effort, Igor finally smiled to his mother, who sat watching his every move.

She dared ask the question again.

"Why did you run away?"

"I didn't run away," he answered shortly. "Father threw me out."

"I'm not so sure of that," she returned, standing up to prepare something hot for him to drink. "You're very hard on him, you don't consider him at all."

Igor angrily banged the plate that still bore some traces of cut vegetables upon it, sending them flying through the kitchen.

"What do you mean, I don't consider him? He doesn't consider me! He lives in another world, in a Soviet Russia that doesn't exist anymore! That maybe never existed, but men like him didn't know it."

His mother placed a cup of coffee in front of him. Igor calmed down a little and sipped it eagerly.

"What are you babbling about? You're like those dissident students trying to subvert the regime."

"That's it exactly, what you, too, can't understand. They aren't subverting the regime — they *are* the regime! If not today, then tomorrow. And if not tomorrow, then in a few days!"

"And you're among those who want to destroy everything we've built up?"

"You haven't built anything. You're simply persecuting me because I'm a Jew."

Igor had not finished his cup of coffee. He stood up. "And that, at a time when I haven't the faintest idea of what it means to be a Jew!"

He turned to his room. His mother barely managed to whisper the question: "And if so, Igor, why did you really come home?"

Igor turned around. He was already standing in the doorway of his room, holding on to the sides of the door. His body leaned forward slightly, in a gesture of defiance.

"A person needs a home!" he shouted. "A person needs a nation! A person needs an identity! I have no nation, no identity. At least let me have a home!"

37

J eff looked at the ice-cold eyes of the customs official, who stood quietly waiting for his order to be obeyed. With an obvious effort Jeff lifted the suitcases and placed them on the low steel table that separated him from the forces of law.

"Open, please."

Jeff responded to the infuriating request, pulling the keys out of his pocket and fitting each one into the appropriate lock. He felt himself trembling inwardly and hoped that his fear was not outwardly apparent. The suitcases were opened one by one; the customs official surveyed, with the first glimpse, but with a lack of surprise, the storehouse of food and repository of books that was revealed before him.

The customs official, without saying a word, began to take out item after item. The Handlers' clothing did not interest him at all. He stared at each book, put each volume on the side, one on top of the other, until he had quite an imposing pile. Then, with infuriating tranquility, he took out each salami, the cans of pickles, the packages of yellow cheese and other foodstuffs that had been packed into the luggage in numbers that made no sense, unless one assumed that they were being smuggled. The customs official organized each of the items slowly, without rushing, in separate piles. Finally, the Handler family exhibit in the airport was complete.

Afterward, the customs official found a blue package in one suitcase. He picked it up, examined it in the light of the bulb that gave off very little illumination. His face registered surprise, but he did not open the bag. Much to his amazement, he found a similar package in a second suitcase, hidden within a jacket. And so on, in the third and fourth suitcases as well. These items, too, he piled up neatly in a corner near a window. His stern countenance moved from Jeff's face to that of Miriam Handler, and then returned. Jeff kept quiet; his wife murmured chapters of *Tehillim* that she knew by heart.

When the bags had been completely emptied the customs official began examining the treasure trove he had uncovered. At first he tried by himself to understand what this was. Jeff, who tensely awaited further developments, suddenly noticed that he and his wife were the last of the passengers remaining. The customs inspection of all the others had been relatively brief. Not far from where they were being checked, Jeff noticed a broad-shouldered man standing and watching him with interest, but Jeff did not pay much attention to him.

The customs official's eyes fell first upon the blue packages. He opened one of them and pulled out two black boxes. His cold eyes seemed to ask Jeff for an explanation; they demanded an answer.

Jeff searched for the correct words.

"Those, those are *tefillin*. An item necessary for my religious belief. I am a religious Jew."

The customs official shrugged his shoulders. He pulled at the straps, removed the boxes, and stared at the *tefillin* with wonder and curiosity, as if he could not believe what the strange item could be. He put it against his ear, perhaps wondering if it was some kind of modern communications device. He noticed grooves in the *tefillin* and tried to pull the sides apart. Jeff, forgetting all the rules of caution that he had to take when dealing with the Soviet authorities, grabbed the man's arm and cried out anxiously, "No, no, sir! It's holy! Holy! It may not be opened!"

The customs official gave him a surprised look. He was not used to such sudden outbursts. Jeff's look penetrated deeply into his eyes with the firm, silent demand that he leave the *tefillin* alone without damaging them.

Jeff noticed that the broad-shouldered man, wearing a blue suit, who had stood a little distance from them, now approached, as if to hear his raised voice.

The customs official hesitated for a moment and finally gave in to Jeff's look and handed him the *tefillin*. Jeff kissed them, rolled up the straps, and placed them back into the package. His eyes seemed to ask the official if he could put them back into the empty suitcase.

"Yes," the official gave his authorization. Jeff wondered if it was a miracle, or just the power of his feelings that had done the trick.

The customs official picked up the second *tefillin* bag. "And what is this?"

"That's also mine."

"Why do you need two?"

"For the Sabbath."

"Why?"

"Sabbath is a particularly holy day. A day of rest. For a day like this, we need another set of *tefillin*."

The official looked at Jeff, unbelieving. With that, he put the second bag into the luggage. Now he picked up the third bag and again, with his eyes, asked the question.

Jeff pointed at his wife. "Her *tefillin*. She is also a religious Jew."

Jeff's wife nodded her head.

The customs official picked up the fourth bag. "And this is for Sabbath too!" He burst out laughing.

Jeff felt that this non-Jew did not believe a word that he was saying. He hurried to declare, "Yes, for my wife on the Sabbath."

The fourth bag was put back in the luggage. Jeff felt a slight twinge of relief.

Now he noticed that the man in the blue suit looking at him from a few steps away was speaking into a two-way radio.

The customs official turned to the pile of books. He stared at them and asked, "How long will you be in Moscow?"

"For a week."

"What is the purpose of your visit?"

"Business — diamonds — and touring."

The customs official lifted one of the books. "And you need all of these for one week? When will you have the time to read them all?"

Jeff noticed that the official was holding the Maharal's *Netzach Yisrael*. At the request of the small community in Moscow, Joe Hausbinder had sent a few copies of the Maharal's works: *Be'er HaGolah, Netzach Yisrael,* and others. In New York they had removed the new covers from the books and replaced them with used ones in order to minimize suspicion of smuggling banned books into the borders of the USSR. Jeff had also written his name in large letters on the front page of each book, and they had singed the edges of a few pages with the help of a lit match — all to allay the suspicions of the customs inspectors. And now, this stupid Russian was asking a lot of unnecessary questions.

Jeff took a deep breath and broke into his explanation.

"I am a religious man and I learn all day. I don't read each book at once. This isn't Dostoyevsky or Tolstoy, Gorky or Chekhov. No, I learn a little of each every day, a little in each book. That is what our religion demands, sir."

Jeff showed himself as being slightly offended, in the hope that this might have some effect on the stolid-faced official. The customs official did not reply. He checked each book and placed it back into the luggage.

Now he turned to the mountain of food.

"Who is this for?" he asked the direct question.

"For us. What's the question?"

"There's no food in Moscow?"

"I don't know. We eat our own."

"The food in the Moscow hotels is actually quite good."

"I'm certain of it," Jeff answered. "But we only eat kosher food."

The official blinked. "Kosher? What?"

"Kosher is special food that religious Jews eat. We've brought food for ourselves for the entire week."

The official looked eagerly over the foodstuffs arranged neatly in piles before him. His eyes particularly returned again and again to the salamis. Jeff picked up on the desire it had aroused in the Russian. But he did not react. More correctly: He did not react just yet.

From the corner of his eyes Jeff could see the man in the blue suit still listening quietly to his communications device. The chilling thought hit him: Perhaps the man was looking at him? And if so, who was he? Suddenly Jeff noticed the man quickly leaving the place, never stopping his murmuring into the radio.

"Here, you can taste it if you want. Take this salami home; your family will enjoy it."

The customs official was slightly taken aback by his directness. His eyes flickered over the almost-empty terminal to see if anybody was watching. Quickly he grabbed the salami and pushed it into the inner pocket of his coat. From that moment on, the inspection turned routine and really quite simple. The other foodstuffs landed safely back into the luggage. Jeff hurriedly closed and locked the bags. He and the official exchanged understanding looks; they practically winked at each other. Amazing, what one salami could do in hungry Moscow! Jeff wiped the sweat from his brow before he and his wife turned to carry their luggage to the main terminal, on the way to the city itself.

Jeff and Miriam said a silent prayer of thanksgiving. They'd overcome this first obstacle. Suddenly, they heard the official's voice.

"Excuse me, sir, there is someone here who would like to speak with you."

A heavy snow coated the streets of Moscow, giving it a white carpet that glistened even in the darkness. Four Lada automobiles slowly began to drive away from Dzerzhinski Square, heading in the direction of Moscovaskaya. After a short ride they parked at a reasonable distance from their objective, allowing them to keep it in view. They shut their motors. The agents sitting inside curled up in their heavy coats, their eyes scrutinizing the street and sidewalk. Cars hardly passed, and no one walked on the pavement near the building that received such scrupulous attention. Dim light came out from various windows, giving a yellowish cast to the snowflakes that fell ceaselessly upon all of Moscow, including Moscovaskaya Street.

"Colonel, do you hear me?" The radio crackled to life.

Malenkov put the miniaturized communications device to his ear. "Yes."

"Colonel, there is light in all the apartments but one. The apartment under surveillance is dark."

Malenkov coughed quietly. "Are you certain?"

"Absolutely. What can it mean?"

"I don't know. Our information says that there is a gathering of hooligans there. Has someone passed by or gone into the building?"

"No. Absolutely no one. Oh, wait a minute: Here is a person who has come from the corner. He's looking back and forth and disappearing into the house."

Malenkov did not reply. The men sitting in the cars were not under his direct charge, and so he minimized his contact with them, only giving them short commands to continue the operation. Now he wasn't certain what to do. The bare facts seemed to indicate that there were no activities going on. But that Jew, Dimitri, usually provided reliable information. Impossible that he had made such an error.

Malenkov turned on his car and slowly traveled up the street until he himself could see the apartment that was to be raided. Yes, there was darkness in the square window. *Perhaps,* the thought flashed in his head, *perhaps the hooligans were sitting and conspiring in the dark?*

Malenkov glanced at his watch. 9 p.m. He had no desire to spend the night in a car and freeze in the cold. He commanded the men to approach the building, leave their cars, and prepare for action.

Two militia men walked up the dark staircase. Their small flashlights sent beams of pale, flickering light in every corner, giving slight illumination to stairs worn down by age. The two militia men climbed up in the darkness with slightly hesitant steps. They reached the door of the apartment and knocked lightly. No answer. Now the KGB men joined them at the entranceway.

The militia men knocked more heavily. To no avail: No one opened the door.

"We're spending too much time here," Malenkov complained, thinking of his warm bed and deciding that this whole affair was a waste of time.

The militia men began to pound the door with their fists. A door opened somewhere in the dark hallway. A man, frightened, peered outside. When he saw who was knocking, he quickly disappeared back into his apartment.

The militia members shouted, "Open up! Militia!"

From amidst the silence that followed they could hear the sound of quick footfalls. They could see a light come on from a crack beneath the door. A rusty lock creaked and the door opened. A short, wrinkled old man in pajamas stood, frightened, his eyes darting back and forth in fear from one representative of the law to the other.

The militia men did not wait for his invitation to enter. They pushed him aside fairly gently and strode into the small apartment, the KGB agents in their wake. They turned on the living room light and saw a messy room, but no one inside. They glanced into the bedroom, searched the bathroom. No one. The windows were all closed; no one had used them to escape into the snowy night. Disappointment at their failure colored their faces in the yellowing light of the weak bulb that dangled without a fixture from the ceiling.

"Where are all the people who were here at the meeting?" one of the men asked in an authoritative voice.

The old man, trembling like a storm-driven leaf, barely managed to answer.

"What meeting are you talking about? There was no meeting here. You see there's no one here but me and my wife."

And they did, indeed, see just that. They felt humiliated, and Malenkov, furious, vowed to have vengeance on Grasimov for causing them such shame. For a moment he wondered if Grasimov knew that he, Malenkov, was actually working to undermine him and had craftily arranged this entire fiasco in order to cause him to fail. Well, he would show him!

Malenkov was the first to leave the room, without saying a word and at a vigorous pace. The other agents walked out after him. The men of the militia, who were obligated to be present at every KGB search, muttered a word of apology and joined the others.

The old man locked the door and shut the light. His exaggerated fear vanished without a trace. He returned to his bedroom and whispered to his wife, who'd also been awakened, in a voice that could hardly be heard, "Now I know why E. suddenly canceled tonight's lesson. How did he know that the evil ones would come?"

The old man asked the question, but did not wait for the answer. He was asleep before his wife could say a word.

J eff and Miriam complied with the request. They stopped and turned around to the man who approached them with measured steps. Somehow he radiated authority. The unknown man was speaking into a small communications device. His face grew scarlet with fury. Jeff could not understand a word of what he was saying though he was speaking out loud. It was clear that the man was losing control of himself and pouring harsh words into the receiver.

The man came within a few steps of where Jeff was standing. Jeff could see the wrinkles on his face that expressed decisiveness and harshness, perhaps even cruelty. The man certainly gave off an aura of power. He was not particularly tall, but he was broad and solidly built. Jeff wondered what he wanted from him.

The man now stood across from him, his cold glance fixed upon the young American couple. Jeff did not move but waited for developments with a particular lack of confidence. He noticed that the Russian's eyes seemed to soften a little; a look of arrogant pleasantry settled on his features.

"American?" he asked in heavily accented Russian.

"Yes," Jeff answered, trying to guess who the man could be and why he seemed more drawn to him and his wife than any of the other passengers.

"The first time here?"

"No," Jeff answered shortly.

The man would not let up. He didn't take his piercing gaze off Jeff's face. Even when the man was silent Jeff felt that he was undergoing some kind of security check whose nature he could not fathom. Who was this man? His brain could not find a satisfactory answer.

"You're coming back here," the man persisted, "because you liked Moscow?"

Jeff felt anger beginning to overpower him. What did he think? What was this all about? He coughed lightly, trying to contain his outburst. In a voice that was quiet but full of fury he said, "Is this a police investigation?"

"You're in Russia; you're in Moscow," came the sharp answer.

Jeff immediately recovered his composure. He realized that he had to stick to the rules of the game as it was played in this police state called Russia and not to be too smart; not, for example, to argue with a policeman here as if he were a cop on the beat in Flatbush. He tried to smile, but it came out affected and forced.

"I am sorry," he murmured quietly.

The Russian's face suddenly changed. He gave Jeff a smile of goodwill and fellowship. This metamorphosis worried Jeff even more than his earlier behavior. Jeff's wife pulled at the straps of the leather bag that hung from her arm. The Russian continued with his sudden air of camaraderie:

"I'm sorry," he said, "if I frightened you. No. This isn't a police investigation. Just the curiosity of a Soviet citizen about honored American tourists. You are tourists here, correct?"

The Russian's eyes again pierced through Jeff, as if awaiting some sort of answer. Jeff hesitated, then replied, "Oh yes, that's right, we're tourists here."

An inner sense told him he had failed. His momentary hesitation, his confusion, had put him into the stranger's hands. Undoubtedly, the Russian now suspected him of motivations other than the wish to tour snowy Moscow. He bit his lower lip in an obvious effort to seem relaxed. The Russian's eyes never left their prey, despite the fact that the smile and pleasant look remained upon his countenance.

"Oh, Moscow," the Russian said admiringly. "A lovely city, one that shows hospitality to all tourists who think well of her."

He put out his hand to shake Jeff's, and added, "I wish you a pleasant visit to this city. It is an interesting place, full of surprises."

Jeff gathered his courage. "What's your name, sir?"

The Russian laughed loudly. "Better you shouldn't know."

He said no more, and Jeff did not ask again. He knew that he was now a marked man. He would have to be very, very careful with every step that he took.

The big-boned man stood in his place, indicating with a look that Jeff and his wife were free to go on their way. Jeff turned and began to push the folding luggage cart that he had brought with him from New York. His wife walked a few steps behind. Without giving the Russian another glance they hurried to the airport exit, towards the few automobiles still parked near the terminal at this late hour.

The broad solid man, Dimitri Grasimov, stared at the couple as they moved away from him, toward the exit. He tried to decide whether he gained anything from the quick conversation he had had with the tall lean American. To his disappointment, he had to admit that he had not made much progress in understanding the reason for the man's visit to Moscow. He wondered why Jeff had not mentioned that he was a diamond merchant. That made a better cover for a visit than coming as a tourist during the Moscow winter.

Grasimov shrugged his shoulders in bafflement.

His communications device buzzed. Grasimov listened. The men who had gone out for the raid had already returned to KGB headquarters, their mood dismal. Their failure rankled, and the hurt was evident in the short report that Grasimov heard from one of his agents. He had actually heard about the debacle about half an hour ago, from Malenkov himself. Why had he felt that his opponent's voice held a tinge of malice?

Now, standing in the empty airport terminal, he received the full report. His fury at the bearded man who had outfoxed him in such an embarrassing manner increased from moment to moment. A heavy suspicion grew within him that the bearded man, known for his craftiness, had actually written the note on purpose in order to fool the Cometee with misinformation. He would pay for his acts. Dimitri clenched his fists and in his imagination saw himself plunging them into the face of the bearded man.

Grasimov pulled a small bottle of vodka from his coat pocket. He looked around him, saw no one nearby, and drank directly from the bottle, taking a generous gulp. Afterwards he slowly left the terminal and walked towards his car.

Grasimov's driver turned on the motor and drove away. As they drove, Grasimov muttered commands into his communications device, routine matters that he took care of with no joy and little interest, just from the desire to do something. The failure on Moscovaskaya Street had drained him of his interest in action.

"Follow the American starting tomorrow morning. Do it in a way that he has no idea he's being followed. I want him to feel that he's free to do what he wants. Keep up a continuous report. More instructions will be given depending on developments, understood?"

"*Da,*" a quiet voice answered from the distance, crackling out of the communications device.

After a ride of two hours Dimitri reached his home, scowling and angry. The light coming from his window, the only one on in the neighborhood at this hour, told him that his wife was waiting for him. He went up the stairs and noisily opened the door, not thinking about the late hour.

His wife sat in the living room, knitting. She put her finger to her lips in a gesture that asked him to be quiet.

"He's sleeping," she whispered.

At first Grasimov did not understand who she was talking about. But in a millisecond he remembered Igor, and the fact that his wife had told him that his son had returned home. The fury that had been gathering as a result of the night's failure, combined with the vodka that he had downed, lit up all the anger that had been simmering for so long.

"He's sleeping, you say?" he shouted coarsely. "He'll soon forget about the idea of sleeping!"

Dimitri walked quickly to Igor's room. His wife ran ahead of him, blocking the door. He tried to push her away and break into the room by force. He could already envision himself putting his hands upon Igor as a small deposit for what would be coming, to this little flea who was trying to destroy his father's position. The woman took the blows meant for her son, but refused to move. She could see the vodka clearly in his eyes, and understood that she had to do whatever she could to keep her drunken husband out of her son's room. With her sharp senses she realized that her husband had again failed in one of his missions.

"You didn't succeed again, Dimitri, and you want to take it out on the boy?"

As soon as she said the words, she realized that she had made a terrible mistake. Her husband's eyes showed a lust for blood. His breath came in short spurts after the insult his wife had hurled at him. He beat her until she fell to the ground. Dimitri burst into the room where Igor slept quietly.

Jeff and Miriam went out towards the concourse in front of the airport. There was no sign of Gregory. Jeff was surprised, and a little worried. One lone taxi stood forlornly nearby, awaiting a traveler to liberate it from its solitude. With no choice Jeff approached it, bent towards the closed window to get the driver's attention, and called out, "Hello! Hotel Russia."

The driver got out of the car, took off the woolen gloves that protected his hands from the cold, opened the trunk, and helped Jeff load the luggage. Jeff and his wife sat down quietly in the back. Jeff repeated, "Hotel Russia, *pozalusta.*" With some difficulty he ground out the Russian word for "please" that he had gotten from his Russian-English dictionary. Jeff was not sure if he had used the word properly, but it was obvious that the driver understood him.

They reached the hotel after a journey of close to two hours. Jeff walked in like an old acquaintance. His wife looked around, tense, as one facing the unknown. An older clerk dozed at the reception desk, and only the sound of the cab's engine and the trunk being opened and then shut roused her from her nap. Her tired, blank face gave off an aura of complete apathy and indifference.

"Documents, please," she said to Jeff without a smile, her hand moving forward. Her English was passable. She took their passports and visas and handed him a green card. "This, sir, is your permit. You must always carry it with you. You'll receive your passports and visas back when you leave the hotel. You must show your permit whenever anyone in authority demands it of you."

"Okay," Jeff said, giving her the shadow of a smile. His wife, too, smiled, as she bid the Russian woman good night. The woman, however, did not respond, not with her mouth, not with her eyes. Nothing. Her empty, frozen Slavic face hardly seemed to notice the two human beings standing in front of it. Jeff's wife felt a sudden stab of disgust laced with suspicion.

The Handlers were taken to their room on the eighth floor by an incredibly silent elevator boy. Near the elevator door on the eighth floor they met the Intourist representative who asked to see their hotel permit. She actually managed a slight smile as she returned the card to them and directed them to the left side of the corridor to Room 814, a room reserved for them while they were still in New York.

The door was opened, the light turned on. Jeff, with his last strength, pushed the luggage inside. Miriam looked around with obvious disappointment at the low standards of cleanliness, at the wallpaper tearing in the corners.

"What kind of room have they given us?" she complained. Jeff swiftly turned toward her and put his finger on his lips, motioning to her to keep quiet. He pointed towards the various corners of the room, hinting at concealed microphones.

Jeff pulled out a plastic erasable tablet from his briefcase. He wrote a few words on it — "It is forbidden to speak" — and handed it to her. She laughed at the words and mischievously added a few more — "during prayers." Jeff read her addition. His face grew serious and he added his own: "It's worse than during prayers, because it's more serious to endanger your life than to do almost anything that is prohibited."

His wife read the words, looked at her husband's face and longed to be back in New York. Then she pulled at the inside part of the tablet and the writing on the plastic was erased.

She then hurried to tear out the shoulder pads from her dresses and pulled out the *yarmulkes* that were hidden within them. She opened the clasps of the jewelry that graced her neck and slipped out several *mezuzos* secreted inside, handing them to her husband. For about a quarter of an hour they arranged their clothing and other possessions in closets whose hinges squeaked. Jeff pulled out a carry-on bag from the luggage and put two salamis inside, one of the books of the Maharal, four packages of yellow cheese, two *mezuzos* and three *yarmulkes*. He added one of the Minolta cameras that he had brought with him from New York.

He took out the plastic-coated pad and scribbled, "I'm going down to call."

She looked at him in astonishment. "Now, at midnight?"

He wrote: "Yes. Those were the instructions they gave me in New York."

She quickly answered him, again in writing: "Why do you have to go down? Call from the room. I'm afraid for you to go down into the Soviet night."

He read what she had written, erased it, and wrote, "Call from here? You've forgotten where we are. I'm going to call from a public phone outside the hotel, like Joe Hausbinder instructed me."

She read it, quickly erased it, and wrote: "We're going home tomorrow! I don't have the strength for this!"

Jeff grew angry as he read her words. "No. I'm going down. Don't worry; everything will be all right."

He erased those last words. His wife turned away, obviously nervous, and began to prepare for bed. She refused to look at her husband as he silently opened the door and slipped away into the darkness of the corridor. But she listened for a few seconds to the sound of his soft footsteps. Then she picked up her *Sefer Tehillim*.

39

eff went down to the hotel's deserted lobby. Even the reception desk was empty. One lone man sat in an armchair not far from the exit, slowly sipping vodka from a small glass. A half-empty bottle stood on a low table next to him. He gave Jeff, slowly walking towards the door, an astonished glance. Jeff tried to avoid looking at him and to ignore him completely. Had he been put there for his, Jeff's, benefit? Or maybe he was just another Russian suffering from insomnia, drowning in a glass his inability to sleep? Maybe. But as Jeff reached the door he realized that this Russian was sitting in the empty lobby of a hotel open only to foreign guests. A KGB mistake? But why would they send someone to follow him around at midnight? Why would they think that he, Jeff, a tourist who had just gotten in from the airport, would go for a stroll at 12 o'clock at night in the Russian cold, that had, according to the radio, reached minus 12 degrees?

Jeff reached the hotel exit. He glanced suddenly and swiftly at the Russian, who was engrossed in his glass. Jeff pushed the glass door and walked out to the area in front of the hotel. A blast of freezing air hit him with such force that he blinked, despite the wool scarf — that his wife had insisted on their bringing — that was wrapped around his face. In the darkness, he looked all around for a public phone. He would not repeat his mistake; he would not use the hotel phones. He turned right and walked past Red Square. After a few moments, he spotted a telephone booth. He put a few kopeks into the instrument and dialed. There was a short ring and then a voice came on the other end of the line, a voice Jeff could hardly make out.

"Hmm?"

Jeff hoped he had dialed the correct number. He took a deep breath and gathered his courage. He put the receiver close to his lips. Instinctively, and quite unnecessarily on this freezing night, he looked all around the phone booth to see if anyone was following him. Then he whispered the code words. "Yaakov's friend."

The voice on the other end of the line now became clearer.

"One hour."

And the man on the other end of the line hung up.

Jeff knew well that the anonymous man's phone lines were tapped. He therefore hastened away from the phone booth. Who knew, perhaps they could identify where the call had come from? They had told him in New York that he was protected. Still, one never knew.

He returned to the hotel lobby. In another hour he was to go to the appointed rendezvous. He had been briefed as to its location before he had even left New York. In the meantime he would wait in the Siberian cold of the lobby.

He chose a far-off corner in which to sit. He took out his small *Mishnayos* and began to look through it. He distanced himself from the Russian drinking himself blind. But after a few minutes the Russian actually took his bottle and glass in hand and wandered towards Jeff, sitting down across from him and laughing loudly. It was vodka, it seemed, that flowed out together with the tears of laughter coming out of the drunkard's bloodshot eyes. Jeff felt uncomfortable in his presence, but he did not dare get up and leave. His senses were alert; he prayed quietly to himself that he not fail in either his words or behavior. He suspected very strongly that the man was there for some sinister purpose.

The man took a drink from the glass, looked at Jeff, and laughed.

He snorted drunkenly. Jeff suspected this action was artificial. The man uttered one word.

"America?"

Jeff nodded his head in assent and buried his face in the *Mishnayos*.

The man lifted a thumb in the air and repeated the word. "America." Then he pointed his thumb down and declared, "Russia." Jeff understood his meaning clearly, but he did not react. He began to recite *mishnayos* aloud, in order to diminish the fear in his heart somewhat, and in order to hint to the drunk — perhaps only pretending to be drunk — that he was not interested in any contact. Jeff could see that the man wanted to draw him into conversation and get him to say something negative about the Soviet regime. Jeff wondered once more how a Russian citizen had managed to get into the hotel lobby. His suspicions grew.

The drunk continued, "Brezhnev, *ach.*" He made a gesture indicating distaste. But Jeff was not lured into the trap; he glanced at his watch and saw that half an hour had already passed. It would take him 15 minutes to get to their meeting point. He should start on his way. He stood up but the drunk seized him by the coat. "Brezhnev, *kaput.*"

Jeff shook him off with a strong shove, and the man fell to the floor. It seemed to Jeff, though, that the fall, too, was artificial; its goal was to embarrass Jeff. In order not to make things worse Jeff quickly helped him up, seated him in an armchair, and cleaned off his suit. "Excuse me," Jeff said in English. "I'm sorry. But why did you grab me like that? Are you from the KGB?"

He knew that the man could not understand a word of what he had said; still, he was horrified by the words that had somehow come out of his mouth. On the other hand, he was pleased — perhaps he had confused the man and his concealed superiors if he was, indeed, a KGB agent. The man did not answer. He looked regretfully at the glass that had fallen with him and shattered into pieces. Jeff hurried to the exit door. Instinctively, he turned back to glance at the man, and saw him sucking on the bottle. Obviously, nothing more than a Russian drunk. Jeff's fears were clearly unfounded.

Igor heard the noise near his door, the exchange of harsh words and the blows. He jumped out of bed and, alert and tense, awaited his father's appearance in his room.

The door burst open. Dimitri, who had prepared himself, it seemed, to startle the boy awake with his blows, stood shocked before his son, standing before him with fists clenched. Dimitri screamed like a wounded animal.

"What do you mean by running away from home? Did you want to destroy me completely?"

His father approached him. Igor did not move. There was no fear in his eyes; he was ready to fight for his life.

"You only think of yourself, Father. I'm nothing to you! The only thing that matters is your career!"

His mother, who had picked herself off the floor with difficulty, stood in the doorway, completely frightened. She dared not come in and interfere. She knew that this time the situation was serious, much more dangerous than ever before.

Dimitri came a few steps closer. His red eyes announced that the vodka had gone to his head. Igor, in an act of great courage, walked toward his father. He opened one clenched fist and picked up a medium-sized hammer that happened to be lying on his night table. He held it, ready for battle.

"Tonight, Father," he said with terrifying calm, "there will not be a winner and a loser. There will only be losers."

Jeff left the hotel and walked slowly toward the rendezvous. A whirlpool of fear and tension swirled and eddied within him, spiced with the feeling of carrying out a vital mission. The pleasant feeling that sometimes accompanies a forbidden, but holy, deed inwardly blended with his anxiety lest he be searched by hostile forces. However, the many hours he had devoted to studying the route of this action gave him the strength to overcome his stormy emotions before they could explode and affect his behavior.

He walked slowly. After a quarter of an hour he reached the corner of Karl Marx and Gorky. Behind him he could see the dreadful shadows of the Kremlin walls and the mausoleum where Lenin's body lay embalmed. The wind shrieked; the air was freezing. Jeff was not used to such cold and he could not understand how human beings lived in the Soviet capital. But it was good that it was so cold, he thought: fewer people wandering through the streets. Even the agents of the KGB, if there were any, would not do their jobs as well at this late hour.

He stood in his place for a moment, looking around him. Not a living thing could be seen in the area. Suddenly he tensed. His ear, cocked for any sound, made out soft footsteps in the snow. A few seconds of suspense, and suddenly a man, who answered the description that Hausbinder had given him, appeared. The man seemed to come right out of the darkness. He approached Jeff directly, nodding his head, then picked up the heavy carryall that Jeff had placed on the ground next to him. Almost casually, he whispered, "Tomorrow, as agreed."

Jeff knew what he was referring to. He stood in his place, waiting. The bearded man continued to walk, gripping the handles of the heavy carryall in his hand. Jeff knew that this was a critical moment for the bearded man. If a policeman should stop him and want to investigate what was in the bag, he would be accused of black market dealings. When they would discover the foreign foodstuffs, he could be sent to prison for years. Jeff was amazed by the courage of the man and stared as his figure disappeared into the cold darkness.

Jeff suddenly heard the roar of a car engine. The vehicle's headlights projected their strong white beams, illuminating the dancing snowflakes that had not ceased falling since he had left the hotel. He noticed that the bearded man signaled for it to stop. So it wasn't the police. The car, which Jeff now saw was a taxi, pulled over and the bearded man jumped in.

Jeff breathed deeply, relieved. But the tension still constricted his chest as he returned to the hotel. He had fulfilled the first part of the mission he had undertaken. In a strange, but perhaps natural, way he felt himself connected now to the Jewish people in a way he had never experienced. His peaceful life in New York, the Torah learning and mitzvah observance of a yeshivah student turned businessman, was fulfilling. But it had never brought with it the feeling that now captured him, as he walked into the lobby of the Russia Hotel. He looked for the troublesome drunk, but he was not in the lobby. The bottle, too, had disappeared from the table. Jeff shrugged his shoulders and went upstairs.

The light was on in the room. His wife was sitting at the table, her head leaning on the palm of her hand. She looked at him, a question in her eyes. The *Sefer Tehillim* was open before her.

"Why didn't you go to bed? It's late!" he asked.

She rolled her eyes, stood up, and said sarcastically, "A very logical question" — as if he did not realize that her worries about him had kept her awake.

Jeff laughed. "Tomorrow we'll go for a walk. It's a pretty city, Moscow."

She took the plastic pad and scribbled quickly, "Is it as nice in the day as it is at night?"

Jeff read it and erased the words without comment. He understood what his wife meant. But he did not want to volunteer any information on the mission they were to undertake tomorrow, in the middle of the day.

Dimitri Grasimov's wife let out a shout. The sight of the hammer in Igor's hand filled her with real terror. But neither Dimitri nor his son, Igor, paid her the least attention. They stood across from each other like two fighting roosters before the decisive battle. Their eyes radiated tension, perhaps hate.

Dimitri was thunderstruck. This was the first time that his only son had reacted so violently to his frequent outbursts. This was a different Igor. Where had he been? Whom had he stayed with? What had he learned? Dimitri's agents had not managed to locate him until evening, when Igor had tried to go into KGB headquarters in Dzerzhinski Square. No! Dimitri had no desire to get into a confrontation with him, to provoke him into physical violence. The hammer in Igor's hand somewhat cooled down Dimitri's fervent desire to give the boy what he so richly deserved.

Dimitri lowered his clenched fists; his body relaxed. In response, some of the tension in Igor's heart dissipated.

After a few seconds of anxious silence the father spoke.

"Put down the hammer. There won't be any fighting here."

Igor did not rush to fulfill the demand. He did not believe his father. He suspected that his father was trying to disarm him, in order to then attack him with his fists. True, his father was older than he was, but as a KGB officer he kept physically fit and ready for a fight, in case of any unexpected trouble. Dimitri was a powerful man; Igor knew that well. He held the hammer tightly.

His father tried again. "Put the hammer down on the night table. You don't believe me?"

Igor bit his lips, then pursed them tightly. "No. No, I don't believe you."

Dimitri walked away, retreating behind the door.

"I've moved away. Now do you believe me? I want to talk to you."

40

gor's eyes were riveted on his father's face. He tried desperately to uncover the motives behind the soothing words. He saw that his father's features were immobile; not a muscle moved in his face. Even his eyes, those inhuman eyes, those eyes that could be as cold as Siberia, did not wander back and forth as they used to during those times when Dimitri was nervous. Times, so many times, Igor could remember. But this time it seemed his father was speaking the truth. Still Igor did not rush to put the hammer down. He held on to it ostentatiously, as he hissed between pursed lips, "Speak!"

Dimitri Grasimov did not like it. He was not used to speaking to someone who showed he had the upper hand. And his son, Igor, was exuding a very infuriating sense of superiority.

"You're making a mistake, my dear son. The hammer won't help you. If I really wanted—"

Igor cut him off. "What do you want?"

Dimitri did not respond. His rebellious son had raised his anger to the point of destructiveness. But still he held himself back and gave no vent to his fury. His eyes, against his will, fell onto the hammer that was still raised against him.

"It's not important," he said after a brief pause. "The main thing is I want to speak with you quietly, so that you can hear what I have to say, so that I can show you the choices open before you as a young Soviet."

Igor did not answer. He scrutinized his father's every move, as Dimitri took a few steps toward him. More accurately, a few steps toward a chair that stood near Igor's side. Dimitri sat down upon it with studied calm, a relaxation that was meant to offer an opening to a more tranquil — if firm — conversation.

"Look, Igor, you stupid fool, you seem to have forgotten that to my generation socialism and the Soviet state are above everything. Above family, above friends. Do you hear me? And also — if you haven't figured this out yet — above sons. Especially in today's times," he raised his voice slightly, "when runny-nosed little kids like you, who have barely gotten out of their infancy, are trying to undermine the Soviet regime that we've created and built for you. Ingrates! Especially in these days, we're called upon to defend it to the utmost. Do you understand that, my dear son? You know very well that we do not suffer from an excess of goodness. Mercy doesn't flow in our veins. We are in the service of our ideal with unflinching will, sometimes even cruel will, to fulfill it, even if we have to coldly crush to death whoever tries to oppose us."

Dimitri became silent. He was breathing heavily. It was apparent that he was laboring under the effect of heavy emotions and that this conversation, despite everything, was not easy for him. His wife, Natasha, disappeared from the entranceway that she had been blocking with her broad body. She returned after a minute, holding under her arm her own personal weapon — a wooden rolling pin. No, she would not leave anything to chance. Igor himself did not move a muscle. He concentrated intensely on what was yet to come.

"Why don't you answer me?" Dimitri raised his voice.

"I have nothing to say, and there's no use in answering."

Dimitri fumed. "We'll soon see if there's no use in answering." Suddenly, surprisingly, he looked at his wife standing behind him. He saw the rolling pin and laughed bitterly. "Very nice. Very nice. You're really protecting me — you with the rolling pin, and your youngster with the hammer. Very nice. My agents in the Cometee should be here to see this!"

His wife answered quickly. "You said you wanted to tell Igor something. So tell him, and let us all go to bed."

Dimitri was hurt by the behavior of his wife and son, but he quickly recovered his composure. With a suddenness that frightened Igor and his mother, Dimitri jumped up and said, "I thought you would understand by yourself. You're forcing me to speak, to tell you what awaits you because of your stubbornness."

Dimitri took a deep breath. "My enemies in the KGB know that you're making trouble for me. They are watching to see how I will react. They're hoping that I will make a mistake so they can bring me down. With their cursed generosity they have already explained to me that there is no choice but to send you to a mental hospital. That's the decision, Igor. Final!"

He squinted his hunter's eyes towards his only child and continued in a whisper, "They demand it of me. It doesn't make me particularly happy. You must know that all your running away won't help you. Do you understand what you've brought upon yourself? And me?" He took a quick glance at his wife. "And your mother?"

Igor did not answer. It was as if his stomach was trembling, a shuddering horror that moved up to his chest, through his spine, and back down to his knees. He felt that in the next moment he would fall, unconscious, to the floor. He understood very well the terrible implications of this judgment that the wicked ones had pronounced upon him. In student groups he had often heard the whispers about those who opposed the regime, how the KGB had them committed to asylums. There they were granted the privilege of brutal psychiatric care. Members of the legal profession, minions of the KGB, declared that anyone who was against the Communist regime, that was based on the unity of the Soviet nations, and that was dedicated to building socialism, must obviously be mad. It was just this policy that caused so many young people to loathe the regime under which they lived.

Igor made a superhuman effort to keep his composure even as a hurricane of fears roared through his perplexed heart. He knew well that his very life was in danger if he were sent to such an institution.

He had heard the hair-raising stories of students treated with electric shocks, injections, dangerous drugs. No. He did not want to end his young life with endless tortures. The knowledge that his father, who had brought him into this world, was willing to agree to such a horrifying scheme, only increased his burning hatred against the tyrannical regime that his father served with such blind faith. Igor felt that he wanted to vomit.

His father's eyes were glued to him like a vampire to his victim. Igor understood that it was his turn to speak. With an obvious lack of desire, he blurted out, "What do you want me to say?"

Dimitri approached Igor, taking two steps towards him. Igor retreated, his hand once again clutching the hammer. He could see that behind him his mother had also gone into high alert and had taken a few steps into the room. It was a good idea to be prepared.

Dimitri laughed at their battle-readiness. "I won't do anything, my dears," he said mockingly. "I don't have to do anything. The things will happen by themselves. You can put down your arms. I can't have a conversation like this!"

Understandably, they did not listen to him. Dimitri, overlooking any request for a "cease-fire," continued. "You want to know what I want you to say? Very simple — that you agree to the alternative."

Igor kept his peace. He knew very well what that alternative was: to become a KGB informer and reveal all he knew of his friends. To report on their actions and their words. The city was full of informers but the KGB, with inexplicable hunger, wanted more and more of them. Their fear of the people pushed them into creating even greater terror within the public. The choice was a cruel one: between the destruction of his sanity in some closed institution and the destruction of his human conscience. A traitor! Treachery! Betrayal! What could he do?

Dimitri Grasimov, whose voice was suddenly incredibly soft, so fatherly, spoke. "You want to think about it, Igor? To answer me tomorrow morning? Fine. But don't run away again. Running away will be a very clear answer. Understood?"

"I understand."

"So do you want to think about it until tomorrow?"

"No."

His father tensed. "What does that mean?"

"I want to give you an answer now."

The KGB officer grew anxious. "And what's your answer?"

A short hesitation and Igor whispered, "I choose the alternative."

Dimitri kept his cool and his artificial serenity. A feeling of triumph overcame him. A tiny laugh escaped against his will. "I am glad to see that you still have at least a tiny drop of sense."

Dimitri gave his son a final look, turned around, and left the room. He completely ignored his wife, who was standing guard with her rolling pin.

The bearded man switched on the light in his small apartment, despite the late hour and the chance that he would wake his sleeping wife and their year-old son. He felt the need to unpack the package he had received from America, even before dawn. The men who constantly kept him under watch could surprise him at any moment. From the weight of the package he suspected it held many treasures. And if the KGB agents came to pay a visit he would have no way to explain away the forbidden merchandise in his possession.

The bearded man first pulled out the foodstuffs and hurried to conceal them in various hiding places around the apartment. He took the white Swiss chocolate into his bedroom and put it under his pillow. In the morning his wife would melt it and form it into small balls, like sucking candies: food that would, by tomorrow, reach his comrades in Moscow prisons. Chocolate was a luxury, prohibited to prisoners, aside from the dangers of questions being asked on how it had come into the hands of the refuseniks. Sucking candies, though, were permitted.

Now he was ready to check the *sefarim* that had arrived. Here it was: the Maharal's *Netzach Yisrael*. The bearded man grinned at the resourcefulness of his supporters in the U.S. The original, new binding of the book had been removed, and it was now bound in an old cover, so that those wooden-headed, greedy customs officials would think it was the tourist's personal property. The bearded man enjoyed the cleverness of the idea. The two volumes also bore labels from the Columbia University library, as if it had been taken from there. Who was it, he wondered gleefully, who was the imaginative man who kept coming up with these ingenious schemes?

He pulled the labels off the *sefarim* and placed them in the small library that he had been building up over the past years, each book smuggled into the country in a different way.

His face radiated absolute contentment as he pulled out the new Minolta 900. He turned it over and examined it with obvious delight. He pulled the cover off the lens and saw his own reflection in the highly polished glass. He looked over every groove in this miracle of the Western world, and finally replaced the cover.

Tomorrow morning, he knew, he would give the camera over to one who awaited it; that one would know, by prearranged code, what to do with it. The one who awaited it would fly to Tbilisi, in Georgia, and would sell it to one of the heads of the local Communist party for a vast sum. Eight thousand rubles at the very least; the equivalent of 120 salary checks for your average worker, a sum he would work for over the course of many years. The bearded man was satisfied. With the help of the sum that he would finally get, after a portion was shaved off for the middlemen, he would be able to maintain five families of refuseniks whose right to work had been denied them as a result of their request to Ovir, the Soviet Interior Ministry, for a visa to emigrate to Israel. What one camera coming from New York could do! The bearded man hoped that the tall lean man had also brought the other camera, a Nikon 03, also a special order from a Communist leader in the south of the country. The amount he would get for the second camera would allow him to run a seminar in Judaism for 30 families in the next month. It would take place in a *dacha*, a summer home, far from Moscow, far from the prying eyes of the KGB.

"It's late. Why don't you go to bed?"

He heard the voice of his wife coming from the bedroom.

"Yes, yes, I'm coming."

"What are you doing there?"

"It's okay, I'm coming."

The bearded man left the items that had come to him from the free world. He turned out the light with a feeling of satisfaction. In the prolonged stubborn and cruel battle against the regime, he could record another small victory.

The telephone jangled in the Handler's room in the Russia Hotel. Jeff awoke with a start, glanced at his watch. This was too much. It was only 7 in the morning!

He lifted the receiver.

41

"Hello," Jeff whispered into the receiver.

"*Dobroya utro*," the mysterious voice, authoritative and firm, replied.

Jeff responded in English. "Good morning. Who is speaking?"

The voice on the other end of the line softened a little and switched to heavily accented English.

"Excuse me, I forgot you are an American."

Jeff ignored the apology. "Who are you looking for? And who are you?"

"I am looking for Mr. Jeff Handler. I am from the Ministry of Industry and Trade. Are you Mr. Handler?"

Jeff calmed down somewhat. "Yes, you've reached the right address. What's this about?"

He glanced at his watch. It was very early for this Soviet bureaucrat to be calling. Suddenly he remembered that no one had been there to meet him at the airport. Where was Gregory?

The voice informed him: "We will be there to take you to the Ministry of Industry, to the Diamonds Section."

"Thank you."

Jeff wondered again where Gregory Butbinick had disappeared to.

"The meeting has been postponed until noon."

Jeff took a deep breath. The wheels of his brain began whirling. It couldn't be: At noon he was supposed to be on the subway. The change in his schedule infuriated him, but he asked calmly and quietly, "Why? Don't my honored hosts know that Americans are prompt in their meetings?"

"I don't know much about Americans," the voice said decidedly. "But this meeting has been put off until noon."

Jeff breathed deeply once again. His wife, he saw, was anxiously following his end of the conversation.

"Can I at least be given get an explanation?"

"Yes, I believe I can help out."

"So what's the point of it?"

"Two large-scale merchants from Antwerp have to return home early, so we're switching your meetings with theirs."

Jeff pursed his lips. "So that's it? Without asking? Without consulting me?"

There was silence for a moment. Finally, the voice answered, "Those were my instructions, sir. There's nothing to be done."

Jeff sat down on the bed. He was completely awake now.

"Ah, you say there's nothing to be done? I suggest you rush back to your superiors and tell them that there *is* something to be done. If our meeting doesn't take place as scheduled, I am returning to New York today. Remind your superiors that we're talking about a $2 million deal! Do you hear? Two million dollars! Think about it, think about how many rubles that comes out to, even at your official rate of exchange! And — "

The man on the other end of the line cut him off, trying to be pleasant. "But, please, sir — "

Jeff interrupted him, working to keep up the momentum of the threat: "Remind your superiors that I will report to your consulate in Washington the reason that their deal didn't go through. Someone is going to be held responsible for the significant loss to your country's coffers. Do you understand?"

"Yes. I understand. I just don't understand what difference it can possibly make to you. Do you have other business in Moscow, that the hour is so important? Where are you supposed to be at noon?"

Jeff, surprised, kept silent, not knowing what to say. He hastily scribbled a few words on his plastic pad.

"We're in trouble!"

His wife read the words and swiftly erased them. Her eyes asked the question: "What's wrong?"

But Jeff had already returned to his argument with the Trade Ministry official on the other end of the line.

"I have no other meetings. It's the principle of the thing. Just the principle. That's the way I am. Your men in New York should have checked me out."

After a pause, Jeff added, "Actually, didn't you have me checked? Don't you know that I am a man of principle?"

"But in any case —" the Russian tried to stem the flood of words flowing out of Jeff's mouth, but to no avail. Jeff continued his attack.

"Principles, sir. I have arranged to take a trip with my wife at that time, and that's it. You check with your superiors to see if $2 million means anything to them. I'm awaiting an answer."

Jeff precluded any response, replacing the receiver. His eyes met those of his wife and he exuded an air of tension and anxiety.

She quickly wrote on the pad. "What happened? Tell me! That is, write me!"

Jeff took the pad from her, read it, erased it, and swiftly wrote his answer.

"They want to postpone my meeting in the Trade Ministry."

She grabbed the pad back, and scribbled, "What do you care?"

He answered, "We can't make it. At noon I have another, more important, meeting."

"What meeting is that? And with whom?"

"On the Metro, the subway, on the Grogovski-Ghamoskvoretskiyah line. I'll get on at the Myakvoskaya station at exactly 10 minutes to 12. Got it?"

His wife slowly read the words, erased them, and answered.

"I don't get anything at all. What's this meeting about?"

"You'll see. It's all contingent on the answer we get from the Ministry of Trade. Let's wait and see."

"And if they don't agree to move up the meeting, what then?"

"We're in trouble."

The phone rang. Jeff jumped for it.

"Hello, Mr. Handler. It was hard for me to explain your problem, but the meeting will be at 10 o'clock. Not at 9, but not at 12. Is that okay?"

It was fine with Jeff. But he would not bring himself to give those Russians the satisfaction.

"No, it's not okay," he shot into the phone. "But I'll do my competitors in Antwerp a favor, this time."

"Thank you, sir," the Russian said, ending the conversation.

Miriam quickly wrote on the pad. "Are you sure they are only listening to us? What if they are photographing us too?"

Jeff shrugged. "So what do you suggest we do?"

"I don't know. I'm just tired of talking to you via a plastic pad!"

"So let's not talk," Jeff wrote. "We'll go over everything back in New York."

His wife laughed.

Dimitri Grasimov reached his office in KGB headquarters, well satisfied. There was a thin, supercilious smile on his lips as he entered the frigid building, one that he wore until he sat in the chair behind his desk. His son, Igor, had told him that the illegal class had been canceled. Since the news of the cancellation had not reached them, his men, under Malenkov's direction, had met with their embarrassing failure. They had arrived at the right apartment, but on the wrong day. Personally, Dimitri exulted in Malenkov's humiliation. Let him feel the bitterness of shame. But Grasimov could not ignore the fact that Malenkov had gone out in liaison with Dimitri himself. The failure, then, was really his, Dimitri's.

Grasimov was pleased with the way he had overcome his son's obstinacy and hostility. It was clear that Igor would, at least for a short time, listen to him. They had agreed that Igor would give full information regarding the meeting of hooligans that was going to take place tonight in that very same apartment. Grasimov had decided to remove the surveillance, that was more or less overt, from the apartment there on Moscovaskaya. Any surveillance, hidden or open, could scare away some of the people. Everything he wanted to know — the number of participants, their names, the topics under discussion — his son would tell him. Igor would do the job for him.

Grasimov called on his intercom. "Ask Malenkov to come in here."

Malenkov appeared, his face frozen and official. Grasimov smiled at him. He could clearly see the sour look on the face of his fellow officer, his enemy.

"You're not to blame," Grasimov said, without further introduction. "You're not to blame for what happened two days ago. Unfortunately, we never heard that the meeting had been canceled. The group will meet tonight."

Malenkov shifted in his chair and asked, "Where did you get that information?"

It was a wonderful moment for Grasimov. He gently tapped his chest and said casually, "From absolutely reliable sources. In any case, Malenkov," he continued, "tonight there is to be no surveillance and no raid. Whatever goes on there will come to me; breaking into the apartment during the meeting will just hinder the possibilities of finding out what's going on there."

Grasimov wanted to make certain that no one from the Cometee would meet his son.

Malenkov did not answer. He still felt the sting of failure. This information of Grasimov's gave him an idea. He would take his men and he would raid the apartment. Tonight.

"Okay?" From amidst the fog of his own swirling thoughts, Malenkov heard the question — really a demand — of Grasimov's.

"No action tonight."

"Okay," he answered casually, still thinking about which men he would use for the night's activities.

A black Lada automobile reached the hotel entrance at exactly 9:30. Jeff and his wife had left their room 10 minutes earlier, and had waited quietly and patiently in the lobby. Jeff was carrying a thin Russian-made briefcase that he had gotten in New York from his friend Joe Hausbinder. The briefcase was quite heavy.

After a half-hour's ride they reached the Ministry building. After an official check they were allowed into the dim hallways, behind their escort. The head of the department and two of his assistants were waiting for them in the conference room. A large cardboard box sat on the table. The men greeted Jeff and his wife politely but without any significant enthusiasm. One man introduced himself as a translator.

"Where is Gregory?" Jeff asked.

The man waved away the question. "From Intourist? I've heard that he's no longer with them. Why do you care?"

Jeff suddenly knew that he must not show any interest. In truth, he was only curious; yet he could clearly hear the tone of suspicion in the Russian's voice.

"No, no, actually I don't care," he hastened to reply. "I was only asking."

The negotiations were tough. Jeff, wanting to buy some time and searching for an excuse to stay in Moscow longer, made a very low offer for the merchandise, much lower than what the Russians had proposed. The Russians refused; Jeff remained adamant. He managed to hint, again and again, that he represented one of the United States' largest diamond concerns, and that it would be possible to close million-dollar deals with them several times a year. Everything was contingent, of course, Jeff explained with a mysterious smile, upon their closing a deal now that his superiors would be happy with. The price that Jeff suggested was so low, so unrealistic, though, that the Russians, eager as they were to do business with him, just could not agree. Occasionally Jeff was struck by the fear that the Russians would actually agree to the figure, in order to develop their business for the future. If that would happen, Jeff knew, he would have a serious problem; he would have to explain to someone in authority why he wanted to stay longer in Moscow.

The Russians, he noticed, were whispering among themselves. The translator did not bother explaining what was being said. One of the assistants left the room, returning after a few minutes. During his absence, there was an uneasy silence in the room. The man returned, and the phone rang. The manager sitting at the head of the table picked up the receiver, wordlessly heard what was being said on the other end of the line, and handed the instrument to Jeff.

"It is for you," he said, unexpectedly, in English.

Why, Jeff wondered, *does he bother with a translator?* Another ploy of Soviet bureaucracy.

Jeff took the receiver.

"Hey, Jeff, it's your boss, from New York."

"Hi. What's happened? Why are you calling?"

"Nothing's happened to me. But I understand that something's happened to you."

Jeff, shocked, answered slowly, thinking out each word.

"What's happened to me? I don't understand what you're talking about. Why have you called here?"

"I didn't call you; your negotiating partners called me."

"What? I don't believe it! What do they want?"

"They're complaining that you're proposing a crazy price, one that makes no sense. What's going on, Jeff? You're losing their trust that I so badly want to build up."

Jeff took a deep breath. Was that all?

"Listen, please. Let me take care of these negotiations. I know what I'm doing. The Russians have been very nice to me, very fair." (He knew that they were listening to every word, and probably taping them.) "But I'm sitting across from them, and not you. You're the general in headquarters, I'm the soldier on the field, right? And every soldier on the battlefield is a general. I'm sorry if I'm being blunt. Okay?"

After a few seconds of silence the reply came from New York.

"Okay, Jeff. I'll leave it in your hands. But make sure it ends up well. Okay? Bye."

"Bye."

Jeff returned the receiver to the department head. His eyes searched the face of the disappointed bureaucrat, who had hoped to get the boss in New York on his side.

"Let's leave the matter open," Jeff said. "We'll continue tomorrow. Whenever it's convenient for you. I won't make a fuss about the time, like I did today."

He waited for a response. The superior answered shortly, in an angry voice.

"We have to decide if a second meeting is worthwhile."

"I understand. I'll speak with New York again in the afternoon. Now, could your driver possibly bring me to the Myakvoskaya station of the Metro?"

They parted ways with a cold politeness. Jeff patted his heavy briefcase in order to somehow check that everything was all right within. He and his wife followed the driver who had brought them to the Ministry.

When the two of them had made themselves comfortable in the back seat, the driver, obviously curious, asked them in broken English, "You have meeting?"

"No. Just a trip on your wonderful subway system. I want to show my wife what we don't have in New York."

The driver grinned and zoomed into the street. And at the Ministry, someone reported to someone in the Cometee, who reported to Grasimov, that the Americans were going to the Myakvoskaya station of the Metro.

Grasimov's men went out on their assignment.

42

The black automobile came to a stop. "Myakvoskaya Metro," the driver announced. Jeff thanked him with a nod of the head. "*Dosvidanya*," he murmured.

"*Poka*," returned the driver, bidding him farewell with a Moscow slang term.

Jeff pulled out another word from his treasure chest. "*Spasibo* — thank you."

Miriam rushed out of the car, not bothering to speak to the driver. He gunned the motor and drove off, disappearing into the flow of traffic like one fleeing some unnamed threat.

Now the two of them stood on the street corner exposed to the fierce wind, wrapped in the fur coats they had bought in New York before setting forth on their travels. They tried futilely to bundle up from the freezing temperatures and the snowflakes falling on them from the leaden skies. Jeff saw, not far from them, a stairway leading down to the Metro station. *Maybe it will be warmer there*, he thought. He glanced at his watch, and smiled inwardly: twenty minutes before noon. According to his calculations, he would have just enough time to reach the train heading to Ghamoskvoretskiyah station exactly on time. He was surprised that he actually managed to remember the strange long names of places that he had been given in New York; he had repeated them dozens of times both at home and during the long flight to Moscow.

Jeff's wife, Miriam, gazed around her at the quiet street, at the subdued flow of traffic and the stone buildings that stood on both sides. She stared at the massive structures, at the ponderous entranceways and heavy brown facades. How different a view from that which she was used to in New York! It seemed that behind those stone walls and drapery-covered windows lay many dark secrets and mysteries.

Jeff nudged her, urging her to follow him. She listened, not asking unnecessary questions. Near the entrance to the subway stood a middle-aged man, placidly reading a newspaper as if it were a lovely spring day. Jeff glanced at him, but he did not look up. As they walked quickly down the steps leading to the station itself, Jeff whispered to his wife, "Idiot!"

Miriam, startled out of her usual caution, said out loud, "Who?"

They reached the bottom of the stairs. Now they had to pass through a long corridor to get to the platform. But they stopped for a moment and stood, amazed, feeling that somehow they had wandered into one of the czar's palaces. The beauty and luxury that stood before them astonished them. They had never seen such luxury, certainly not in the grimy subways of New York. Turquoise archways graced the terminal leading to the platforms. At the center of each archway was a bowl-shaped object illuminated by the light of countless bulbs. Each of these was decorated with a professional painting of one of the legends of the Communist revolution. The Handlers began walking slowly, just like a couple of tourists intoxicated by the sights before them. Jeff suddenly roused himself from the spell cast by the unique architecture of the station, one of Moscow's largest. He began walking quickly. After all, he had a mission to complete. Business before pleasure.

Miriam remembered her question. "Who's an idiot?" Now she was careful to speak quietly, despite the fact that there were few people passing by in the station.

"The man standing at the entrance holding a newspaper."

Miriam did not understand.

"Why? What did he do?"

"It's obvious that he's following us. He's an idiot if he thinks I'm not going to notice him. When did you ever see a person standing in the cold, reading, as if he were sitting in a park on a spring day? A Russian brain!"

"Don't be so sure that it wasn't done on purpose."

Jeff, in the midst of his swift walk, managed to turn his head towards his wife.

"What do you mean?"

With difficulty she caught up to him; breathing heavily, she tried to explain.

"Maybe they want you to know that they're following you, so that you'll be careful and not do anything crazy."

Jeff was quiet for a moment. Finally, he said, "That's a possibility. It could be. But you should know that we're not going to do anything that's against Soviet law. So we've got nothing to be afraid of."

"I hope so. Don't turn around; there's someone following us now in a way that's too obvious. When we stopped to look at the artwork in the station, he stopped too. When we started to move quickly, so did he. Is the platform far? I'm getting tired of this running."

"I hope not. I don't want to miss our train. This train, at this time, is the one we need."

"Why this one especially?"

"You'll see."

"Jeff," she whispered.

"Yes? Oh, here's the platform." He pointed to an area in front of them.

"But Jeff—"

"Yes, what's the matter?"

"I want to go home."

Jeff bit his lips. This was not the time to get cold feet. He answered quickly, with open anger, "In another few minutes the train will be here. Maybe it can take us home. Can't you hear the sound of the wheels on the rails?"

She could hear the sarcasm in his voice, but decided not to respond.

"You are to pay attention to everyone who is sitting around the table. Understood?"

Igor nodded his head, not meeting his father's gaze. His father, Dimitri, sat across from him, leaning on a round table in a small bar located not far from KGB headquarters. Though he had overpowered his son, though he had filled him with fear and terror, still Dimitri suspected that he was not going to get full cooperation from him.

"I repeat: It's important that you be familiar with the faces of the hooligans who are gathered there. I want to be certain that we recognize all of them. Afterwards, we'll go through our photo archives in order to compare them. These subversive activities must be under our control. Don't worry, we won't take action against them. Certainly not now. It's a question of politics in high places. A part of detente, the compromises between America and our nation. The Americans, they have soft hearts, they're so sensitive, it's amazing." Igor could hear the scorn in his father's voice. "And that's why they make so much noise every time we take in some religious hooligan and teach him a little about the laws of socialism."

Igor did not respond. He simply nodded his head in comprehension. This was not the time to rouse his father's fury.

Suddenly, his father leaned closer to him, like one sharing a secret.

"Look, it's possible that some American might join the group you'll be with tonight; a young man, tall and slim. He's got sharp eyes that seem to say that despite the disgusting hamburgers he eats there in America, he's still got a grain of intelligence in his head. I watched him for a long time in the airport."

Igor lifted his head; his eyes showed wonder. Dimitri Grasimov felt a stab of satisfaction.

"Yes, yes, that night, two nights ago, when you were so wild at home, I was in Chermentyevo Airport. I went only in order to personally check out that suspicious American. I was there for a full hour. We work hard, Igor, in order to preserve this nation for the coming generation, and you don't appreciate it at all."

Igor maintained his silence despite his growing curiosity. Dimitri lit a cigarette, inhaled the smoke deeply, and then exhaled.

After a few moments of silence Grasimov continued giving his son his orders.

"Now, pay attention. Look for any excuse to start talking with the American. Strike up a conversation, show that you're interested in America. It doesn't matter; even though it's illegal, I permit it this time."

The request seemed ambiguous to Igor. He broke his resolution not to speak to his father, just to accept his commands in the hope that he would somehow find a way to circumvent them. But now he asked, "I don't understand! What's the point?"

"The point of what?"

"Of my speaking with the American."

Grasimov gave his son a searching look, took a deep drag on the butt of his cigarette, still clenched between his fingers. Finally he threw it on the floor and said, "Nothing. Talk to him about this and that. But somewhere in the conversation, at a place that seems right to you, mention that you know where Krasno Bogatirski Street is. That's all! And tell me how he reacts."

Igor was taken aback. "Krasno Bogatirski? But that's where—"

Grasimov cut him off. "Shhh! Not another word. Just do what you're told, and that's all!"

The Russian standing outside the Metro station folded the newspaper that he had been reading, nodded his head in the direction of the men sitting in the black Volga automobile parked on the other side of the street, as if to say, "The Americans have entered the station."

The train arrived, coming into the quiet station with a startling roar. The platform sprang to life. Jeff counted the railway cars. He was to enter the second car. The train came to a halt. A number of passengers jumped out; others entered. Jeff did not notice the man standing behind him, whispering into a miniature communications device on the lapel of his coat. Jeff did not know that every station contained receiving equipment for transmissions of the *tauton*, those covert surveillance agents of the KGB.

On the street near the station the driver of the Volga turned on his motor and drove slowly on his way.

Jeff and his wife jumped onto the train a moment before its doors closed. With a show of indifference he ran his eyes over the car which he entered. All the seats were taken, but Jeff was not looking for a place to sit. He walked towards the end of his car, his wife following behind him. He saw the man he was looking for: short, thin, in his late 20's. As agreed upon, he was wearing a black cap rather than the Russian fur hat adopted by most of the passengers. The leather jacket he was wearing was too big for him; a green scarf wound around his neck peeked out from under his lapels. Jeff knew that this was the man he was to meet. Jeff stood near him, putting his brown leather case down right next to an identical briefcase that belonged to the Russian. Jeff's wife stood next to him, and Jeff began to speak to her in a loud voice.

"Did you see that gorgeous station? They've told me that all the stations in the city are fantastic!"

His wife was startled by his conversation, but realized that she should play along even if she did not know why. She answered, in the same loud tone, "Really fabulous! Too bad we didn't have more time to look at those incredible paintings on the ceiling."

"Good, good," Jeff answered in loud English, that brought upon him the angry glances of several passengers who were sitting as quietly as monks who had taken a vow of silence.

Jeff's hand clutched the metal pole that was intended for the passengers' use. He could clearly feel the hand of the man standing beside him touching his fingers. He continued to stand, motionless. Slowly, so slowly, he felt the Russian dexterously push something into the palm of his hand. Their hands touched for a moment, and then the Russian returned to his original position. All the while the man looked around him indifferently, and Jeff continued to chat with his wife as if they were two carefree tourists. Jeff could feel what the

Jewish man had placed into his hand, but he did not move; he clutched the metal pole in order to protect the hard object the man had placed there, making certain it should not slip down to the floor.

The train stopped. The thin Russian prepared to exit. He took Jeff's briefcase and slowly left the car. Jeff could see two men following him from a distance. He felt a flash of fear. If the spies would examine the briefcase, the young man was lost. He would certainly be accused of black marketeering when they saw the two long salamis inside, the chocolate bars, the yellow cheese, the *yarmulkes*, and *tzitzis*. From what Jeff had heard, the man could end up spending years behind bars. Where had he gone wrong, that they were following him so closely? He was furious with himself: Hadn't he himself announced, in a loud voice, what station he needed, there in the Trade Ministry building?

43

he thin young man walked slowly out of the train. From the platform he turned with measured steps toward the tunnel that led to the exit. He knew that a cab was waiting for him not far from the station. According to plan, one of his cronies would be sitting inside, and he would take the briefcase to where it was supposed to go. That was what he hoped would happen, as he approached the escalator that would bring him up to the street.

But as he reached the escalator his sharp senses warned him of an ambush. He stopped for a minute, but realized almost immediately that he should not do so. He must walk on, as if nothing was wrong. This was not the first time, and would not be the last, that someone was waiting for him. He stepped onto the bottom step of the escalator, held on to the rail, and began to go up. Only when he was about halfway up did he dare turn around to see what was going on behind him. It was not difficult to spot the two men who had sat near him in the train, and who now were approaching the escalator. The thin young man, known to his friends as Alexander, swiftly decided what his next step would be. The moment he reached the top, as the light of the busy street just outside became visible, he quickly turned and hopped onto the escalator going down, back into the station. As he descended, for a split second his eyes met those of the two men going up beside him. He saw, with a flash of pleasure, their shocked looks. His suspicions were now confirmed. The *tauton* were on his heels. He realized he had surprised them by evading them: a small victory by a refusenik persecuted by the awesome machinery of the KGB. Despite his success he stayed tense and alert, realizing that he was still in grave danger. The precious merchandise in his briefcase added up to a serious indictment against him if those men would get their hands on it.

He had won himself a few seconds respite, until the men could get to the top of the escalator and head back down; a time-out that would enable him to put his emergency escape route into action. He was extremely nervous and at the same time completely determined. They would not catch him with his hazardous load, the cheeses and salamis that so threatened the Soviet regime.

The two men stalking him were trapped. The escalator going up was blocked by passengers rushing to their jobs in the city. The men tried to open a path through the crowd, rudely pushing away their surprised fellow citizens, in order to get to the top — and get back to the bottom. They knew they were losing time; time that would let that thug slip out of their hands somehow. Perhaps he would board another train, or hide in one of the many corners of the huge station. Suddenly, without warning, the two leaped over the railing that divided the two escalators. They paid no attention to the dangers of their move, nor to the shocked stares of the other passengers. Their ploy worked: now they, too, were heading downward, standing on the stairs just steps away from Alexander. He felt their presence clearly, but forced himself to move slowly, and not to exhibit any signs of fear.

Alexander reached the bottom and began to walk swiftly through the long corridors, fully aware that the two agents were behind him. The two kept their distance, as if wanting to see what he would do next. He made a sharp turn into a narrow passageway that appeared on the right of the large hall. He quickly opened a door that bore the words "Men's Room," closing it behind him. Now he leaned weakly on the door, breathing deeply. He knew that they would not come in after him, nor would they budge from their post just outside.

Alexander worked quickly. This was not the first time that he or another refusenik had found himself in this position, and it was the bathroom that offered the solution. It was no coincidence that they had chosen this particular station as their "transit area" for merchandise. He put the briefcase on the floor, pulled a small screwdriver out of his pocket, and quickly removed a wooden board that hung behind the toilet. Before it was an empty space, and Alexander rushed to place all the contents of the case within: two salamis, yellow cheese, *yarmulkes*, *tzitzis*. In two minutes he was done; the wooden board was back in place, the screws tightened, the screwdriver lost in a pocket of his leather jacket. In his briefcase he left only a woolen sweater that the American stranger had for some reason placed within.

Alexander waited a few more minutes, took a deep breath, forcing himself to exude a feeling of calm indifference. Only then did he slowly open the bathroom door. His eyes, alert, immediately spotted the two men waiting for him on the sides of the passage. He passed them by, not giving them a second glance. But one of them stepped in front of him, not allowing him to continue on his way.

"*Stoi,*" he commanded, his voice grim.

Alexander acceded to the command, and stopped.

"What's the matter?"

They didn't bother answering.

"Open the briefcase, please."

Alexander shrugged in puzzlement, as if he did not know what they wanted. Yet he hurried to obey their command. They rummaged in it curiously, and their disappointment soon became evident. Uncomfortable, and in an effort to quell their bafflement, they began their interrogation.

"Why did you return to the station?"

"I had to go to the bathroom."

They stared at him furiously.

"We know exactly who you are. Next time you won't get away from us."

Alexander did not answer. Silence is an important armament in the arsenal of the lone refusenik. They let him go on his way. He went up to the street, passed the waiting taxi, and did not go in. His comrade waiting inside understood and told the cabbie to drive on.

A few hours later a young Polytechnic student came to the train station. He slowly went down the escalator and entered the bathroom. He quickly removed the wooden board and with swift motions filled the backpack that he had brought with him. He held one of the *yarmulkes* in his hand for a moment, put it on his head for a few seconds. Then he fervently kissed the strings of the *tzitzis*. It was only last week that he had heard a *shiur* that introduced him to the *mitzvah* and its importance.

The train left the station. Jeff cautiously placed his hand in his pocket, leaving the note inside. He was very curious to know its contents. The Handlers stayed on for two more stops, and then left the train for Moscow proper.

"Let's take a taxi and get back to the hotel," Jeff said as he once again gazed at Moscow, rapidly turning white under the onslaught of the falling snow. He wanted to hurry back and read the note.

"And what about our visit to Gorky Park?"

"Tomorrow is another day. And if we don't have time, we'll do it on our next trip to Moscow. I'm sure you'll want to visit this incredible city again."

She glanced at him angrily. She did not find him funny.

About half an hour later they were in their room in the Russia Hotel. Even before he took off his heavy jacket, Jeff had pulled out the folded note, opened it, and began to read. It was written in English, in a style that impressed him.

"We, the imprisoned, thank you for having come to Moscow to teach us a little Torah. The lesson will take place tonight. Before nightfall, go down with your wife to the lobby of the hotel. Go to the Intourist reception clerk and ask her in a loud voice where you can buy tickets to the Bolshoi Theater. Add that in New York you had always dreamed about attending the theater here. If there's no unexpected difficulty, she'll see to it that you get tickets.

"Afterward, at exactly 8 o'clock, you and your wife should sit in the lobby and look out at the people walking past. A very fat young man will pass by the hotel entrance in the direction of the Kremlin. He will be wearing a grey coat, with a large green scarf wrapped around his neck. Watch him: After 10 minutes he will again pass the hotel, this time walking in the opposite direction. Only when you see him a third time should you and your wife get up and follow him, from a distance of at least 100 yards.

"Bring with you in your briefcase the pair of *tefillin* that you will be giving a lesson on. And let your wife not forget the cakes. They are very important, for our enemies are always upon us."

Jeff read the note a few times, then handed it to his wife, Miriam, motioning to her to rip it up once she had read its contents. She perused it carefully, and then did as her husband had bid, tearing it into tiny pieces. Jeff could see in his wife's eyes the readiness to go into action. They radiated no fear at all. The sense of mission, a mission of Jews living in the free world on behalf of their brethren in Eastern Europe, now surged deeply through her. Jeff was thrilled: This would surely enable him to cope with the obstacles that lay before them on their way to a difficult goal.

Jeff got the two tickets to the Bolshoi Theater. At 8, he and his wife went down to the lobby. The reception clerk looked at them indifferently and turned back to her work, which consisted of reading some cheap periodical. Outside two taxis stood, awaiting passengers who did not come.

Jeff saw the fat man walking some distance from the hotel, and then disappearing into the cold night. It wasn't long before they saw the man again, this time walking in the opposite direction. Jeff could see his portly form and the green scarf draped around him. Now they waited for almost 10 minutes, and he once again turned up. When he disappeared around the side of the building, the two quickly went out into the darkness.

Anatoly Dobrovitz reached the Lenin Library at exactly 5 o'clock. He entered the reading room, which was full of students quietly poring over their books. The silence was absolute. His eyes searched for the bearded man who was supposed to be there. He walked slowly inside, scanning the faces of the students. Only a few bothered lifting their heads to glance at the young man staring at them; these, too, immediately turned back to their reading. He continued his efforts at identification. Many minutes passed with no sign of success. He got to the end of the reading room, and was already prepared to go back to the exit. He hardly noticed the young man, not far from him, stand up and walk towards him. The young man bumped into him lightly, and excused himself in a whisper. *"Izvineta puzhlustya."*

Anatoly, startled, whirled around toward the man, who told him a second time, "Excuse me, I didn't mean it."

The young man's hand gave Anatoly's shoulder a friendly tap and then pressed his palm. Anatoly could feel the piece of paper being handed to him. Skillfully he closed his fingers around it. The man swiftly moved towards the exit.

Anatoly stood for a moment, still taken aback by the speed of the unexpected encounter. After a few seconds he recovered his composure and sat down at one of the empty places. He looked around him and, not seeing anyone paying him any undue attention, opened up his fist and read: *"The Magic Goldfish* by Pushkin, page 43."

Colonel Malenkov reached his office in KGB headquarters toward evening. A swift glance at the windows showed him that his enemy, Dimitri Grasimov, was still in the building; a light burned in his office. *What's he doing here?* Quickly he went up the stairs to his fourth floor office. He must swiftly organize his men for the upcoming raid on the apartment in Komaskaya Prospekt. He was curious to discover why Grasimov had insisted that none of their men approach the apartment that night. Interesting: What could he be hiding?

Malenkov knew that he had to take every precaution. Grasimov was sneaky, and up until today had managed to squirm out of every trap that Malenkov and his cronies had set for this *zhid* who had managed to climb up to the top of the Cometee. Not only sneaky, he was also cruel and possessed not the hint of a conscience. And yet these Jews were always so proud of their consciences.

Now he had to take care that Grasimov, still in the building, did not realize what his men were planning. He ordered the two Chekas, that would be joined by two Ladas, to put some distance between them and the area, to separate into different streets and wait until he would communicate with them. The militia forces, members of the police, without whom the KGB was forbidden to search homes, would arrive later at the site.

Malenkov looked at his watch. Eight o'clock. He went down by elevator, hoping no one would notice him. Particularly not Dimitri. His exit successful, he disappeared into a car that awaited him at the edge of the square, its engine already revved up. It sped off the moment he sat down.

44

natoly Dobrovitz easily found *The Magic Goldfish*, whose title had appeared on the note. He pulled it off the shelf and returned to the seat in the library that he had grabbed a few moments earlier. There, on page 43, he found what he was looking for: on the bottom of the page, written in pencil — "Ilya Dobrinin, Brozhonskaya 5."

He read the address a second time, closed the book and returned it to the shelf. It was clear to him that one of his new comrades was watching him now to ensure that he had indeed gotten the address of the mystery house to which he was being sent. This person, after Anatoly would leave the library, would undoubtedly retrieve the book and erase the address that had been scribbled in so lightly.

Anatoly quickly left the library; half an hour later he was at the address that he had been sent to. An elderly woman opened the door for him. She did not ask any unnecessary questions. By her reactions Anatoly realized that she knew of his impending arrival and had been awaiting him. She brought him to a small room in her tiny apartment and pointed to one of the beds, as if to say, "From today on, this belongs to you." She then served him a little food, that he ate quickly and in silence. He spent the next two days there, awaiting the upcoming lesson in Judaism.

Two days later, when he finally reached the small apartment on Komaskaya where the participants were beginning to gather for their lecture, he felt a wave of panic and fear even before he had entered the room.

Jeff and his wife walked quietly in the darkness, following the heavyset man who strolled slowly about 100 yards in front of them. The frozen Moscow streets were abandoned at that hour; no pedestrians passed by. One lone drunk lay on a curb. The fat man passed him right by, ignoring him completely. Jeff and Miriam followed suit.

"A man means nothing in Moscow," Miriam whispered. "Look how he's lying there, and no one cares!"

Jeff murmured, almost to himself, as if he was afraid to break the silence. "You're forgetting New York already! Our homeless are no better off."

The cold penetrated right into their bones, despite their warm fur coats. After about half an hour's walk the moment of blessed release arrived: The heavyset man walking in front of them entered the doorway of one of the buildings, after having given the quiet street a quick and searching glance. Jeff, almost instinctively, copied his movements, scanning the street, and then disappearing into the dark stairwell. He did notice a few cars parked nearby, but did not attribute any significance to them. After all, they had passed parked cars all along their route.

The portly man awaited him on the stairs. Jeff could hear his heavy breathing. The darkness was thick and complete. When the man had ascertained that Jeff and Miriam were right behind him he turned on a tiny flashlight. The thin feeble beam illuminated the steps. The three climbed up slowly, trying their best to muffle the sound of their footsteps. Jeff counted four stories. Eighty steps. Now they walked down a dim hallway. The fat man walking in front of them knocked on a door, which opened immediately. The pale light from within lit up the hallway for a quick second and the three were invited in.

Jeff's heart beat wildly. Here he was, putting into motion the secret mission that had been thrust upon him. Here he was, about to teach Judaism in the very center of Moscow. The purchase of diamonds seemed insignificant in comparison to this mission.

Jeff looked around him, at the small group crowded around the table, examining the people with whom he was to spend the evening. Most of them were young, in their 20's and 30's. He tried to examine them closely, but their faces were as sealed and shut as the Kremlin walls.

"Good evening," Jeff whispered towards the rocklike countenances that greeted him.

Much to his astonishment, several returned his greeting in English. The elderly owner of the home pointed towards an empty seat at the head of the table and invited him to take it. At the same time Miriam unpacked her case and placed several cakes and other treats that she had brought especially with her from New York just for this evening. The old lady, owner of the home, danced around her, speaking ceaselessly in Russian, thus preventing Miriam, who did not understand a word that the pleasant woman was saying, from giving an answer.

The faces were intent upon him, awaiting his words. Jeff felt a lump in his throat, like a ball bouncing slowly from his gut to his diaphragm. It had been a long while since he had spoken in public, and certainly never under these circumstances.

"I am the translator," a man sitting at his left whispered.

"Pleased to meet you," Jeff answered, with a slight feeling of relief. "How do we do this?"

"You say a few sentences and stop. I'll translate them."

"That means that a half-hour talk takes an hour?"

"Exactly," he replied with a thin smile.

Jeff pulled a pair of *tefillin* out of his bag. The lesson began.

Malenkov sat in one of the cars parked across from the building under surveillance. A second automobile stood at the beginning of the huddle of buildings and a third at the end of the street. During an endless hour, as the cars sat, their motors silenced and their lights extinguished, Malenkov counted at least fifteen men sneaking in, at intervals of about ten minutes, into the entrance across the street. There was a light upstairs, on the fourth floor; that must be the apartment where they were all going.

"It looks like an important meeting," Malenkov muttered to himself. He turned to the driver. "Alexei."

"Yes, sir?"

"Am I right?"

"Of course. About what?"

"That today is a special meeting."

"I don't know."

"But you've been in the field, in ambushes like this, many times."

"Of course."

"And tonight there are more arriving than usual?"

"Yes, yes, that's what it looks like."

Malenkov didn't pursue it; he thought deeply. Mostly, he wondered why Grasimov had objected to a raid tonight. Malenkov looked at his watch. It was already 9 o'clock. If he wanted to get any sleep tonight, he would have to hurry. He had budgeted another half-hour of waiting time. In the meantime, he contacted the militia, the Moscow police force, without which, according to law, a KGB agent could not enter an apartment of a Soviet citizen if the citizen objected. It was a stupid law. After all, he and his men forced the police to bend to their will. But in Russia, Malenkov grinned to himself, there was democracy, citizens' rights, the rule of law and order.

The police car arrived, unexpectedly, ten minutes before schedule. It parked not far from Malenkov and its occupants awaited further orders.

Anatoly stopped in front of the door. For one panic-stricken moment his tense eyes fell upon Igor, who was already sitting at the table, across from the entrance. Anatoly felt that he, and all those sitting here, had walked into a trap. At first he wanted to announce it: "Be careful, there's a spy in our midst." But he held his tongue. He knew that this would be a first-class error, one that would be impossible to rectify. He noticed that Igor was looking at him intently.

Anatoly entered and approached the table. The few people already sitting around it chatted quietly about this and that, as they awaited the lesson on the fulfillment of *mitzvos*. They had been promised, as the lecturer, a young man from America. They did not notice, at least at first, the silent tension that had been created between Igor Grasimov, sitting by the table, and Anatoly Dobrovitz, who was taking his seat with them.

"What are you doing here?" Anatoly hissed between clenched teeth.

Igor understood Anatoly's anger. He tried desperately to keep his composure.

"I came to the lecture. What's the problem?"

"You said you wouldn't come."

"I changed my mind."

"Hard to believe."

"You see for yourself that I'm here."

"That's right. The question is, why are you here?"

It remained unstated, but both knew what he meant. Igor knew very well that Anatoly had heard him tell the cab driver to go to KGB headquarters.

Igor chose not to say anything. Anatoly took a seat across from him. His eyes darted back and forth restlessly. Igor attempted to smile, without success. The few participants lapsed into silence, listening now to the dialogue that concealed more than it revealed.

Jeff tried to overcome the shyness that had struck him at the sight of the small congregation awaiting his words. His hand patted the *tefillin* that lay upon the table; his eyes scanned the group. He felt a sudden sense of adventure. It was both poignant and exciting, to sit among this group of heroes. His glance, jumping from face to face, tried to unearth the secrets that lay behind each stolid countenance. He longed to know if these youngsters had ever been in prison. Had they been interrogated? What had brought these students, these engineers and other professionals, to endanger themselves and listen to a lesson in Yiddishkeit? Deeply moved, he felt a feeling of deep respect for these young people.

There was a light knock on the door. Another refusenik slipped silently in, exchanged a glance and a smile with an acquaintance, and

quietly took an empty chair. Jeff had just cleared his throat in anticipation of beginning his lecture when the door opened yet again. The
words disappeared from his mouth at the sight of the newest arrival:
none other than Gregory, his Intourist guide, whom Jeff had long suspected was a KGB agent. Outwardly Jeff merely nodded at him, but
his heart was in turmoil. What was Gregory doing here? Did the others know that he was, apparently, an agent of the enemy? He, Jeff,
would have to be very, very careful with what he said.

"They asked me," Jeff began, not taking his eyes off Gregory, "to
speak to you about the practical fulfillment of *mitzvos*. In New York
they told me that you wanted to learn about the *mitzvah* of *tefillin*,
tefillin which we don every morning."

Jeff held up the *tefillin* so that everyone could see what he was talking about. The translator explained his words, since only a few of the
participants understood English.

Jeff continued. "Practical *mitzvos* are the core of Judaism. Faith is
not enough; nor are emotions. Judaism is everyday deeds. The
Rambam, Rabbi Moshe ben Maimon, one of the great Rabbinic authorities, who lived 900 years ago, said that it is better to give one
penny to a poor man one thousand times, than one thousand pennies
all at once. Do you want to know why? Because Judaism wants man
to change, to change internally for the better. And the thing that really
changes a person is actions. In Judaism man doesn't create deeds; on
the contrary, the deeds create the man."

The lecture went on. The participants listened to the translator's
words. Occasionally one of them would stretch a hesitant hand out towards one of the plates that held the cakes. Igor and Anatoly
exchanged suspicious, hostile glances between them. And again and
again Jeff's eyes were drawn, against his will, towards Gregory.

The time was 9 o'clock.

The three cars parked on the street, not far from the house, were
joined by a fourth. Malenkov had decided that it would be worth his
while to make one or two arrests. That would give the raid more impact among his superiors, and increase Grasimov's chagrin. It would

be interesting to see how he, Grasimov, would try and justify his refusal to act this evening. Malenkov looked at his watch. The time was 9 o'clock. The raid, he decided, would take place at half past. Perhaps a few more hooligans would show up in the meantime, and make the fun even greater.

One of the participants asked a quiet question. The translator interpreted.

"I don't understand. Don't you give money to a poor man in order to help him? Doesn't G-d want us to help our fellow men?"

"Of course, but it is more than that," Jeff answered.

The man persisted. "But isn't it better to give one person a thousand rubles, knowing that you've really helped an unfortunate person? What's one ruble? Nothing!"

"Of course it's very important to help someone. But a great Talmudic scholar by the name of Rabbi Akiva—"

A few of the participants nodded. They'd heard this name before.

"Rabbi Akiva once answered a Roman who asked him a logical question. If G-d loves the poor, why doesn't He give them what they need? Rabbi Akiva gave him an answer that seems a little strange at first glance. 'So that we can, through him, increase our merit.' "

"It really isn't a very logical answer," one of the participants who understood English interrupted in that language, translating his words immediately into Russian for the benefit of the others.

Jeff took a deep breath, smiled, and said, "That's true. When you look at the little picture before us we see one man giving, another taking. But the truth is that the Roman's question enlarged the picture. Because he inserted G-d, the entire cosmos, into it."

Several voices spoke at once. "I don't understand."

"Simple. The fact that G-d, Who can do anything, does not sustain the poor, and, rather, demands it of us, teaches us that there is more to the *mitzvah* than simply feeding the hungry. If that was true, G-d could surely do the job better than mankind. This means that the requirement that we assist the needy has a function with respect to me, the giver."

"And what function is that?" It was Gregory asking, meeting Jeff's gaze squarely.

Jeff felt an electric shock course through him. It was difficult to answer Gregory, whose behavior had been so open to suspicion, with the same tranquility and composure that he spoke with to the rest. His breath came quicker. He hoped the Gregory had not noticed. After a moment's hesitation Jeff replied, without looking at him, "That's what I said at the beginning of the class. A person doesn't create his deeds, his deeds create him. Every philanthropic action engraves a line of generosity in the heart of the one who gives, and helps change him into a better person. The physical action, the reality of giving, sets off a spiritual reaction in my unconscious, in my heart and, as the Zohar, the Jewish book of mysticism, tell us, indeed changes the entire spiritual world."

The time was 9:10.

Malenkov savored one last draw on the cigar burning low in his fingers. He looked at his watch. The time was 9:10. Should he give the order for the raid a bit early? In the last ten minutes no one had passed near the house that he and his men were watching.

No, he decided, despite this he would not change his original plan. In twenty minutes he would give the sign.

"But you admit that in Judaism there is also worth and importance in the fact that the poor man benefits."

"Of course. But the most important effect is the influence of the deed on me, on its teaching my heart to have mercy."

"Yes, I understand," murmured one of the participants, a man of about 40 who, before speaking, had carefully cleaned a few cake crumbs from his thick beard. Jeff had noticed that he had not stopped munching the cake brought from New York.

"Actually," the man continued, "I understand. That is, I can understand when you're talking about a *mitzvah* to help another person. But there are other kinds of *mitzvos* in Judaism. I'm not from Moscow, I'm from Riga, and I learned a little Judaism there from a *chassid* — a Lubavitcher *chassid*, and he spoke to me about the *mitzvah* of *tzitzis*, about *tefillin*, things like that." His finger pointed at the pair of *tefillin* that lay in front of Jeff.

"These," he said in an even tone, pronouncing each word heavily, "I don't understand. What can they do for a person?"

"What did the *chassid* tell you?" Jeff asked.

The man took a deep breath and sighed. "He didn't answer me. He didn't get the chance."

The eyes of all those sitting around the table were now riveted upon the speaker.

"The day after the lesson," he told them, "he disappeared. The KGB took him. After two weeks they sent him home, completely destroyed. He died two days later. He was a good man. Completely alone. No wife, no children. They'd been killed by the Nazi fascists."

The people in the room said nothing. The leaden silence that fell was grim. It seemed almost as if there was an air of expectation in the small room.

"What did they accuse him of?" the translator asked.

"They caught him circumcising a Jewish baby. The boy's father, a top doctor in a hospital, was exiled to Siberia for two years, to a re-education camp."

No one reacted. They had heard this kind of story before; it was the bread of their daily existence.

The man added, "After a few days I sneaked into his house and took his abandoned *tefillin*. I am not a religious person, I don't do the *mitzvos*, but I put on the *tefillin* every morning in his memory. But I don't understand what it's all about."

Jeff gave a broad smile. "Heaven sent you to this lecture. I want to talk about *tefillin*. I think that I explained a little bit, through the *mitzvah* of charity, that the action, the physical deed, liberates spiritual energies, does something to a person. I also said that we know that each action that changes a person also changes the spiritual world, the internal world, in those parts connected to a man's specific soul."

He took a breath. "If so, there is no difference between a *mitzvah* linked to doing something good to another, that we call the *mitzvah* between man and man, to the *mitzvah* that we call *mitzvos* between man and his G-d. Both liberate positive energies within us and have profound effects on the world. Fulfillment of *mitzvos* is using the keys that G-d gave man, the means by which man rules the world, rather than having the world rule him."

Jeff stopped for a minute. In New York he had been told how the Soviet Jews liked to hear about the spiritual context of the *mitzvos*. It was, he felt, a reaction to the Marxist, materialistic world in which they had grown up. The atheistic belief that the world consisted only of the material, with no place for the spiritual, had actually brought them to an interest in the spiritual side. Jeff had heard that these leanings existed among Russian gentiles as well, who secretly had begun filling the few churches that existed on the edges of the law of the Communist regime.

Jeff picked up the *tefillin*. "A Jew puts on these black boxes every morning. He knows what lies within them. Four portions of the Torah which speak of the Exodus from Egypt. Acceptance of G-d as King. The Exodus, you probably have heard of it, represents the liberation of the Jewish nation, and proves the existence of a Creator and His presence in nature and in history. It proves, also, His providence upon mankind. There is a deep difference between a person who lives in the light of such faith and one who does not profess it. The fact that one puts on *tefillin* every morning — the actual deed itself — places these beliefs, these truths, within our hearts. We remember when we put it on, the great days when our ancestors were saved thousands of years ago. That means that every single day — we improve. We have again liberated within ourselves a spiritual energy that assures us that there is a Creator, the world is a spiritual place, that G-d watches over us. It gives us the taste of freedom, freedom from other men, freedom from fear, freedom from slavery to the physical. It's like, it's like—" Jeff searched for an analogy, "like that Jew, a Chabad chassid, whom our comrade from Riga told us about. The chassid who circumcised the Jewish child despite the terrible danger. He lived within G-d's kingdom, free and liberated from the terrible reality outside of him. That, despite the bitter consequences."

Jeff grew fervent as he spoke. He could only think about the internal freedom of these people sitting around him. Within this city, so enclosed by fear of the KGB, time after time they came to hear lessons in Judaism. Some even began to fulfill the *mitzvos* despite the fact that they became outcasts from society, despite the imprisonment, the interrogations, the persecutions.

The participants listened quietly. Jeff didn't know if they were taking in his words or not. He felt that his enthusiasm was actually getting in the way of his ability to explain. He'd forgotten for a moment that though he was sitting among a group of intelligent people, they knew little about Judaism. He didn't know if he had managed to explain things that they could not yet comprehend.

"And what about the cosmos? You said that the *mitzvos* change the entire world."

It was Igor asking the question, Igor Grasimov. Anatoly lifted his eyes, that had been lowered for most of the discussion, and for a split second met those of Igor. Then he turned to Jeff, trying somehow to get his attention, to let him see by his look that he should be careful. But, much to his disappointment, Jeff failed to get the message.

"Look," Jeff answered, "I don't know how every single *mitzvah* works. But let's say I'm sitting here among a young, intellectual group that has learned science. I tell them that the *mitzvah* of *tefillin*, for example, has a very curious aspect."

He took the *tefillin shel rosh* into his hands and said, "In this black box are four paragraphs. When we say the prayer as we put on the *tefillin* on our heads we say the words, 'opposite our brain.' Interestingly enough, a Jewish neurologist in Britain discovered that the structure of the brain actually parallels the structure of the *tefillin shel rosh*. Amazing."

Jeff looked at his watch. 9:20. He must speed up his explanations. He wanted to be back in the hotel by 10; he had to prepare himself for his next meeting in Red Square with the bearded man, who, for some reason, had not come to the lesson. Jeff hoped he would have enough time to finish.

Malenkov took another nervous look at his watch. 9:20. He began to prepare his men for the raid.

he participants sitting around the table shifted in their chairs. It was obvious that their interest in Jeff's words was increasing. The surprising connection between neurology and religious imperatives seemed to them very strange. Strange, particularly, to young intellectuals whose university background was in the natural sciences. Jeff saw the reaction, and was pleased with it. Here, he had managed to touch the nerve endings of his students in a positive way.

Miriam stood up from her place and refilled the simple wooden bowls that stood on the table, which had been emptied of their selection of cakes and other treats brought in from New York. She had not yet cut the birthday cake.

The time was 9:21.

Jeff put his hands behind his head. "I believe I'm not telling you anything new if I mention the two hemispheres of the brain, each of which is divided into two lobes. That is, there are four parts to the brain — paralleling the four parts of the *tefillin shel rosh*. Do you see?"

Jeff lifted the *tefillin shel rosh* and pointed to the four compartments.

He passed it from hand to hand, and everyone touched it. Jeff noticed that for some of the participants it was the first time they had actually held *tefillin*. Perhaps, for some, it was the first time they were even seeing them. The seriousness and respect which each gave to the "black box" gave him a strong sense of satisfaction. Here he was, fulfilling a mission in Moscow. True to his profession, the metaphor flashed through his brain: a precious diamond!

When they had returned the *tefillin* to him, he continued his explanation. "Without being an expert in neurology, I want to explain what we're talking about. We, believing Jews, see an absolute correspondence between the natural world, the internal world of man, and the *mitzvos* we are obligated to fulfill. These are three components that are, in reality, one. So too, between *tefillin* and the world of consciousness that lies within the brain there exists this correspondence. In order to follow this there is a need to know a few concepts that touch upon the anatomy and physiology of the brain.

"The correspondence between the structures is obvious. As I said before, the *tefillin shel rosh* contains four compartments; the human brain contains four compartments. The human brain is composed of two hemispheres. The differences in the functions of these two hemispheres strengthens this correspondence between brain and *tefillin*. These differences have been carefully examined in the past few decades. For our purposes, it's enough to note that the left hemisphere is responsible for functions such as language and other logical, analytical processes like mathematics. The right hemisphere specializes in holistic functions such as intuition, emotions, music."

Jeff paused for a moment, took a deep breath, and continued.

"Now, pay attention. If we compare the different ideas that are set forth in the various paragraphs of the *tefillin* we will see significant differences among them. Let's look at the passages of the Torah in the two left chambers, that is to say the left side of the person wearing them."

Jeff tapped the *tefillin* that lay in his hand on the left side.

"These paragraphs are *Kadesh* and *V'haya ki yiviacha*. I can't explain everything that's written within them, because time is short." He cast a swift glance at his watch and saw that it was 9:23. He forced himself to speak slowly despite the time. "These verses relate to 'outward' incidents such as a newborn's exit from his mother's womb and the Jews' exodus from Egypt. The two portions that begin with *Shema* and *V'haya im shamoa*, which are placed in the two right compartments, relate to more 'inward' topics, particularly the recognition of G-d's oneness.

"Now look," he continued, feeling increasingly excited, "in the left-hand portion it says, 'So that G-d's Torah shall be in your mouth.'"

Jeff put his fingers to his lips.

"The verse in its entirety reads like this: 'For with a strong hand He took you out of Egypt.' Do you hear? G-d took you out of Egypt and now you take out words of Torah from your mouth. We see clearly that the words of the left chamber, dealing as they do with language, correspond to the left hemisphere, seat of language ability. The function of the left hemisphere, like the verses, deals with the outward. The portions on the right tell us, 'and you shall place My words on your hearts and your souls.' Inward, within the boundaries of emotion and intuition — the function of the right side of the brain, home of the emotional world."

The time was 9:25.

Malenkov, ensconced in his car, looked at his watch. This was it! The time was 9:25. Five minutes more and they would burst into the apartment. He instructed his men to prepare and to leave their cars. They zipped up their warm coats and wrapped their faces in woolen scarves against the cold, then began to sidle over towards the building. The group numbered four KGB investigators and five policemen, members of the militia whose presence was necessary during a raid. To this group were added two men in civilian clothes, "witnesses" who would testify at any future trial, if there should be one, of the participants in a forbidden meeting.

Jeff was completely caught up in his fervor. He could sense that the group was impressed by his words. He noticed that a man with a short grey beard sitting at the other end of the table wanted to ask something. Despite the pressure of time, so quickly running out, Jeff turned to him with a pleasant nod. The man said a long piece in Russian; Jeff did not understand a single word. He waited patiently for the translator.

"I understand the spirit of your words; the comparison, not as much. I, at least, think this way. They are certainly interesting, but I am not comfortable with them. *Mitzvos* are spiritual matters. How is it even permitted to connect them to earthly things, physical concepts, to our understanding of the natural world? I once heard from someone that some of the *mitzvos* are given to us in order to preserve our health. I think that is, how do you say it, a desecration of that which is holy."

Jeff smiled with pleasure and was quick to reply.

"Of course that's a desecration. The *mitzvos* were not given in order to keep us healthy. *Mitzvos* are *mitzvos,* the means by which a person grows closer to G-d — Who is endless — the way in which he does His will, and improves himself. That is our faith, and is the topic of a long and deep discussion. But, I think that it is simply amazing to learn that the structure of the *mitzvos* corresponds to the structure of the cosmos, and that every *mitzvah* has its corresponding factor in the natural world. In our books it is said that the existence of the universe is contingent upon the Jewish nation, who watches over creation by means of the *mitzvos* that belong to it. I know this is a bit mystical, but this also increases the spiritual responsibility of a person towards the world. And here are the *tefillin,* corresponding to the structure of—"

Jeff suddenly was silent. His ears, like those of the others, caught the sound of the heavy footsteps in the corridor. Footsteps that were coming closer and closer. Jeff quickly hid the *tefillin* in his briefcase. His wife jumped like one bitten by a rattlesnake, flew into the small kitchen and quickly opened the cardboard box that contained a birthday cake. She rushed it into the room where the others were jammed. Even as she began to cut the cake into pieces two of the participants broke into a melancholy Russian melody, one replete with longing for relatives suddenly gone: everything as planned before in the event of an unwanted visit.

The footsteps drew closer, in a slow and confident beat. The echoes of their footfalls sounded in the apartment like the march of soldiers drilling in Red Square on the first of May. There was something frightening about the rhythm, something that took one's breath away. Everyone sat in the silence of people who have no alternatives, of those waiting quietly for the inevitable blow to fall. Veterans who had already gone this route before tried to smile in order to ease the tension somewhat, without much success. Not many minutes had passed when the rhythmic knocks were heard on the door. They were not particularly demanding or brutal. The forces of the law knew that those in the apartment would open the door for them in any case. Thus they could allow themselves the affectation of gentleness that they liked to display in these actions. At least, at the beginning of the search.

"Militia! Open up!"

The elderly owner of the apartment, who had been dozing in a chair in a corner of the room, awoke with a start. "Hello? Who's there?" he asked.

"We told you! Militia!"

The people's eyes met each other restlessly. The old man got up and began to approach the door. Only then did the others see his bent figure, that fit in so well with his wrinkled visage. Jeff knew nothing of the man, except for the fact that he had shown considerable courage in opening his apartment to those who desired to learn Judaism through the underground, despite the evident dangers. When Jeff had entered the apartment, he had heard the man mutter in Yiddish to one of the older participants, "They can't frighten me anymore. I graduated from Stalin University."

Jeff knew no more. In Russia, he had already managed to learn a lesson: People did not volunteer unnecessary information.

The old man got to the door, the eyes of all assembled accompanying him. "What do you want?" he asked.

"To come in."

The old man seemed to wake up. He leaned on the door and turned around, giving a mischievous wink at the people gathered around the table, as if trying to inject a little life into them before their encounter with authority.

"Please, please, but why at night? You can't do it during the day? I'm an old man, and my wife isn't very healthy."

The voice on the other side of the door could be heard clearly.

"Open, please. In the name of the law."

The old man threw his hands out at his sides, as one who says: "*Nu*, what can you do?" And he slowly opened the door.

The seven militia men came in and politely greeted the assemblage. The people in the room answered with curt nods. The KGB agents were silent.

"The neighbors are complaining about noise," one of the policemen said. "We wanted to check on their complaint. And now it seems that there is some kind of illegal gathering going on here. Am I correct?"

At first no one answered. The policeman approached the table, saw the pieces of birthday cake lying in front of each person. His eyes bulged.

"I assume that this is a celebration of the upcoming anniversary of the November revolution. But where did this cake come from?"

The KGB agents each stood silently in a different corner of the room, their faces grey. The policemen didn't move. The one who spoke asked again, this time in a firmer tone: "It seems that someone should explain the purpose of this meeting."

The old man, owner of the apartment, volunteered. "A birthday party. My wife's birthday. She's 90 years old today. Why not join us for a bit of cake? And give some to your friends."

His wife, sitting on the other side of the table, lifted her wizened head and smiled.

The policeman was startled, and didn't know how to continue the investigation.

"Okay," he finally said. "Let's make a list of all those taking part in this 'party' of yours. Are these people all related to you?" he asked in open mockery.

The old man didn't lose his cool. He answered casually, "Not all of them. Who in Russia has so many relatives? Some are friends. Friends of the family."

Malenkov, sick of the policeman's lawful approach, interrupted, getting right down to business.

"I am Colonel Malenkov of the Cometee. We know that this is an illegal gathering, and your party decorations don't fool us at all. We want to make a list of all those here. I must tell you that no one may leave until the end of the investigation."

Malenkov whirled around in a sharp and sudden movement and came face to face with Jeff. "Who are you and what are you doing here?" he barked in Russian.

Jeff did not understand what he had said, though he could clearly hear the threat in his voice. With a nod of his head he indicated that he did not understand. The translator told Malenkov quietly, "He doesn't know Russian. Can I interpret for him?"

A wicked gleam sparkled in Malenkov's beady eyes. "Doesn't know Russian? He's not a Russian?"

"No. He's not Russian. He's American."

Malenkov approached Jeff's place at the head of the table, then turned to the translator.

"Ask him, if so, what he is doing here in the home of a Soviet citizen, breaking the law?"

The translator whispered Malenkov's question to Jeff. He added, "Try not to be afraid. They get their power today only from our fear."

The translator turned back to Malenkov and said quietly, "He is a relative of the owner's wife's family in America. His grandfather is this woman's brother. He brought her regards from him, her younger brother, who lives in the United States."

Malenkov was quiet for a minute, then he growled, "It was not permitted for him to do this without getting prior authorization. Tell him that tomorrow morning he must report to our headquarters for interrogation." Turning to Jeff now and talking directly to him, he said, "Your name, I believe, is Jeff Handler and you are staying at the Russia Hotel, are you not?"

Jeff nodded his head, as if he understood.

"It will be interesting to check into the history of your family when they still lived in Russia."

After hearing these comments translated into English, Jeff's spirits plummeted. He hadn't anticipated this. Woe to him, if they should look too deeply into his grandfather's history, after the tale his grandfather had told him of his adventures in Siberia. But he knew they could not do much to him. In these days of detente, the warming period between Russia and the United States, the worst they could do was deport him. But with all that, an unpleasant hour was in store for him tomorrow, among this threatening group. His eyes wandered from them to Gregory. He suspected that Gregory was the reason the KGB agents had come to this apartment just when Jeff was giving his lecture.

Malenkov gave his men the sign to begin interrogating the people sitting around the table. Each one was to give his full name and exact address. Then each had to give up his identity card.

From the very beginning, Malenkov had noticed that the young man sitting on the other side of the table resembled the son of Dimitri Grasimov. He had never seen him in person, but this boy certainly looked like the picture of him among the students in the forest.

Malenkov himself interrogated him. "Name."

"Igor."

"Family name."

Igor hesitated for a moment. Before he could answer, the firm voice demanded once again, "Family name."

"Grasimov."

"Address."

"Leninski Prospekt Kotoviski 17."

Malenkov took a deep breath. It was he! Son of that scoundrel, Dimitri Grasimov! Now it was clear why Dimitri had so opposed this visit. Malenkov favored Igor with a long and piercing look. Igor lowered his eyes. Anatoly, sitting nearby, showed signs of increasing discomfort, signs that captured Malenkov's attention.

"And you, what's your name?" he quickly turned to him.

"Anatoly."

"Family name?"

"Dobrovitz."

"Address?"

"Krasno Bogatirski 19."

Jeff sat motionless, paralyzed, in shock. His eyes jumped back and forth between Gregory, whose behavior was so suspicious, and Anatoly, who could lead him to the street where — perhaps — his grandfather's *tefillin* lay concealed. In this surprising manner he had finally heard the name of the street that had actually brought him to this city. Gregory, who also was agitated by the mention of the street, didn't take his eyes off Jeff. Igor, whose father had instructed him to speak to the American and bring up the topic of this street, was also confused.

Malenkov, with his keen interrogator's eye, saw the emotions the words aroused, particularly in Jeff.

"Is there something special about this street, Mister American, that you get so excited at the mention of its name?"

46

J eff heard Malenkov's question and paled. Why was he turning to him, when it was another one of the participants who had announced that he lived on Krasno Bogatirski? After all, Jeff had been in Moscow for only two days, and that street name had never once passed his lips! Was the arm of the Soviet secret police so long?

Against his will he found himself looking at Gregory, who sat, lost in thought. Illumination came to Jeff: Certainly Gregory was involved. Gregory, Intourist representative, who had accompanied him on his first visit to Moscow. Jeff had incautiously turned to Gregory at that time, asking him how to find that street. Was it he, then, who had supplied the KGB with the information that he was looking for Krasno Bogatirski? Or had the KGB investigator merely noticed his, Jeff's, excitement when it was mentioned? Jeff could not know. And yet his heart connected this unpleasant surprise with Gregory's presence. Who knew, perhaps Gregory was a "mole," a double agent sent to set up a trap, a snare to be used by this officer of the secret police who stood before him with his finger raised in accusation. And maybe, just maybe — Jeff's eyes took a swift glance at Anatoly — maybe this young man was also involved. Perhaps he did not even live there. Perhaps he had been told to mention the street name in order to confuse Jeff, in order to enable the police officer to interrogate him.

Jeff, perplexed, took a deep breath. He noticed his wife sitting, almost cringing, at the other end of the room, her eyes closed. He kept his silence short, in order not to further arouse the suspicions of the investigator. The man's gaze pierced though him, despite Jeff's efforts not to meet his eyes.

"I don't know what you're talking about," he said quietly.

Malenkov grinned in mockery. "I'm sure you don't. But when they mentioned that street name you got very excited, as if they were mentioning New York, your city, for example. Or maybe you like Washington better? Who knows?"

Oddly enough, a kind of calm settled upon Jeff. "I am an American citizen, sir," he said with decision. "I am entitled to more respectful treatment, as a tourist in this land."

Malenkov gave a dismissive gesture. "A tourist, perhaps, but not a tourist breaking the laws of the country."

Jeff turned an incredulous face towards him. "Breaking the law? How?"

Malenkov answered with grim politeness. "How? Interesting question. Visiting the apartment of a Soviet citizen without permission, for example."

Jeff protested. "Celebrating a birthday with relatives is also forbidden?"

Malenkov met his gaze steadily. "Yes, yes, I know these little stories. A birthday, a wedding— By law, I am now permitted to bring you in for questioning. But, as an American citizen, I will treat you with more respect. You may now return to your hotel. At 10 o'clock tomorrow morning you will be picked up from the Russia Hotel, Mister American Citizen. Just a short investigation, I hope. We have a few interesting questions for you."

Jeff felt the pressure rising in his chest. Malenkov turned away from him to face his men, who had been standing silently after completing their investigations into the identities of all those present.

Malenkov skimmed through the identity cards with interest. Suddenly he lifted his eyes and asked, "Who is Vladimir Popovitz?"

A heavyset man with a grey beard seated at the end of the table blinked and shifted uneasily in his chair. Malenkov, with his eagle's eyes, noticed the movement.

"You?" he asked harshly.

The man nodded his head in assent. His left hand straightened the cap on his head in an attempt to conceal his nervousness.

Malenkov flicked a look at his men. Two of them approached and took their places behind Popovitz, one on either side of him. Tension and anxiety could be seen on the faces of everyone in the room. They knew what was about to happen. Only Jeff didn't understand, but he didn't dare ask questions.

"You're to come with us," Malenkov ordered in a dry voice.

Popovitz's face reddened. His eyes narrowed. He didn't rush to stand up. The two agents standing silently behind him hurried him to his feet. He stood up heavily and left the apartment together with the policemen, Malenkov at their head. The door slammed behind them. The others sat wrapped in the heavy silence.

And now there was the sound of pounding on the door again. The participants jumped up, startled by the repeated visit. The door was opened; they didn't bother waiting for the owner's permission. Malenkov stood in the doorway, a cold smile on his meaty face. "I forgot to tell you: Happy birthday."

The door slammed once more. The people exchanged glances. Finally, one of those sitting near Jeff demanded loudly: "We can continue the lesson. Just a small disturbance. It's gone; now we've got to go on learning."

Jeff did not know what he was supposed to do. He had made an appointment to meet the bearded man on the corner of Gorky Street, and he had to hurry. On the other hand, he was shocked by the swiftness with which the young Russian Jews had recovered from the terrifying visit of the KGB men. Those agents surely knew full well what was going on in this room, despite the pieces of cake lying on the table. But these people wouldn't allow their fears to paralyze them, to stop them from continuing that which they had begun: the study of Torah. Jeff felt a strong surge of emotion in the face of these people's iron determination to go on with the lesson. He felt that he was touching upon the fringes of a legend. His friend in New York, Joe Hausbinder, was right when he described these refuseniks as the Jewish heroes of our day. At that moment he thanked him silently in his heart for having sent him on this mission to Moscow. And then he remembered the interrogation awaiting him the next day, and the magic of the moment dissipated.

"I've got to go," he whispered. "But I have to tell you: This is the most moving lesson I've ever given."

Before getting up he asked the translator, "Why did the KGB agents take Vladimir Popovitz with them? What did he do?"

The translator turned to the assembled with the query. One of them, a little older than the others, volunteered the answer, which the translator interpreted.

"This Vladimir has already been imprisoned a few times by the KGB. Last time he was forcibly registered for more than two months in an insane asylum — for in Russia if one wants to learn about religion he is clearly mad — and he was treated with injections and electric shocks. When he couldn't take the tortures, he signed a document stating that he would not attend any Torah lectures, despite the fact that Soviet law does not exactly forbid him to. He was warned that if he were caught again he would be considered a subversive against the Soviet regime. Vladimir, naturally, ignored the declaration as soon as he returned to Moscow and recovered from his 'treatments.' The desire to hear more about Judaism overpowered his fear of the tallest building in Moscow."

Jeff didn't understand the reference to the building. He noticed the others grinning. The translator, too, smiled.

"He means the KGB building in Dzerzhinski Square."

Jeff still didn't understand.

"How tall is it?"

"Four stories."

"And that's the tallest building here?"

"Yes. It's so tall, you can see all the way to Siberia from there."

Jeff joined in the laughter. Bitter laughter.

Finally he stood up. Much to his surprise, he felt a sharp pang. He did not want to leave this room.

Wordlessly, he left the pair of *tefillin* on the table. He hoped that one of the men here would adopt them and begin to use them, perhaps even on a daily basis. Igor Grasimov sent out a hesitant hand to touch them, but Anatoly's burning eyes forced him to pull it back. Jeff noticed what was going on, without understanding Anatoly's reaction. He wished them all farewell, doing his best not to look at Gregory.

Igor Grasimov stared at the others in the meeting as it broke up. Anatoly didn't exchange a word with him as he walked out of the small apartment. Igor had sent a parting glance to him that went unanswered.

Finally, only Igor remained. The elderly couple, owners of the apartment, eagerly licked up the last of the cake that their dear friends from America had left behind. When they finished they noticed Igor, still sitting in his place. They looked silently at him.

"I have nowhere to go," he said in a quiet voice in answer to the question in their eyes. "Can I sleep here tonight?"

The two exchanged swift glances. Without saying a word they quickly prepared the couch for him. They brought a pillow and several woolen blankets. They did it all in complete silence, without uttering a word; they did not even ask him why he wanted to stay there. Igor marveled at their lack of curiosity, but he did not volunteer any information.

Igor lay on the couch for a long while, his eyes open, staring at the darkness that lay upon the room. His thoughts thundered through his mind like the racing wheels of a subway train. He knew his father was awake, awaiting his return in order to receive a full report on what had gone on during the lecture. But Igor was too bewildered to give over any reports. The information about the *tefillin* had stirred him greatly. The new world that had been revealed to him almost by chance, and that offered him just a crumb of knowledge about his Jewish identity, had shaken him up. In addition, Malenkov's appearance had completely disconcerted him. Malenkov had recognized him, that was clear. He had seen it on Malenkov's face when he had given his name and address. What would he do with this information that had fallen into his hands like a ripe fruit off a tree? Igor knew all about the concealed but fierce competition between his father and Malenkov. There was no doubt in his mind that Malenkov would use the cruelest of ammunition in this internecine war in the KGB. Igor felt that he did not possess the strength of character to tell his father about it in the middle of the night; he could not face his father's impulsive, unpredictable reaction. Besides, it was not at all clear to him whether he truly was prepared to report to his father on what his eyes had seen tonight. An innocent and beautiful evening, something so spiritual, that did not hurt anyone. Why should he inform on people who were free of guilt, people whom his father was persecuting as enemies of the nation only because he wanted to excel in the eyes of his KGB superiors? There were moments when Igor hated himself for becoming, from this day forward, a liar, an informer for a dark apparatus. A wave of self-pity engulfed him.

He didn't feel when he finally fell asleep, when he sank into the abyss of dreams.

Jeff and Miriam returned to their hotel in silence, not exchanging a word the entire way back. When they were in their room his wife wrote him a note.

"Don't worry, Hashem will help you. In the merit of the Torah that you taught, the investigation will go well. I didn't tell you, but before we left New York I worked it out that in our daughter Golda's school they will say *Tehillim* every day for our success and our safety."

Jeff read the note and gave a grateful smile.

She quickly added more. "The minute they come to get you, I'll phone our embassy here and report to them. I'm sure they'll go into action immediately. The Russians today are very careful about their relations with Washington."

Jeff read it and gave another smile. Then he handed her a note.

"Everything's fine. Thanks. But I have to go out now for another meeting with the bearded man, to give him more foodstuffs, *tzitzis*, and *siddurim*. Maybe you should start saying *Tehillim* now."

She answered, in writing: "Maybe you shouldn't go? Maybe they're following you?"

"I understood from them that the situation is better at night. They don't believe that the Jews are so crazy that they would meet in Moscow at 15 degrees below zero. Besides, I want to ask him how I should act at the interrogation. He's been interrogated many times and will know what to tell me to do. I think it's important."

She thought for a minute and then scribbled, "Try to get it over with quickly."

The two sprang into action. They pulled a few packages of yellow cheese out of their suitcase, together with two large and impressive salamis, some white chocolate, two *siddurim*, four pairs of *tzitzis*, and the *sefer* of R' Chayim HaLevi's *chiddushim* on the Rambam. Jeff closed his heavy pack, and left the hotel. The cold hit him in the face, taking away his breath. He stopped for a moment, wrapped himself more closely in his jacket and two scarves — his and his wife's — and walked slowly towards Gorky Street, that snaked out from Red Square not far from the hotel. The dim light of the street lamps cast a bit of illumination upon him. He tried to hug the walls of the homes. Every few minutes he gave a nervous look around him in all directions.

He reached the agreed-upon meeting point and didn't see the bearded man. The darkness in this corner was absolute.

Not far from him he heard the sound of a car growing more distant. The only sound in the frozen night.

47

For the first time, Jeff felt paralyzed by fear. The darkness all around him seemed threatening; his warm fur coat did not still the trembling of his body in the face of the freezing cold. His heart beat frantically, exhaustingly. What should he do? He stood at the corner of Gorky Street, in the heart of the malevolent city, letting snowflakes fall thickly on his shoulders and his fur hat. His eyes tried to pierce the darkness. The bearded man was not there. Was his failure to appear somehow connected to sound of the motor receding into the distance that he had heard a few minutes before?

Jeff did not know how long he waited in that one spot. Suddenly his sharp ears caught the sound of stealthy footsteps shuffling through the snow that was piling up on the sidewalk. He shrank into his corner, tense and alert, leaning on the wall of a building like one who wished he could disappear within it. Who was it coming towards him?

From out of nowhere a figure appeared and stood next to him. For a second his breathing seemed to stop. But the tension eased almost immediately, leaving in its wake a painful headache. The bearded man stood beside him.

"I'm sorry I'm late," he whispered into the darkness.

Jeff did not answer; he waited for more.

"It seems they are following us."

Jeff still kept quiet. He knew well who "they" were, the ones the bearded man referred to.

"Did you hear the car?"

Jeff nodded his head, yes. The bearded man, too, gave a nod. The two of them understood this language of gesture. Jeff had learned it in Russia.

"How was the lecture?"

Jeff stamped his feet, trying to ease the cold that had him in its Siberian grip. His teeth chattered as he answered in a voice that trembled, "The lecture. Okay. At least, I think so."

After a short pause he added, "They visited us."

The bearded man didn't reply and began to walk slowly, Jeff keeping pace at his side. After a moment he said quietly, "I understand. It was clear that they would come."

"How? Prophecy?"

"No. Logic. Calculating reasons and consequences."

"I don't understand."

The bearded man did not explain away Jeff's wonder. Instead, he continued, "That's why I didn't come. Because this time they would have arrested me."

"Why?" Jeff asked in a whisper.

"Because this time they could find me guilty of trying to persuade young people to come and learn about Judaism. Do you understand the absurdity of the law? For one to learn personally is permitted in this country. But to influence or convince someone to come and hear a lecture about Judaism, or to learn in a group — that is forbidden. That is incitement. Do you understand? I always work within Soviet law. They gnash their teeth, but I am protected. It's not the era of Stalin anymore. Do you understand?"

Jeff did not. Yet he mouthed the word, "Yes."

The silence grew heavy. "What do they have on you now?" Jeff finally asked.

The bearded man then told Jeff the story of the note that he had given to the young man, Anatoly, which included information on the apartment in which the underground lecture was to be held. He explained that the note had fallen into KGB hands, a note that offered incriminating evidence against him, particularly if he was caught at a lecture.

Jeff did not respond. He wanted to end this meeting and return to his warm bed in the hotel. His unpleasant adventure of the evening was sufficient for him; the cold was just too much for him to bear. He hastened to hand the bag over to the bearded man. But the man showed no signs of wishing to leave him.

"How was their 'visit' to the lecture?" he asked.

"For me it was a very difficult, frightening ordeal."

The bearded man laughed. "Come live in Moscow. You'll get used to it."

No thanks, Jeff thought. Out loud, he said, "You should know that they took one of the participants."

Even in the darkness, the bearded man's eyes gave off sparks. He removed the scarf covering his face in order to speak more clearly, and asked in a worried tone, "Do you maybe know his name?"

"No."

"Can you describe how he looked?"

"Grey beard, cap, reddish face, average height. A bit heavyset."

"Older?"

"In his 40's, approximately."

The bearded man was not certain of who was being described. "Are you sure you don't know his name?"

"No."

"Did they say why they were taking him?"

"No. The officer looked at the identity cards, called out his name, and saw to it that two of his men took him with them. He didn't believe our cover story, about the birthday party."

The bearded man smiled again. "Not important. They can't prove it's not true. Besides, you are an American and enjoy a certain immunity in this country."

"Yes, but they've called me for an interrogation tomorrow morning."

The bearded man again stopped in his tracks. He stared in some surprise at Jeff.

"Interrogation? Why?"

Jeff told him in detail of the strange tension that sprang up in the room when one of the participants gave his address on Krasno Bogatirski Street, and how the KGB officer had picked up on Jeff's excitement at hearing that particular street name. The matter had roused the officer's suspicions. Why should a Russian street name so excite an American tourist who had spent exactly two days in Moscow? Jeff described the fear that had fallen upon him at the sight of the sharp, suspicious, and frigid look of the officer. All the terrible stories of the KGB came into his mind.

The bearded man was indeed surprised. "What, exactly, does interest you in that street?"

Jeff felt that this was the opportunity he had been seeking. They began to pace up and down the dark street once again, one next to the other, speaking in whispers. Jeff, absorbed in his tale of his grandfather's holy *tefillin*, forgot for a short while the cold penetrating his bones. He told the bearded man that his true mission to Moscow was locked in his desire to fulfill the wish of his ailing grandfather: to find the *tefillin*, hidden somewhere on that street. And he, Jeff, would be thrilled if the chance to do so would come up.

After a moment he added, "Can you perhaps help me with it?"

The bearded man didn't hurry to reply. Even with their slow pace they were not far from Red Square, carpeted now with white. The walls of the Kremlin looming in the distance cast a foreboding shadow. Jeff waited for an answer.

"Tell me, first, when are you going for interrogation?"

"They said they would come to take me from the hotel tomorrow at 10. Should I go?"

"Of course you should! You are an American. Today is the era of detente, the warming of relations between the rulers of the Kremlin and Washington. You're not in very much danger."

After a short silence he added, "But with that, you must still be careful. You never know with them."

"When they come, my wife will immediately call our embassy."

The bearded man was satisfied. "That's good."

They stood for several long minutes in the center of the deserted square without exchanging a word, each lost in his own thoughts. Suddenly, the bearded man pulled himself out of his reverie and said, "I hope that the interrogation doesn't last long. I think they're just trying to frighten you. So that you don't visit any more private homes. In any case, the minute you return to the hotel go down to the street and find a public phone far from the hotel entrance. Call the second number — you know which one — and say that Yaakov is speaking. Perhaps there's a way I can help you with the *tefillin*."

Dimitri Grasimov was nervous when he got to his office. He had waited in his home for his son, Igor, until very late. He was curious to know just how much loyalty he could expect from the boy, and what details he was going to report on from the meeting in which, as far as Dimitri knew, "his" American had taken part. Particularly, he was interested in what Igor had picked up regarding the American's character. Perhaps he had managed to chat with him, as Dimitri had asked. But Igor had not arrived home. Had he once again swerved from the proper path and disappeared?

Dimitri opened the door to his office and stopped short, completely taken aback. There sat that cursed Malenkov, smiling at him from ear to ear.

"Good morning, Comrade."

Grasimov did not answer immediately. The man's obvious glee was highly suspicious. His face solemn, Grasimov entered slowly, turned towards his chair and dropped down into it, and then gazed directly at his competitor's cheerful face. "What are you doing here without permission?" he hissed between clenched teeth, his anger increasing.

Malenkov continued to sit tranquilly. With a slow movement he crossed one leg over the other and in a proprietary gesture leaned back comfortably in the chair.

"I've come, that is, I've rushed here, because I am sure you will be happy to see me."

Grasimov's suspicions grew.

"What makes us so happy these days?"

"Adding to the stability of the Soviet society is always a bright light that should make us joyous."

At this moment Grasimov actually hated Malenkov, more than he had ever hated him before. His eyes narrowed even more as he stared at him.

"Tell me what you want," he interrupted impatiently.

The infuriating smile did not waver. "I'll tell you, Dimitri, I'll tell you everything. You don't have to get angry with me. It's simple: Last night I arranged a 'home visit' where some Zionist hooligans were meeting with a visitor from America."

Grasimov's face turned scarlet with rage. He gripped the edges of the desk in order to avoid an outburst. Malenkov had gone against specific orders; the damage he had inflicted was irreversible. Grasimov imagined himself pulling out his revolver and shooting at this self-satisfied man sitting across from him. Shooting, and shooting, and shooting —

After he calmed down a little, his breathing once again measured and even, he asked in a voice that still trembled with rage: "You went against orders, do you know that?"

Malenkov grimaced. "Perhaps against your formal orders, but undoubtedly in accordance with Soviet law, and even more in accord with the function of the Cometee."

Grasimov's anger did not abate. "The order not to work against yesterday's meeting was in accord with the investigative techniques of the Cometee. Not every decision of every brainless junior officer is the right one."

But Malenkov would not take offense; conversely, he enjoyed seeing his Jewish superior officer so clearly under pressure.

"Yes, Dimitri, I understand, but maybe you'll be interested in knowing whom I met there. Aside from our interesting American, of course."

Grasimov did not want to hear. He was troubled by the thought that because of Malenkov's criminal behavior the American would be much more careful, and his trap for him would become that much more difficult. His brain worked feverishly to plan new means of entrapping the man from New York.

"Imagine," Grasimov heard, from amidst the fog of his thoughts, Malenkov's quiet voice. "Imagine. I saw your son there."

Outwardly, Grasimov remained astonishingly calm. He was awaiting the revelation from the moment he had heard about the raid. Now he must use the very limit of his endurance to control himself.

"Really," he said in obvious irony. "Do you think you're telling me something I don't know?"

For the first time Malenkov gave him a piercing glance. He quickly said, "Of course, after I brought you the pictures of your son participating in a meeting, in the forest, of student hooligans, enemies of the regime, you should know where he is to be found. The question is what are you, as a KGB officer, doing about your rebellious son? That's the question."

Malenkov jumped up from his chair and turned to the window. Grasimov, too, flew up, standing behind him at a reasonable distance for striking a blow, if it should come to that amidst the harsh words that were yet to be exchanged here.

"Of course I know what he was doing there. I sent him there."

Malenkov whirled around. Their eyes — frigid, hostile — met.

"That means, Dimitri, that you are ignoring your son's parasitic deviance."

"If you, Malenkov, are trying to use my son in order to get me out of the Cometee, you'll be the one who is out at the end. Let's talk straight: Igor was sent there by me! Do you get it?"

Malenkov put a little distance between them, trying to avoid the shouted words, as well as the unpleasant smell of cheap vodka.

"Sent there by you? Very nice. Did you send him to the forest too?"

"I don't have to answer to you; you have to answer to me. In spite of the power that you've gotten in the KGB, and your subversion, I'm telling you that you can sleep peacefully, without worrying about defending your homeland from its enemies. After the forest I broke him, my son, Igor, and now he works for me. That means, for us."

"Why?"

"Because he learned that he had to make up for his wayward behavior, for the damage that he caused his father."

"And you're certain he's working for you? You're so naive?"

Grasimov, slightly calmer, returned to his chair.

"There's only one thing that's certain, and that's death. The only other certainty is the socialist victory at the end of the battle that we're a part of."

Malenkov grinned to himself. He knew quite well that Grasimov did not believe the slogans that emerged so smoothly, so mechanically, from his lips. Just as he, Malenkov, didn't believe in them. Yet Grasimov did believe that his son was serving him now, and that he would bring him information as to what was going on in those groups. The situation, then, was bad.

Malenkov did not react immediately. He, too, took a seat, crossing his legs. Finally, after a short silence, he declared, "I'm sorry, Dimitri. I was there. It didn't look like your son was working for you."

"And how do you know?"

"I've learned, with your help, a little about interrogations."

Grasimov could hear the mockery in his competitor's voice.

"So let's see if you did your homework properly. Why are you suspicious of Igor?"

"Because of his behavior at the time we broke into the apartment."

"Explain."

"I admit it's just a feeling. But it seemed to me that there was some kind of hidden connection between him and the American."

Grasimov couldn't sit still in his chair; his knees wobbled slightly.

"I would be happy to receive a detailed report, Yuri."

"There was a word that was said there that led to an exchange of glances between him and the American and some of the others there."

Grasimov could feel the tension growing within him. Fortunately, his face revealed nothing.

"I'm waiting," he said shortly. "What word?"

"Krasno Bogatirski."

Grasimov paled. The panic that overtook him didn't go unnoticed by Malenkov's bulging, crafty eyes. Was Grasimov, too, connected with some kind of strange conspiracy?

Grasimov recovered quickly. "What does it mean?"

"It's the name of a street, Dimitri, as if you didn't know."

Malenkov saw the strange, threatening spark that lit up Grasimov's eyes as he replied, "I know, of course I know. That's why I sent my son there. To find out the secret. Now you've sabotaged my undercover investigation into the matter."

"You're hiding something!"

"That's right. I'm in the middle of an investigation, trying to uncover a possible conspiracy, and Igor was supposed to bring me some answers. When you disobey orders — you do damage."

Malenkov said, "I've called the American in for a short interrogation this morning. That will help you, I'm sure."

Grasimov bolted from his chair. "What?" he yelled. "You've called him in for interrogation! Are you out of your mind? To damage internal security like this! Cancel it right now, do you hear me? If I have to I'll take it to Andropov, do you hear?"

Victor Malenkov grew frightened. Truly frightened. When Grasimov lost control he could do anything. Grasimov was still his superior in the KGB, and he, Malenkov, had to be careful.

"Okay, I'll cancel it," he said, relenting just a little. "But tell me why. Let me hear that from you."

"No!" The shout echoed through the corridor. Grasimov jumped up and leaped to the other side of the desk. He grabbed Malenkov by the lapels, pulled to his feet, and growled, "I don't want him to know we're suspicious. I want him to go to that street. I will do everything so that he goes there, to see what he's looking for. To know who sent him, and why. Was it the CIA? British Intelligence? The Mossad? Call the hotel now, do you hear? Cancel the interrogation. Now!"

Grasimov let him go, shoving him backwards. Within seconds Malenkov had disappeared into the corridor. With trembling hands, Grasimov lit up a cigarette.

48

gor awoke with a start. Daylight peeked in through the frost-encrusted window. *Where am I?* the frightening thought flashed through his still-sleepy mind. He sat up in his bed, shook his head from side to side — and remembered. He leaped out of his warm bed and was shocked to find that it was already 9 in the morning. The awful fears that had disturbed his sleep throughout the long hours of the night had apparently caused him to oversleep this morning.

He sat down on the edge of the bed and thought about the lecture on *tefillin* that he had heard last night from the American. Suddenly he remembered his father, and the report he was to hand in to him. He could explain away the fact that he had not returned to his house to sleep somehow, even to his suspicious father: the late hour that the lecture had ended, the terrible cold outside, the lack of transportation, and a host of other excuses. But he had no idea what he should report on and what he should not, and how. Particularly, since he hadn't managed to chat with the American on the topic that most interested his father.

And now he remembered the KGB officer who had visited the

apartment during the lecture. The man had undoubtedly submitted a report on what he had seen. It was almost certain that he recognized him, Igor, and knew that he was Dimitri Grasimov's son. He would tell his father about his participation in the lecture. That fact would surely not help his father's ambitions within the KGB.

From the kitchen Igor could hear the sound of clattering dishes, of running water, and of footsteps. Probably the babushka, the elderly woman who owned the apartment. And where was her husband, the old man? Igor dressed quickly and entered the kitchen.

"Good morning, Babushka."

She turned around. The spark of fear that had glimmered in her eyes disappeared in a millisecond, when she saw that the speaker was the young man who had stayed in their home overnight.

"Oh, good morning! You must have slept well, to sleep so late. Or maybe you're one of those parasites."

Her elderly, faded eyes winked mischievously at him; 'those parasites' were refuseniks who had lost their jobs as a result of their request for a visa to Israel. The KGB, it was known, saw to it that they did not find employment anywhere, so that, starving and banished from a society that labeled them parasites, they would be forced to surrender to the demands of the regime.

Igor smiled the sleepy smile of one who has just awoken.

"Sleep? Yes. Sleep well? Not really. Parasite? No, I'm not yet a parasite, just a student."

"And you're learning a little Hebrew and a little Judaism?"

Igor leaned against the side of the doorway, radiating tranquility. "Not yet. Yesterday was my first time."

The old woman wiped her hands on the dirty apron tied around her waist. "Was it interesting?"

"I don't know if it was. It was all new to me. I didn't understand a lot."

"But surely you got something from it?"

"Yes. I understood that those little black boxes that the American was holding have great worth to a Jew."

The old woman did not answer, just gave a murmur of assent.

Igor surveyed the kitchen and approached her. "It's always here in your apartment, this lecture?"

The elderly woman held her breath for a moment. A warning voice whispered to her: Caution. She continued scrubbing the charred pot that she had been scouring when he had come in, and did not rush to answer. In truth, this group met in her house once every two weeks. Each time they looked for another cover story in the event of an unwanted visit from the men of the secret police, as had taken place just last night. But she did not admit to that. She did not know enough about the young man who was asking her.

She turned towards him with a sudden movement and said, "Oh, here we are, just chatting, and I haven't offered you anything to drink."

And off she raced to turn on the fire and put a kettle of water on the small stove.

"We don't have a lot to eat today. My husband went out to work. He's a sanitation worker for the city. He gets back in the afternoon, and maybe he'll bring back something to eat. He doesn't like standing in line for hours in the winter. So sometimes we hardly eat anything."

"It's okay," Igor answered. He was fully aware that the old woman was avoiding answering his question. It appeared that she was suspicious of him. He smiled inwardly, a bitter smile. The last thing he wanted was for them to suspect that he worked for the regime, and yet how it hurt him that at the moment he was, indeed, working for them....

He sat down on a wooden stool in the tiny kitchen. The old woman silently handed him a cup of scalding hot water. On a tray lay a few pieces of bread, not quite fresh, with the barest smear of jelly on them. She was pleasant, yet said little. After he finished eating, he thanked her and went out into the cold, snowy street. For a moment he stood still in front of the building, not knowing where he should go. Finally, with a little jump, he moved away and walked briskly towards the KGB building in Lubianka Square. He had to speak with his father as soon as he could.

The jangle of the phone awakened Jeff. It was 8 in the morning. The voice on the other end of the line spoke English with a heavy Russian accent.

"Mister Handler?"

"Yes?"

"Mister Handler, we're speaking from the Cometee."

"Yes?"

"Malenkov has asked that we inform you that you do not have to come for questioning."

At first Jeff didn't know how to react. He suspected some kind of trap. "Who is this?" he asked, openly suspicious.

"Yuri Poliakov, from Malenkov's office. I was there yesterday, in the apartment."

Jeff tried, without success, to picture the man, based on his voice.

"So what are you saying?"

"I'm saying that the interrogation is canceled. They will not be coming to take you to headquarters. Is that understood?"

"Yes, it is. But why?" Jeff was still doubtful.

The man on the other end of the line lost a little of his patience. "That's the order I was given. I didn't ask why; that is certainly an unnecessary question."

"I understand," Jeff said. "Thank you very much."

"Good-bye," the Russian answered, breaking the connection.

Jeff was baffled. He didn't return to his bed. His wife's eyes asked wordlessly for an explanation of the call. He shook his head, no. She indicated with a gesture that she did not understand what he meant. "No interrogation," he whispered. Her eyes lit up.

After he had *davened* and eaten something he hurried to the hotel lobby and, with slow, measured steps to avoid arousing suspicion, he walked out to the street. After he had turned a corner, so that the hotel entrance was now out of sight, he stopped near the first telephone booth that he passed. He shot swift glances all around him, hoping he had not been followed. Nothing suspicious — at least, as far as he could tell.

He picked up the receiver, slipped in two kopeks, dialed a number, and listened tensely to the phone's ring. Someone picked it up on the other side, Jeff could tell, even though no one spoke.

"This is Yaakov speaking," Jeff said the code words.

"So early?"

Jeff understood the bearded man's question. He knew, after all, that Jeff was supposed to begin the interrogation at 10.

"Yes. I'm staying in the hotel." He hoped the bearded man would understand him.

"I understand. Call me in an hour."

Jeff glanced at his watch. It was 8 o'clock. He returned to his hotel room.

At precisely 9 in the morning he was back at the telephone booth. Again, he said the code words: "This is Yaakov speaking."

The voice on the other end said, "In two hours, at 11, walk with your wife to Red Square. Stand close to the large store, Gum. At exactly 11:30 stop a cab that will just be passing by. The driver will open the door. Tell him, 'Gorky Park.' If the driver answers, '*Shema Yisrael*,' get into the cab without any other questions."

"But where..." Jeff did not have the chance to finish his question. The man had hung up.

Igor reached KGB headquarters after a short walk. The guards at the entrance allowed him entrance without excessive delays: the son of Dimitri Grasimov! He took the stairs to the second floor, where his father had his office. As he walked through the dark corridor he passed by the officer who just yesterday had raided the apartment and interrogated the participants. Igor wasn't certain if he noticed him. Better that way. But it seemed to Igor that the officer had been coming out of his father's office. That fact didn't bode well.

Within minutes Igor stood at the door of the office, looking in. It was always a good idea to first check on his father's mood. Here he was, his father, standing by the desk, one hand leaning on it. Igor could clearly see that his father was feeling stormy. Dimitri

Grasimov's eyes flashed sparks of fury. Igor took a deep breath and closed his eyes for a moment, trying to dispel the discomfort that he felt. He stood by the door without entering. Who knew what that officer had whispered into his father's ear? Perhaps he had told him that he, Igor, had listened with great interest to the American tourist's lecture? In any event, Igor knew that he had to be very careful.

Finally, he took a chance. "Has something happened?" he asked hesitantly, still not finding the courage to enter the office.

Dimitri's face immediately relaxed; he underwent an almost magical transformation. Igor understood: His father was trying to conceal something from him beneath a mask of tranquility.

"No, no," his father said quickly. "Nothing out of the ordinary."

Igor took a step inside. "I saw the officer leaving your office."

Dimitri gave Igor a direct, suspicious glance. "So what?"

Igor took a few more steps, almost like a crawl.

"Nothing special. But he's the officer who arranged the search during the meeting that you sent me to. Why didn't you tell me that there was going to be a raid? Do you like the fact that KGB officers will publicly announce that I am taking part in lectures given by enemies of the regime? That they should suspect that I've become a dissident?"

Dimitri was silent for a minute. Finally, his discomposure evident, he blurted out, "I didn't know. I didn't know that he was going to do the raid."

Igor was taken aback. His father clearly outranked that other officer. "What do you mean, 'I didn't know?' I don't understand."

Dimitri sat wearily down on his chair. "What can I do? He went against my specific instructions! He disobeyed orders!"

Dimitri said the final sentence in a barely audible whisper. Igor heard in his voice the acceptance of an unavoidable fate. But Igor did not believe him. It just didn't seem possible. To violate a clear order of the KGB? How could it be?

"Can I sit?" he asked his father.

Dimitri nodded his head in assent, and Igor took a chair.

"It can't be!" he said in open surprise. Dimitri nervously tapped his pen upon his desk.

"To my great sorrow, that's the reality today. The good days of the Stalin era have vanished."

Igor listened in silence to what his father said and, particularly, to the words his father did not say. Suddenly, the entire story became clear. He understood, in the flash of a micro-second, the significance of the subversion against his father's standing in the KGB. The officer who had just left the office, the one who had yesterday raided the old couple's apartment had, it seemed, purposely worked against express instructions and direct orders. All in order to undermine his father. Perhaps that officer even knew that Igor had taken part in the group. That fact, when judiciously revealed, could help the officer in the battles going on in these dim corridors of power. As much as he found his father's job abhorrent, Igor was not prepared to serve as ammunition against him.

"What's that officer's name?" Igor asked, in order to break the heavy silence that had fallen upon the room.

"Victor Malenkov. Why do you ask?"

Igor nodded his head in a gesture of indifference. "Just curious."

Dimitri's bulging eyes slowly scanned his son's face. Those eyes seemed to show that Dimitri didn't believe him.

"Malenkov showed interest in you? Did he ask you questions?"

"No," Igor replied. "He just muttered under his thick mustache when he found out my name. The others, he asked about their father. Me — no."

"Interesting," Dimitri answered shortly.

"That means, he recognized me."

"He most certainly did," Dimitri said. "And this morning he reported that you had been there."

"Was that why you were so angry just now? I noticed it when I came in."

Dimitri Grasimov decided to reveal everything. Much to his son's astonishment, his voice softened.

"Yes, that's why I was angry. They don't believe that I sent you there in order to help me, in order to infiltrate the group and expose it."

"They." Igor understood that "they" meant the group of officers who were fighting against his father's authority in the Cometee. A strange, unsought feeling of pity insinuated its way into Igor's heart. He tried to banish it, but it had settled there and would not be dislodged.

"Father?"

His father opened his eyes wide in surprise. That was a word he hadn't heard for some time from his son.

"Yes?"

"Did he say anything special about the search that they conducted?"

"No. He reported on the usual lies that the American subversives tell, as they take advantage of their freedom of movement that we give them, as well as the American passport in their pockets, to infiltrate into the homes of Soviet citizens. Aside from that —"

"Aside from that, what?"

Dimitri stared for a moment, startled by the eagerness in his son's voice. Then he continued.

"Aside from that, he hinted that there was some strange incident, when one of the participants mentioned that he lived on Krasno Bogatirski Street."

Igor held his breath. "What did he say?"

"He said that he noticed that you grew tense when you heard the street name. He claims that he saw how the American, too, reacted with shock and confusion. According to him, there was a third hooligan there, who also became tense and nervous at the mention of the street. The way Malenkov reported it, 'my' American exchanged quick glances with him. Do you know who this third man is? He may be the key to my suspicions."

"I didn't notice. I was concentrating on the strange reactions of the American."

"But what about the third one?"

"I told you, I didn't notice."

Dimitri shifted uncomfortably in his chair. "But this is important to me."

"So ask the officer what his name was. That's right, ask Malenkov."

The fury erupted once again. "I don't want to! Do you hear me? I don't want to ask him! I don't want anything from him! Do you understand?"

Igor understood. Oh, how he understood.

Dimitri wiped his brow, clearly nervous. His eyes wandered; his gaze seemed to leave the room. Finally, he asked, "Did you manage to chat with the American about the street?"

"No, the atmosphere was too tense after your friends —"

"They're no friends of mine!" Grasimov interrupted him sharply.

"Sorry, I didn't mean that. After the Cometee agents and the militia men left, the people all went away quietly, hardly exchanging a word. The American and his wife, too, went back to their hotel. There was a lot of tension in the room."

Dimitri was silent for a long moment. Finally, a smile accepting defeat appeared on his face. He put his arms out at his sides. "There's nothing to do, that's it," he said decisively. "What did the American talk about?"

Igor shrugged his shoulders. "I didn't understand a lot. The need to translate from English to Russian made it even harder. The others understood more, but I didn't. This was my first time at such a meeting."

Igor tried to conceal the truth from his father. Actually, he had understood. Understood quite a lot. The subject of the connection between the *tefillin* — which he had seen for the first time in his life — and the brain, had enchanted him. This, despite the fact that he had not understood all the connections.

"The American spoke about Russia? Or the Soviet regime? About socialism? Or perhaps others did?"

"No, no. Your Malenkov destroyed all possibilities of speaking."

Grasimov bit his lips. The telephone shrilled. Dimitri didn't rush to take care of the disturbing ring. When it wouldn't stop, though, he wearily lifted the receiver and placed it against his ear. He listened intently to what was being said. Igor could see his father becoming rejuvenated. His eyes opened wide and the color returned to his beefy face. The conversation ended, the receiver was placed firmly back in its place. Without wasting a moment, Dimitri jumped up from his chair.

"Igor, quick," he called out excitedly. "Come with me. The American is taking a trip, and I think we'll be able to get our hands on him."

The two of them raced down the stairs and burst out of the building, the two guards running after them in confusion. They sped towards one of the Volga automobiles that stood on the edge of the sidewalk, their engines already humming in anticipation.

Suddenly Dimitri remembered something. "Stop!" he called to the driver, who had begun to pull away. Igor, surprised, followed his father as he returned to the building. After a moment Dimitri was back, his revolver in his hand.

"I forgot it on the desk. I hope we won't need it."

The Volga jumped forward, circled Dzerzhinski Square and hurried to its destination.

Red Square was almost deserted when Jeff and Miriam walked through it. The time was exactly 11 o'clock, just as the voice in the hurried phone conversation two hours earlier had instructed. The cold was terrible, penetrating into the bones even beneath the fur coats that they each wore. In the hotel they had been told that the temperatures were going lower than 15 degrees below zero. But now, as they walked through the frigid street, if they had been asked they would probably have said it was closer to 30 below. The skies were wonderfully clear, while snowflakes descended gracefully to the ground in an elegant dance.

They were quiet all the way there. Fear or, rather, anxiety about what awaited them, had overpowered other feelings. Jeff knew that it was the bearded man who was arranging plans for him, and it was his job to listen to him, as he had been instructed in New York. Maybe he had accepted Jeff's request to take him to his, Jeff's, grandfather's house in order to find out whether the *tefillin* were still secreted there. Maybe? In any case, Jeff was relying on him. In the short meetings the two had had, the bearded man had given off an air of authority and efficiency. Undoubtedly, he knew what he was doing. And yet, something about the man had set every one of Jeff's nerves on end. What was that verse? "Praised is he who is always afraid. —"

They reached Gum, the large department store located exactly opposite the Kremlin walls that loomed so threateningly on the other side of the square. Jeff avoided looking beyond those walls.

A cab passed. Jeff's heart skipped a beat. He put out a hand to hail it. The taxi didn't stop and continued on its route. Jeff looked at his watch. It was 11:20. He had been told that the cab would arrive at 11:30 exactly. That meant his taxi would be here in another 10 minutes. He closed his eyes; he could almost hear the pounding of his heart, ticking like a watch: Ten minutes, nine, eight, seven, six... one...

A car suddenly appeared from around a curve in the street. Jeff put up his arm. The taxi stopped in front of them. The driver opened the door and Jeff asked, "Gorky Park?"

The driver gave an ear-to-ear smile and whispered, "*Shema Yisrael, Hashem Elokeinu, Hashem Echad.*"

Jeff did not hesitate for a minute; he entered and sat down in the seat next to the driver. Miriam did not waste time either, and jumped quickly into the back seat. The taxi went on its way, driving carefully through the streets of the city. Jeff could not tell how long the ride took, but it certainly was not short. Finally, the taxi stopped in front of a tall building. The driver got out, walked around his cab, and opened the doors for Jeff and his wife. Leading them to one of the building's entrances, Jeff and Miriam wordlessly followed him. A metal gate was pulled to the side and they found themselves in a courtyard that led to several homes. They turned to the house at the farthest end and went up to the third floor through a darkened stairwell. Jeff had already learned that the light bulbs were routinely stolen by Soviet citizens. Twice he almost tripped on the broken stairs. The Russian driver, Jeff thought to himself, was well practiced at climbing in the dark, but why did he have to run up these dim stairs? After a few minutes of quick pacing through a corridor on the fourth floor, the driver opened one of the apartment doors and Jeff and his wife entered.

Jeff stopped in wonder as he walked in. Across from him stood Gregory, Gregory from Intourist. Gregory who had been the first to hear, in a moment when caution had been forgotten, of Krasno Bogatirski Street. Gregory who had, it seemed, reported him to the authorities, a report that had caused several confrontations with the regime. And now here he was, standing there, smiling broadly at him.

Jeff remembered that he had also been at the lecture he, Jeff, had given the night before in the old people's apartment. He had heard a lot about traps the KGB set for their victims. Was this... was this... was this what was happening to him now?

Jeff paled. His head spun. He felt that in another moment he would collapse.

A car, three KGB agents within, parked not far from where the taxi had stopped. They managed to discern which building the cab driver had entered together with the American couple. Using microphones, they relayed the information to Dimitri Grasimov, who was traveling towards Krasno Bogatirski Street. A sixth sense told Grasimov that some Muscovites must be assisting this American in getting to that street. His nerves tingled in anticipation of battle.

eff stood, speechless, in the entrance to the small apartment. He trembled. His wife whispered to him in English, "Calm down! What's the matter?" Jeff did not answer. He stared at Gregory's face, with its broad grin. Next to Gregory stood the young man who had come to speak with the bearded man in the synagogue, the one whom he had met again at the lecture last night. He remembered: This was the young man who, during the KGB visit, had mentioned Krasno Bogatirski as his place of residence.

"Don't be afraid," Gregory said in soothing tones.

Jeff walked haltingly into the room. He realized almost immediately that his fears were exaggerated. But the suddenness of the encounter had left him in shock, unable to control his alarm. Now he calmed down a little.

"Where am I?" he asked hesitantly.

"Among friends," Gregory, sole speaker of English among the Russians here, said.

Jeff was quiet. He looked attentively at the various people in the room. He saw two other men standing quietly in a far corner. Jeff noticed that they were wearing dark overalls. What could that mean?

"Yes, I understand," Jeff mumbled. "But what kind of friends?"

Gregory laughed. "Friends! Good friends who want to help you."

Jeff could not decide whether he was telling the simple truth, or whether Gregory just thought of it as a good joke. All the stories about KGB interrogations that he had read about or heard of flew into his mind, mixing with his frenzied thoughts.

"Is this... is this an interrogation?"

Gregory approached Jeff slowly. He put his palm on Jeff's shoulder in a friendly gesture that was meant to relax him and banish his fears.

"Mr. Jeff Handler, don't be worried, you are really here among friends. We've gathered here in order to help you get to the address that you asked me about the first time we met two weeks ago. Do you remember? During your first visit to Moscow."

Jeff relaxed. He tried to collect his thoughts. *Only two weeks?* he thought. *Only two weeks since I met him as an Intourist representative? Impossible.* It seemed to his fevered brain as if months had passed. But, he realized, Gregory was right. Two weeks. How unexpected adventures and exciting events confused one's sense of time!

"I understand. But you work for Intourist."

"That's right. I worked for them."

"And in America they told me to look out for you. That you were agents of the secret police. I hope I'm not offending you."

Gregory laughed merrily. "That's right. And you weren't careful. You asked me a suspicious question, while you were still a tourist on your first visit to Moscow. Maybe you want to tell me what you were looking for, on Krasno Bogatirski Street?"

The tension came back, stronger than ever. "Is this an interrogation?"

"No, no, Mr. Handler. I want to know, because we are now going there."

Jeff didn't understand. His fear mounted.

"What's going on?"

Gregory was surprised. "I don't understand. Don't you want to go there? Our leader asked that we organize something for you."

Jeff threw his wife a quick glance. Her eyes were tranquil and calm, sparkling with encouragement.

"Who is your leader?" he asked Gregory.

"The man whom you met last night in Red Square. You met, right?"

Jeff nodded in assent.

"And you told him that you were interested in a certain house on that street, right? And he asked us to organize something for you beneath the noses of the KGB. Anatoly here," — he pointed at the young man, "lives on that street, and he will show you the address that you're looking for." Gregory zipped his jacket and put on a fur hat. "And now we're driving there."

Jeff's gaze fell upon the two quiet men.

"Is it dangerous?"

Gregory gave an ironic smile. "Yes, it is."

"So why are you doing it?"

"To do you a favor."

"Why?"

"First of all, it's not forbidden to do a favor. Aside from that, it seems to me that you came to teach us a little Torah. We owe you!"

Jeff enjoyed the unexpected compliment. And yet he objected, "Even to put yourselves in danger?"

Gregory didn't answer. He merely nodded.

Jeff was still not satisfied. "But you were in Intourist!"

Gregory finally showed a little impatience. "I have already admitted my guilt before this. Don't hold us back. We've got to hurry."

Jeff persisted. "And it wasn't you who told the KGB that I was looking for that street?"

"You're mistaken. It's a shame that you've been wrong for so long. It wasn't me."

"Then who was it?"

"You behaved recklessly, Mr. Handler, very recklessly. You'll never make much of a spy. Do you remember that in the synagogue you also asked one of the *gabbaim* the same question?"

"Yes, I remember."

"*Nu,* they didn't tell you in New York that the *gabbai* of the Great Synagogue can also be a KGB informer?"

Jeff was silent, trying to digest this new information. But Gregory didn't give him the chance.

"Hurry, Mr. Handler, we don't have a lot of time."

While he was speaking Gregory handed him a pair of dark overalls. "Put these on quickly."

Jeff hesitated, staring in surprise at the garment. But Gregory's urgent stare forced complete obedience. He put on the overalls. He looked at his wife and saw that, in her eyes at least, the overalls did not suit him.

"What's this for?" he asked.

"I'll explain on the way. Now tell your wife that she is to stay here. The young owner of the apartment will be her hostess; with the language of the heart they will understand each other. When we get back she can leave."

Gregory, too, put on overalls, as did Anatoly; then he urged Jeff out of the apartment. The two other men who had been in the room left it last, closing the door quietly behind them. Jeff hastened his footsteps in order not to fall behind his strange hosts, who ran quickly down the stairs to the courtyard. When they reached the courtyard they did not turn to the entrance they had used; instead, they went to a gate that opened to a parallel street. There a small car bearing the seal of the City of Moscow awaited them.

Jeff stopped for a moment. "Where are we going?"

"Why that question again? To Krasno Bogatirski, naturally. Get in the car before anyone notices our strange clothing."

"What's really going on?" Jeff asked, even as he pushed himself into the back seat of the car.

"We are now," Gregory began to explain, "municipal workers. Do you understand? I see from your face that you don't. When you are wearing these overalls, you are an employee of the city fire department. Get it?"

"No!"

"We are now going to carry out a fire inspection in the apartment that you want to get to. You come in with us, and keep quiet. Understand? Don't open your mouth. You may not let anyone know that you're a foreigner who can't speak Russian. Check whatever it is you want to check, and do it quickly. In the meantime we'll do our inspection and hope we can help you. Everything has to be done quickly, before any others can come and 'visit' us. Understand? We've been very lucky that the secret police haven't yet found out about the two young men who work in the fire department, who also participate in our lectures."

Gregory spoke so quickly that it was hard for Jeff to follow him. A silence fell on the car as it made its way through the streets of Moscow, amidst the few other automobiles that, because of the snow on the ground, traveled slowly.

"Do you know whose idea this was?"

Jeff looked curiously at Gregory.

"Our leader's. It was right before dawn, an hour before, that he thought of these two firemen who take part in the lectures. He was trying to find a solution for you the entire night. Nice of him, no?"

Jeff nodded his assent. He appreciated the efforts. But at the same time he was very tense and wound up, particularly since he still did not know what these new, unknown friends had prepared for him. Everything had fallen upon him suddenly, as a complete shock. Could he possibly succeed in his mission and find his grandfather's *tefillin*? If so, he would see it as a reward from Heaven for having agreed to travel in order to teach these heroes about the *mitzvah* of *tefillin*.

After about half an hour the car reached Krasno Bogatirski Street. Jeff looked out the car window. One side of the street was taken up by relatively new stone houses; on the other side were old buildings. Though he had so wanted to reach this place, the idea that he was truly here standing on a street whose existence he had not known of even a month ago seemed like a mad dream that somehow had come true through an impossible reality. Could it be that he would find that which he was looking for? His grandfather's *tefillin*?

Gregory and Anatoly were the first out of the car. They tensed their muscles and gave themselves a shake, trying to ward off the cold a little. When all five were standing across from the two story, impoverished-looking house, Gregory went over the instructions:

"I understand that you, Mr. Handler, know what you're looking for inside. I wasn't told. Now here area some last minute instructions: Don't appear to be rushing. Search for whatever it is with the confidence of a professional. We can't be in the apartment for more than five minutes. 'They,' as I told you, will come to get us, if we don't get out of there fast. If you need any tools here, we've brought them with us. We'll see to it that the building's residents are kept occupied."

Gregory gave a look around him, watching for any suspicious movements. The street was quiet, clean, and white. At the end of the street he noticed a parked car, but he didn't attach any importance to it.

In the parked car sat Dimitri Grasimov, tense and excited. Igor did not take his gaze off his father, who was peering out the window through the binoculars that he had brought with him. Igor, too, felt the excitement of the moment.

"There are five of them," Dimitri announced shortly.

After another minute of quiet watching he added, "They're standing at the entrance to the house. I don't recognize any of them. Oh, wait! He's turning towards us. Yes, it's the American. My instinct was correct."

"What could he want there?" Igor wondered.

"That's the big riddle. I simply don't know."

Anatoly led them to the apartment they wanted. He knew this street, the place where he lived, intimately. This was one of the oldest buildings in the neighborhood. The excuse of a fire inspection would certainly be accepted by the residents. Such inspections were not unheard of here.

Gregory knocked on the door with his fist, which was wrapped in a fur-lined glove. The door was quickly opened just a crack. An old, wrinkled *babushka* peered out in fright.

"Hello, *Babushka*."

"Hello," she said hesitantly, her eyes suspicious.

"We're from the city. May we come in?"

She stared at them for a long moment, then slowly opened the door wide. The suspicion flickering through her eyes didn't disappear.

"Come in, please."

"*Spasibo*. Thank you."

They entered the apartment, which was built partly of wood. They inspected the wooden walls, which in many places had cracks between the boards. The *babushka* followed them with her eyes, trying to be polite to her uninvited, unexpected guests. Jeff made an intense effort to remember the details that his grandfather had given him regarding the hiding place of the holy *tefillin*, but his overpowering emotions simply left him paralyzed.

"Would you like to sit down?" the *babushka* offered.

"Thank you," Gregory answered for all of them, "but we've come to do our job. We've come to inspect whether the safety measures against fire and short circuits are in proper order here. You know, a short circuit even on a winter day such as this can cause a fire. Right? We just want to make sure everything is in good condition. Part of a general inspection in this neighborhood. Is that all right?"

"I'm not objecting."

Gregory, encouraged by her cooperation, asked her pleasantly, "Come and show me where the electrical connections are in your kitchen."

Gregory and one of the other men walked behind her to the kitchen, which was relatively new. It could be seen that it had been built on later, an addition to the communal kitchen shared by all the neighbors. There they kept her attention, chatting with her about this and that, and inspecting the walls unhurriedly as she watched them.

At the same time, Jeff climbed up on a chair in a room facing the street. He easily located the brick on the left side of the window. With the help of a small screwdriver, he pulled it carefully out and handed it to one of the men standing near him. His trembling hand felt through the black hole that he had revealed, and after seconds touched a hard, small package. His heart beat wildly; his entire body quivered. His breathing came fast and uneven. It was a cloth-covered package, completely worn away. From within the torn fabric, he could feel a pair of *tefillin*.

Jeff could hardly believe his eyes. The reality — that he was standing in a house in Moscow, dressed in blue overalls, holding the *tefillin* of his grandfather who was lying in a sickbed in Beilinson Hospital — was complete madness. Something not of this world. But he quickly recovered. He replaced the brick, jumped off the chair, and stood like one dreaming in the middle of the room. Had it really happened? Miraculously, he had managed to do the impossible.

He heard the sound of voices coming from the kitchen. He noticed the men who had stayed with him in the room. One of them was the young man whom he had seen in the synagogue, and again, last night, at the lecture. Gregory, he had noticed, had called the young man Anatoly. Jeff felt a sudden need to explain what was happening. But he knew he could never convey his strong feelings just by gestures, no matter how fervent they would be. Through Anatoly's open curiosity, Jeff realized that the Russian, too, was very excited, feeling that something extraordinary was happening. It seemed that Anatoly had picked up at least a little of Jeff's feelings, perhaps because of the lecture he had heard last night about *tefillin*. Jeff closed his eyes. He could clearly see his grandfather's joy when he would arrive, a few days from now, in Israel, and place the *tefillin* next to him. Would the elderly man's heart be able to stand the emotion as an unrealizable dream came true, a dream he had held for 50 years?

The door burst open. A wave of cold air froze those standing in the small room. But what froze them even more was the sudden fear as they stared at the KGB officer standing before them, his eyes deadly, a revolver aimed directly at them.

50

J eff grew white. He trembled uncontrollably. Here was the trap that he had so feared. Gregory had led him into this. Now they had caught him in the act. The barrel of the gun, its muzzle staring wickedly at him, frightened him almost to death. His panicky look took in the terrifying face of the man holding the revolver. The Russian's eyes were frenzied; he licked his lips firmly, decisively. The man was wearing a uniform. Jeff recognized it: KGB. Much to his chagrin, he recognized the man as well. He had seen that face somewhere before. Where? Under what circumstances? Jeff couldn't remember. Amidst the frenzy of emotions that attacked him, he could feel the chagrin of not being able to remember.

Jeff noticed, too, the young man standing at the side of the threatening man. He had taken part in last night's lecture. Was he the one who had brought the KGB agent here?

The man walked over to Jeff with bellicose steps. Jeff could see that he was trembling with controlled anger. His eyes gave off sparks of hatred. Jeff did not understand why. He stood, rooted to the floor, paralyzed, unable to open his mouth because of his panic and shock. Tensely he watched every movement of the man approaching him. Where had he seen him before? Certainly, it had been in the past few days.

Jeff tightened his grip on the holy *tefillin.* The barrel of the gun was now close to him, right between his eyes. He began to silently recite *Viduy.*

"What are you looking for — in this house," the man barked right into his face. He spoke a heavily-accented English. Now, upon hearing his voice, the light of recovered memory went on in Jeff's brain. This was the man in the blue suit, the one who had watched him at the airport during the customs inspection! Yes! That was it! What that meant was that he had been caught in this ambush from the moment he and his wife had landed in Moscow.

Jeff took a step back. The Russian walked forward, lessening the distance between them even more. Now what should he say? Jeff could feel the man's heavy breathing. Jeff had no idea what story he could tell him, what story he would believe. He suddenly remembered his wife; he grew faint. He had left her at some anonymous apartment on some unknown street. What was happening to her? Perhaps she had already been brought to KGB headquarters for questioning. To the place where he, too, was undoubtedly going to be taken in the next few minutes.

Jeff knew that he was trapped. No cover story would answer what a young American dressed in a Russian worker's overalls was doing in the apartment of a Soviet citizen. Jeff knew that even in the free land of the United States the police would take a bleak view of a break-in such as this. How much worse, here in Russia! Why had he been enticed to follow Gregory? But, on the other hand, it was the bearded man who had gotten him into this. If so, was he also — Impossible! No, what was going on here? *Oh, Hashem, help me, please!*

His head pounded, and he felt an unbearable pressure around his eyes.

"Talk!" The uniformed man's shout echoed in Jeff's continued silence.

The sudden yell startled Gregory and his two friends, who were still chatting in the kitchen with the elderly apartment owner. The scene they saw when they walked into the other room left them horrified. Gregory immediately considered sneaking out of the apartment and disappearing. But he quickly erased the thought. Who knew how many agents of the secret police were now surrounding the building? Besides, would it be fair to leave the young American to his fate?

The old woman, too, turned her stare to the other room. She, too, was aghast at what she saw. She pushed aside Gregory's arm, which was blocking almost the entire entranceway, and burst into the room with a shout. "Dimitri! What's going on?"

Dimitri Grasimov did not turn around to look at her. "Calm down, Mother," he hissed through clenched teeth. "In a minute I'll know exactly what's happening. Don't be afraid."

Gregory felt a surge of panic. What a mess! What a tragedy! They had broken into the home of the mother of a KGB officer!

Jeff did not understand a word of the exchange between the old woman and the man brandishing the gun. But he could tell from their voices that the KGB agent and the old woman had a close relationship.

The elderly woman began to shiver with the cold. "Dimitri," she said aloud, "how many times have I told you to shut the door behind you! I know, you're working now. But shut that door!"

She suddenly noticed Igor. "Igor, my sweet, go and close the door. Then come back and give Grandma a kiss."

Now Gregory understood: The young man who had been at the lecture last night was the son of the KGB officer, grandson of the woman who owned the house. He, Gregory, had to warn the other refuseniks, tell them to keep their distance from him. But first, how to get out of the mire that they had sunk into?

The muzzle of the gun lightly touched Jeff's face. The cold steel of the barrel moved slowly, threateningly, across his cheek. Jeff felt that he could take no more. And here, came the shout again. "Talk already! Do you hear, you American agent! What do you have in your hand?"

Dimitri grabbed the package that Jeff was still clutching in shaking hands.

"What's that?" he screamed at the top of his lungs. "Open your mouth already!"

The time for silence had ended. Jeff's eyes met Gregory's in a beseeching look. Gregory lowered his.

"May I sit?" Jeff asked Grasimov.

Grasimov's eyes calmed down a little. Now, they shone with mockery. He could see how Jeff was writhing in the face of the revolver.

"Yes," he answered with obvious indifference.

Jeff looked for the closest chair. Though one of its legs was broken, he sat down. The mere act of sitting made him feel a little better.

"Mother," Dimitri gave an order. "Bring him a glass of water, please. It will help him reveal some things that interest me.'"

Jeff took a few sips from the glass handed him, and calmed down a little. Then he heard Grasimov's voice again, a little softer this time. "Mister Yankee, give me all the information that I want to hear."

Jeff knew that he had no choice. "My grandfather lived in this house. He lived here before World War II."

Grasimov was surprised. His face showed his complete disbelief. His mother, who did not understand English, looked curiously at her son.

"And so you came to see if we are taking care of the house?" Grasimov asked coldly.

"No."

"So why did you come here?"

"My grandfather forgot something."

Dimitri Grasimov broke out in laughter. "Dimitri, why are you laughing?" his mother asked.

"I'll explain soon." He turned to Jeff. "Look, Mister American, during interrogations people tell us a lot of different stories. I think your story is absolutely the best, the most entertaining that I've ever heard. Your grandfather lived in this house. Very interesting! And he sent you to Moscow to find something that he forgot here 50 years ago? You Americans obviously think that we're complete idiots."

Dimitri pushed the barrel of the gun into Jeff's cheek. Jeff could feel the cold steel. But with an intense effort of will he kept his composure, which had begun to return.

"Perhaps you'd like to give me your grandfather's name?"

"Vladimir Paruskin," Jeff's answered, after some hesitation. He remembered well his grandfather's story, how he had run away after killing two members of the secret police in Siberia.

At the sound of his words the old woman seemed to come to life. She gave off a yell of astonishment. That name meant something to her. She grabbed her son's arm and asked, "What did the American say?"

"Only nonsense."

"But what did he say? He mentioned a name, didn't he?"

Grasimov didn't take his eyes off Jeff, not for a minute, while he spoke with his mother. "He's talking about someone who apparently lived here before you. It's silliness."

"No, Dimitri," the old woman wouldn't let up. "He mentioned a name. What did he say?"

Dimitri pulled his arm away from his mother's grasp. "He claimed that in this house lived, you heard the name, Vladimir Paruskin."

The woman's eyes opened wide. She grabbed the sides of her head, her hair thinning and white, and screamed, "I can't take it!"

All those present saw the woman sway. It seemed she was losing her balance completely. Another minute, and she would land on the cold stone floor. She made an effort to remain standing but—

Her son, Dimitri, grabbed her firmly, and she landed in his arms.

"Hurry!" he screamed at the people there, who were actually his prisoners. "Hurry and bring some water and a towel from the kitchen. Igor, come and help me put her on the sofa. I don't understand what's going on."

Grasimov put his gun back into its holster with a swift movement. But even at this moment he didn't forget his job.

"No one dare leave this room! Don't take advantage of the situation in order to run away. My men are waiting outside."

He translated the sentence into English for Jeff's benefit. Panting slightly as he lay his mother down on the couch, he turned to Jeff. "Understand, Yankee?"

Jeff stayed in his place, looking with perplexed eyes at the confusion that had resulted so suddenly because of the mention of the name Vladimir Paruskin.

Dimitri lovingly took care of his mother. He patted her face with cold water, massaged her temples and wrists, and gently slapped her cheeks. After about 10 minutes of intensive activity the old woman opened her eyes, eyes which, at first, didn't take in where she was or what was happening.

"Do you feel better?" Dimitri asked gently. Jeff could hardly believe what he was hearing: impossible that that tough mouth could emit such a soothing, kind voice.

"Yes," the old woman replied. Her breathing still seemed somewhat labored.

"Can I ask what happened? What upset you so?"

She was very weak. She passed a feeble hand over her temple and asked, "Did this American really say the name Vladimir Paruskin?"

"Mother, what's the matter with you? You heard it, and I told you he did."

The old woman covered her face with two emaciated hands. Dimitri could see that she was sobbing. He was confused and impatient. He bent over towards her, patted her head, and asked, "Why are you crying, Mother?"

"Because...because... Vladimir Paruskin did live here."

Dimitri stood, amazed. "When?" he asked. "Before you moved here?"

"No," the old lady sobbed. "He was here together with me."

Dimitri grabbed his mother by the shoulders. "I don't understand. Explain!" He shook her lightly.

"I'll tell you. I'll explain. Vladimir was my brother. My sweet Vladimir."

Dimitri Grasimov's hands dropped. The information that had been thrust upon him was like a storm lashing at his face; it took his breath away. A strange weakness overcame his entire body. With an obvious effort he straightened up and stared above his mother, lying on the couch. She was still entangled in the mesh of her emotions that had snared her with the mention of her brother's name, brought back from the world of the forgotten past.

He slowly turned his glance to Jeff, who stood motionless, watching all that was going on. If what the American had said was true, Dimitri thought with growing anxiety, he had spent the last days running after a relative, the grandson of an uncle whom he had never heard of until today. As strange as the story seemed to him, it did not seem possible that Jeff Handler could have known of the existence of one by the name of Vladimir Paruskin, who lived in Moscow 50 years earlier, specifically on Krasno Bogatirski Street — unless it was true. A mad world, a world turned completely upside down.

Dimitri looked for a chair to sit down on for a few minutes. He felt he needed to recover a little from this new information. He saw well that this entire group that he had captured in his mother's house was looking at him, not daring to make a move because of the fear that he had instilled in them by his very presence. Dimitri suddenly realized a very strange fact: Here he was, acting as a liaison between his mother and her brother's grandson, and only he knew the full story. The American, who did not know Russian, had no idea that the woman lying on the couch was his grandfather's sister. On the other hand, his mother, speaking no English, would never think that in this small room stood the grandson of her lost brother, of whom she had not heard in decades. Only he, Dimitri, had the entire picture. A frightening picture, that held within it the beginnings of tragedy. What should he do with this information? What should he do with this blood connection between capitalist America and Soviet Russia? To reveal it, or not? To build connections or avoid them? And with all this, he still felt he did not know the most vital points. What was the young American looking for in this house? What was the secret that he was willing to come here for, even at the cost of breaking Soviet law, even if it meant entangling Soviet citizens in illegal activities? Was it possible that the young man was not an American agent, but simply a stupid, nosy man looking to see his grandfather's apartment? If so, what would they say about him, Dimitri, in the corridors of Lubianka? He would be a target for all kinds of ridicule and scorn.

Dimitri was deep in thought, thoughts that lay heavily upon his aching temples. He put his head down for a minute on the table, trying to concentrate and organize his racing thoughts. Suddenly, he felt a blast of cold air. He picked up his head and managed to see one of the men racing out of the open door.

"*Stoi*! *Stoi*!" he screamed like a wounded animal. He leaped out the door and fired his gun in the direction of the escapee. Then he jumped back into the house and shut the door with a loud slam. The smoking barrel of his gun pointed in turn at each one of the men. His eyes once again gave off sparks of fury.

"No one move. You are all in the midst of an interrogation. A complicated one, this interrogation! But don't worry. In a few minutes I will know the truth! The entire truth!"

With an energetic step he leaped towards Jeff. His face was once again set and stern, without mercy, just as it had been when he had broken into the room.

51

imitri Grasimov, his eyes alert and piercing, examined the young American who had suddenly been revealed as his relative. He felt a strange aversion towards him. His hand, still gripping the revolver, trembled a little. It hurt his pride to think that one of those involved in this illegal break-in, into his mother's apartment no less, had managed to escape. He knew that he would find no rest until he managed to get his hands on him; on that day he would take vengeance for the humiliation he had suffered. But mostly Dimitri was impatient with the unprecedented situation in which he had become entangled. He had hoped today to garner the kind of success that would reflect well upon him among his superiors in the Cometee. He was certain that he was on the track of the American, who would be uncovered as a threat to state security. And here he was — standing and facing his cousin! A capitalist cousin from the hated capitalist country! In the past, the mere existence of such relatives could send one to reeducation camp in Siberia. That was all he needed, for his superiors to know about this! If Malenkov would find out, he could have him thrown out of the KGB. In his imagination he could already see his bitter competitor in the Cometee preparing the incriminating report and bringing it to Andropov. It was an unbearable situation. What could he do?

He took another threatening step towards Jeff. Oh, how he longed to finish him off, to be rid of him forever. To destroy all the documents showing that this creature had ever visited Moscow. Dimitri remembered, with intense chagrin, that it was he himself who had caused this American to return to this city. He, Dimitri, had wanted to put his hands on him, and had forced Intourist to refuse visas to any other agents from his firm. Now even if this American would be thrown into prison, he would ultimately be freed with the intervention of his embassy. And if not —

Dimitri hissed through clenched teeth, in controlled fury: "What were you looking for here, you hooligan? Why did you come to this house?"

Jeff trembled in fear. He was certain that doom was upon him, that his end was near. He had clearly seen the old woman's emotional response to the name Vladimir Paruskin, but he didn't understand her reaction. He looked at Gregory; perhaps there he would find the secret of what had gone on some minutes ago, as well as the reason for the renewed wrath of this KGB officer. But Gregory was trying with all his might to downplay his own presence in this room.

With no other option, Jeff decided to reveal all. He gave a short summary of the story of the hidden *tefillin* that his grandfather had begged him to rescue from Communist hands. After describing exactly where they had been hidden, Jeff lifted his hands and showed Dimitri the package that he was holding as proof of the truth of the tale. He pointed to the exact spot over the window where he had found them. Jeff noticed Gregory's wide eyes, as he listened avidly to the strange, astonishing account. Even more startling to Jeff, was the obvious curiosity exhibited by the young man who had come in with the KGB officer, the one who, last night, had participated in the lecture on *tefillin*. The young man's eyes darted back and forth between the KGB officer and the small package that contained the *tefillin*, his glance sometimes landing on Jeff's face as well. His behavior seemed odd to Jeff; after all, this one was clearly the informer.

Dimitri listened with affected calm to the story, one that he did not like at all. He grabbed the *tefillin* from Jeff, and gave them a long and penetrating look. The simple cloth bag in which they were placed was tattered and moldy. At first Dimitri longed to fling them to the floor, to humiliate Jeff's find, right before the American's eyes. But a voice whispering within him stopped him. What was this? Honor, feelings for some uncle whom he didn't even know existed? An unpleasant sense that he would have to explain to his mother what was going on here? Dimitri didn't know. It had been a very long time since he had felt so perplexed, with no idea of what to do. But he maintained control; not a feature on his stern face hinted at his bafflement. Finally, he laid the *tefillin* carefully down on the table. Dimitri's son, Igor, walked over to the table and stared at the *tefillin*. After a long moment, his right hand ventured out towards them and gave them a gentle pat.

"Get your hand away from there, Igor!"

Igor turned away in confusion. The murderous look on his father's face at the sight of this brief scenario upset him. He retreated to a corner of the room.

Dimitri's mother lay upon the sofa, watching. "What did the young man say, Dimitri?" she asked.

Grasimov hesitated. He had absolutely no desire to reveal the relationship that he had discovered in such a strange manner. He did not know the consequences of the revelation, particularly for him. The best thing, in his opinion, would be to send Jeff, the faster the better, out of the borders of this country, and let the whole matter be forgotten. On his chest, he knew, would be pinned a medal of dishonor marking his failure in a prolonged assignment. But that would be all.

Despite himself, he spoke. Some kind of internal pressure forced him, almost against his will, to reveal the bizarre secret. Perhaps it was that he was curious to see her reaction. Perhaps he was seeking confirmation of the truth of the tale. Why? He didn't know. But he spoke.

"The young man standing here, Mother, is the grandson of Vladimir Paruskin. That is, of your brother."

The old woman leaped up, her weakness forgotten. "That's not true! The American is a liar!"

Dimitri was taken aback. "Why, Mother? Why are you sure he's lying?"

She passed a trembling hand over her forehead. It was clear that the words were difficult for her to say.

"Because Stalin killed my brother. He was sent during the Great Purge, in 1936, to Siberia. He was sentenced to five years imprisonment. He never returned. At first we got news from him, but then we heard nothing. After the war we tried to find out what had happened to him. But, it seems... as I said... Stalin..." She made a gesture of despair, afraid of saying more. She knew that her son, to this day, secretly revered Stalin, even after the frightful things revealed about him by Nikita Krushchev during the Communist Party convention.

Dimitri seethed with anger. He smelled a conspiracy here. The American was lying! He had built for himself — or someone had built for him — this cover story, which was proving to be completely false. The revolver jammed into Jeff's ribs, causing him to cry out in pain.

"Imperialist liar!" yelled Dimitri. "Vladimir Paruskin was this woman's brother! That is — my uncle! He disappeared in one of Comrade Stalin's labor camps even before the Great War. Now tell the truth! What are you looking for here? Who sent you? You're under arrest."

The pain had left Jeff short of breath. With a great effort he managed to speak.

"She doesn't know. My grandfather wasn't killed. He managed to escape the camp with the outbreak of World War II. I'm telling the truth; believe me!"

Dimitri increased the pressure of the revolver on Jeff's lungs. "Stupid cover story that the CIA, or who knows who, gave you, Mr. Handler! How was he able to get out of the country, as a fugitive?"

"He got to Vladivostok, sir."

"Nu, Vladivostok is still Russia, Mr. American. How did he get out of the country? Illegally, hmm?"

"He was hidden. Smuggled out by Japanese sailors who'd weighed anchor in the port."

"And from there?"

"To the United States."

Grasimov was silent. He looked with open mockery at his prisoner.

And yet he could not discount the possibility that this man might just be his relation.

"Why do they call you 'Handler' if your grandfather's name, by your own admission, was Paruskin?"

"He...he... changed his name. He was afraid of them."

Jeff knew immediately that he'd made a bad mistake. He should have saved his life with a lie: he ought to have said that he was the son of his grandfather's daughter. He should have said that his father's name was Handler. But — it was too late. He could see it by the frigid smile that came upon the beast interrogating him.

"Ahh, I understand. That means, by your own testimony, that he changed his name in order to continue fleeing from Soviet justice? We shall check the matter in the GPO archives, see what he did, what he was being punished for. In the meantime, you are under arrest for the next few days. We will report to your embassy of the flagrant breach of law on the part of an American citizen who forgot the basic laws of behavior in the Soviet republic."

Jeff felt his knees buckling. His eyes jumped from one person to the next, in a mute plea for help. In his heart he murmured verse after verse of *Tehillim*, whatever his frenzied brain could remember. Exactly what he had been afraid of: that somehow, the terrible story of how his grandfather had murdered the two Soviet agents would be revealed, and he, Jeff, would pay the price. All that he had feared had come to pass. And under what bizarre circumstances! He remembered his wife, abandoned in some Moscow apartment. What was happening to her now? Had Gregory been a partner in this trap? In despair, Jeff searched wildly for a way out of the labyrinth in which he had become hopelessly lost, because of his grandfather. Was the sacrifice worthwhile? His three young children in New York suddenly appeared clearly before his eyes, almost as if they were in the room with him.

Suddenly an idea popped into his head. "Tell her, sir. Please tell your mother that her brother Vladimir is still alive."

Grasimov was silent. And then his cold, evil smile played upon his lips once again.

"He's alive?"

"Yes," Jeff said, in what was almost a groan. The pressure on his lungs was causing him increasing pain.

"Where?"

"He's alive, in Israel! In Ramat Gan. He's got heart trouble, but he's alive. Tell your mother, sir."

A feeble hope rose in Jeff's bleak heart. Perhaps this fact might change his terrible situation. Perhaps he would get a little mercy, at least, in the merit of the KGB agent's mother. But, much to his disappointment, he didn't see the agent rushing to tell his mother the poignant secret, that her lost brother was still alive.

Instead, Dimitri said, "I will tell her. Absolutely. Certainly. She'll be most moved. But don't you think that it would be wonderful for them to meet in person? For one to fall upon the other's neck? How moving! Such a reunion, after 50 years!"

Dimitri was silent for a moment, not removing his eyes from Jeff, who was standing defeated before him.

"Such a meeting, Mr. Handler, would also allay all suspicions against you, right? Then we will know absolutely that you are telling the truth. So tell him, your grandfather, to come to Moscow and visit his sister. And so, just that we can be certain that he will come to chat with her, you will stay in our custody until his arrival."

Jeff's eyes opened wide in terror. The wicked glint in the eyes of his nemesis only worsened the pain; he could smell the dreadful danger. He knew that his grandfather would never come to Russia, where a death sentence awaited him for what had taken place 50 years before! Besides, he was suffering from heart disease, and his health could never withstand such a trip. Jeff's fate, then, was sealed. Paralyzed with dread, he didn't respond to the offer.

Grasimov added a frosty suggestion, in a comradely voice. "Don't worry, Mr. Handler, from our side there won't be much of a delay. One day, maybe two. From Tel Aviv via Vienna, your grandfather can be here in less than two days, right?"

How Jeff loathed the man who toyed with him with such pleasure, as a cat might play with a trapped mouse. This, when he knew that the two of them were related. Why was he behaving like this, this man who had turned out to be his cousin? Had the atheistic Communist education managed to tear out every iota of humanity from him? But this was no time for philosophical meditations. He felt his throat growing tight, his heart about to burst. He lost control, and burst out in tears.

The old lady watched carefully the dialogue between her son, the KGB agent, and the young American. Suddenly she intervened.

"Why, Dimitri, why is he crying? Tell me everything!"

Dimitri stared at Jeff, still sobbing, and without taking his eyes off him told his mother all that had taken place. She listened open-mouthed, her feelings mounting from moment to moment. For some reason, she believed the story. With slow steps she stood up from the couch where she'd been lying and approached Jeff. She then gently pushed her son Dimitri away and commanded, "Enough of this! Put the revolver back where it belongs. This is my brother's grandson; you've got to treat him differently."

She patted Jeff's head gently, still looking at Dimitri. "But you didn't tell me why he's crying."

Dimitri answered her, profoundly serious: "To make you happy, Mother. I want to make certain he's telling the truth. In the meantime I'm still suspicious, and I won't let him get away with it. He's crying because I told him that until his grandfather, who may or may not be your brother, comes to Moscow for a visit, he'll get a nice room from me in Portovo Prison. I'm doing this for you, Mother. Don't you want to see your brother after all these years?"

The old lady cried, infuriated, "Want? Of course I want! But don't you dare imprison him, my brother's grandson, do you hear? I believe him! Of course I believe him! Particularly because of the story of the *tefillin*. Now that he tells me, I remember. My brother was very particular about it: Once every week he would take out the *tefillin* and put them on. We laughed at him. But we loved him, and we didn't give him over into GPO hands. We knew we were breaking the law, but we loved him, our Vladimir. How I would love to see him before I die! And you, my police interrogator, you know how to interrogate. How can you explain how he knew about these *tefillin*, if Vladimir was indeed killed by Stalin? Oh, I can't take it! Vladimir is alive! Oh, who would have believed it? Ask him how Vladimir is feeling, and what's happened to him until now."

She stood next to Jeff, as if guarding him, in an attempt to defend him from Dimitri. The position was almost funny, and yet Gregory and Anatoly, and, certainly, Igor, felt at that moment a shiver go up their spines and through their entire bodies. Dimitri Grasimov himself had no answer to the question of how the young American had learned about the *tefillin*, unless his story was true. In addition, Dimitri, too, could feel the odd atmosphere that permeated the room. And as much as he wanted to preserve his air of toughness, he was not 100 percent successful. His mother's determination as she placed herself by Jeff's side, her deep faith in Jeff's words, and the emotions that the discovery of her brother had aroused in her, affected even him. And the turn of events made the course of action on which he had planned impossible.

Until he heard the sound of his small communications device.

Miriam Handler did not feel comfortable in the apartment in which she had been interred. The young owner was very amiable to her, trying to make the hours of her forced stay pleasant, but the language barrier made it impossible to hold a conversation. Miriam, in any case, felt nervous. She walked over to the window and pushed the curtains to the side. The scene that met her eyes was depressing: the back yard of a typical Russian house, surrounded on all sides by unattractive buildings whose rectangular windows, covered with heavy drapes, peered down upon it. The yard itself was covered with a thick blanket of snow upon which one could see the footsteps made by a man's boots.

The apartment owner dashed forward, quickly closed the curtains, and hurried Miriam away. Using sign language the woman indicated that it was forbidden to look outside. The neighbors might see a strange face in the apartment and who knew what they would do once their suspicions were aroused? Miriam understood and gave a nervous smile. The suffocating feeling, the lack of confidence, became more pronounced. Where was her husband now? She knew that he had been driven to the house that he had hoped to reach on Krasno Bogatirski Street. But why was it taking so long? Why had Jeff not returned yet? How much longer must she sit here, doing nothing?

The young woman placed a steaming hot cup of tea before her. Her embarrassed smile, together with her gestures, told Miriam that she had nothing else to give her. Miriam nodded her head in understanding. The impoverished furnishings clearly indicated the economic situation of the family.

Suddenly, Miriam gestured that she would like to use the telephone. The woman agreed. With trembling hands Miriam dialed the United States Embassy.

"Hello. I am an American citizen and I'm in trouble here in Moscow. With whom should I speak?"

"You can speak to me," came the authoritative reply. It was a woman's voice on the line. "Where are you located?"

Miriam sighed. "I don't know."

"What do you mean, you don't know?" The protest could clearly be heard.

"That's exactly the problem."

"I don't understand."

"I don't understand either. My husband brought me to this place and left. And he hasn't gotten back yet."

"Is your husband Russian?"

"Heaven forbid. He's American, like I am."

A moment's silence. "Can you tell me what's going on? Otherwise, I can't help you."

"I understand. Why don't you ask me questions and I'll answer them. I am very confused, and very frightened, right now."

"Your name?"

"Miriam, Miriam Handler."

"Your husband's name?"

"Jeff. Handler, of course."

"Is this your first time in Russia?"

"Yes."

"Why are you here?"

"Diamond business."

"You're a diamond merchant?"

"No, my husband is."

"If so, what are *you* doing here?"

Miriam held her peace for a moment. She couldn't find the words to tell about the Torah lectures given to young Jews, and certainly not the matter of the *tefillin*. In any case, she was afraid to report on those activities.

"Why don't you answer me? Don't you want me to help you?"

Miriam recovered her composure. "Yes, yes. Of course. Thanks a lot. But... I... I don't know how to explain it."

"That's not good, ma'am."

"I know it."

"Try to explain, please. Otherwise, we can't go forward and we'll have to end this conversation here."

Those last words frightened Miriam. This conversation was her only connection with the outside world.

"So.. I am here... how do I say this? As part of a cover. My husband is doing other things in Moscow."

"You must be aware that we cannot help in every instance. It would be against standing orders. Not even American citizens."

The voice was firm and inflexible.

"But he's not doing anything against the regime! It's a personal matter."

The voice on the other end toughened. "Mrs. Handler, what you happen to think, doesn't matter. What's important is what the government thinks and they — are very suspicious. Besides, what private business could an American citizen possibly have on his first visit to Moscow?"

"It's because of his grandfather."

"Explain," the woman at the embassy said in a brusque manner.

"His grandfather lived in Moscow 50 years ago."

"And so?"

"He left in the year 1936."

"And?"

"His grandfather, when he heard that my husband was traveling to Moscow, asked him to bring back a certain holy item that he'd forgotten in the apartment that he'd lived in during that time. We are Jews. Do you understand?"

"Oh, his grandfather isn't entirely normal, I assume."

"I don't know. But he asked him to do it. That is, he demanded it. And my husband decided to try and fulfill his request."

"And then?"

"So some Jewish refuseniks have taken him to that apartment."

The woman on the other end of the line began to shout. "If his grandfather is normal or not, I don't know. But, if you'll pardon me for saying this, your husband is certainly not normal! The refuseniks are under constant surveillance by the KGB. It's a certainty that your husband is in trouble now! Do you know where they went?"

"Yes. Krasno Bogatirski Street. With whom am I speaking?"

"Jennifer Smith, First Secretary of the Embassy. I'm sending a number of embassy security men to that address right now. Good luck."

"See you. And thanks."

Everyone in the room could see the changing expression on the face of Dimitri Grasimov. He concentrated completely on what was being said on his communications device. For the first few minutes he listened without reacting, then his eyes filled with a mixture of fury and fear. He began to wander through the room, as if trying to control the storms raging within him. His mother did not take her worried gaze off him. He paled; despair seemed to be painted upon him. Even Jeff forgot, for one moment, his own dread, and tensely watched the transformation that the KGB agent was undergoing. Igor stood, paralyzed. He understood that something frightful was happening. He knew his father well, knew that such an emotional upheaval could not have a happy ending. A tense aura of anticipation filled the small room as the words came out of the tiny device strapped to Grasimov's chest.

The mother approached her son, Dimitri.

"*Shto proischodit?*" — What happened?

"*Oni podorogeye suda*" — They're on their way here.

"*Kto eto oni?*" — Who is 'they'?

"I've told you about them, Mother. Victor Malenkov from the Second Department."

She balled her thin fist and bent her arm in a sign of conflict.

"Oh, that villain. What does he want?"

"Yes, that hooligan. He wants to destroy me. And I'm very much afraid that this time he may succeed."

The old woman, by this time standing right next to her son, put her palm gently upon his arm. His hand, trembling slightly, still held onto the revolver. She pulled at him, trying to move the gun's muzzle away from Jeff's direction. Miraculously, Dimitri allowed her to do so. Clearly, he'd been overcome by a momentary weakness.

"What do you mean, he'll succeed?" she asked in concern.

"I don't know. They've been trying to undermine me for a long time. They want to get me purged from the Cometee. To bring me down, to throw me to the dogs. They're just missing the excuse. It seems that they've been following me around for some time, trying to catch me in any slight deviation from the party line."

Gregory listened with great interest and surprise to the words of the KGB officer. He wondered what advantage he, and the other refuseniks, could get from this development. Dimitri Grasimov was an avowed enemy.

His mother asked him, "So what can they get you on? No one is more devoted to their job than you are!"

Dimitri's fury rose within him. "What? You're asking what? Here's your wonderful grandson, Igor, my darling son," he thundered, his voice dripping with sarcasm, "taking mountain trips with anti-socialist student hooligans. And they — Victor Malenkov, that is — were thrilled to put Igor's picture on my desk. Do you understand? Victor loved watching the color in my face change. He even hinted, in honey-sweet words, how could I be trusted, how could my loyalty be depended upon, if my only son is a dissident?"

He was quiet for a second and then added, in a scream that startled all those around him, "And now, here is our new cursed American relative!"

His mother took a defensive posture. "How will they know? We only just found out."

"Malenkov! Malenkov just told me the good news over my receiver."

"But how does he know about it?"

"The thug who ran out of the house half an hour ago was one of their men. Malenkov, behind my back, planted him among the dissidents." Dimitri noticed how Gregory paled, but at this moment nothing mattered to him. Let the whole lot of them just disappear. "He told them what was going on here with this American." The hand holding the revolver again pointed it towards Jeff. "Now that scoundrel has evidence against me. He is coming to imprison me, do you understand? He's coming in the company of two high-ranking officials. He's accusing me, a KGB agent, of holding unauthorized contacts with a foreigner. Contacts with an American citizen, who is also a relative! Do you understand?"

The last words were a scream—

Suddenly, he lost control. He burst out, raising the revolver: "I'll kill him! He's ruined my life!" Jeff did not understand the Russian words, but he clearly saw the venom and hatred of the gesture, and he felt overcome with horror. Why had he come to Russia, to this accursed land? He picked up his arms to protect his head, awaiting the unavoidable blow.

And then it happened: The old woman and Igor together blocked Dimitri's path. They grabbed his arms and tried to force him to sit down. "Calm down, Dimitri, everything will work out," his mother attempted to console him. "They'll believe your story. Stop this nonsense!"

Dimitri struggled against them, while Jeff fled to a corner of the room.

"Leave me alone!" Dimitri roared. "Or I'll kill every one of you!"

The car, with three security men inside, one of them an officer, slid through the rear gates of the embassy, near the barracks where the Marines who guarded the embassy were stationed. A Marine standing on guard duty saluted sharply; the men inside responded with a casual gesture. The car passed the spot where the militia had a lone policeman stationed; he gave the automobile an indifferent look. They passed Tchaikovsky Street and from there turned onto Arbat; then they passed the skyscraper, built in Stalinist style, that housed the Foreign Ministry, with its turrets and towers. After a short time they reached Kalinin Boulevard. There wasn't much traffic; thus, despite the snow, they were able to speed up. The driver, before leaving the embassy, had inspected a city map and identified their destination, Krasno Bogatirski Street.

One of the security men asked the officer, "What's the point of this trip, in this cold?"

"We've got to save some American who's gotten himself into trouble."

"He couldn't find another day to do it, when it wasn't 15 below?"

"I agree, that's the first question we'll ask him, after we've rescued him."

"Do you know what his problem is?"

"No, I know that I've got to get him back to the embassy alive. Mrs. Smith is already taking care of the matter with the government."

There was silence in the car. Finally, the officer added, "And this idiot also managed to put his wife in some apartment in Moscow, and we don't know where."

"Meaning, a hot day in this cold."

"We'll know when we get there."

After about half an hour's ride, the car reached Krasno Bogatirski. "Stop!" The officer's brief command broke through the silence.

The driver pulled over. The passengers in the American car looked at the house. They could see three Cheka automobiles and one Lada

— all cars used by the KGB — parked nearby. At that moment a number of men wrapped in bulky coats got out of the cars and walked slowly towards the house, disappearing inside in a matter of seconds.

"Don't go in," the officer whispered. "I want a minute to assess the situation. I have a feeling we might be a little too late."

53

The old woman, Dimitri's mother, patted him gently.

"Calm down, Dimitri, everything will be all right. They wouldn't dare!"

With the help of her grandson, Igor, she led him to a chair and sat him down. Slowly, with great care, she drew the revolver out of his hand. Dimitri did not protest. Clearly, he saw himself as doomed. The two firemen grabbed at their chance: They fled the house. Dimitri saw them opening the door and bolting, but didn't react. Nothing mattered to him anymore. Their car could be heard roaring away. For some reason, Anatoly and Gregory remained. Igor, shivering from the cold, hastily shut the door. As for Jeff, he was terrified of making any movement at all.

The old woman ignored everyone else and continued lightly caressing her son's cheeks, while whispering words of encouragement and comfort. After a few moments she placed a soft hand on his thick hair.

"Feeling a little better?"

Without awaiting an answer, she turned to her grandson. "Bring some vodka."

Jeff approached Gregory. "What's going on here?" he whispered.

"Not now! Don't say anything now!" Gregory hissed in a barely audible voice. "The danger isn't over."

Dimitri drank the vodka that Igor brought him in one gulp. The alcohol was strong; he shook his head back and forth, trying to clear it. But the vodka seemed to send new strength coursing through his veins.

"Did that help?"

The old woman did not manage to hear the reply. All those in the room turned their heads toward the door. The banging was firm and unyielding. Dimitri straightened up; his eyes bulged. Then his body collapsed weakly.

"It's them, Mother, they've come," he murmured, trembling uncontrollably.

The old woman stood up, a fire burning in her eyes. Powers welled up from deep within her. She would stand firm, no matter what.

"Igor," she said in quiet, determined tones, "go and open the door. Don't be afraid. They won't do anything to your father, I promise."

Her confidence was overwhelming.

Igor opened the door. Three stern-faced KGB officers stood on the threshold. After a millisecond's hesitation they walked in with slow, determined steps. Dimitri immediately saw Malenkov. The enemy. The other two were higher-placed officers whom Dimitri also recognized: Sasha Pasternak and Nikita Soslov.

"Yes? What do you want?" the old woman challenged openly. Her words rang out like cold, unyielding metal.

Malenkov was pleasant, trying to dissipate a little of the tension that they had created with their appearance. Though he was the junior among them, it was clear that it was he who was behind this visit.

"We want to speak with Dimitri."

The old woman didn't bend.

"You meet him every day in the office! No? You don't talk enough there? You have to come and speak with him when he's visiting his mother?"

Malenkov was taken aback. He exchanged a quick glance with the other two officers. The fact that it was Dimitri's mother's home into which they had just burst, both startled and perplexed him, confusing him completely. Perhaps he had been wrong in his analysis of Grasimov's actions. Despite his doubts, he turned to him, ignoring the old woman who stood near her son, ready to do battle.

"What's the matter with you, Dimitri?" he asked with affected concern. "Don't you feel well?"

The ridicule fueled Dimitri's wrath. For some reason — perhaps it was his mother's courage and spirit — a smattering of his characteristic toughness returned.

"When I see you I always feel well, Victor."

Malenkov chuckled. "Well, that makes me feel good."

"I'm glad that my presence makes you feel good," Dimitri answered in open irony. "You've come to help me, I take it? You didn't think I'd manage with this American by myself?" He pointed to Jeff.

"We know," said Pasternak, "that you can manage anyone. Except yourself."

"Meaning?"

"A KGB official meeting with a foreign American in a private home without official authorization from his superiors? Is there an explanation?"

Grasimov strengthened himself and got out of the chair. Now he was standing opposite them.

"Explanation? Victor knows quite well what's going on!"

"We know too," Pasternak answered. "We know that Victor called him in for an interrogation, this American, after he caught him in a secret meeting with a group of dissidents. And you, Dimitri Grasimov, Cometee officer, forced Victor to cancel it. Is that true?"

There was no reason to deny it. "Yes."

"All so that you could meet him here in a private apartment at the edge of the city?"

"Wrong. That's not the situation." Dimitri was quick to protest.

"We understand. We'll get your explanations at headquarters. Now you will come with us."

Though Dimitri had anticipated this, he was still taken aback. The radical transformation from all powerful to one being interrogated — and possibly a prisoner — weighed heavily upon him. He walked towards them hesitantly, with slow steps. And then, without advance preparation, the old woman moved quickly and stood between her son and the KGB officers, her two arms outstretched as if to defend him at any price with her weak powers. She said, quietly and decisively, "He's staying here. You're not taking him."

The three men looked at the old woman. Her behavior had disturbed their plans.

"*Babushka*, what's it your business? We just want to have a friendly chat. Please move out of the way."

"What's it my business?" she bellowed. "He's my son! A friendly chat? Ha! I know all about your friendly chats. He hasn't done anything wrong!"

Malenkov smiled. "If so, he has nothing to be afraid of."

"From the truth he's got nothing to fear! But from you he should be afraid! He's afraid of you because he knows you!"

The three gave frigid smiles. "Fine," said Pasternak. "Now tell your son to come with us."

She lifted her chin, placed her hands on her hips. Her eyes gleamed with rebellion. "He won't go. He won't go and don't you touch me! Do you hear? I repeat: He's done nothing wrong! Nothing against the law or against the country's security!"

They didn't dare touch her. The fact that she was the mother of a fellow officer made them loath to use force. They took a few steps towards Dimitri, who was sitting quietly, planning to put their hands around his arms and pull him with them. At the same time, Pasternak spoke. "Really, *Babushka*, really, to meet with an American citizen in your house isn't wrong? You too are going to have to give us some answers."

Her wrinkled visage seemed to crumple even more. She jumped in front of her son: They wouldn't be able to put their hands on him without a fight. Then she pointed an accusing finger towards the speaker.

"Oh, that's the way it is! I'll give you the answers right now: This

American is my brother's grandson. Do you understand? My brother, whom I haven't seen in 50 years! He's not a spy! He's not an enemy! He came from America to see his old aunt. We're not living in the era of Comrade Stalin, even you must know that, my son's good friends! Today it is permitted to visit an old aunt, I believe."

She saw the perplexity on the faces of the two KGB officers, and quickly added, "And you, you won't even give me the chance to hear a little about what's happened to my brother since he left Russia."

Pasternak was the first to respond. "A very nice story, very moving. But we know that it's not true."

They motioned to Dimitri to hurry and join them.

Gregory walked over to Jeff and whispered, "They don't believe that you're a relative. That your grandfather is the old woman's brother."

The thought came to Jeff like lightning. He whispered back, "Tell them they can call Israel. You know what? Tell them that the old woman can speak to her brother. Let her speak to him in Russian, so that they will understand. Just have them give me permission to call."

Malenkov heard the whispering. He turned sharply towards Gregory and Jeff. He could remember the two of them sitting by the table during the lecture that he had raided last night in the apartment on Moskovaskaya.

"And what are these discussions, may I know? You, also, have to come with us now, not just your partner, the KGB officer. It will be interesting to hear from the American how he figured out this story about relatives whom he managed to find just one day after being in the city."

The blatant lie upset Gregory; his anger gave him the courage to answer, though he knew the words might bring down the wrath of Soviet law upon him.

"The American said that he is ready to call his grandfather in Israel and that she, the old woman, should speak with him, so that he can prove the story is true."

Malenkov grew angry. "We're not interested in this nonsense! We've already spent far too much time here. Now, Dimitri, come along without making problems, so that we don't have to call for help and use force."

Dimitri's mother had listened intently to the exchange. The thought moved her profoundly; she began to weep, still standing between the KGB officers and her son.

"Look," she wailed, "they can check if the American is lying or not. Let him call!"

She covered her face with her hands, her entire body shaking at the suddenness of the thought: She would speak with her brother, Vladimir. Her brother, who had suddenly risen from the abyss of memory, whom she had been certain had been dead these 50 years.

The idea did not sit well with the KGB officers; they did not bother answering her plaintive plea. Sasha Pasternak signaled with his eyes to the other two, and they began to push, carefully, the old woman blocking their way to Dimitri. She grew frenzied, the tears disappearing as if they had never been there.

"You're not going with them, Dimitri!" she shouted furiously. "Fight them! This is just a conspiracy of a few officers! Don't let them take you!"

Along with her desperate cries, she began to use her fingernails and teeth. She bit Malenkov in the hand, ripped at his face, until he gave a weak cry of pain. In his wrath he gave her a hard push to the side, and the old woman fell to the floor like an old discarded bag. But somehow, with powers that seemed not to belong to her, she leaped up again like a wounded lioness, grabbed a wooden bowl and threw it with all her ebbing strength at the officers, who were trying to grab Dimitri. The bowl hit Pasternak in the face, and he cursed loudly. With the swiftness of a cat she grabbed a picture from the wall and threw it, too, towards them; it fell uselessly onto the floor, hitting no one. Dimitri realized that this was a lost battle. Even if this was a conspiracy, the law and the forces of the law were on their side. And yet he derived strength from his mother's grim and determined behavior, and decided to use the last few minutes of freedom that were left to him in order to lash out at his enemies. At least, let them feel the pain as he went on his way to prison. Dimitri, who was well versed in the skills of self-defense, hit Soslov, the senior man there, on the head; he collapsed onto the floor from the strength of the blow. Soslov had been the first to dare and grab Dimitri. Then Dimitri kicked Malenkov squarely on the ankle as he made his way to Soslov's aid. Malenkov grabbed his aching ankle and hopped through the apartment.

"That will cost you dearly, Dimitri," he hissed.

"I've got nothing to lose, you fool," Dimitri answered, fully enjoying the minutes before he would plunge into the chasm that awaited him.

"I'm afraid," Jeff whispered to Gregory who, like Jeff himself, stood at the side, watching the terrible scene, not knowing what to do. "What did I need this for? Why did I come to Russia at all? Let's get away from here."

Gregory, who was also consumed with fear, whispered through chattering teeth, "We've got nowhere to run. Nowhere."

They noticed that Anatoly had fled to the small kitchen. Igor stood near the window, shock and fear etched deeply upon his face.

"Igor!" the old woman shrieked, as Sasha Pasternak grabbed her, trying to push her out of the room. "Igor! Why don't you help your father?"

Igor didn't answer. He stood, paralyzed, unable to react. He didn't move, not even when he saw a mighty kick to his father's face ram him, unconscious, into the wall, from where he slid down to the floor. The three KGB agents raced towards the routed officer, picked him up, and prepared to take him with them. But Dimitri's mother would not let up. She pulled Pasternak towards her.

Even in those stormy moments, Victor Malenkov hadn't forgotten the living — and incriminating — evidence against Dimitri Grasimov. He turned to Jeff and commanded, "You're being held for questioning. We are very interested in this story of yours, and in your new-found relative, Dimitri Grasimov."

The KGB officers pulled Dimitri towards the entrance and opened the door.

Before their surprised eyes stood three men.

54

I t was a moment fraught with awkwardness. The KGB agents stared in obvious surprise at the three American men standing in the entranceway blocking their path. Their Marine Corps uniforms identified them instantly. *Serving at the American embassy,* Malenkov thought. Without thinking, he held on tighter to Jeff's arm, as if fearing his prey would escape. He assumed their appearance was connected with the presence of the American who he planned on bringing in for interrogation. As an intelligence officer, he was anxious to know how these Marines had learned that the young American was in an apartment on Krasno Bogatirski Street. That meant that he was working for someone, somehow, who knew where to find him. The suspicion that Dimitri Grasimov was in the pay of the Americans grew steadily stronger within him.

The Russians stared in open hostility at the Americans, who had broken in on their turf.

"Are you looking for something here?" Sasha Pasternak asked frostily.

"Yes," said a blond-haired man, the heftiest of the three Marines.

"A young American has disappeared on us."

Victor Malenkov pulled his revolver out of his jacket and rammed it between Jeff's ribs, an obvious reminder that he should not dare open his mouth at this critical moment. He would not give up the opportunity to interrogate Jeff. It was, after all, the sole card in his hand. He gave Jeff, who was paralyzed with fright, a sharp push.

Through thin lips Malenkov spoke to the American officer. "Let us pass, please. Who are you, anyway?"

Their attempt to force their way out had the opposite effect from what the Russians had intended: It raised deep suspicions among the Americans that these Russians were trying to hide something from them. Their stance became firmer, more provoking, and their eyes gave off steely glints of determination.

"I am Captain Jerry Norton of the American Embassy. Which one of you is the American citizen answering to the name Jeff Handler?"

"I am!" Jeff found the daring to cry out, ignoring the pressure of steel on his ribs. Captain Norton stared at the American flanked by the stony-faced KGB officer.

Captain Norton was fluent in Russian. He had learned the language from his grandfather, who had emigrated from Russia to the United States with the outbreak of the Communist Revolution in 1917. Norton's job, supervising security in the American Embassy in Moscow, enchanted him. His grandmother had cultivated a great curiosity about the land of her birth, and he found working here both fascinating and rewarding. In his two years' service he had several times been forced to rescue American citizens who had managed to get themselves entangled in the winding labyrinth of Soviet law. He had even enjoyed some hand-to-hand combat, particularly with members of the KGB, who were usually loath to give up their prey. Now he stared at Jeff's terrified face — although the color had returned to it somewhat, with the appearance of the embassy men — and at the men holding on to him. *Here's another story,* he thought to himself.

The highest-ranking among the KGB officers immediately responded, in a more patient tone. "Captain Norton, my name is Sasha Pasternak, an officer of the Cometee. I believe you are overstepping the authority granted to you by the Soviet government. You have broken into a private home, just as did the citizen of your country, whom we have arrested."

Captain Norton took a deep breath, inhaling the frigid air and then exhaling it slowly out of his lungs. "I'm sorry, we didn't mean to break in, just to rescue an American citizen who, it would seem, you are holding in violation of agreements made between our countries."

Pasternak shook his head in vehement disagreement. "This citizen, apparently broke the law and, it seems, in a most serious way. We have the right to interrogate him."

Norton looked with great interest at Jeff's face, as if to try and figure out what dire acts he had been charged with by the Soviets.

"Maybe you can tell me what he is accused of?"

Sasha Pasternak was generous. "Gladly. But only after the interrogation at our headquarters. That is clearly spelled out in our mutual agreements."

Norton knew that the Russian was correct. By treaty, it was the Soviets' right to interrogate an American citizen who had fallen under suspicion of having harmed national security or of having created a public disturbance. But they had to make an immediate report to the American Embassy, which would give all the necessary defenses.

Norton lightly bit his lip. "You're right, I know it. But if we're already here, why not go a little further and tell us what his crime is?"

The three Americans were very large men. One of them, a dark man was almost seven-feet tall. Despite his bulky clothing, one could see his rippling muscles. He took a step towards the Russians; his comrades followed. It was a clear challenge to the Russian men, who were much shorter and slighter. The Russians knew quite well that the Americans would not dare do them any violence without having to face later consequences; and yet, in the face of the unexpected, Pasternak looked around for a way out other than breaking through the human wall that now loomed in front of them.

He looked at his fellow officers, and did not find the determination and firmness he had been seeking.

"I don't see any reason why I should. Persuade me."

"From the little I know about this, I believe you're going to be very disappointed, and you'll be wasting your energy on nothing."

Pasternak listened to his words with interest; Malenkov, in increasing fury. It was Jeff, though, who suffered the most from them: The revolver stuck between his ribs increased its pressure. Jeff's face contorted in pain. Pasternak threw a question at Norton:

"Are you prepared to tell me what you know of this?"

Norton saw an opening for negotiations. "I am prepared to tell you what I know. But it's cold here; let's go into the house."

The Russians, who all understood English, exchanged quick glances. They, too, were freezing. In addition, they realized that without some chatting they would not be able to accomplish their mission. They agreed.

The men all entered the house. The Americans looked around at the dreary ill-furnished home. They saw the old woman standing next to one of the KGB men, as well as the three who had remained behind: Gregory Butbinick, Anatoly Dobrovitz, and Igor Grasimov.

The atmosphere was loaded and heavy. No one sat down; everyone stood, as if ready to do battle.

Pasternak began to radiate impatience. "Well?"

"The man has gotten himself messed up, I admit," Norton replied. "But all he really wanted to do was visit the house where his grandfather had lived."

Pasternak and Malenkov laughed derisively. This time it was Malenkov who answered.

"You believe that story? As a cover it's really weak, really transparent. It's not worthy of you, Captain Norton. We expected more from your CIA."

Pasternak added frigidly, "Have your intelligence services been going through a crisis?"

Norton would have no part of these foolish games. "Any crisis is going to be yours, in the next few minutes, if your interrogation is going to take the line that this young man is a spy."

Pasternak was offended by his presumption. He walked menacingly toward Norton, his fists balled in a manner that worried Norton not at all. The American did not budge, just turned blue eyes made of cold steel upon Pasternak.

"Are you threatening me, Mister American, right here in Moscow?"

"Absolutely not. No threats. I'm just sizing up the situation."

"Yes?" Pasternak spit out the word.

"Yes, yes! This American citizen is 'clean.' He has absolutely no connection with any covert operations of our country."

"Are you sure?"

"That's the official reply we've been given by Washington. We accept it."

Malenkov weakened his grip on Jeff; even the revolver didn't press so hard against his ribs. The feeling of confrontation strengthened, and he took another menacing step towards Norton.

"Are you prepared to prove it? This won't be the first time your country has lied."

"No more than your country. That's not much of an argument."

The two sides stood still, facing each other, exchanging hostile looks.

"In any case," Malenkov declared, a little more calmly, "it's up to you to prove it."

"I haven't got proof. You've got to take the word of a fellow officer this time."

The three Russians reacted with mocking laughter and gestures of dismissal. "That's no answer and no proof."

Without giving further notice they began to walk toward the door in an attempt to avoid Norton and his comrades. Malenkov's revolver again found its place between Jeff's ribs. Soslov and Pasternak strengthened their grip on Dimitri Grasimov. But the Americans were quick to react: They blocked the way. It was clear that within seconds a battle would break out.

The old woman, Dimitri's mother, had listened to the harsh dialogue between the KGB officer and the Americans. Now, again terrified that her son would be thrown into the cellars of Lubianka, the notorious prison, she moved from her place and said out loud, "One minute! I have proof that the American is innocent!"

All eyes turned toward her. She gave them all a quick look and said, "The American has asked to call his grandfather in Israel, so that I, his grandfather's sister, could speak with him. Dimitri didn't agree. Now you can listen, and you'll see that he's telling the truth."

She was quiet for a moment and then added, "And now I think Dimitri, too, will agree to him calling, won't you, Dimitri?"

Her son nodded his head in assent. But Malenkov wasn't pleased.

"Fine, *Babushka*. We agree. But only after the interrogation. We'll call you for questioning too, and then we'll arrange this phone call."

"No!" she screamed. "Now!"

Norton intervened. "Actually, why not now? It will help you get out of this stupid mess, that is of no use whatsoever to you, and will only embarrass you."

He turned to Jeff. "Mr. Handler, are you prepared to call your grandfather?"

"This minute!"

"But we don't want to," Malenkov objected.

Norton was beginning to lose control.

"You don't have to want to. But if there is a way of checking on this American's innocence, and you refuse to do it, you must release him immediately! Understood?"

Pasternak broke in. "You are on Soviet soil, Captain."

"We know that. But we have diplomatic immunity. Either get your hands off him, or allow him to call. If we find out that he's a liar, well, then he's all yours!"

Norton's eyes began to skim over the room. After a moment's search he found what he was looking for — the telephone. He leaped towards it and before anyone could stop him he had picked up the receiver and dialed the embassy. He whispered something into it. No one, not even the KGB operatives, tried to stop him.

"Mr. Handler," he barked, "tell me quickly your grandfather's phone number in Israel. The embassy will make the connection. Quick!"

Malenkov tried to stop Jeff, but the giant black man tapped his hand lightly, pulling it away from Jeff's mouth. He did it with a gentle smile that lit up his face. Malenkov, feeling the power of the man, let up. Jeff quickly gave them the number of Beilinson Hospital, where his grandfather was under treatment.

Pasternak didn't dare stop them, but he protested: "This is unconscionable interference in an internal matter of the Soviet Union."

Norton grinned. "I am operating by the authority of our embassy. From this moment on, the First Secretary in the embassy is in continuous contact with the Foreign Ministry. As important as you are, my friends, the subject is no longer in your hands."

Pasternak's face grew scarlet with rage. "How dare you! How dare you defy our authority in such a manner!"

Norton grinned again. "Your unreasonable behavior forced me to take these steps. If you wish, you are free to turn to Yuri Andropov himself. I don't believe he can do anything about the situation at this point. Oh, here, Mr. Handler, the phone in Israel is ringing."

With a sudden sharp movement Jeff wrested himself out of Malenkov's grasp and raced towards the telephone. He held the receiver in trembling hands and listened to the ringing that might get him out of the terrible trap in which he had become ensnared.

Sasha Pasternak got KGB headquarters in Dzerzhinski Square on his miniature two-way radio. He whispered furiously into the tiny microphone. No one could hear what he was saying though all eyes were turned upon him, some anxious, some merely curious. All except Jeff, whose excitement was growing from moment to moment.

"Hello? Grandfather? It's me, Jeff, Yisrael Yaakov." Emotion almost overcame him; he felt as if he was suffocating. "Yes, I'm in Moscow! That's right, in Krasno Bogatirski! Yes, in your house, Grandfather. I found them! A miracle! Grandfather, don't cry. A miracle! You've got to be strong."

Sasha Pasternak finished his whispered call and approached Jeff with hurried threatening steps. The three Marines immediately gathered protectively around him.

"I've received instructions to end this conversation immediately. It is against the law for a detainee to speak freely with someone living abroad."

Captain Norton wasn't particularly impressed. He and his two cronies moved a little closer to Jeff.

"Tell the one who's giving you orders, Captain Pasternak, tell him to speak with your Foreign Ministry. We are working in accord with them."

"Impossible!" Pasternak shouted.

"It is a fact," the American answered tranquilly. "You can see for yourself that it is possible."

"I will call my men and have you all arrested."

"That should be interesting, Captain. I will be able to visit your headquarters and see if all the terrible stories that come out from behind its walls are true. To your sorrow, you know very well that my visit there will be brief. You'll be reprimanded by your diplomatic circles almost immediately. I wouldn't have expected such rash behavior from someone in your position."

All through this Jeff kept his ear glued to the phone. The confusion going on around him made it difficult for him to catch exactly what his grandfather, who sounded very weak, was saying. Still, he could certainly hear the enormous emotion of his grandfather at the realization of his life's dream.

"Grandfather, I have something else to tell you. Your sister is standing right next to me. Which one? I don't know her name. She is standing next to me, crying. Do you want to speak to her? Grandfather, you've got to be strong! I'm giving her the receiver. Grandfather, if Hashem helps, I'll be with you in another two or three days. Yes, yes, with the holy *tefillin*. Here, take the phone. Goodbye, Grandfather, and be well."

Jeff had spoken to his grandfather in English, so that Norton and his friends would understand. When he finished, Norton called to the old woman. The huge Marine cleared the way for her without any trouble; all opposition from the three KGB officers had come to a halt, since they hadn't the slightest idea of how to behave in this mad situation. The old woman grabbed the phone with both hands, while the black Marine brought her a chair to sit on. And a good thing, too; she almost collapsed in her excitement.

"Vladimir, is that you?" she whispered in Russian, her voice almost a sob. "You're alive? Where have you been all these years? Vladimir, it's me, Marisha, your younger sister. Do you remember? Vladimir!"

She couldn't go on. Her entire body was trembling under the strain of her emotions. She lifted moist eyes towards those standing around her, the tears running nonstop down the rivulets of her wrinkled face. Even the KGB officers held their peace, looking curiously at the drama unfolding before them. Pasternak and Soslov eased their hold on Dimitri.

"Vladimir? Can you hear me? Your grandson is standing here next to me, and my son, Dimitri, and my grandson Igor. He is a student, a nice boy, yes, Vladimir? Where have you been all these years? I thought they killed you in Siberia. Why didn't you ever write? Vladimir, what's that you ask? Yes, I am all alone. Irina died 12 years ago. Yes, yes, you're healthy, Vladimir. Oh, I just can't take any more."

Pasternak suddenly forced his way to the phone. "I have something to say to him too. I have something to ask him."

Norton hesitated and finally cleared the way for him. "Just remember that he's an old sick man."

Pasternak glanced at him mockingly. "Do you think I'm going to kill him through the phone?"

He took the receiver from the shaking hands of the old woman, who sat, drained, in her chair.

"Comrade Vladimir Paruskin?" Pasternak asked.

"Yes," came the tinny voice from over a vast distance. "Who are you?"

"I am Captain Sasha Pasternak of the Cometee. That is, the KGB."

The old man, Asher Yosef Handler, almost choked. All his old fears returned. He could only manage one word: "Oh."

Pasternak took no notice. "I want to know when you left the USSR, and how."

"What do you want with my grandson? He's not guilty."

"Guilty of what?"

The old man felt that he had failed. The failure, though, gave him new strength. Suddenly he felt that it was up to him to save his grandson, Jeff, from whatever trouble he was in.

"Yes, I left Russia illegally, I don't remember how anymore. But that was in Stalin's time. Today things are not like they were then, yes?"

"Where did you live in Moscow?"

"*Nu*, you know; you're there now."

Pasternak was determined. "Where did you live, Comrade? The street name, please."

"Krasno. Krasno Bogatirski."

Pasternak wondered what else he should ask. He wanted so to regain control over the situation in the room, to hold an interrogation in which he reigned supreme. But he didn't know what else to ask. His eyes communicated with Malenkov, standing in a corner.

"Ask him why he was sentenced to imprisonment in Siberia."

Pasternak put the receiver to his ear once again, but all he heard was the dial tone, like the wailing of a wounded man. The call had been cut off.

Norton took advantage of the moment. "I think that everything is quite clear. This is no spy story, no secret agent stuff. It's a silly young man who thinks he's wandering through the streets of New York, where such behavior is permitted."

Pasternak objected. "It's not so simple. He's involved in the matter of a Cometee officer."

"It is simple indeed. Your problems in the KGB are of no interest to an American citizen."

Norton turned to Jeff. "Mr. Jeff Handler, you will come with us now. I think that it is clear to the Russians that you are nothing more than a foolish young man. Come."

Jeff accepted the insult with obvious delight. He began to walk behind Norton. But Malenkov brandished his revolver in front of him. "Don't move!"

The black man, smiling, walked serenely towards Malenkov and almost effortlessly pulled the revolver out of his hand. Then he picked up the KGB agent and set him down in a corner of the room. Malenkov was astonished by his strength. The other two agents chose not to test it further, and Jeff walked out the door at Norton's heels.

Gregory, who'd been standing quietly at the side, leaped out and joined them. The Americans hurried to their car, taking Gregory along after Jeff had explained his part in the affair. Gregory used the car's walkie-talkie to instruct another embassy automobile on how to find Jeff's wife, still stranded in an apartment in Moscow. Norton, who had been giving Jeff a severe lecture all through the ride on his childish and irresponsible conduct, told him, "You will not return to the hotel. These men are dangerous. And they'll find you there. You will come with us to the embassy and stay there until your flight tonight. Our men will bring your things from the hotel."

After a short ride they reached the embassy building. A room had been readied for him, and for his wife, who arrived a few minutes later. All Jeff longed for was a few minutes of sleep to try and allay some of the tension roiling within him. He flung himself on the bed, but could not sleep. Suddenly he jumped up as though stung. His shout sent his wife flying out of her chair.

"What happened?" she screamed.

"I can't believe it! I left the *tefillin* on the table, there in the house, on Krasno Bogatirski. What can I do now?"

They stood, the two of them, paralyzed.

55

eff was on the verge of tears. He sat on the bed, his elbows on his knees, his head nestled in the palms of his hands. His wife, Miriam, tried to calm him. She was still reeling from the terrifying hours that she had spent that morning.

"Just thank G–d for taking you out of that insanity."

"I am thankful, truly thankful, to Hashem. But is that the reward for all this suffering, that after all that we've gone through, I don't have the *tefillin*? What will I tell Grandfather?"

She cracked her knuckles nervously. "But what can we do?"

He stood up from the bed. His figure grew straight with determination.

"I'm going back there!"

His wife, too, leaped up from the bed. She stood by the door, trying to block it.

"Are you crazy?"

"I've got to go back! Don't you understand? I can't fail, not at the very last minute!"

His wife started to cry. "You're not going! I won't let you! Your sacrifice for your grandfather has already gone far enough! You don't have to do more! You have children in New York! Have you forgotten them? We'll simply tell him the truth."

Jeff did not respond. He raced towards the telephone that stood on a small table in one corner of the room and dialed the switchboard operator.

"Hello? Who is in charge here, who can I speak with? Who am I? My name is Jeff Handler, the crazy American who your men rescued from an apartment in this cursed city."

"What do you want?" the voice on the other end asked.

"I want to speak with whoever is responsible for this embassy. Do you understand?"

"Why are you taking that tone? What have I done to you that you're so angry?"

Jeff lowered his voice. "No, no, I'm not angry at you. I just want to speak to the person in charge."

A lengthy silence. Finally, "Here is the First Secretary."

"Hello? This is Jeff Handler, who is being held in your embassy."

"And this is Jennifer Smith, whom you can thank for bringing you to freedom here in the American embassy."

Smith fumed at the ingratitude of this man who could have, in the worst case, spent a good few years in prison.

Jeff pulled himself together. He realized he had made a tactical error.

"And I thank you. I am really grateful."

"What do you want now?"

"I want to go back to the apartment on Krasno Bogatirski."

"What?" The woman on the other end of the line was shocked to the core.

"I have to go back! I forgot something there!"

"You can't go back there, Mr. Handler. You are flying directly to the United States. Maybe there, in New York, we'll see to it that you get some psychiatric care. You're simply not normal, if you'll pardon me for saying so."

Jeff ignored the slur. "But I forgot something that's vitally important to me!"

"But the KGB hasn't forgotten you, my dear sir! A good number of black Cheka automobiles are lying in wait for you right now at the entrance to the embassy. If you want, at this very moment, you can calm your nerves by peeking out of the window and looking at them. You're protected here, while you're in the embassy, Mr. Handler! Just step beyond this territory and you are in grave danger."

"You mean the danger isn't over yet?"

"Absolutely not. We're waiting for Moscow's reply to the State Department in Washington, so that we can finally finish up this messy affair that you've caused. Your diamond business, too, has been frozen."

"So what's going to happen?"

"Nothing, sir. You will, it seems, be deported, and that's the end of Moscow for you. And you can thank Heaven if it ends with nothing worse than deportation."

"But what's going to happen with the *tefillin?*"

"With what?" Jennifer Smith asked, surprised. "I didn't understand what you just said."

"It's not important."

There was a momentary silence. It seemed clear to her that this "client" of theirs was not completely sane....

Finally, she said, "I would suggest, sir, that you rest a little from the frightening ordeal that you've been through. They seem to have done some damage to your nerves. When everything is arranged we'll be in touch. Oh, by the way, we've managed, after a good deal of trouble, to get your possessions from the Hotel Russia. They refused, however, to return your passports to us. I hope you'll get them in the airport; otherwise, you'll fly with a transit document."

The woman didn't say anything more; the connection was broken.

Krasno Bogatirski Street was left with chaos, anger, and humiliation. But the three KGB officers reined in their fury: they were forced to restrain themselves in the face of the American actions and the abduction the Marines had carried out, by instructions that they had received from central headquarters. The officers changed, also, their relationship with Dimitri Grasimov, the man they had hoped to catch in the act of meeting with a foreign spy. They realized that the story they had hoped to weave about Dimitri had unraveled somewhat. The living witness, the young strange American, had slipped out of their hands with infuriating suddenness. The telephone conversation to Israel with the old man who had been revealed as Dimitri's long-lost uncle had also not added anything to the trap they had set for him. Dimitri could sense the difference, and he felt his spirits returning. He had wriggled out of Malenkov's grip, and he said mockingly, "I'm embarrassed by this group of officers. I would have expected more skill, more professionalism. If you want to undermine a person, if you want to trap him — you cannot be so careless. You understand that you're going to suffer for this criminal behavior against me. I'm not going to ignore it!"

There was murder in Malenkov's eyes. "You're still talking, Dimitri? Your failure is even worse! You were running after ghosts! You thought you'd caught a spy ring, didn't you? And here you find some weird relative instead. If he really is your relative, we'll never know. That's our problem, because the American managed to sneak away. Another failure, my dear friend. That will also go into your file. I'll see to it."

Dimitri barked a command. "And now, go home! Leave me here with my mother. She's still completely upset by that surprising, sudden phone call to her brother."

"Now, you'll come with us," came the conflicting order.

It looked like the violence would begin once again. Eyes stared at each other like glinting bayonets. Dimitri swiftly assessed the situation and decided to go with them. His fear of what they might do to him had eased somewhat. Better to stand against them at headquarters and see what they would say when facing superior officers.

"Mother," he turned to the old woman, still sitting, completely drained but anxiously following the action, "don't worry. I'm going with them. The danger is over, I promise you." After a moment's pause, he added, "At least for now."

The woman didn't react; she was too weak. She just nodded her head in a feeble motion. Dimitri left the house in the company of the three agents. A few tears dropped from the old woman's eyes, weary from years of suffering.

In the room, next to the old woman, stood Igor Grasimov and Anatoly Dobrovitz. They stared at each other in silence. Neither knew what to say to the other. Igor remembered well the fact that he had arrived, together with his father, a KGB agent, in order to arrest Jeff. That is, he was connected with the actions of the secret police. Igor could also sense that Anatoly had pulled himself away after their stormy parting on Moskovaskaya Street the day before. In Russia, land of suspicions, he knew that he could not successfully convince Anatoly of the change that had come over him, a change that had deepened all the more during the last frenzied hour, when he had suddenly discovered that the man who had spoken the night before of *tefillin* was his father's cousin. And here, in the home of his grandfather, he'd found a pair of *tefillin!* What a strange coincidence!

Igor approached the table. He took another look at the bag containing the *tefillin*, at the material, ragged and moth eaten after all these years. It lay there, abandoned; the American, in his hurried exit from the room, had forgotten it. Anatoly watched Igor with interest. At first, Igor dared not touch the *tefillin* bag; his eyes scanned it from all sides. Finally he gently placed his hand upon it. Anatoly took a few steps towards him. Igor picked up the bag with hands that trembled just a little. This was the first time in his life that he was actually holding a Jewish holy object. Anatoly stood by his side.

The bag seemed to come apart in Igor's hands. And here, the pair of *tefillin*, the black paint chipped a little at the corners, were revealed. Anatoly's eyes jumped back and forth from the *tefillin* to Igor's face. He was testing his loyalty. Yes, Igor's face showed seriousness, and it seemed to Anatoly that he could also see yearning and a sense of awe upon it. The speech yesterday, it seemed, had left its mark.

"Do you understand what happened here?" Anatoly asked.

Their eyes would not meet.

"No."

"A pair of *tefillin* in your grandmother's house!"

"Yes."

"And your father works for them."

Igor knew quite well who he was referring to as "them." He answered weakly, "Yes."

Anatoly took a deep breath. After a short pause he asked, "And—you?"

Igor raised his eyes in angry surprise. "What do you think?"

Anatoly took the *tefillin* out of Igor's hand, turned them carefully around from side to side. He did not look at Igor as he said, "I don't know yet."

Igor was insulted. He took the *tefillin* back from Anatoly, feeling the loss of his new treasure. At the same moment he made his decision, a bold and audacious one:

"It doesn't matter, Anatoly. Don't believe me. You don't have to believe me. I, in any case, from this day forward, will be putting them on. I already know where to go to learn how to do it. You asked me if I understood what happened here. Now I know exactly what happened: Someone wanted me to have these *tefillin*. And that you,. who don't believe in me, should see it with your own eyes."

Igor gave a weak smile. "And now, Anatoly, leave me alone. I have to cheer up Grandmother. It was hard for her. You saw that yourself."

Anatoly didn't answer. He understood that he had gone too far and he was sorry. At the door he said, "Please forgive me. I didn't mean anything. We'll meet again."

Jeff paced back and forth in the room like a caged lion. All the incredible effort of will that he had put into this affair had been for nothing. He had failed in his mission. The feeling of failure ate at him. He rubbed his hands together in increasing nervousness: "What can I do?"

Miriam tried to calm him down. "Nothing, Jeff. You've done enough. Show me another person who would have endangered himself like this!"

"But Grandfather—"

"Grandfather will understand, Jeff! He's human! He will understand that this was Hashem's will! What's the problem?"

She was upset. She still worried that Jeff might do something unexpected, something crazy, out of a sense of desperation and defeat.

Suddenly Jeff stopped his frenzied pacing. He looked out the window and saw the Cheka automobile. He understood: The hunt wasn't over yet. There was nothing he could do. He accepted his fate; he sat on the bed and grew silent.

Towards evening, the phone rang in their room. Jeff quickly picked up the receiver, as if waiting for news of the lost *tefillin*.

"Mr. Handler, prepare for your flight. Moscow is letting you go."'

It was Jennifer Smith, First Secretary of the Embassy.

An hour later, they were at Chermentyevo Airport. The three Marines escorted them, together with Ms. Smith. They had come just in case there was some unexpected and unwelcome development. Jeff sat in the car wrapped in his own thoughts. Despite the tension, Miriam felt an increasing sense of joy: In a few hours Moscow would be behind them.

In the lobby of the airport they saw Gregory. Jeff paled at the sight of him: Even at this last minute he didn't quite trust him. *What does he want with me now?*

"Mr. Handler?" he said. Jeff and his escorts stopped.

"Yes?"

"Mr. Handler, you forgot the *tefillin* in that house, right?"

"That's right."

He tried desperately to figure out what Gregory could want from him.

Gregory looked around from side to side to see if anyone was eavesdropping on their conversation. He spoke quickly. "The son of the KGB officer, the old woman's grandson, Igor, who was at your lesson on *tefillin*, remember?"

Yes, Jeff did remember.

"He's decided to use them every day."

Jeff closed his eyes and swayed. The *tefillin*, then, weren't lost.

Gregory saw Jeff's emotions. "The *tefillin* have stayed in the family," he whispered.

Jeff was absolutely astonished. Here, he thought, look how Hashem arranged these things. The *tefillin* were fulfilling their mission. And because of him, Jeff, another Jew would put on *tefillin*.

Jeff opened his eyes and smiled at Gregory. "And you, Gregory, where do you stand?"

Gregory was silent for a moment. Finally he said, "I think you know."

"And you were never working for them. Not even when you were with Intourist?"

"No. Even then I was a student of the bearded man."

Jeff grew pensive. "And when you took me to the synagogue that morning, it was so that I could see him?"

"That's right. I wanted you to know that in Moscow there were young people returning to their Jewish heritage."

Their eyes smiled in farewell, and Gregory disappeared in the milling crowds of the airport.

The next evening the Handlers landed in the airport in Lod. One hour later, they were already at the bedside of Jeff's grandfather, who had returned home. Jeff's father, Moshe Aryeh, met them. He gave them a short report on his father's illness, which had worsened since yesterday after his conversation with his sister. The excitement had affected him badly, and he could not speak. The doctor was at his side right now, and had ordered that they leave him. But, he added in a whisper, Jeff's grandfather was anxiously awaiting him.

Moshe Aryeh heard, in increasing shock, that his son, after all his adventures, had not brought the *tefillin* back with him. Jeff, though, insisted on seeing his grandfather and telling him the whole tale.

The room was darkened; there was a stale, sickly odor within. Jeff approached the bed, lightly kissed his grandfather on his forehead, and gently held his wrinkled, emaciated hand. His grandfather's eyes opened wide, and he whispered, "Where are the *tefillin?*"

Jeff whispered softly, "I got them. I found them and held them in my hand. But because of the KGB, I couldn't bring them."

Jeff saw the tears that slowly dripped from the dim eyes. He patted the thin hand. "But don't cry, Grandfather, they are in good hands. Your sister's grandson has started to put them on every day. His name is Igor. His father is a KGB officer. But the son has started to become religious, it seems. Hashem's ways are mysterious. Yes, yes, there in Moscow. In your merit, Grandfather, he will put them on. Every day, he will put them on. They are fulfilling an important mission."

At first the old man could not comprehend what Jeff was saying to him. Jeff repeated his words. Suddenly, Asher Yosef's eyes lit up. He understood: his Holy, special *tefillin* would be put on every single day by someone in Moscow. Someone who was his relative, his own father's great-grandson.

The old man tried to squeeze Jeff's hands in a gesture of thanks. But he didn't have the strength. The weary eyes opened again, gave Jeff a long look, a look of peace. He smiled in satisfaction.

Suddenly the eyes closed. Grandfather had gone to the world where no evil exists.

Jeff held his father's hand, which trembled uncontrollably. The two gazed in anguish at R' Asher Yosef, who had just returned his soul to his Creator.

"It was the hope of seeing his *tefillin* that kept him alive," Jeff whispered.

His father nodded, as a tear coursed its way down his cheeks.

"The sense of mission that gives a person the power to live. Take comfort in the knowledge that Grandfather's dream came true, and he died tranquil, with words of thanks."

His father didn't answer directly, he merely whispered, "*Baruch Dayan Ha'emes.*"

And the thought flitted through Jeff's mind: Happy is he who merits to fulfill his mission in this world.